"Name your price . . ."

"I am a god, Sylvie, whether you choose to accept it or not. Your fee could reflect that. What do you want?"

Sylvie's heart skipped—a god? The possibilities reeled before her. Money zipped by; she always needed that, but money was easy. If Dunne wasn't lying, if he was a god, he could give her something far more valuable. Something that would lift the guilt from her back and make Alex smile again. There was really only one thing to ask for.

"Anything I want?" she said, trying for casual in her voice, trying not to let him see how much this mattered.

"Pretty much," he said.

"Can you bring back the dead?"

SINS & SHADOWS

A SHADOWS INQUIRIES NOVEL

Lyn Benedict

ACE BOOKS, NEW YORK

THE BERKLEY PUBLISHING GROUP
Published by the Penguin Group
Penguin Group (USA) Inc.
375 Hudson Street, New York, New York 10014, USA
Penguin Group (Canada), 90 Eglinton Avenue East, Suite 700, Toronto, Ontario M4P 2Y3, Canada
(a division of Pearson Penguin Canada Inc.)
Penguin Books Ltd., 80 Strand, London WC2R 0RL, England
Penguin Group Ireland, 25 St. Stephen's Green, Dublin 2, Ireland (a division of Penguin Books Ltd.)
Penguin Group (Australia), 250 Camberwell Road, Camberwell, Victoria 3124, Australia
(a division of Pearson Australia Group Pty. Ltd.)
Penguin Books India Pvt. Ltd., 11 Community Centre, Panchsheel Park, New Delhi—110 017, India
Penguin Group (NZ), 67 Apollo Drive, Rosedale, North Shore 0632, New Zealand
(a division of Pearson New Zealand Ltd.)
Penguin Books (South Africa) (Pty.) Ltd., 24 Sturdee Avenue, Rosebank, Johannesburg 2196,
South Africa

Penguin Books Ltd., Registered Offices: 80 Strand, London WC2R 0RL, England

SINS & SHADOWS

An Ace Book / published by arrangement with the author

PRINTING HISTORY
Ace mass-market edition / May 2009

Copyright © 2009 by Lane Robins.
Cover art by Shane Rebenschied.
Cover design by Lesley Worrell.
Interior text design by Tiffany Estreicher.

ISBN: 978-0-441-01711-9

ACE
Ace Books are published by The Berkley Publishing Group,
a division of Penguin Group (USA) Inc.,
375 Hudson Street, New York, New York 10014.
ACE and the "A" design are trademarks of Penguin Group (USA) Inc.

PRINTED IN THE UNITED STATES OF AMERICA

10 9 8 7 6 5 4 3 2 1

For Kim and Nannette,
for reasons that should be evident

Acknowledgments

As always, there are many people who should be thanked for helping bring this book to completion. Thanks to the KU CSSF novel workshop for starting me off right. Thanks to GS Dastur for saving me from Babel Fish French. Thanks to my noble critiquers, Luisa Prieto and Larry Taylor, for keeping me on the straight path! And thanks to Caitlin Blasdell and Anne Sowards for their tireless efforts on my behalf.

1

Closing Up Shop: The Real World

SYLVIE LIGHTNER STUDIED HER COFFEEMAKER WITH A WEARY AND contemplative eye, trying to decide if she should dump the carafe and pack the machine now, or keep the caffeine until the very last moment. Maybe she could just leave it behind, along with everything else: her obligations, her pride, her pain. Just walk away from it and pretend it wouldn't follow.

A shadow crossed over her floor, fed in through the rippled glass of the front door, blocking the Florida sunlight and the gilded letters that reflected her sign on the floor: SHADOWS INQUIRIES. Sylvie automatically turned her eyes toward a marble bowl containing a walnut-sized bell on the recently cleared main desk. The warning bell stayed silent, meaning it wasn't a boogeyman at the door, but when Sylvie heard the jangling of keys, she almost wished for the monster. She'd hoped to be gone before Alex got back.

Alex swore as the keyhole refused to surrender the key, and finally yanked it away. "Syl, we have *got* to get that fix—" She gaped at the front office filled with cardboard boxes, her usual complaint derailed.

"What's going on?" she asked. The circles under her eyes darkened. Such anxiety used to look out of place amidst the pierced brow, the blond-and-black spiky hair, but of late, it had become all too common. Sylvie noticed with a pang that Alex wasn't even wearing her tricolor eye shadow anymore. This was all for the best.

"And you call yourself a detective," Sylvie said, keeping her tone brisk. "I'm closing up shop. As of this moment, Shadows Inquiries is out of business."

"What?" Alex said. Her voice cracked. "Just like that? You can't, Sylvie. I'm a part of this business, too."

"Yes," Sylvie said. She continued taping a half-full box shut with a ruthless hand, sealing away files that could probably be left behind, as most of them were merely constructs of code and falsehood. Still, better safe than sorry was Sylvie's new motto. "The employee part. Whereas I am the boss."

"Don't I get a say?" Alex said. Anger lit Alex's face, chasing away some of the ground-in grief. She snatched the tape gun from Sylvie's hand, forcing her attention.

"No," Sylvie said. "See above, me boss, you employee. And, Alex—you're fired. I'll send your last check in the mail." Sylvie refused to wince at the hurt in her friend's open face. Alex was too loyal for her own good, that was the trouble. If Sylvie just laid it out, that she expected to be embroiled in a losing battle, Alex would refuse to leave her side. She had to be driven away. Better to lose a friend to temper and hurt than to another bullet.

"Bullshit, you can't just fire me," Alex said. "I've been with you from the beginning. You *need* me, Sylvie."

Agree or disagree, Sylvie ignored the comment as irrelevant. "I'm closing the shop," Sylvie repeated. "I'll need your key back."

Alex dropped onto the cracked leather couch; a box slid to the floor with a thump and the chime of breaking glass. "You're serious?"

"Yes," Sylvie said.

"You're trying to protect me," Alex said. "That's not your job. You can't protect everyone."

"Get your stuff and get out," Sylvie said, finding real temper for the first time. Can't protect everyone? Didn't need to tell her that. Not now. Her gun hand twitched; the little dark voice that lived inside her head roused, and laced her tone with fury. *"Get out."* She throttled back the rage.

Alex, despite Sylvie's current pretense, was her friend. The dark voice had no friends at all, and why should it? It existed only to survive, had woken during Sylvie's first brush with the *Magicus Mundi*. Sylvie wasn't sure what it was; a microsplit in her personality, the echo of ancient genetics, or something else entirely. Her witch friend, Val, when consulted, argued for option A or B, said it was too bitchy not to be pure Sylvie. But hers or not, she couldn't argue with its priority: to keep her alive.

Alex licked her lips, nervous. It wasn't a tone Sylvie usually turned on her. "Syl—"

"You don't feel like packing up? Fine, I'll mail anything you leave. Now, key and out." Sylvie held out her hand, met Alex's eyes without flinching.

Alex dug in her pocket and dropped the key into Sylvie's palm. Sylvie chucked it into an open box and turned her back, though the prickling at the back of her neck let her know that Alex still watched her.

"You forget what the door looks like?"

Footsteps edged away, then the door opened, bringing in the sound of the crowded South Beach streets, the sounds of foreign tourists talking, the cars honking as people jaywalked before them. The office filled with the warm scent of salt and sun.

The noise faded, but Sylvie knew that Alex wasn't gone; she refused to turn around.

"This is because of Suarez," Alex said, her voice low. "He died, and you think—"

"Be accurate," Sylvie snapped. "He was murdered. In front of us."

Alex scrubbed at her eyes, and Sylvie said, "It's not just Suarez. It's all the shit we deal with, the creepy crawlies and nightmare fodder most sane people refuse to acknowledge. And that's not even including the government agents who think we're worth watching day and night. I've had enough." All true. All utterly misleading. But how did she say, "I'm quitting before I have to start killing people as well as monsters," when Alex had no idea she killed anything at all?

She chucked a handful of pencils at a box just as two patrolmen pushed into the room, shoving Alex out of the way.

"What now?" Sylvie asked. The little silver bell chimed faintly in its marble bowl, too quietly for Sylvie to tell if it had been jarred to movement by the cops' sudden entrance or by something else.

Sylvie didn't care for the police at the best of times. Not that they had much reason to like her either, an unlicensed PI who'd ended up standing over one too many bodies.

"I've quit, guys, so take your shit elsewhere," Sylvie said, but the police ignored her. One of them climbed the stairwell to her private office and kicked the door open. It banged against the wall hard enough to scar plaster.

The other cop, a fortyish black male, headed toward Sylvie. Something was wrong with his eyes. He had junkie eyes, strung out, hurting eyes, looking for some intangible fix. Sylvie wasn't sure he saw her at all.

He circled the small kitchenette, opening the storage closet and peering inside.

It was their silence that worried her the most. It was too loaded and too separate. The officers seemed as unaware of each other as they were of her. She traded a look with Alex, still pressed back against the wall, and tilted her head slightly toward the door. *Go on,* she thought. *Get out.*

Alex shook her head. Stubborn as always. Loyal to a fault. Exactly the reason she had to go.

The cop came down from the office above and focused

in on Sylvie for the first time. She glared back, unflinching. Young, Hispanic, and a little too pudgy for his uniform, he still made her blood run cold. Like the other cop's, his eyes were empty.

Careful, Sylvie's inner voice whispered. Her hand ached to pull her gun from the desk drawer.

"Is there something you want?" Sylvie said, her tone steadier than her nerves. "Got some java going if you're needing caffeine."

The older cop pushed past her again; her hand spasmed on the drawer, but he headed straight for the exit and was gone. A moment later, pudgy followed.

Sylvie put her hands on the desk and leaned forward, staring at the fake-wood grain, following the patterns until her adrenaline faded.

"What was that?" Alex asked.

"An omen rolling up to wish us bye-bye," Sylvie said. "See you 'round, Alex."

She locked the door behind Alex and sighed, looking at the mess. Enough. She'd tape the boxes closed and hire someone to come collect them. She wanted to be gone. Just headed toward noon, and the day had already been too damned long for her tastes.

But first—she opened the desk drawer and took out the gun, feeling more secure with the weight of it in her hand. She checked again that it was loaded, scrabbled the loose bullets out of the drawer and into her purse.

It was one thing to turn her back on the *Magicus Mundi*; it was another entirely to trust it to ignore her. And a well-placed salvo of bullets could take apart a sorcerer or drop a werewolf in its tracks. Bullets even held sway over the sex-drenched glamour of the succubi, provided, of course, you sniped them at a distance. Bullets made everything better. As long as you were fast enough.

Better practice that, the cold dark voice jibed at her. She pressed her palms over her eyes and breathed, sniffing back the tears. Grief was valueless. It couldn't change facts, and guilt meant nothing but that she had failed.

Not her fault, Alex had told her. There were too many of them, all of them determined to see the ritual completed. What could two women do about a crowd hell-bent on earning power through a blood sacrifice? When Suarez had laid his neck on the chopping block with a smile?

Make it a lose-lose. Suarez died, but the satanists hadn't gotten their ritual done. Of course, as a result, Sylvie had thirteen very angry people hunting for her. People didn't like having their rituals disrupted, even if the ritual was as benign as morning coffee and the newspaper. Interrupting a proceeding that promised supernatural power and influence? Sylvie was number one on their shit list. Their problem was that they didn't have the power yet; they were still human.

Sylvie didn't have a lot of rules in her life, liked it better that way, but she held tight to two. She didn't put innocents between herself and trouble. She didn't kill people that the cops could handle. The satanists were perilously close to making her throw rule number two away. Better for her just to get out of town.

The door handle rattled.

"Closed! ¡Cerrado!" she snapped. "Go away."

She turned toward the upper-office stairs, intending to see how much damage the cops had done, how much of her deposit wasn't coming back. On the desk, the bell jangled suddenly, spinning in its marble orbit, ringing louder and louder, like the wail of breath over wet glass.

Behind Sylvie, the locked door opened, bringing in the sounds of distant sirens and the pungent scent of the low-tide shore. Slipping her hand into her purse, she curled her fingers around the reassuring weight of the gun before turning.

Three women looked back at her, closer than she had anticipated. They moved with a silent, animal grace, loose-limbed and long-legged, like escapees from some models' runway.

A dark-haired girl in punk regalia of layered, fishnet

tees, plaid skirt, and hefty Doc Martens sauntered forward and crouched near the base of the stairs. Her near twin, a woman demurely dressed by J. Crew, flanked Sylvie, pacing around her until she and her sisters had Sylvie pinned between them.

The third woman, pale blond in dark leather, returned to the door, watching the street. She tapped her high-heeled boot idly against the floor, waiting, counting off against an internal clock.

Not a lookout, Sylvie thought, not someone to prevent the outside world from interfering while the other two did what they'd come for. These women were bodyguards, an advance troop of some kind, and according to the ringing bell, not human.

She took a step back, feeling her way up the riser, trying to move smoothly, trying to give herself some space to work with. Two sets of eyes tracked her movement instantly.

The preppie girl raised her upper lip, showing teeth, and made a faint, querulous whine. Sylvie stopped dead in her tracks. She'd never heard a sound like that before, but it resonated in the atavistic part of her brain that recognized a predator's cry.

The blond woman at the door stiffened, coming to alert. The sisters beside Sylvie cocked their heads, listening. The bell went silent as a tall man ducked beneath the doorjamb, filling it momentarily.

Another cop, Sylvie thought, watching his scoping of the room, the way he carried himself. A plainclothes detective who had picked one hell of a bad time to come ask some more questions about Suarez. His dark brown eyes flickered around the room, noting the boxes and the clutter, before homing in on her.

Sylvie found herself torn between demanding his assistance and warning him to flee, but while she was stymied speechless, the blonde rubbed her cheek against his arm. He stroked her hair without looking at her, his expression of weariness and concern never shifting.

"You three been good?" he asked.

"She was leaving," the punk girl said in the dulcet tones of a schoolgirl. "We stopped her."

"Thank you," he said, his eyes never leaving Sylvie's.

A sudden shudder racked her, a quick acknowledgment that he meant trouble with a capital *T*. She had met men like him before. Humans with power and a yen for unnatural entourages. He was exactly what the satanists aspired to be.

The two sisters sat on the floor near him, not like people, cross-legged and uncomfortable, but crouched like dogs. The punk girl yawned widely, and Sylvie had a quick flash, like an X-ray rising through flesh, of something *Other*. Something huge, angry and implacable.

"Ms. Lightner?" the not-cop said, his voice pleasantly deep and rough. "I need your help."

Sylvie shivered again. Most of her clients addressed her as Shadows, assuming that she'd given her name to the business: Shadows Inquiries. But the ones who checked her out . . . She didn't like the idea of him looking into her life without her knowing. The Internal Surveillance and Intelligence agency snooped enough for anyone.

She sucked in a breath, and said, "I've quit. Besides, it looks like you've got more help than you can handle."

His broad shoulders tightened as if she'd struck at him, and she pressed her case.

"Really, you should be careful. I've seen men torn apart by help like that. Their own help." She didn't know why she felt compelled to warn him, except maybe—there was pain in his eyes, deep and raw, and she had no intention of helping him ease it. Her warning was the least she could give.

"The sisters?" he asked. He petted the pale one's hair again. "No danger of that. But they're not the help I need right now. I need a detective who can deal—"

"With the supernatural," Sylvie finished. "I told you. I've retired. And I'm not the only one of my kind. There

are others if you know where to look. There's the Good
Shepherd—"

"That's the hell of it," he said, and the veneer of calmness slipped, giving her a glimpse of desperation. "I always know where to look. I can find anyone, track them
anywhere. And no one escapes my eyes—"

He fell silent, but the impression lingered in Sylvie's
mind. Raw power, harnessed. Something flickered in his
eyes like a whirlwind. *This,* Sylvie thought, *is one hell of
a dangerous man.*

"I want *you,*" he said. "I've heard about you. You don't
give up. And you don't back down."

"News flash," Sylvie said, regretting it even as she
sassed him. "I've given up. I've backed down. Permanently." This was exactly the kind of thing that got her
into trouble.

The sisters responded with the eardrum-shivering, whining mewl, all three at once, and Sylvie fought the urge to
slap her hands over her ears.

"Sisters," he said, chiding, and they stopped.

"Ms. Lightner—"

"No," she said. "And really, if you've checked me out,
you know I'm mostly hired out to fight your kind. I
couldn't work for—"

"My kind?" he asked.

"Sorcerers, magicians, whatever the term du jour is,"
Sylvie said.

"I'm not a sorcerer," he said.

Her fragile patience unraveled. "You're sure as hell too
damn big to be a Boy Scout. And I don't think there are
badges for 'plays well with minions.'"

She trailed off as the punk girl leaned forward onto her
hands like a shifter about to go beast. Sylvie had a nasty
feeling it would be something far stranger than a wolf that
erupted from the girl's skin.

The pale woman said, "He is your *god*, girl, and you
will revere him, or I will have your throat." Her voice, the

first Sylvie had heard of it, was as raspy as if she spoke around a mouthful of feathers.

Swiveling her head, the preppie girl glanced from the not-cop to her sister, trying to decide.

"Alekta," he said. "We came here to ask for help. Not threaten."

"She should prostrate herself—" the pale, leather-clad woman argued.

"Alekta," he repeated, and she fell silent, sulking.

"I think you put a bit too much hero worship into whatever summoning spell you used to get them," Sylvie said. "Either that, or you have serious egomania."

He sighed, brown eyes downcast. "It doesn't make sense, I admit, but I'm afraid it's true." His cheeks flushed as he spoke. "At least, I am *a* god, and unless you're more devout than I think, there's a good probability you're mine by default."

Sylvie pulled the gun from her purse, raised it, and said, "I said no." She had let this nonsense go on for far too long, drawn by the pain in his face. Her business was closed, and even if it weren't, she didn't take clients like him. Crazy and powerful was a deadly combination.

"Ms. Lightner—" he said, half-raising a hand.

"Still feel divine?" she said. "It's amazing how a little lead can bring out the mortal in men."

"Not a good idea—" he said. He seemed concerned but unafraid, and while Sylvie tried to decide if that was good or bad, his minions lost patience.

"Insolent child," the preppie girl spat.

"Magdala, don't," he chastised her.

Alekta, the pale one, lunged into the air like a raptor in flight. Panic seared Sylvie as the lean length of the woman changed, sprouting feathers and fur and scale, sprouting fangs, sprouting claws, showing a nightmare face that belonged nowhere in this world. She pulled the trigger without a moment's thought, and the creature dodged, dropped, and rose again.

"Alekta! Here!" he snapped, then gasped. The gun's

explosion slammed distantly into Sylvie's ears, the recoil twitching it out of her hand as if she were a rank amateur. It skidded down the stairs.

"Enough," he said. His breath was labored. "This isn't the way it should have gone—"

The women gathered around him, snarling at Sylvie, but tethered by his will. The blonde had snapped back to human form, and that freed Sylvie to look at him. Dreading the sight, the moment—Alekta had dodged, and he was behind her.

To kill a man, in her own office, with the ISI outside her door somewhere, watching . . . The problem with killing sorcerers was, after the deed, there was nothing to prove they had forfeited the right to be human. Sylvie had just bought herself a world of trouble.

There was blood on his hands, on his white shirt, like some crimson insignia over the heart. He had a faint frown on his tired face, more bewildered than angry. What would happen when he died? His sisters, freed?

Sylvie's hands grew icy. The man scared her, but there had been no proof that he meant her harm.

He sighed, then the moment unwound.

Sylvie held the gun in her hands again, her finger curling on the trigger, the bullet in the chamber waiting, the metal cool and unfired. He held Alekta's arm in a bruising grip, while she fell back toward him as if her lunge had been thwarted before it had actually begun.

"Why don't you put the gun away," he said. "They're touchy of my honor and overprotective. Especially now."

Sylvie opened her mouth, for once at a loss for words. His white shirt was pristine, no perfect chest shot, red rimmed with black, and the only pain in his eyes was the pain that had caused him to seek her out in the first place. Still wordless, she tucked the gun into her waistband.

"My name is Kevin Dunne. I am the god of Justice, and I need your help."

2

Tall, Dark . . . Crazy

SYLVIE FUMBLED TO A SEAT ON THE STAIRS. SHE HAD NEVER SEEN A sorcerer so strong—she refused to contemplate the other. "Help?" she echoed.

"I need you to find my lover," Dunne said.

What kind of name was that for a god, anyway, she wondered a bit hysterically. Gods had names like . . . like Thor, like Legba, like *God*—she met his calm eyes again and dropped her own. She supposed that gods could choose any name they liked. But he looked so ordinary in his white shirt and Levi's. His hair had flecks of grey in it; his face had lines around his eyes and jaw. A nice face, attractive enough, but the face of a god?

Belatedly, his words filtered through. "You're a god. Find her yourself." Her lips were numb; she was running on autobitch, as Suarez had called it.

"I can't," he snapped. "Don't you think that's driving me mad? I should be able to—I don't know why I can't. I can find anyone I've ever seen, ever laid eyes on."

"So don't even think of running," Magdala, the preppie woman, muttered.

Sylvie tore her eyes away from the woman, met his.

Underneath their earnestness, she found herself talking again. "Dead maybe? Not among the living?"

His mouth twisted, his eyes squeezed closed, and the women's expressions grew fiercer.

"No," he said. "No." She wasn't sure if it was knowledge or hope that drove the denial. He opened the door to her shop and gestured to the women. "Go on, wait outside. I can't talk to her when you're distracting her."

"But—" Magdala objected.

"Go," he said. "I'll call you when I need you."

The sisters rose and filed out, obedient but not happy. The punk girl paused to stick her tongue out at Sylvie. Dunne shut the door on her.

"What are they?" Sylvie asked. "Some sort of Aztec werewolves? I saw feathers and fur—"

"They're the Eumenides," Dunne said, taking a seat on the cardboard box nearest the stairs. It sagged a moment, then firmed beneath him, transforming from a standard cardboard box to a heavy chair, lattice-backed, in a golden oak that looked like it belonged in some homey kitchen somewhere. He hooked his feet around the support rungs automatically.

Sylvie swallowed, her attention diverted. A sorcerer at the very least. A common magic-user couldn't transform an item worth a damn; give cardboard the *appearance* of strength, the *look* of oak, no problem, but actual strength? Even sorcerers preferred illusion to actual transformation, saved them the effort of reshaping the world. Dunne didn't look bothered. Dunne didn't look like he had thought about it at all. More to the point, Sylvie thought, there was rather more chair than there had been box. Creation of matter—

The files inside, she thought. He'd transformed paper to oak. Her files had just become woodwork, and wasn't that one way to hide the evidence.

He leaned forward. "Before I came, I hadn't realized you'd killed quite so many people."

"I'm no murderer," Sylvie said. "I don't kill people."

Monsters, on the other hand, yeah, she'd killed those in quantity.

"They think otherwise, and they get a little . . . over-zealous in their desire to help justice."

"Good to love your job," Sylvie said. Empty words to go with her empty mind.

He sighed. "I am a god, Sylvie, whether you choose to believe me or not. But I was once a policeman, so let me save you some time. Death is no mystery to my kind. I ask you to find my lover, and I do this knowing, without any doubt at all, that he's alive. Equally, I know that he's being held somewhere I can't reach or find. And he can't get free—" His voice cracked, the calmness deserting him.

He, Sylvie thought, *now that's a surprise.* "I'm sorry," she said. "I really am. But I've quit."

"Can you?" he asked. "Some things are in the blood. You can't be other than you are."

She started to rise, and he took her wrist. She yanked it away. "Call the cops if you think your boyfriend's been kidnapped."

"I already have," Dunne said. "They're hunting for him, but their methods have become mindless."

Sylvie remembered the cops earlier and hesitated. It couldn't be related. Even a sorcerer couldn't influence people that greatly. Charm, Deceive, Destroy. The three major spell groups; the first coaxed people into action they wouldn't otherwise take, the second shrouded a person's mind, and the third ruined a man or woman, body or soul. Perhaps a big enough charm—

"Just hear me out," he said. He reached into the space between them and opened his palms. A photograph lay on them.

Sylvie, reluctantly, took it. It wasn't a great photo. The subject had been moving at the time, slipping to the outside of the shot, as if he didn't like the camera eye's weight on his skin, but it revealed a good-looking man with red hair, a lithe build, and an expression on his face that struck a worried chord in her.

"His name is Brandon Wolf," Dunne said.

Robbing the cradle a bit, Sylvie thought, looking at the young man's face; she wouldn't put Dunne at a day less than forty-five. But maybe gods aged differently—the fog in her head cleared. She knew what had woken that worried burst of déjà vu. Brandon Wolf, twenty years his lover's junior. Her old friend, Valerie Cassavetes, twenty years her husband's junior. They both held the same expression in their eyes, a little tinge of fear. Valerie's fear had been of her husband. Before Sylvie had killed him dead and helped bind his spirit forever. Brandon's fear?

"I'm sorry—"

"No," he said. "I don't want to hear that again. You don't trust me, I see that. But you're not the kind to gladden an old cop's heart, either. I know you're unlicensed, unsupervised, unauthorized. An amateur with a gun."

"If that's what you think of me," Sylvie said. She tried to hand back the photograph. He closed his hands into fists.

"I told you," he said, eyes dark with unhappiness. "I checked into you. You're a vigilante. The only saving grace I see is that there's no system set up to deal with the supernatural. I'm trying to ignore the thought that says even if Metro-Dade had processing forms for rogue angels and werewolves, you'd still act as you saw fit."

"This from a man who calls himself the god of Justice," Sylvie said, finally setting the photograph facedown on the stairs. Out of sight, out of mind.

"I was a cop first," he said.

Sylvie shook her head. "What, you just woke up one morning and were a god? It doesn't work like that. Men don't become gods. Men don't have that kind of power. At most, humans can borrow it or manipulate it. Not own it."

"You don't know as much as you think you do, Sylvie," he said. "You want to watch out for that. That's the kind of thing that comes back to haunt you." In his eyes, grey skies rolled, slaty and darkening. "But maybe you know that already."

She shied when Dunne rose from his chair and collected his lover's photograph from the steps beside her. Up close, he smelled almost electric, like a stormy day. She raised her head, forced herself to meet his gaze.

"I can't help you." Finally, *finally* she mastered the flat conviction to her voice that should drive him off.

He leaned against the wall, slumping. "I'm sorry, Sylvie. I don't think you understand. You don't have a choice." His voice sounded dragged out of him, ending in a whisper.

Familiar rage buoyed Sylvie after the first shock. Always the same with his type. It always came down to threats. "You may claim godhood, but last I checked I still had free will."

"Free will," he said, "is overrated and not as powerful as you think. To be truly free, Sylvie, you have to care only for yourself. To care for no one else."

"You're threatening my friends," she said, "my family? Is that it? After all your talk about justice, you're going to play mob boss?"

He said, still in that strained half whisper, "Gods radiate their influence around them. Very rarely do we linger in the mortal world. When we do, it has ramifications. I need Bran found. And the world will bend to that, whether it knows it or not." He turned his head, looking toward the front of the store, and Sylvie's eyes followed.

It had grown dark in the last few minutes of their conversation, but unwilling to take her eyes from him, Sylvie hadn't noticed it much. Cloud cover, an early storm rolling in. Her blood chilled when she saw the reality.

It wasn't the sky that had darkened. Instead, her glass doors and windows were blocked, filled by policemen, motionless, peering in with blank eyes. Waiting.

"Come here," Dunne said. He opened the door, and the police stepped back. Sylvie went to the door and looked out, looked at the blankly determined faces all turning toward Dunne like sunflowers to the sun. In the midst of the uniformed mass, she spotted two suits, two faces she vaguely recognized. Her ISI watchdogs had fallen prey to Dunne also.

Surveil that, she thought, a quick, fleeting satisfaction trying to surface. Dunne's words drove it back.

"Everyone who is mine, everyone who falls under the aegis of Justice, will hunt. But they hunt without understanding, without control, just a reflection of my need to find him. And the more desperate I grow—"

"The harder they search," Sylvie finished. "I get the picture. It's not just my friends and family you're holding over my head. It's the city."

Across the street, nearly swamped in the uniformed mass, the sisters grouped themselves. Alekta raised her head and grinned at Sylvie.

Sylvie shut the door, thinking dark thoughts about power. Dunne either had far more than any human had a right to, or he was siphoning off the inhuman but undeniably powerful sisters. Eumenides: the word sounded familiar in a high-school way, something heard and dismissed in one of her classes. Back before she knew there was more to reality than what they taught.

"You'll find him?" Dunne said, interrupting her thoughts.

"What if I fail?" Sylvie asked.

Dunne closed his eyes, biting at his lip, exhaustion pulling his features. Outside the police slowly dispersed. "Don't. I couldn't bear it."

"And they're the stick to make sure I do my best," Sylvie said. "Them and your sisters."

"Not mine," he muttered. "*The* sisters."

"You want me to take your case; you won't take no for an answer, and you've got the power to make my life extremely difficult and very short," Sylvie said. "I suppose that means there's no carrot to the stick. Just a do-it-or-else kind of clause." Bitterness laced her voice. Maddening to take on a case when she wanted to quit; to do so without remuneration made her want to spit.

His face cleared a little in surprise. "No, of course

you'll get paid. Name your price. I am a god, Sylvie, whether you choose to accept it or not. Your fee could reflect that. What do you want?"

The Eumenides sisters were the only faces left in her storefront window; they watched Dunne as faithfully as the police had, but with far more intelligence behind their eyes, a visual reminder of the power Dunne wielded.

Sylvie's heart skipped—a god? The possibilities reeled before her. Money zipped by; she always needed that, but money was easy. If Dunne wasn't lying, if he was a god, he could give her something far more valuable. Something that would lift the guilt from her back and make Alex smile again. There was really only one thing to ask for.

"Anything I want?" she said, trying for casual in her voice, trying not to let him see how much this mattered.

"Pretty much," he said.

"Can you bring back the dead?"

3

The Unreal World: *Magicus Mundi*

"IS THAT WHAT YOU WANT?" HE ASKED, HOLDING HER GAZE.

"I asked, didn't I?" she said. Hope and disbelief warred in her, came out as bad temper. "And I don't mean a zombie, dead flesh animated and forced to feign a life that it can barely recall. Don't give me any Star Trek Prime Directive objections, either . . . that you're not allowed to interfere. You claim to be a god. Put up or shut up. *Can you do it?*"

"Sometimes," he said. "There are a lot of gods, Sylvie, and each of us has our own followers, devout folk who are ours to do with as we will. Then there are the rest. So few humans are truly devout anymore, mouthing words without belief. They're up for grabs, and we divide them. We're not too comfortable with sharing, though sometimes deals have been struck.

"If he's mine or no one's, I can bring him back. If not, not without permission. But most of law enforcement falls under my aegis. Including you."

"I belong to no one," Sylvie snapped.

He shrugged, not taking offense. The sisters, on the other hand, scowled at Sylvie through the window. Sylvie thought she could feel the thick glass vibrate beneath the weight of their collective growl.

"I've heard that before," Dunne said. "As a general rule, policemen claim to lack belief in abstracts, but most of them believe in me. In justice. In the idea that wrongs can be made right."

"Suarez isn't getting any less dead," Sylvie said.

"How did he die? What one god has done, it is not wise to undo."

"He was killed by a bullet. By a human," Sylvie said.

"Show me," he said.

"Show you?" she repeated. "I didn't videotape it. I had other things on my mind at the time. Knee-deep in satanists tends to do that to a girl." She watched his face, and said, "I suppose you're going to say since a satanist fired the gun, he's lost—"

"That's not a problem," he said. "Satan's not a god, only a fallen angel and one not inclined to waste his limited power defending his followers. But you must show me, Sylvie. I don't know your man. To bring him back, I need to be able to find him."

"How?"

"Just remember it. I'll watch through your eyes."

"I can't do that," she said.

"You're doing it all the time," he said, his voice softening. "You worry at it like the lion with the thorn."

When she thought she was ready, she said, "His name was Rafael Suarez, my assistant and friend. He got into blood magic and went junkie for it, got wrapped up in the pain and power. Masochism done magic style."

Sylvie let the words unroll, the images fill her mind. By the time she'd realized the scope of his problem, he'd gone to the satanists' altar eagerly, hunting the ultimate rush. Sylvie had crashed the party, Alex refusing to be left behind, and there had been a brief stalemate as the celebrants saw Sylvie's gun. They might have been reaching for power, but they were mortal and selfish at the moment. The gun sobered Suarez as well, sent him reeling from the altar toward them. A look back, and he crossed himself, a brief, desperate prayer for forgiveness.

At the time, Sylvie had seen it as a meaningless gesture, but now, in her head, the image of the sketched cross burned so bright it made her eyes water.

Dunne sighed. "He was Catholic? And truly believed. I'm sorry. He's been taken to the light god's hands, and He is a most jealous god."

"So that's a no, then? Figures," Sylvie said, when the disappointment that thickened her voice past speech faded.

"I'm sor—" he said. She flung up a hand. Stop. Sorry meant nothing to her.

"Then you have nothing to offer me," Sylvie said. "But I guess it doesn't matter. You've got my obedience anyway." She couldn't believe she had almost liked this man.

"That's not true," he said. "I can give you the other thing you want, the thing you don't want to admit to." There was a note in his voice suddenly that resonated with her own internal voice, the one that spoke so often in terms of kill or be killed. She raised her head and met his eyes, no longer gentle, but cold, grey, and full of purpose.

"I'll bring them to justice."

Sylvie's heart thudded in her rib cage. "The cops can do that," she said, dismissively. "*I* can do that."

"When they were masked?" he asked. "When the trail from the club has gone cold? When they'll be hunting you? Kill you, and they not only get their power, they get rid of a witness to their crimes. Or . . . just say the word, and I'll take care of them."

Sylvie shivered; another line crossed. Asking Dunne to remove her human enemies was only one step from her doing it herself. Of becoming the monster. Still, the word hissed out, over her doubts, over her fears. "Yes."

"Are you sure?" he asked, his voice gentling again, as if he could read that weak trace of dismay in her thoughts.

"It would be . . . justice," she said, voice flat. Her hands shook, and she slid her wet palms down the sides of her jeans. If Dunne and the sisters took out the satanists, it would solve her most pressing problems. Protect Alex, her family, anyone else the cultists ran across in their search for her. "A life for a life."

"His life for all of theirs," Dunne said.

"He was only their first victim. They'll want more." Sylvie thought of Alex crying silently for days, of her own tears, which stalked her at awkward moments, of Suarez's bewildered parents uncovering their son's private life. She closed her eyes, allowing that dark whisper to overrule the rest of her mind. "Can you deliver?"

"Yes," he said. Simple, confident, impatient. He gestured to the sisters, and they sauntered back into the office. Magdala and the punk girl settled on Sylvie's battered couch, speaking to each other in liquid syllables that Sylvie didn't recognize. The blonde beelined for Dunne's side. Obviously, he played favorites, Sylvie thought.

"Kevin?" Alekta asked. Glee surfaced in her pallid eyes. "Is it time for work?"

"Yes, Alekta," Dunne said. The other two women looked up with sudden interest, but he waved them back. "Just Alekta."

He nodded at the chair he had made, and Sylvie sat in it, ill at ease. "It's easy enough, Sylvie. Just think of one of them; we'll seal our bargain after the first one's been dealt with. The rest will come . . . after you find Bran."

There was the reminder of her leash again, she thought. Take out one of her enemies, but the rest would be free until she recovered Bran. It all added up to an unspoken *Find him fast.*

Sylvie closed her eyes, remembering. She wanted to be *sure*—they had been masked. She didn't want him to just kill anyone and pretend it was one of them. There had to be some way. . . .

She focused. The leader raised his arms, spoke behind his mask, and Sylvie frowned. Nothing distinctive about him. Tall, but not remarkably so. He wore gloves, a full face mask, a full cloak. She couldn't even tell if he was white, black, Hispanic, or other. She wouldn't recognize him if she saw him on the street.

Reluctantly, she chose another target. Parting the crowd, pushing through silken cloaks, bumping up against one of the most avid participants. Behind her mask, the eyes had been blue; a spill of red-dyed curls tangled at the nape of her cloak, and her perfume, the ripe, sex-sweet musk of tropical orchids. *Her,* Sylvie thought, remembering the girl's laughter when Suarez fell.

"That one," she said. "That one first." There was a brush of softness against her face, the faint prickle of blunt-cut hair and the creak of leather.

She opened her eyes and found Alekta pressed nearly into her, her eyes wide and blank, her mouth gaping. Sylvie recoiled, reaching instinctively for her gun and coming up short. "Get away from me."

"Did you get the scent?" Dunne asked.

Alekta nodded, tongue lolling out of her mouth in a horror-movie moment; her waist and belly sucked in, her ribs expanded, her arms thickened, and she dropped to all fours, still shifting leisurely, as if she intended to enjoy the hunt.

"No!" Sylvie snapped. "No."

Dunne said, "What now? Changed your mind?"

"No, but not like that. Not shredded by an animal." Sylvie had seen deaths like that before—ugly, loud, and bloody. She wasn't going to watch it again, and she had every intention of seeing the satanist die. If she ordered it, she had a duty to bear witness. Her heart pounded. "You do it," she told Dunne. "Not your minion. You."

Alekta whined, but reversed her transformation on Dunne's command. "Fine," he said. He reached over Alekta and seized Sylvie's arm so tightly she knew there'd be bruises.

Bastard, she thought, just before the world dropped out from under her. She shrieked outrage, but the sound was swallowed by the overwhelming blur of color and noise that surrounded her. Like being inside a tornado, she thought, her breath hiccuping in her chest. And then it was done, and she and Dunne stood on the Gables campus of the University of Miami, midway between the Rathskeller, the Olympic pool, and the University Bookstore.

When she could speak, she growled, "Never again. I don't like magic used on me."

And such magic, she thought, her nerves still jangled. Dunne was far too talented. Mind-viewing, summoning of those horrible sister-demon things, transport spells, and of course, that tiny hiccup in time that she'd experienced earlier.

Humans could do each of those things if they were sufficiently talented and foolhardy. It took a type of power that always fought back, twisting in on itself, devouring its users if they faltered for even a moment.

Dunne seemed to use magic as easily as he breathed. Sylvie bit her lip; she was going to have to give Val a call—what she knew about magic was sketchier than it should be, confined mostly to her reasons for distrusting it.

"There she is," Dunne said, gesturing. He had taken a seat on one of the benches that lined the concrete path.

Two girls walked side by side, coming down the path toward them. Sylvie recognized her would-be target immediately, in the way she moved, held herself, *smirked.*

The girl shook back her red curls and nudged her prettier companion just hard enough that the girl stepped off the path and into a slick spot of mud. She went down, and the red-haired girl laughed.

Still spreading her own particular brand of joy, Sylvie thought. If she had had any doubts, that little act of spite erased them. She nodded at Dunne, and his lips tightened.

"She wasn't the one who shot him," he said, but even as she opened her mouth to protest, he nodded. "Done."

Sylvie turned, and the girl was suddenly gone. Sylvie had expected flames for some reason, people screaming and fleeing, campus police scratching their heads over an undeniable case of spontaneous human combustion, maybe even the girl's ashes blowing back across Sylvie's skin.

Instead, there was nothing. No outcry, no notice. Even the girl's companion, rubbing exasperatedly at the mud on her jeans, seemed unaware that anything had occurred. But one moment the girl had been there, sauntering down the path, the next—nothing. *Nearly* nothing, Sylvie realized. Something lay on the path, something small and fragile.

With shaking legs, Sylvie walked over to the place where the girl had vanished, and bent, her fingers ready to recoil. An illusion, surely, not the thing itself. Sorcerers excelled in illusion and deception. But this—she reached out and touched it. Her eyes and her fingers agreed. She picked up the orchid, white bleeding into pale pink, the roots dangling, and said, "Transformed? Not dead?"

"She isn't a murderer," Dunne said. "Revenge is outside my nature. If you want her dead, you'll have to do it. It won't be that hard. Just throw her back on the ground, let someone trample her. Run her through a Weed Eater. Or even simpler, let her dry out and die."

Sylvie let out a shaky breath; she should be relieved that her orders hadn't put that responsibility on her. Instead, she only felt as if he was squirming out of their bargain. Testing her determination.

Sylvie felt the frailty of the narrow stem, the fleshiness of the petals, and cast it down onto the path again, raised her sneakered foot, imagining how the plant would shred, pulpy and tender beneath her heel. But when her sole touched pavement, she felt only the grit of concrete. She opened her eyes. Dunne stepped back from her, holding the orchid in his hands.

4

Murder, Morals, Motive

"AS SIMPLE AS THAT FOR YOU?" DUNNE SAID, TOUCHING THE FRA-
grant petals. "Transformation is not enough? An evil
turned to harmless beauty, made benign—"

"You want me to take the damn case, don't lecture me
on my morals," Sylvie said. "They killed Suarez. They'll
be after me. Yeah, it's pretty simple. Kill or be killed."

"But she's harmless now," he said. He frowned, but the
expression was more puzzled than disapproving. "It's one
thing to kill in self-defense or in protection of another. To
kill once there is no pressing need—"

"If your lover is dead, or alive but tortured," Sylvie
said, "will you dare tell me you won't exact his pain on
their hides?"

As he quailed, she pressed her advantage. "An eye for
an eye, a tooth for a tooth, tit for tat; it's the oldest, simplest justice there is. Or is that different from being Justice with a capital *J*? Are you a kindlier, gentler justice?"

He closed his fingers, and the orchid vanished. Sylvie
caught the protest in her throat. "You let her go?"

"No," he said. "Put her elsewhere." His eyes were tired,
and he rubbed at them with the heels of both hands, the

face of a man with a dilemma. "Is this going to work? I need you to think—you're almost as bad as the sisters."

"Fuck you," Sylvie snapped. "I'm smarter than your minions." She was shaking, cold all the way to her bones at what she had tried to do. She didn't kill people. Even if they were flowers. She clung to that thought, but she had always responded to fear with rage. Fear paralyzed you. Rage kept you moving.

"How many others could you identify clearly from your memories? The girl passed close to you—you saw her hair, heard her laugh, saw her move, smelled her perfume and sweat. The others? If you destroyed her, their identification becomes harder."

"Your sisters could follow her scent back, right?" Sylvie said.

"Oh, they could have followed it anywhere. On anyone she'd been near. Like her classmates, her teachers, the people in her dormitory, and those she stood next to on slow elevators. How many throats would you see the sisters hunt?" His eyes were steady on hers.

Sudden sickness welled in Sylvie's throat; she turned from his gaze.

"This way, you have a choice. We can still ask her questions. Identify the others the simplest way."

"Kinda hard to ask a flower questions," Sylvie said, trying not to let him see how shaken she was. "All that language of flowers crap aside."

"Don't be difficult," he said. "I'll change her back first, of course."

"Of course," she said. No big deal. Transformation. *Real* transformation of matter. Most transformations were only a matter of rearranging mass. Werewolves were big because men were bigger than wolves. Turning a person into a toad would only result in a toad the size of a man. To turn a woman into a single, delicate orchid—to change her back at will—that required destruction and creation of mass. Destruction was a human skill, possible for a juiced-up sorcerer. Creation—wasn't.

He took her arm again, and she yanked away. "No. We are not traveling that way again."

Dunne's face darkened. "We don't have a lot of time—"

"Enough for you to lecture me on ethics. Enough for you to prove your skills. I think we have enough time to take a car wherever we go next." She met his eyes, refused to back down. He could force the issue, she supposed. But he was weak, too. He was desperate, and he needed Sylvie.

"Fine," he said. He gestured in a manner that looked a lot less like a spell trigger than a man throwing his hands up in exasperation. With the sudden rearrangement Sylvie was beginning to get used to, her truck appeared in the parking lot nearby, its battered and clawed red hood a familiar beacon.

"Great," she said, her poise restored with its appearance. The clawed hood reminded her she'd survived a lot more intrinsically malevolent creatures than Dunne was turning out to be. "But tell me this. Where are we going?"

"To look for him," Dunne said. Bewildered panic entered his eyes again.

Sylvie found a bench and sat on it, noticing campus security showing up more and more in her line of sight, blooming like fungus after a rain. Watching Dunne. Not approaching him. Just watching.

"Everyone's looking for him. Sit down, Dunne, and let's do this right. You accused me of not thinking, so let's think. Where was he the last time you saw him? When exactly was that?"

"I've told the cops that," Dunne said.

"Look, what do you suggest I do?" Sylvie said. "Wave a wand? I'm no witch. I am what you see, what my reputation declares me: an inquisitive bitch with a gun. I suppose I could wander the streets like your mindless cops, calling his name like he was a lost cat. . . ."

The police reports appeared in her lap. He slumped forward, head in his hands. "That's efficient," she said.

She flipped through the first report. Not local, these boys. Chicago. She frowned. She hated Chicago—all that concrete, those looming high-rise buildings, and the poor man's ocean. Couldn't hold a candle to the tropics. She found the Polaroid again of Brandon moving away from the camera's eye.

"That's the most recent one," Dunne said, his voice rough. "It was taken the night he was abducted. Two weeks ago."

Sylvie noted the cream-and-green sweater, the nice watch, the glittering gems in his ears. "Is he wealthy?"

"Yes," Dunne said. "But it's not a kidnapping."

Yes, Sylvie thought. *Of course he'd be wealthy. If you're the play toy of a god, why not be rich.* "Any vengeful exes?"

"I checked them out," he said, raising his head to meet her eyes. "Thoroughly."

"They still alive?" she asked.

"Of course," Dunne said, offended. "I'm not a killer."

"No, but your pets are," Sylvie said. "No tricky technicalities here. *You* didn't kill them. Did the sisters?"

"No," he growled, for one moment sounding uncannily like the creatures he commanded.

Sylvie shut up, self-preservation kicking in. She flipped the picture facedown, turned it faceup, trying to restore her first impression of Brandon Wolf.

Delectable.

She closed her eyes and tried not to think about opportunists, killing for money or sex, feeding some dark fetish she'd never even imagined.

Dunne said, in echo of her thoughts, "The FBI thinks there are approximately twenty known serial killers working, and assumes there may be up to three hundred working the country unnoticed. There are more than that, but the odds are still against one of them having taken Bran, especially when you consider that Bran is more aware than most of the evils of this world. Besides, I told you. He's not dead." He snagged the photograph from her, looked down at it.

"You'd—feel it?" Sylvie asked, unable to keep the

skepticism from her voice. "Like something out of a romance novel? Kindred souls and all that rot? You were a cop, Dunne, you know how full of shit that is. People die, and it's an ugly surprise to their loved ones, each and every time."

"I'd know," he repeated. "I'm not human. I am a god."

"Who once worked as a cop," Sylvie said, forcing gentleness into her tone, turning the acid to humor. "Were things slow on the god front—had to moonlight?"

He pinched the bridge of his nose, closed his eyes. "Bran—" he whispered.

Without fanfare, the skies clouded over and began to rain, a sudden Miami downpour that turned the air silver and thick with water. Sylvie grabbed the police report and bolted to her truck.

He appeared in the seat next to her, the passenger door still locked, and she said, "All right. All right."

He seemed very close to shattering, and, god or not, he had power. She didn't want to be at ground zero if he blew. She leaned back against her seat, let rainwater trickle down her face, and thought. Two weeks missing, no ransom, no clues. Conventional wisdom argued that Brandon Wolf was dead.

But then, Sylvie thought, stealing another glimpse at Kevin Dunne, this was not a conventional situation. There was another alternative; Brandon Wolf might have fled. Her searching could jeopardize some exotic occult protection the young man had found—but she wasn't sure she believed it.

Dunne, despite his power, despite his minions, despite *everything*, kept defaulting back in her mind to Nice Guy. It made her uneasy.

She started her truck, tucking the rain-spattered police reports in the door pocket, and headed for Miami International. Chicago, huh. At least it would take her out of the satanists' immediate reach.

"Hey, Dunne, don't suppose you can magic me up a passport and a credit card?"

He blinked. "Okay." Then her entire purse was on the seat beside her; she rummaged through it with one hand, identifying things by feel: too-thin wallet, cell phone, ID, spare bullets. The bullets made her pause, thinking of the latest threat she'd faced.

"The sisters are on their own?" she asked. "We left them there."

"They'll be fine," he said.

"I'm not worried about them," Sylvie said. "I'm worried about the people around them if you're not there to snap their leash."

He shrugged. "They'll be looking for Bran mostly."

"Mostly," she muttered. But there was nothing she could do about it now. "Tell me what happened the night Bran disappeared."

"We were at a friend's party. Something came up, and I had to go—"

"Something like the Bat-Signal?" Sylvie interrupted.

"Something like that, yes," Dunne said, evenly. "But Bran wanted to stay, which was fine by me. He's too tenderhearted to watch me work." He leaned his head against the window, fell silent. Sylvie glanced over, watched the pain surge and fade on his open face.

"It took a while," he continued, after a moment in which the only sound was the sweeping thump of the wipers fighting the rain. "I was a little surprised when I got home and Bran wasn't back before me—we came home at dawn."

"We?"

"The sisters and I," he said. "Mostly they live in our backyard."

"Charming," she said. "Wonder what they do for property values in the neighborhood." He shot her a quelling look. "You weren't worried about his absence?" she prompted.

A muscle jumped in his jaw as if she'd assigned blame. "No." Guilt laced his voice, then morphed into irritation. "He's my lover, not a child. He has a life of his own. He's perfectly capable of taking care of himself. And I was . . . tired. To be the god, to enact justice—"

"It tires you out?" Sylvie asked, trying not to sound hopeful.

"No," he said. "*Containing* my power so that I don't affect the whole world is tiring. It's like walking. A fit man can walk forever. But a fit man forced to stand on one leg and hop—it takes effort. It's far easier to be what you are than to fight it. But the consequences of a god on the mortal plane . . . Well, you're seeing some of them, aren't you? My concentration is going."

The traffic up ahead crawled; police cars, lights strobing, blocked three of the four lanes, funneling all the traffic to one lane. "Like that?" she said. "Or do you suppose they're doing a midday sobriety checkpoint?"

"Shit," he muttered. There was the little hiccup of the world shifting, and the bottleneck was in her rearview mirror.

"So you went to bed," Sylvie said, plowing ahead, shuddering reflexively. "And you weren't worried."

"Bran and Tish are close," he said. "I assumed he stayed over to help her clean up. He's done it before."

"Tish?"

"Tish Carmichael," he said. "It was her party. She's a dancer. Ballet."

Sylvie took her eyes from the road again to assess his mood. After all, with a self-proclaimed god in her truck, she probably didn't have to worry about car accidents. He sounded more relaxed, as if he found the tradition of question and answer soothing, no matter that he was the one answering the questions.

"What kind of party was it?" she asked.

She had startled him; she saw it in his eyes. Outside, the rain began to slacken. "What?"

"What kind of party? A celebration of something. New job. New boyfriend. Birthday. Or was it just a party for the sake of it—a 'hey, it's Wednesday' kind of thing? C'mon, Dunne, you know what I'm getting at."

"Tish throws parties all the time. She's sociable."

"So not a collection of close friends attending, then. Not an exclusive list. Were there strangers crashing?"

"Always are," Dunne said, frowning. "but I checked them out. I would have felt anyone powerful enough—"

"You keep saying what you would have felt. But tell me this—what were you feeling when Bran disappeared? If you didn't feel that, then I don't see—"

"I *did*," he said.

"But you weren't worried when he wasn't home. Something worried you enough to check out the strangers at the party, but you feel something when your boyfriend disappears and you aren't worried. You go to bed."

"It was so quick," he said, his voice rough. "I was in the middle of a gang fight, and I was trying hard not to let the sisters go, trying to keep the battlefield confined, the witnesses to none. It was just a touch. It was just . . . I felt startled . . . and there was no reason. It was just a moment; he wasn't hurt or scared. Just surprised."

Sylvie fell silent. "You left the party. The kidnapper could have come later."

"Yes," Dunne admitted.

"You were suspicious of strangers earlier. Why?"

"Bran doesn't like strangers," he said, something in his tone withdrawing.

A lie, she thought. Clients all had to lie about something. Was it Dunne who didn't like strangers? Or was it even simpler than that? Bran stayed out overnight often enough that Dunne wasn't concerned. Maybe he'd been having an affair, and Dunne had caught on. Only a fool cuckolded a sorcerer. There probably weren't words for anyone brazen enough to cuckold a god.

The road curved into the entrance to the airport, and she sighed. She'd learned the hard way there was no point pushing at a lie a client told her; she had to come at it from a different angle, and she was out of time.

He touched her arm, tense with the pressure she was putting on the steering wheel. "What are you going to do?"

"Talk to Tish," Sylvie said, raising her hand to stifle his protest. "I know, I know, the cops talked to her already."

"She doesn't know anything. About me," Dunne said. "She thinks I'm human."

"So don't do anything weird while I'm talking to her."

"I'm not going with you," he said. "I'm going to keep searching. I have to."

She nodded, oddly relieved that she wouldn't have him lurking behind her. He handed her a plane ticket. "There's a flight in twenty minutes," he said.

"Of course there is," she muttered. She pulled into the parking lot, and a guard came over to inspect her truck. "Fuck," she said. "My gun. Can you do something about that?"

The guard turned on his heel and went back the way he had come. Sylvie took her gun from her waist holster, and said, "Can you Jedi mindtrick the metal detectors?"

Dunne touched the gun in her hand, and it changed in her grasp, felt aware and warm. She twitched but controlled the instinct to drop it. She had been far too careless with it once today. "What did you do?"

"It will scan as flesh, as your own body," he said, "and appear part of you while you wear it."

"You turned my gun to meat?" Her voice soared, a little panicky, belatedly realizing how much comfort she took from the weapon.

"It's still a gun," he said. "Try not to kill anyone. You're under my aegis, and it's embarrassing."

5

Digging for Facts

O'HARE AIRPORT WAS BUSTLING WHEN SHE DISEMBARKED, AND NOT in the usual harried-traveler fashion. The terminal seethed with police and airline security, and Sylvie, all too conscious of the gun seated warmly in the small of her back, hustled her way past them. No one even gave her a glance. It made her crazy.

Even after Dunne's transformation, her gun was still a gun, still a weight beneath her thin Windbreaker. Someone should have noticed. Someone should have stopped her. That they didn't was symptomatic of a larger disease: willful blindness. Humans clustered together even as they had in the beginning. Closing ranks against the things "not our kind."

The *Magicus Mundi* wasn't invisible, intangible, or safely elsewhere. It seethed around and in and through the mass of humanity; all it required was a willingness to look beyond the expected, to ask why and how and who and most often—*what*.

Once seen, the *Magicus Mundi* had a way of keeping your attention. Sylvie had had a crash course—crash *curse*, she thought wryly—years ago, when Troilus Cas-

savetes turned out to be more than your average busi-
nessman and set a killing curse on Sylvie.

Maybe blindness was the safer choice: The *Magicus
Mundi* might not be hard to discover, but it was hell on
earth to live with.

Sylvie bypassed four parked police cars and the eight
cops standing beside them on the way to the taxi stands,
and shivered as they all turned to watch her go. Dunne's
eyes on her, long-distance? Or some instinct that she held
an image of their search in her sweating hands? She didn't
feel like finding out.

She slid into a taxi, read off Tish's address, and was
pleased when her voice was steady. The weight of their
eyes lingered on her skin.

"You sure you want to go there, lady?" the driver said,
meeting her eyes in his rearview mirror. His voice held
the rich Cuban tones she knew from Miami, but the accent
was flattened and clipped. He'd been in Chicago a long
time.

"Yes," she said. "Is there a reason not to?" She couldn't
imagine the area being dangerous, not if rich-boy Bran
partied there in cashmere and silk.

"No," he said. "No reason." An obvious lie.

He rabbited away from the curb, rocking her back in
the seat, his eyes all for the cops coming their way.

She shifted in her seat, the gun pressing into the small
of her back like a warm, strong hand—muscle and bone at
her command. The sensation soothed even as it repelled,
the near-heartbeat feel of what was once metal.

A god? She bit her lip and turned her thoughts away
from that conundrum.

Sylvie flipped the police reports open again, turning
back to statements. Wealthy? *Oh yes,* she thought. Even if
there hadn't been a list of platinum-card numbers now
considered stolen, accounts shut down, she would have
known simply by the fact that the police had accumulated
this much paperwork.

The file, nearly as thick as a phone book, threatened to

spill with every page she turned. This kind of effort *only* happened with wealth or influence behind it.

The pity of it was all that effort was useless; the reports didn't give her anything much to chew on. Bran left the party and disappeared somewhere in the ten blocks between Tish Carmichael's downtown loft and the parking garage, leaving no traces. The cops had canvassed the area, asking questions of the nighttime scavengers, making threats, making promises, and came up blank. Even the reports betrayed her. The first pages were standard collections of interviews and facts, but the latter pages of the report were all the same. Typed. Handwritten. Word processed. But all the same. Two words. Page after page.

Find Him. Find Him. FindHim Findhimfindhimfindhim . . .

Sylvie forced the pages back into a neat pile, wrapping the rubber band around them. Police reports looked nice and official, a neat alignment of facts. But these "facts" came from human lips, and people loved to lie, about big things, little things, for any number of reasons. All the reports hinged on Tish Carmichael as a starting point. The last-known person to see Brandon Wolf ali—

Sylvie shook her head. She had to assume he was alive, no matter the underlying tone of the reports—before Dunne's all-Bran, all-the-time channel took over, at any rate—no matter what common knowledge said. If she presumed him dead, how hard would she look for him? It had to be her best—whether or not Kevin Dunne was the god he claimed to be, he was capable of causing a great deal of harm.

Tish Carmichael. Kevin had said Bran and she were close. Sylvie wondered how close.

Close enough to tell lies about it?

The cabbie swore under his breath, and Sylvie was recalled to her surroundings. He pulled over, and said, "Walk from here."

"Something the matter?" she asked, but the streets ahead answered her question. The police swarmed the street like ants. She briefly wondered what it was—criminal history, points on his license, or a missing green card—that made him want to avoid inquisitive cops.

"You walk," he said. "Five blocks more."

"All right," she said. It didn't matter; she wasn't burdened by luggage. Hell, it even saved her some of the fare, and saving money was always good. Especially since she'd bartered this case for something other than cash.

She groaned. Crap. Alex would kick her butt—no, Alex was fired. Sylvie was on her own.

Sylvie walked on, keeping quiet, keeping out of the way of the cop cars, and beginning to swelter in the summer heat. In the small of her back, the gun sweated also, soft uneven droplets that touched her skin like tears or blood; Sylvie shuddered and picked up her pace.

Sylvie recognized Tish's apartment immediately. How could she not? The checkered bands in the Chicago PD's hats were deeply distinctive. Tish's apartment had four policemen sitting on her stoop. Just sitting, watching the door, like dogs left leashed outside a shop, waiting for their owners. Stray dogs, maybe. They looked unwashed and hungry. The crackle-pop static of their radios went ignored.

She took a breath, then climbed the five steps between them, aware of their eyes shifting to stare at her. She knocked on the door. "Go home," she said. The dog image rose in her mind again. "You're not helping. And you have other jobs to do. Dunne—"

Their eyes sharpened, and she said, "Yeah, I know him. *He* wants you to go back to work." They hesitated.

"But he was here," the youngest of them said, voice unsure. The other cops nodded in unison.

"He's not now." Sylvie knocked, harder the second time, taking into account the distorted strains of classical music being cranked out at full volume.

Frustration rose in her, woke the little dark voice within. *"Go away,"* she said, letting its utter contempt for human frailty bleed through.

They stiffened and blinked. Their faces took on indi-
viduality again; panic, confusion, embarrassment. She
turned her back as they scattered with confused murmurs.

After checking that the cops were out of sight, Sylvie
tested the knob. The door opened. Maybe Tish Carmichael
was a trusting soul who believed in a literal open-door
policy. Maybe not.

Sylvie slunk through the door, wincing as the volume
increased. Her hand settled in the small of her back; the
gun gave an eager pulse.

The apartment was long but roomy and seemingly
empty. The bottom floor, one large brick-walled room that
doubled as bedroom and living area, held signs of Tish:
discarded clothes, a plate left on the tiny kitchenette
counter, a scatter of cameras beside the plate—Polaroid,
35mm, and digital—a proof sheet left out, images circled
in red. The futon was opened out, sheets rumpled, sagging
toward the floor. A miniscule bathroom stood empty, save
for a clutter of hair products and dropped towels. Sylvie
climbed the narrow stairs, following the music, and soft
thumps and scuffles.

Dancer, Sylvie remembered as she came out onto the
second floor and found the girl alive, well, and working
hard in a homemade studio. One wall was mirrors; the
wood floor was sanded smooth and oddly springy. Sylvie
caught Tish's eyes midspin, and the girl came to a graceless halt.

"Kevin Dunne sent me," Sylvie said. She pitched her
voice to compete with the music. Tchaikovsky, she thought,
now that the distortion was gone. "I'm Sylvie. Your door
was unlocked."

Tish hit the remote, and the stereo fell silent.

"Okay," Tish said, and picked up a hand towel. She
wiped the sweat out of her tousled black hair, fluffing it
with the ease of old routine.

"Sorry to interrupt," Sylvie said. *Make nice when you
meet people,* Alex told her. Sometimes Sylvie tried.

"I think Bran's more important, don't you?" Tish said.

Sylvie sighed. Nice worked for Alex; people opened right up to her, even with the exotic haircut and cosmetic insanity. But Sylvie—even when she tried, it went wrong. "Of course I do," she said.

"I hope I can help," Tish said. "But I don't really see how. I told the police everything, told Kevin everything— God, I wish I'd never made Bran come. I knew he didn't want to. But I thought it'd be good for him." She pressed the towel to her face again.

Sylvie watched her sniffle, trying to get a read on the girl. Tish was careless for sure—to leave the door unlocked after Bran's disappearance, to accept Sylvie's identification without question—but careless didn't mean stupid.

Tish dropped the towel in favor of a well-faded Joffrey sweatshirt and pulled it over her soaked leotard. She reached for a pair of running shorts on the floor.

"Good for Bran, how?" Sylvie asked, leaning back against the mirrored wall so that she didn't have to watch herself interview Tish.

Tish folded herself to a cross-legged seat on the floorboards. She tugged nervously at her ankles, pulling threads from the edges of her slippers. Her blue eyes, reddened now around the rims, met Sylvie's and flicked away.

"He—he's been different of late. He stopped wanting to go out, to do things he used to do. It worried me. Especially since Kevin's been so busy."

"Doing what?" Sylvie asked, curious to see what Dunne's cover story was.

"He's security for . . . Olympus Group Ltd., I think he said. Some big, global tech company."

Sylvie kept her face still. Olympus group? Surely it couldn't be coincidence. A Greek god? Kevin Dunne didn't sound like a Greek name. Maybe he just liked the reference. Cocky bastard. "I see," she said.

"I've never heard of it, but honestly, if it doesn't involve dance, I'm probably not going to know about it."

SINS & SHADOWS **41**

Tish sighed. "Bran says I have a one-track mind. I wish I did. Then I'd be more than just a fill-in member of the troupe. Bran's got me started on photography, though. That way, when I can't dance, I can maybe still get a job in the arts—"

"Artists give the best parties," Sylvie agreed. Get her back on track. "But Bran didn't want to come to yours. He give a reason?"

"Sort of," Tish said, rubbing her fingers over the callused soles of her feet, hesitant.

"Don't make me guess," Sylvie said. "I don't have the time."

Tish let out her breath in a rush as if Sylvie's words were a blow. "I know. It's just . . . I don't want you to get the wrong idea."

"About what?" Sylvie said, sitting down opposite Tish.

"Bran was getting paranoid. I mean, *really* paranoid. You know the kind where you think your enemies are everywhere and know everything about you? He came over and checked my phone for wiretaps. Like he would even know what one would look like—he's a painter! He was so scared all the time. I was worried. And now this happened—" Tish's voice faded.

"You thought he was delusional," Sylvie said.

"No," Tish said. "I mean, not like that." She gnawed her lower lip, darkening the pink of it to red when she released it. "He's had some troubles, you know?"

"No," Sylvie said. "I didn't." The clients always lied. *Always.*

"Yeah," Tish said, and in a gesture that put unwilling chills up Sylvie's spine, drew the tips of her fingernails up each soft inner wrist and the veins underneath. "He's got scars. Old, though. I guess I just thought—I didn't think it was real." The tears gained ascendancy in her voice again, and Sylvie tossed her the towel.

This changed things. Dunne knew it would, undoubtedly why no whisper of Bran's instability had touched the police reports. The police would look hard for a young, rich abductee. Would they look as hard for a delusional young man? In this case, Sylvie knew the answer was yes, but only because Dunne was seeing to it. Still, it changed things, she thought, reduced the odds of Bran's survival.

It also put Sylvie on a tighter schedule than she had first thought.

"Stop crying," Sylvie said. "Talk to me. Did he say who he thought was following him? Or why?"

"Government." Tish hiccuped through her sobs.

"Of course," Sylvie said. The number one paranoia fantasy. But in this case, with Dunne in the picture, it was possible. Sylvie knew at least one government group that just loved sticking their fingers into every magical pie they could, heedless of the damage they caused.

"Yeah," Tish said, finally dragging her tears to a stop. "That's why I had a hard time taking it for real, you know? Why would anyone be after Bran—he's just a sweetheart; everyone l-loves Brandon. They just can't help themselves. I mean, even those bitches that Kevin works with, they're sweet as sugar to Bran."

"There's all sorts of love," Sylvie said. "Some of them will turn your stomach."

Tish shut her eyes but soldiered on. "I made him come to the party, and he did, brought Kevin along, and everything was all right. He was having a good time. But then Kevin had to go."

"And Bran—"

"Was fine with Kevin leaving him here. He was having fun. I stopped worrying, but he must have wigged out," Tish said. "All I know is he was suddenly telling me he had to go, all wired and shaking. I tried to get him to come up here, wait, and I'd take him home 'cause he was too drunk to drive for sure."

Sylvie slid the reports free from their rubber band. "He didn't wait."

"No," Tish said. "I thought he went to walk it off. He usually did. He would never drive drunk."

"But he left anyway, to do that?" Sylvie said.

"No, I told you," Tish said. "He wouldn't. He probably took the El. He likes to ride the El late at night, just looking at the city through glass. He said it was soothing to be on the outside. It let him see things as they really were."

Sylvie paused in her leafing through the reports, looking for the list of party attendees. "The El? The reports said he disappeared between your house and the parking garage north of here."

"Well, the El's in there," Tish said. "There's a station about halfway between here and the garage. So the report's right, isn't it?"

"*Technically,*" Sylvie said. She felt her breath quicken. Not much of a lead, but maybe a start, given that she knew more than the cops, knew that magic was involved. She itched to get going, to walk Bran's path on her own, and see if she could find where the path disappeared.

Instead, she riffled through the report and found the roster of partygoers. After all, someone had spooked Bran, made him flee a place where he had earlier felt safe.

She put the list in front of Tish. "Who came after Dunne left?"

"Oh crap," Tish said, looking at the sketchy collection of names, sometimes just first names, sometimes just a description of who they'd come with.

"It's not that bad," Sylvie said, though her first reaction had been just as dismayed. "It's not like you have to go through it all. Only the people that came late, and people that you don't count as Bran's friends. Of course, that leaves us with mostly the unknowns—"

"Wait!" Tish said. She jumped to her feet and ran downstairs.

For a dancer, she made enough noise for a marching band, Sylvie thought. She was back in another rush of sound and movement, clutching a double handful of what looked like Polaroids. The same kind Dunne had handed her earlier as the most recent photo of Brandon.

"Pictures," Sylvie said, smiling.

"They make fun party favors, and people like posing

for them," Tish said. "But I'm going to switch to digital—Polaroids are costing me an arm and a leg. Well, mostly Bran keeps me supplied—"

"Didn't the cops want these?"

"They took a whole bunch, one of everyone pretty much, to look for criminal records. Didn't find anything more than a couple of dopers and a few DWIs. But I still have these, and maybe they'll help me remember the names better." Tish laid them out on the floor, and Sylvie smiled again. A good many of them were taken against the wall where the wet bar had been set up, right below the kitschy ballerina clock, her legs pointing the hours and minutes. Dunne had left about eleven. . . . Sylvie started weeding through those taken when the hour was past that, listening to Tish mumbling, trying to match names to faces.

A quick flash startled her, and she looked up to see Tish lowering the tiny digital camera, frowning at it. "Hmm. I'm not sure I like it—you want to see?"

Sylvie shook her head and went back to flipping pictures. One-track mind, indeed, she thought. But if Tish couldn't get through a single conversation without snapping pics, the odds just went up that whoever scared Bran was documented. It was only a matter of recognizing it.

Sylvie flipped another shot, looking first at the clock, then at the partygoers beneath. She dropped the photo and stared at the blank black back of it for a moment.

Surely not. She picked it up again and took stock. A woman and a man, the woman whippet thin, her face petulant and of no interest to Sylvie. But the man with dark, sleek hair, eyes concealed behind dark glasses, and leaning on a white-tipped, crystal-hilted cane—recognition shocked her anew. She flicked her eyes to the clock above his head, as if she even needed confirmation of the time. Michael Demalion could only have been at Tish's party for one reason.

"Whatcha got?" Tish said, peering over Sylvie's shoulder. "Oh, the yummy blind guy. Came with Denise, that slut. Can't see it in that shot, with the glasses, but he has really pretty eyes. Sort of—"

"Dark brown with little bits of gold? Like a cat," Sylvie said. She took the shot from Tish again, not waiting for the girl's nod. *There* was *a government agent after all,* Sylvie thought. Brandon's paranoia was founded in fact.

"You know him?" Tish said.

"Yeah," Sylvie said, calm as ever, though her heart thumped at the unexpectedness of it. Michael Demalion of the ISI, the constant thorn in her side, had shown up in Chicago just in time for Bran's vanishing act. It couldn't be coincidence.

6

Allies, Enemies, and the Spaces Between

WITH MORE HASTE THAN GRACE, SYLVIE SHOVED ALL THE PAPERS back into their tattered folder. "Thanks, Tish."

"Wait," Tish said, and caught at her arm. "That's it?"

"For now," Sylvie said.

"Who is he?" Tish said. "You can't just say you know him and walk off. Bran's my friend. I have a right—"

"People have fewer rights than they think," Sylvie said. "I don't have to tell you anything."

At Tish's startled and hurt eyes, Sylvie blinked.

"Sorry. It's been a long day, and it's not near done yet. The man in the photo is a government agent. He doesn't work for very nice people."

"If he comes back?" Tish said.

"If he comes back, we're in real trouble," Sylvie said. "If he comes back, it means they didn't take Bran. And while they're generally assholes, and dangerously short-sighted, they're not casual killers. If they have Bran, there'll be a happy ending."

"Why would they even want him?"

"Don't know," Sylvie said. "Gonna ask."

"They'll tell you? If they have him?" Despite the hopefulness of Tish's voice, some deep doubt lurked beneath.

"I can be very persistent," Sylvie said. She freed herself from Tish's sinewy grip and headed down the stairs. Tish clattered down after her.

"You'll come and tell me what you found out?"

"Sure," Sylvie said. An empty promise, really. Her first duty was to Dunne, and she might uncover things he preferred to keep quiet.

Tish studied her, then nodded. "I'll be waiting."

Sylvie let herself out, and behind her, Tchaikovsky started up again, the sound mingling with the thumping bass of a sedan passing on the street. Tish working out her anxiety on her body.

Sylvie sighed. Now what? Her temper nagged, urging her to go drag information out of the ISI, out of Demalion in particular, but there were good reasons to wait.

First, she wanted to walk Bran's path, see if she could find something the cops hadn't been looking for— something magical and malevolent, some tangible proof of a kidnapping, even an occult one.

Second, she and the ISI were not friends. She'd lived under their watchful and condemnatory gaze for too long, and Dunne's place-hopping might have swept her out of their sight. She wanted to have a damn good reason before she put herself back in their sights.

If the ISI had taken Bran, had locked him away in some magically shielded cell, she'd find it. The ISI were many things; subtle was not one of them. They didn't have to be. They had the monetary weight of the US government behind them and the instinct of pit bulls. Once they seized something between their teeth, they never let go. At least, not without a firm smack to the nose. Sylvie had administered such a smack before. The price she paid for winning was their nonstop attention.

The last time she dealt with them directly, they'd taken a three-year-old child right out of preschool when the boy had given in to his genetic potential and gone wolf on the playground. It had been a bad situation to start with and ended immeasurably worse.

One of the lesser casualties was Sylvie's brand-new relationship with Demalion grinding to a savage halt when she realized he was one of *them*.

No, better by far to avoid the ISI as long as possible, to gather all the proof she could before confronting them. Before confronting Demalion.

Sylvie started down the sidewalk and was jostled by a young man running past. Reflexively, Sylvie checked her bag, her gun, her papers. All there.

She sighed. It was really the wrong time of day to be doing this. Not only would she lack that all-important *feel* of the late-night street Brandon Wolf had traveled, the taste of who and what hung about at 3:00 a.m., but it was difficult to keep an eye out for some nebulous clue when she was playing dodge 'em with a growing crowd of the homeward-bound.

Sylvie evaded a tangle of leashes and a woman walking three huskies at once. The lead dog growled low in its throat as Sylvie passed, and she shuddered. Dogs just reminded her too much of the freaky, frightening Eumenides sisters.

She bit her lip, wondering how much damage those women-things would cause in her city, wondered if Alex would, for once, have the sense god gave small kittens and stay the hell away from the office.

The way things were going, though, Sylvie thought Alex might have gone straight back to the office to have it out with her and run headfirst into the sisters.

Her stomach clenched and roiled. The gun at her back throbbed in time with her accelerating heartbeat. She couldn't lose Alex. *Then you'd better stop whining and find Brandon Wolf,* her internal voice said. *Soonest found, soonest Dunne and his bitches are gone.* Sylvie started walking again; she hated that voice, its spit and spite and rage. But hell, it could always be counted on to keep the goal clear.

The entrance to the El appeared, a dark stairway in the sidewalk. Sylvie headed for it, thinking how *Chicago* it was, that to board an elevated railway, she had to go underground. This city made so little sense, contrary with age. She missed Miami with a passion. Sure, Miami could be brutal, and the forces of good nominal at best, but everything was out in the open. The sun saw to that. A city like Chicago, with its underground and its history, kept its secrets close and guarded them jealously.

Sylvie forded a wave of ascending businessmen and -women, and started down the dimly lit stairs, trying to take them slow, to keep her eyes open, but between the crowds and residual light dazzle, she saw only blurs of movement and color.

Didn't make a difference, anyway, Sylvie thought in discouragement. What kind of evidence was she expecting to find? What could remain firm in this kind of daily traffic? The only constants were the gritty walls, graffitied and stained, and the sweating cement beneath her feet— Sylvie yelped as the meat gun twitched against her spine, like someone receiving a static shock. What in *hell* had he done to her gun? She put her hand on it and felt it throbbing like a frightened heart.

People veered around her, and Sylvie's fingers slowly peeled from the vise grip at her back. Her shoulders slumped. Her hands shook. She couldn't do this. She *had* to. Dunne had made sure of it.

Her eyes, closed and lowered, opened as the crowd began drawing in again, and she blinked.

What was that? Feet crossed her vision, a quick parade of recent fashions, and beneath them, something else, something painted onto the concrete.

Sylvie turned in place, jostling people and gathering complaints, ignoring them all. Blue paint, thick and shiny, looking more poured than brushed, made a jagged circle, half of it on the stairs, the other half below. Red paint edged it in a looping line that weaved around the blue, and within the spaces created . . . Sylvie knelt, touching the symbols.

It looked Greek, not frat-boy, capital-letter Greek, but something more fluid. Inside the circle, a descending spiral coiled, all blues and greens, the color of a whirlpool. Not your usual graffiti, Sylvie thought, and while Chicago boasted a big art community, this wasn't art.

She cleared the stairs and slouched against a wall, watching the crowds thin out as the trains came and went, waiting for another look.

With the people gone, with the air stilling in the wake of the trains, she knew she had seen it right. A spell circle. She might not hold with using magic, but she had a passing recognition of the way it felt. The sensation that here, in this spot, reality had been reshaped, even if only for a moment.

She sketched the circle and its patterns on the back of one of the police reports—Greek for sure, wasn't that rounded *w* omega?—being careful not to close the loops completely on her sketch.

To work spells required talent and intent, but magic was tricky. A spell could look inert and be active. Sylvie had seen men killed with a simple talisman held the wrong way; a spell that vanished a young man beyond the reach of a god was best treated like toxic waste. She needed a witch.

Luckily for her, she knew one, and one who owed her favors. Sylvie left the underground and rejoined the sky, tugging her cell from her pocket. Val Cassavetes was due a phone call; Sylvie just hoped she didn't check her caller ID. Val might owe her favors, but that didn't mean she liked doing them.

Sylvie scrolled through the stored numbers and swore. Idiot, she cursed herself. So busy trying to end her connections to the supernatural world, the first thing she'd done, even before packing the office, was purge her phone of all non-real-world contacts—Val Cassavetes included.

She punched in another number before she could think about it, one memorized in her fingertips. She hadn't wanted to, and God, Alex was going to gloat. Going to laugh and say I told you so, and don't you regret taking my key? *If* Alex even spoke to her.

The phone picked up, and Alex answered, a little breathless; lost track of her cell phone for the millionth time, Sylvie thought.

"Syl? God, are you okay? Where the hell are you?"

"Chicago." Sylvie answered the only real question in the lot, her voice strangely rough. "I need Val's number. Can you get it?" Straight to business, in and out, disconnect, and go back to shutting her out. The only safe way.

"No sweat," Alex said. There were faint background noises that Sylvie recognized, the sounds of surf and traffic, and a conch-fritter vendor in full dinnertime patter.

"Where are—"

"The office, duh," Alex said. "I've been waiting. Worried sick, if you care. Do you even have a clue how worried I was—you've been running on empty since the satanists—" Her voice caught, but continued, growing in strength. "You shut me out, pack up all your stuff, and then . . . then you just disappear!" There was no sound for a moment but Alex's breath, panting with anger and fear.

"Alex—" Sylvie said, meaning to say something, to apologize somehow. "How'd you get in?"

Alex laughed, a bark of unamused sound. "I'm quicker than you give me credit for, Syl. I stole the key back. Fast fingers, remember? You should call your sister, she's worried, too."

"You called Zoe?" Sylvie asked. What the hell—

"Well, yeah," Alex said. "Called your parents, too, but they were out of town. I thought you were having a meltdown. I thought—" Her breath caught, and Sylvie understood.

"You thought I might do something terminally stupid. Sorry, Alex. You should know better. Other people die. Not me." Sylvie kept one eye on the dwindling crowd, wanting to be back downstairs looking at the spell

"No," Alex said. "You're too mean to die."

"Damn straight," Sylvie said. "You got the number or what?"

"Had to unpack a few unlabeled boxes," Alex said. "But I got it."

Sylvie waited. And waited. A gust of warm air rolled up from the railway entrance as a train passed through and rose clattering over the street.

"What are you doing in Chicago, Sylvie?"

Sylvie thought about throwing the cell phone to the street in a satisfying shatter of plastic and walking off. If she could recall even a glimmer of Val's damn number—

"Sylvie—" Alex singsonged into the receiver.

"Missing person," Sylvie gave in, pitching her voice lower as a group of teens walked by.

"Weird, obviously, or you wouldn't be using Val. How weird?"

"The weirdest," Sylvie said, biting her lip. She shouldn't, she *knew* she shouldn't. *Keep her safe,* she thought. Safe meant away from all of this. But Alex was her researcher, and so damn useful. "Ever hear of a family named Eumenides?"

"Eumenides?"

"Yeah, three sisters. Not good with friendly, and not scared of guns. Shifty, scary, savage kind of girls."

"Hellascary girls," Alex breathed. "Jesus, Syl. They are . . . You . . . Why are you asking?"

Sylvie could hear it, the thing she'd been hearing in Alex's voice more and more frequently, beneath the brashness, a tendril of fear as she was pitchforked into one dangerous situation after another.

"Met 'em, didn't like 'em. Now I'm working for someone who owns them."

"Jesus, Jesus, Jesus," Alex chanted. "They're not real—I mean, I never thought they were real. They're myths."

"*Greek* myths?" Sylvie said. *I am the god of Justice.* Greek lettering in the spell circle. The Olympus group.

"Yeah," Alex said. "You think they're the real deal? Not just sorcerers with a shtick?"

Sylvie remembered the bone-chilling paralysis she'd felt under their eyes, the small-rodent urge to curl up and die or run. With shape-shifters, the fear was always physical, that atavistic dread of being eaten alive; the sisters made her feel more than that. In their presence, Sylvie was aware of the fragility of her *soul*. "Yeah," she whispered.

"Do you *know* how dangerous they are?"

"No," Sylvie snapped, taking refuge in anger. "That's why I'm asking."

"They're called the Kindly Ones, the Erinyes, sort of in a talismanic hope that respect will keep them off your back. But they're also called the Furies."

Sylvie twitched. That name she knew. Her blood cooled in her veins, raising goose bumps beneath her long sleeves. "A human could control them?"

"Hell no," Alex said. "No one controls them. Not really. They're punishers. Classically, they drive men mad for their sins, though I've heard they kill as well, or even destroy souls, depending on how much they want their victim to suffer. They're family-obsessed in a way even the moral majority would shrink from—most of the sins they punish are crimes inflicted by a child upon parents. They're unstoppable. They respect few gods, and obey only one."

"The god of Justice," Sylvie said.

"God? There is no god of Justice in the Greek pantheon, Syl. You gotta read more. There's goddesses, weak things, Themis, Dike, but no god. If the Furies listen to any god, it's Hera, who's as mad as they are."

"Doesn't make sense," Sylvie said. She kicked at a dropped cigarette butt, sending a faint red spark across the sidewalk. "They're working for a man now. Kevin Dunne, proclaims himself the god of Justice. They cower before him, fawn on him. Hunt murderers for him, like some vigilante team of cops."

"Oh that's so not right," Alex said. "He's pulling something. There is no god of Justice. You want me to snoop into Dunne's life?"

"Absolutely not," Sylvie said, though she desperately wanted more information on Dunne. Knowing who she was working for had always been top of the list important to her, second only to the ultimate goal of a case.

Normally, she set Alex on every client's bio, knowing that they always lied about something. Alex, who made nice with people, made even nicer with computers. Not this time. She'd have to piece his history together herself and hope she beat the clock.

"Sure?" Alex asked.

"Absolutely sure. Besides, I've got a suspicion someone's already been doing that. It's his boyfriend who's missing."

"Ransom? Blackmail?"

"Not yet," Sylvie said. "And probably not; it's been two weeks."

"Cold trail," Alex said. "If you don't find a missing person within—"

"Yeah, yeah, we all watch TV. But it's a little messier than that. The ISI's involved," Sylvie said. "It looks like one of the reasons we haven't seen Demalion sniffing around at home is 'cause he's here. Or at least, he was here the night Bran Wolf disappeared."

"*Bastard*. Kick his ass for me," Alex said.

Sylvie grimaced against the phone. Alex had taken Demalion's betrayal as hard as Sylvie had, if not harder. Demalion had used Alex to introduce him to Sylvie; in retrospect, Sylvie knew that it was the only way it would have worked. She trusted Alex. And Alex trusted people. Though not so much as she used to, courtesy of Demalion. One more black mark against the man.

"You want me to look into their files, see what I can find?" Alex said.

Sylvie hesitated, and what did it say about this case that she thought Alex would be safer taking on the Internal Surveillance and Intelligence agency than a single man who might be a god.

"I'm gonna go nuts otherwise," Alex said.

"Yeah, all right," Sylvie said. "But it'll take some time. I'm still going to meet them head-on. Makes it harder for them to lie."

"Ah, you just like the look on their faces," Alex said. "All red and puffy."

"Guilty," Sylvie said.

"Give 'em hell," Alex said. "And Syl, just so you know—you rehired me at a higher pay scale."

"Alex—"

"I wrote the contract up already. Done deal. You can sign it when you get back."

"Yeah, yeah," Sylvie said. "Got Val's number, you little mercenary?"

Alex read it off, and Sylvie punched it back into her memory list, cursing in her mind with each digit. "Hey, Alex," Sylvie said. "Don't—don't hang around the office, okay? I don't know where those sisters are now, but last time I saw them, they were prowling around the beach."

"It's okay," Alex said. "I don't want to run into them. I'd pee my pants for sure, but I'd be okay. They hunt specific sinners, and I'm clean. My parents are alive and well, all the multiple steps included, and there's no blood on my hands."

Sylvie sucked in a breath. *You kill people,* Dunne told her again. "Gotta go. You stay out of this," she said, and disconnected without further words.

"I kill monsters," she whispered, clinging to that. Monsters. Her stomach churned, roiled, declared her a liar. Her definition of monster had grown looser over the years.

Before Alex could call back, Sylvie dialed Val, punching in the number while it was fresh in her mind. Wrong number.

She cursed her inability to retain numbers, and hit the newly reprogrammed Memory 1—the first, and hopefully, only *Magicus Mundi* contact back in her books. The phone rang, but it wasn't Val on the other end. A second wrong number. Sylvie frowned. Had Val changed it?

She tried again and got a disconnect notice. Always something with witches, Sylvie thought, getting it all at once. They couldn't just screen their calls like normal people. No, Val had to bespell her phone with a dial-me-not when she didn't want to be disturbed. Tough.

Sylvie took the phone, glared at it, and gritted her teeth. "I'm calling you, Val, so give it up." She dialed the number, one careful, steady key at a time, focusing on Val, on her streaky blond hair, her pale linen dresses, her penchant for white-gold bangle bracelets and hoop earrings. It just shouldn't be so damn hard to call someone.

The phone rang and a youthful voice picked up, didn't speak directly to her, but shouted, "Mom! Sylvie's on the phone!"

Sylvie winced. Julian's lungs were growing along with the rest of him. Nice to see there were no lasting nasties after his go-round with the sorcerers.

"You shouldn't be able to do that, you know," Val said, into her ear. "Just break through my dial-me-not like that."

"There are a lot of things that people shouldn't be able to do," Sylvie said. "They still get done. You up for a trip to Chicago?"

"Tell me you want to go shopping and need my fashion advice," Val said.

"Wouldn't that be something," Sylvie said. "I've got a spell I want you to deconstruct for me."

"I'm busy," Val said. "There's some strange stuff happening in the occult world, power shifts or something. *Big* stuff."

"I wasn't too busy to save your life," Sylvie said. Favor number one. Val owed her three in total. "Look, I'll fax you a sketch I made, and yes"—she overrode the automatic warning—"I was careful when I drew it. You can get a start on it that way, but I want you here. It might still be active."

That would get her. Val had the good witch's hatred of

open spells. "'Sides," Sylvie said, "there's a good chance that this is related to your big stuff."

"Why am I not surprised. You stir up the worst shit, Sylvie."

"Hey," Sylvie snapped. "You brought me into this world, so watch the attitude. Just get here. Call me when you land."

"Fine," Val said. "It'll be late, though. And I'll only owe you two after this." The phone went dead in Sylvie's ear, not with the normal flat tone but a shrieking laugh. She winced away. Witches.

Well, at least her argument with Val had done one thing; it had put her in the mood to go rattle the ISI.

7

Old Flames Make the Best Enemies

SYLVIE SHOVED THE PHONE INTO HER POCKET AND HEADED DOWN the street at a quick clip. She'd seen a CopyKwik Shop on her way into the neighborhood, and she could fax the spell to Val there.

Plus, as a twofer sort of thing, she could hit one of her favorite research tools: the all-purpose phone book. ISI wasn't going to be listed under SNOOPS—BLOODY-MINDED, she knew, but they would be listed. It had taken Alex a while to translate their cover stories, but now Sylvie and she could find them pretty much anywhere. Usually they only did it to keep out of their way.

The ISI had a presence in every major US city; two hours later, Sylvie had learned that in Chicago it was in a onetime bank, hidden behind a lobby of gilt and marble.

Sylvie strode in through the metal detectors and glanced at the man behind the lobby desk. Tall, hefty, didn't look too bright. She flipped her hand at him and kept moving, heading for the hallway and the elevators.

"Ma'am, this isn't a public building."

"Oh, I know," Sylvie said, turning, continuing to walk backward. "I'm just here to search your lost and found;

it's amazing what your men pick up on the streets, sometimes. Like some old lady, snatching up cats who were
only out for a walk."

"Stop!" he said. His hand slid behind the desk; she
wondered which he was going for: silent alarm or gun.

Maybe both, she thought, considering how long it was
taking to get his hands back where she could see them. Or
maybe he was just slow to decide.

The elevators were twenty steps closer when he rushed
forward, hands empty. He loomed just before her, trying
to intimidate her by sheer bulk. "You have to stop."

"Do I?" Sylvie said. Sweat beaded along his hairline.
There wasn't anyone coming to his aid. Maybe Chicago's
ISI was skeleton-staffed. Maybe the budget cuts had
finally reached the ISI—and didn't they deserve it—or
maybe he cried wolf all the livelong day. Whichever it
was, he was on his own, and he knew it.

Still, he *was* a lot larger than she was; it couldn't hurt
to try friendly again. "I could stop—all I want to know is
if the ISI snatched—"

His eyes flared wide, and she broke off. "What, you
thought I was in the wrong place?"

His jaw settled. "Look, bitch, if you know that much,
you know how much trouble you're in. I could have you
locked up, and no one would ever know what happened to
you. I could even have you killed."

"What, with the guards who came to your first call?"

Behind them, the elevator dinged, and an all-too-
familiar voice rang out. "Back off, Agent."

"But, sir—"

That her heart jumped a tiny bit when she recognized
his voice was something she'd deny to her last breath.

"Christ Almighty, Stockton, take a look at the big picture here before you commit yourself to a world of trouble."

"Demalion," Sylvie said, releasing her grip on the butt
of the gun. "Super. Just the man I wanted to see." She kept
her tone flat just in case he might try to read that as a
compliment.

He brushed past her, still talking. His cologne drifted across her senses, spicy, earthy, and too appealing for her comfort.

"You should have recognized her. Her name is in the files. Her *face* is in the files. She's posted as trouble on all the boards, all over the country, and hell, even if you didn't, you should have put the pieces together. How many pretty women carry a big gun and an even bigger mouth?"

Sylvie turned her back when it began to get embarrassing. Huh, from this side of it, Demalion almost sounded pleased with her presence: He must really dislike Stockton.

Then he was at her side, his hand sliding out to take her elbow. She shrugged him and his tasty scent off automatically. His lips thinned. "Let's talk, Ms. Shadows."

"Don't call me that," she said. He always did, and it made her wild; he knew her name, knew her family, had made a point of studying her life and habits, and yet, deliberately called her Shadows.

"You know, the one bright spot in this entire day was that I got whisked out of Miami, out of your jurisdiction. Then I got here, and damn, if you didn't just creep out of the woodwork."

"I transferred. Got family here," he said, ushering her toward the elevator, sliding the keycard into the lock on it. "You didn't think I followed you, did you? Sorry, Shadows, I was here first."

There was a faint gleam in his gold-flecked eyes that could have been amusement or malice. He put a hand at the small of her back as the elevator doors slid open, not out of friendliness, Sylvie thought, but to confirm she was armed. Beneath his hand, the gun twitched. They both flinched.

He jabbed the button for the third floor, and said, "Interesting new weapon you've got. Am I going to get a look at it?"

"Are you going to answer some questions?"

"I always talk to you. It's in self-defense," he said, his lips curving up, mocking her again. The elevator doors slid closed, sealing her in with him. They hadn't been so close together since that night in Key West, and she wasn't thinking about that at all.

She leaned up against the far wall and studied him, the sleek dark hair, the Byzantine eyes, the Egyptian cast to his face. He always reminded her of pharaohs, somehow exotic and ancient. When she'd first met him on the blind date Alex had set up, she'd had the creeping sensation that he might not be human, even while he chatted her up, oh so interested in her and her life. Then, of course, she learned about the ISI and knew he was all too human, and a bastard suit at that.

"No cane today?" she said. "An interesting look on you, I thought."

"Is that what this is about?" he said, the skin around his eyes tightening, as if up to this moment, he'd been enjoying himself. "I should have known."

"I didn't know an ISI agent could have a sense of humor," she said, still staring at him. "A spy masquerading as a blind man, though, that's pretty funny."

"Glad to amuse," he said. The door dinged open, and he took her arm again. "My office."

Sylvie opened her mouth to protest but hesitated. He seemed oddly on edge. As if the ISI world, that orderly snow globe, had been shaken.

He keycarded his office and let them both in. She looked around with reluctant interest, the first time she'd ever been behind the scenes at the ISI. Earlier visits in the Miami facility had been in the equivalent of interrogation rooms. ISI offices were apparently small but elegantly laid out, dominated by a cherrywood desk covered with high-tech toys and a stack of paper beneath a pyramid paperweight. There was even a framed photograph on the desk, propped up alongside a palm-sized crystal ball. A real home away from home.

Sylvie reached for the photo, feeling it was only fair;

after all, they knew whose pictures she kept on her desk, on her walls, in her albums. Demalion beat her to it, tucking it inside the drawer, catching the crystal when the motion started it rolling.

"So 'kay—" she said. "Don't want to look at that one, how about these?" She dropped the Polaroid of Brandon Wolf on the desk, followed it with one of Demalion in blind-man guise. "Do you have him in your lockup? And please, keep in mind, I'm not in the mood for plausible denial or any other government bullshit—he's the only thing between me and my retirement."

Demalion picked up the photograph, stared at his own picture, some unreadable emotion touching his face, before moving to the one of Brandon Wolf. He raised a brow and Sylvie's temper in one move. "You think the ISI has nothing better to do than detain a pretty-boy artist?"

"That's not a no," Sylvie said. "Just in case you weren't clear on my question."

Demalion settled down behind his desk with a sigh, leaving her looming across it. He rubbed his hands over his eyes, reached out, and rolled the crystal ball from palm to palm.

"We didn't take Wolf. Hell, I didn't even know he was missing."

Sylvie felt like swearing. She hadn't really thought they had, not once she found the spell circle; the ISI was generally a technological menace, not a magical one. Still, it would have been nice to pit herself against a known entity instead of fumbling in the dark for someone new.

She wished she could believe he was lying to her. "But you *were* watching him, stalking him, playing blind man at parties with him?"

"Not him," Demalion said. "Like I said, the ISI has no interest—"

"No, of course not," she said. "Not Brandon for himself. But how about as an avenue to his lover? To Kevin Dunne."

"Shut the door," he said quietly. "Shut the door and sit down."

Sylvie's jaw wanted to drop. Was he really going to share information, just like that? This couldn't bode well. She did as he asked, listening to the door suck closed, realizing the room was soundproofed. She perched on the seat before the desk.

"You think we watch you, make your life a *Candid Camera* moment, and you're nothing much—"

"Make a girl feel loved, why don't you," Sylvie muttered.

"A small-time vigilante with a dangerous mouth. A useful barometer of the occult in the country." He sighed, closed the crystal in both palms, then rolled it between his fingers. "No power yourself but good at ferreting out those with powers. Then came Dunne, who made us reset our conception of scale and power. We don't know what he is or how he got that way. He was an average guy, a better-than-average cop, and the only thing not strictly by the books was his relationship. Then *boom*. A year ago, and suddenly he's everywhere. All our psychics could see was him, like a bomb gone off in their minds."

Sylvie shrugged. The ISI had been cruising for trouble; they thought they knew everything. A momentary thought sidetracked her. "You have staff psychics? Slick. Bet it makes the interoffice pools a bitch, though." Maybe she should rethink the magical-menace part of the ISI.

"You have no idea," Demalion said, setting his crystal down again, uncharacteristic fidgeting done. "What did Dunne want with you? I heard he visited your office this morning."

Sylvie's temporary good humor evaporated at the reminder of the ISI eyes on her life. "If you can't even add one and one to get two, I don't know why I thought you could help me," Sylvie said.

"Maybe I don't want you to retire," he said. "You're not the retiring type."

"I learn my lessons," Sylvie said. "My associate *died*. Maybe you heard about that, too. Hell, maybe you and yours watched it happen, took notes on it." Her temper prowled her skin, tensing nerves, quickening her breath. She forced her hands to unfist.

"Bullshit," Demalion said. "People die around you, Shadows. You're used to that. You're . . . running scared."

"You get a whole coven of would-be demons on your tail, planning to cut out your still-beating heart, then we'll talk." Sylvie scraped the two pictures from his desk with shaking hands, crammed them into her pockets.

"Monsters have never scared you before."

"Don't be more an idiot than your paycheck makes you."

"Not scared like this," he said. His dark eyes were on her again, searching, and she'd forgotten how penetrating they could be. She turned her head, looking longingly at the door. But she still had answers to get. "There's only one thing that scares you that badly. Yourself."

"Could we stay on topic?" she snapped. "Brandon Wolf. Missing. Dunne. Unhappy. Bad news all around."

"We're not here to help you," Demalion said.

So angry even her voice failed her, Sylvie yanked the door open; there'd be no answers here, and if she stayed . . . Demalion might get a closer look at her weapon than she could afford.

Behind her, he said, "Sylvie." Not Ms. Shadows. Not Ms. Lightner. *Sylvie.* She waited, breath coming fast.

"I didn't hear about Suarez until after," he said. "If I'd been there, I would have helped." Quiet footfalls in the carpet warned her of his approach; he put a hand on her shoulder in what felt like honest sympathy.

"Words are easy," she said. "Belief's harder."

She'd trusted him once, and the memory was powerful, with him standing so close, smelling so good, so familiar, his warmth mingling with hers.

Six months prior, Sylvie had taken him out to celebrate, though she hadn't explained what. Hard to say to a new guy, yeah, I had a good day at work. I pried a were-wolf cub from the government's hands through sheer persistence and at least one screaming argument about children belonging with their mothers, whether they were furred or fleshy on the outside. She felt good, picked Demalion up at his apartment, and headed for the Keys.

They'd been dancing close in the un-air-conditioned bar, slick and easy in the tropical night, and he'd licked a traveling bead of sweat from her breast. She'd clenched her hands in his hair, mussed out of its sleekness, and thought *this one*, this one she was taking home and keeping.

Then his cell had gone off, and she, teasing, had plucked it from his hip over his protest—fast fingers, trained by Alex—flipped it open, and found herself listening to the ISI: Come on home, Demalion. We got the mother, too.

Result? One crushed cell phone, one shattered relationship. One battered heart. Played from the first.

She met his eyes, remembered that he couldn't be trusted, and shied away from his sympathy. Crocodile tears or not, she didn't want it. "Back off, Demalion. We don't dance anymore."

When he retreated to his desk, she found another question. "When you played your spy games with Wolf and Dunne, you get a sense of anyone *else* watching? Anyone who might want a shot at Dunne through Bran?"

"No," he said, glancing away. Her breath caught.

"Such a lie," she said. "C'mon, Demalion, we are talking about dirty deeds being done, and you're going back to Mr. I-Know-Nothing, I-Say-Nothing?"

"I don't *know* anything," he said, voice dropping to a growl. "Yeah, there was someone else watching. No clue as to who or why. It was like having a shadow. We knew it was there, but couldn't touch it."

"Not so fun when it happens to you, is it?" Sylvie said.

"Do you want to hear this or do you want to take pot-shots?" Demalion said. "It's your client, right?"

Sylvie sagged back against the doorjamb and waited.

"Dunne found out about the surveillance," Demalion said. "He didn't like it. He nailed them, and he got the mystery observer right alongside the ISI team."

He continued, voice low and intense. "I don't know what's happened to Dunne's boy. But things are getting ugly. Be careful, Sylvie."

"Who's this?" Another ISI agent stopped in the hallway, seeing Sylvie framed in the open door. "Is she authorized to be here? To know about Dunne?" He seized her arm. Sylvie twisted free and stepped back into Demalion's office, the nearest shelter from a storm.

"Back off," Demalion snapped. "Jesus, Rodrigo, give us all a break. A pretty girl comes downtown for a pastry and a chat, and you go Nazi on her ass. Don't you have a dick?"

"I'll see her out," Rodrigo said. "You might do things differently in Miami, Demalion. Here we follow the rules." When he tried to take her arm again, Sylvie flipped him off and stormed down the hall. Rodrigo caught up to her at the elevator and keyed the doors open.

"I know who you are," he said, shoving her into the elevator; he jabbed the lobby level and locked it in. "I'm not impressed with your mouth. And you'd best stay away from Dunne." Slackness touched his face, left him staring blankly at her as the doors slid shut.

Sylvie looked at the closed doors thoughtfully. "Okay, that was freaky, even for the ISI."

At the lobby, she wasn't surprised to be met by Stockton, as well as two other guards, mustered from God knew where. She smiled at them, showing all her teeth, and stalked out the front door.

Pastry? She had passed a pastry shop two blocks from here. She walked down the street, bought herself a cruller, two double espressos, and took a seat. She knocked back the first espresso, chased it with powdered sugar, and tapped her nails on the cheap Formica table. She had the second espresso at her lips when Demalion arrived.

"That better not be mine," he said.

She passed it over.

"It's almost cold," he said.

"It was almost *gone*," she said. "What the hell do you want, Demalion? Not help, you're not in the helping business."

He bit his lip, as if he could unsay his earlier words, but then shrugged. "A bargain of sorts. I'll keep an eye out for Wolf. More than that. I'll institute a search. If—"

"If," she parroted. "If what, Demalion?"

"If you tell me what you know about Kevin Dunne."

"You've been watching him. What makes you think I'll know more than you?"

"I hate to admit it, but you seem to know what's going on when no one else does—why do you think we watch you so much? You're like ISI Cliff's Notes to the *Magicus Mundi*."

"That's flattering," Sylvie said. She stood and snagged another coffee from the counter clerk, plain old black this time; if she had another espresso, she might find herself throttling Demalion.

"Surveillance has failed on Dunne," Demalion said, when she sat back down. "Three teams—"

"Dead?" Sylvie interrupted. Her nervous fingers ceased their drumming on the side of her paper cup. "You said— he nailed them."

"No." Demalion leaned forward. "Look, it's this way. The first team we sent—they got nothing. Dunne spotted them right off, went over, and asked them to leave. They did. Now, we even mention Dunne's name, and they get all huffy, demanding that we leave him alone.

"The second team kept their distance. Dunne and Wolf found them anyway, invited them to dinner. They went, contrary to instruction, then discontinued surveillance and returned to base against orders."

"So, Dunne threatened them, made them back off. I can see it; he's a scary guy," Sylvie said. At least he was spreading the scary around, and she couldn't think of anyone more deserving than the ISI.

"They weren't scared of him," Demalion said, shaking his head. "It's like they worship him." She twitched at his choice of words, but, caught up in his problems, he didn't notice. "One of the men on that team, Erickson, keeps talking about how *nice* Bran and Kevin are, that we should just leave them alone. He gets heated about it."

"Guess he met a different Dunne than I did," Sylvie said. "But hell, there's no accounting for taste. Look at you, talking to me. Voluntarily."

Demalion sighed. "Before the ISI took Erickson on, he'd had some disciplinary actions for harassing gays. Enough of them that his career was in a nosedive. You're not in law enforcement—"

"That's not what *he* says," Sylvie muttered.

"But if he'd been disciplined, it wasn't just a matter of name-calling. It was sticks and stones and broken bones."

"So, not an easy convert," Sylvie said, trying to imagine Dunne winning someone over with charm. She failed. Admittedly, she hadn't seen him at his best. He'd been stripped-down angry and scared. Maybe Bran was the lovable one. Tish seemed to think so.

"And you saw Rodrigo back at the office. He was all over you merely for mentioning Dunne's name. He was team one."

"So that wasn't just an ISI fit?"

"No," Demalion said. "That was lingering contamination." He shrugged, fumbled in his suit-coat pocket, pulled out the crystal again, went back to moving it hand to hand. "For a while, we tried purely electronic surveillance, but all our bugs failed. A third team went out, consisting of three experienced field agents, one a clairvoyant, who would warn them of any magical influence." Demalion set aside his espresso, mostly untouched, rubbed his face.

"What happened?" Sylvie asked. "More bestest of friends?

"No," Demalion said. "Dunne lost patience with playing nice. None of team three will ever be watching them again. I would imagine the same holds true for our mystery observer."

"But not dead?" Sylvie asked again, trying to imagine what she felt about that, some evidence that maybe Dunne was what he seemed. A nice guy who didn't like to kill. She remembered his snatching the orchid-girl from beneath her heel, and grimaced. She wasn't used to being more reprehensible than her clients.

Her phone buzzed; she looked down and caught a glimpse of a text message. Flight information. Val was on her way.

"Bespelled. Or something. It wasn't a spell. It just *was*. One moment, things were one way, the next moment, they weren't. We don't understand what type of ability Dunne's tapped into but—"

"All you know is that he's powerful? That's pathetic," Sylvie said, rising. "I learned more than that in the first ten minutes of meeting him. If you'll excuse me, I'll get back to work."

"Bullshit," Demalion said, his temper fraying to match hers. "You talk big, Sylvie, but you're full of it. I'm trying to help you, talking shop when I should just keep my mouth shut and let you sink. But the hell of it is, I'd rather not see you dead. Let me help. You tell me what you think you know, and I'll set men to look for Wolf."

"Your bargain sucks," she said. "Your men are already looking for Wolf, whether they know it or not. Dunne wants it that way. Dunne's not a witch, sorcerer, psychic, or even some type of master hypnotist."

"If you know so much—what is he then?"

"He's a god," Sylvie said. She swept out of the pastry shop, leaving Demalion behind her, sinking back into the booth.

8

When Only a Witch Will Do

SYLVIE WAITED OUTSIDE O'HARE, SITTING ON A METAL BENCH brought to oven warmth by the heat from passing car engines. She shifted, pulling sweat-damp cotton away from her nape, and went back to watching the airport police.

Earlier, they had been everywhere, running in packs of five or more, like confused hounds casting about for scent. Now, they were back to that deceptively slow cop stride, in pairs or singles, and the only signs of interference was the occasional freeze of movement coupled with a blank stare, like the stutter-stop of a petit mal seizure. Like a seizure, the symptoms disappeared with the cops unaware of them.

Sylvie couldn't decide if this was an improvement or not; she lacked facts and was left with empty speculation. Did their return to near normal mean Dunne's influence had faded? If so, why? Had he lost interest or hope in their ability to find Brandon Wolf? Or was it a simpler thing altogether? Had he regained some of his concentration, keeping his powers close to home? Sylvie gnawed her lip, checked her watch, and moved on—nearly time to meet Val.

A third option presented itself to her. Had Dunne

weakened? Maybe gods weren't affected by human limitations of distance or endurance, but that didn't mean nothing could weaken him. If he was a god—and she chose to let that declaration stand—she could think of only two things that *could* stop him. A belatedly delivered ransom demand. Or another god. Sylvie shivered. She needed to check in with her client and soon.

Val strode up at that moment, smiling a little, looking like a sleek jet-setter anticipating nothing more taxing than the shopping trip she'd teased Sylvie about. That changed the moment she leaned in to give Sylvie a social hug. The gun at Sylvie's waist . . . twitched. Sylvie felt the distinctive click of the safety shifting off, a tiny flicker of movement against her skin, a finger tap saying "ready."

"What the hell is that?" Val said. "What have you done, Sylvie?"

"Nothing," she said.

"You're wearing something of stolen power," Val accused. "Spirit bound to flesh. That's black work. How did you—"

"It's fine," Sylvie said. "Just trust me, okay?"

Val grimaced but let the questioning drop, for which Sylvie was grateful. She needed to parse what Val had said. Flesh and spirit, bound? Her flesh—she knew that; otherwise, the gun wouldn't feel so comfortable against her skin. Whose spirit? Dunne's?

Val waved for a cab, her lips still tight in disapproval. "Let's get this over with, Sylvie."

"We're not taking a cab to the subway," Sylvie said. "That's just plain stupid. How spoiled are you, anyway?" She waved off the cabbie and headed toward the El connection.

Val huffed but followed her down the sidewalk in silence. Once in the El, Sylvie leaned up against a pole near the doors, touching her cheek to the cool metal, studying the other passengers, mostly airport run-off of flight attendants and travelers. No one looked back at her; the one man in a business suit who did ducked her gaze a second later, leaving her with nothing to do but seethe and listen to the rattle and clank of the El rising above the street.

Three stops later, Sylvie decided Val had sulked long enough, and said, "You look at the spell?"

"Enough to know it's probably what you're looking for," Val said, pausing in her own calming study of the posters within the car. "Not enough to tell you how, who, or why, yet. I've made some assumptions, of course, from the sketch, but I'd rather see the actual circle itself before I draw real conclusions."

"Thanks, Val," Sylvie said. She relaxed; it looked like Val was going to be helpful.

"Don't thank me," Val said. "If I had a choice, I wouldn't be here. Things are strange right now, and all I want to do is hole up someplace safe."

"Strange," Sylvie repeated.

"My coven thinks a god may have come to the mortal realm."

"So?" Sylvie said. "It's their earth, too, right?"

Val made a face as if Sylvie had said something unbelievably stupid. "The only good thing about gods is that they prefer their realm to ours."

The El swayed heavily as they took a long curve, rattling loud enough to make it sound like a roller coaster, and drew to a screeching halt. Val winced. "Not quite a Benz, is it?"

"You'll survive," Sylvie said.

Once the engine reached speed again, Sylvie said, "In myths, gods walk the earth all the time."

"Yes," Val said, "and mythology is full of monsters and cataclysms. Trust me, they're linked. Gods change things. It's their nature. Their very presence."

"The world bends to their will," Sylvie said, echoing Dunne. "It's all about power."

"It's *always* about power," Val said. "There's only so much of it to go around. Like anything rare, it's prized, guarded, hidden, and sought."

"And stolen," Sylvie finished on the crest of a minor

epiphany. Stolen would explain an awful lot about Dunne's sudden appearance on the scene. There weren't that many possibilities if the two facts she had gained were both true. Dunne was a god. Dunne had been a normal human. Between the two states lay power.

"If humans can steal their power, gods can't be omniscient or omnipotent," Sylvie said, "not really."

"Technically true," Val said, sliding forward on the plastic seat, shifting into lecture mode. "But it's in the same sense that we're not all-powerful to, oh, a bird's egg. We can see it in its entirety, know what's in it, know what it will become, juggle it, nurture it, alter it at will, break it, spare it, or devour it. The egg is completely vulnerable. The egg doesn't even understand that it's in a god's hand. Except maybe, every now and then, it feels a ripple moving through, something vast shifting on a level it cannot comprehend.

"To steal a god's power requires more than determination and a blatant disregard for personal safety, it requires an understanding of the world that most humans are simply not capable of. Suffice it to say that anyone who could seriously attempt such a thing would be a person to avoid, would make my ex-husband look like a saint." Her volume dropped steadily as she spoke until Sylvie had to lean close to make out the soft words. Val crumpled the edges of the fax, the spell rippling with false life. She took a breath, smoothed the paper, and bent her attention to it, tracing lines with a manicured nail.

No real answers there, Sylvie thought. Dunne had been a normal human according to Demalion, and while the ISI was not infallible, its basic information gathering was stellar.

The conductor's voice called out another station, and Sylvie looked up. Getting close. She nudged Val, and Val tucked the spell into her purse, neatly folded.

Ten minutes later, Sylvie sat at the top of the El's steps, squeezing herself out of the way of the occasional passerby and watching Val walk the spell circle.

Fish out of water, Sylvie thought, tickled at the expression on Val's face—such finely tuned distaste. Subways were definitely slumming it for Val, who was accustomed to casual luxury. Still, she bent and knelt beside the circle without hesitation, staining her cream-linen slacks.

"It's—" Val raised a haughty brow at a commuter who was standing a little too close to her. "Do you mind?"

He stepped back and continued waiting for a train, jingling the tokens in his pocket. "Sylvie!" Val said, gesturing at him in an imperious fashion.

"Shoo. Go away," Sylvie said. He flipped her off and stayed where he was. Sylvie shrugged, not surprised. He was the suited man who hadn't met her eyes on the train. The one she thought she'd seen waiting at the airport terminal, passing her a few times too many for coincidence.

Well, lie down with the ISI, get up with ticks.

"I can't do this," Val said, rising. "Too many people coming in and out. You were correct, by the way. This spell is still active. It's also sloppy. I thought so when I got your fax but chalked it up to your poor art skills. I remember your flunking Woodmansee's class."

"Hey," Sylvie said, "This isn't a high-school reunion, you know."

Val said, "Hand me my bag, will you?"

As if a thousand-dollar Valextra briefcase could be termed a bag. Sylvie tossed it toward her, and Val sighed as she caught it. "Look, all the tooling they do makes it magically inert. Okay?"

"I didn't say anything," Sylvie said.

"Sylvie, even your silences are damn loud," Val said, flickering a smile. "Make sure no one else is coming, all right?"

"You're gonna—"

"I'm tired of interruptions. I thought this was a matter of some urgency, but if you'd rather I work around street people?"

"Knock yourself out," Sylvie said.

Val closed her eyes, raised her hands, and began talking.

At least, that was how it sounded to Sylvie. Talking, but incomprehensible, some bastard mixture of sounding too far away, or too foreign. It sounded like those important speeches she heard in dreams, full of portent without meaning.

The air rippled; the subway wavered in her sight and reappeared, warped out of true, the walls gleaming darkly, the shadows oppressive, the screech of metal heart-pounding. The commuters fled up the stairs in a disorderly mess.

Val was obviously still pissy; usually her leave-me-alones were gentle things, tending to make people recall sudden chores that required them to be elsewhere. But this—

Sylvie watched the nightmare spread across the station, adding a layer of revulsion to the glamour, and blinked it away, refusing to give in to her suddenly racing heart. She knew better, dammit. It was all illusion. She closed her eyes as the glamour tried harder to get rid of her, leaving behind subtle nightmare imagery for streamers of blood on the ground, the patchwork paint of body outlines. If she looked long enough, the shape took on the contorted one that Suarez had fallen into when the bullet took out his throat.

Ignore it. It's false. It means nothing. The dark voice was calm as it declared there was no threat here.

Sylvie opened her eyes, and things were back to normal. Or as normal as it could be with a witch casting a spell in a subway station.

"You really shouldn't be able to evade my spells," Val said. "Someday I'm going to test your aptitude for magic."

"Yeah, and someday I'm going to make a nice little housewife," Sylvie said.

Val shook her head and bent to her bag. "Well, now that I've gotten rid of them, let's keep them gone." Val pulled out a silk-wrapped feather, a grey Baggie of what looked like spiderwebs, and a knife from her bag.

"You have trouble with airline security?" Sylvie said, noticing that the suit at the platform was still there, still watching, looking sweaty and rather sick. "Ah, Val?"

"I took the jet," Val said, teasing the spiderwebs apart with the knife tip. "Shut up, Sylvie. This takes concentration."

Val teased one of the cobwebs back into web shape, dangling it from the tip of her knife. "Come down the stairs," she said.

Sylvie sighed and joined Val. "What about him?" she asked, gesturing to their watcher.

"He should have left when I asked him to," Val said. She raised the knife and blew gently on it, simple breath giving way to more of her exotic murmurs.

The cobweb fluttered from the knife, expanding, thinning, gleaming red and gold like metal reflecting firelight. It drifted up the stairs, and Val whispered more coaxing words. The suit on the platform began to look concerned. Sylvie flipped him off and grinned. After all, there weren't many people who were determined enough to stick around through a repulsion glamour. He *had* to be ISI. He edged closer to the rails, as if a foot or so could make all that much difference.

Val gestured with the feather, and the web spread wider and darted forward, sticking suddenly to the edges of the entrance to the El. Sounds from above stopped filtering down to them, wrapping them in silence.

"One more," Val said, another web dangling from the knife tip.

She turned to the wary agent watching them and smiled, that perfect social smile that allowed all sorts of backstabbing to go on behind it. The web flew wide and pushed the agent to a teetering position on the very edge of the platform. The man jumped off, rather than be pushed, and the spell snapped into place behind him.

"I knew we were friends for a reason," Sylvie said, smiling at the agent's predicament. "Hope he's informed about the train schedule and the dangers of high voltage."

Val permitted herself a more honest grin, a rare, open look on her face. There was the impish gamine Sylvie had known in high school. "What? I'm not allowed to enjoy my work?" Val said, turning back to the spell circle. She took a white-silk glove from her bag and traced the circle in silence.

She sat back on her heels, finessed the glove from her fingers, careful not to let the outer part of the glove touch her skin, and tossed it into the trash can. "Nasty," she said, wiping her hands down her slacks. "I was afraid of that."

"Don't be vague," Sylvie said. "If you've got something bad to say, might as well get it over with."

"*Maudits,*" Val said. "Specific enough for you?"

"Fuck," Sylvie said, closing her eyes. "I thought they'd disbanded, decovened, or whatever sorcerers do when you destroy their leaders."

"We stopped them," Val said. "Once. Hardly a final battle. They must have found a new figurehead."

"Lovely," Sylvie said. "'Cause their last choice was oh so good for the world." The *Maudits* were bad news; a cabal of blood-crazed sorcerers could hardly be anything but. Last time Sylvie had run into them, they'd been intent on resurrecting Val's ex-husband, a voodoo king with one hell of a mean streak. Sylvie doubted their tastes had improved in the time since.

"Sloppy, though," Val said, looking over the spell, breaking Sylvie's darkening thoughts. "Far from their usual standards—maybe you're dealing with a splinter group. Last I'd heard, they had begun to argue their methods—since they were so spectacularly unsuccessful last time. Beaten by two women and a child." Val's lips quirked. "Serves them right, those chauvinistic blowhards."

"Yeah, yeah, we kicked their collective ass. Yay us, moving on," Sylvie said. "The spell is sloppy? Meaning what exactly?"

Val slipped off her loose jacket, laid it on the concrete, and settled herself on it. "Well, for one thing it's active, which it shouldn't be. Not if it's swallowed its prey."

"So it is a snatch-and-grab machine," Sylvie said, toeing the painted curlicues thoughtfully, "not a curse or a kill."

Val fiddled with the platinum hoop in her ear, a habit Sylvie recognized from high school, from a hundred scenes of Val before a test, before a big date, before lying her ass off to get away with coming home drunk. Sylvie braced herself for trouble.

"Not exactly. It's an oubliette spell. A magical ambush keyed to a specific person. It sucks the target down the minute they cross it, then it shuts down and disappears. We shouldn't be able to see it at all. A spell like this is either hidden and active, or triggered and gone. The fact that it's visible at all tells me it's triggered, but not complete. Normally, I'd say that its prey got away. God only knows how—we're not talking a beginner spell here. But you say that Wolf is missing?"

"Vanished," Sylvie said. "In the space of a heartbeat according to my client."

"Witnessed it?" Val paused in her fidgeting.

"Felt it," Sylvie said. "How's that for proof?"

"Don't scoff," Val said mildly. "Talents can feel such things. Is he—"

"Talented? Oh hell yeah," Sylvie said.

"So we can assume he's right, and the boy's gone down." Val set her earrings to swinging again, stilled them. Noting the nerves, Sylvie was prepared for the hesitation in Val's words, the softness of her tone. "You know he's dead, right?"

Quick shock touched her back and cheeks with an internal chill, and a denial so strong she didn't think it was hers; some bastard leftover of Dunne's touch or influence. She fisted her hands. "He could—"

"You said weeks. Weeks in an oubliette. No food, no water, no air. An oubliette's a coffin, Sylvie, for sorcerers who are too impatient to wait for their victims to die."

"It makes no sense," Sylvie snapped. "If he's dead, and the spell's supposed to be gone, why isn't it? I think they plan to retrieve him."

"It's a one-way deal," Val said. "You can't just reach in and pull things out."

"*You* can't. What about the *Maudits*?"

Val paused in her automatic rebuttal, the idea that they could do something she couldn't, and actually thought about it. "I—maybe. The original sorcerer could undo the spell, pick it apart layer by layer. That might reverse the effect." She shook her head. "It's irrelevant. The time problem still stands. The most that anyone could retrieve is a corpse."

"That might not matter to Dunne," Sylvie said, thinking aloud. Dunne seemed confident he could restore the dead to life, given proper jurisdiction, and surely Brandon Wolf, his lover, belonged to him.

"You have the *worst* clients," Val said. "First the gun, and now—"

"I didn't mean that," Sylvie said. She wished she hadn't said anything, but wasn't that an endless source of regret? Her mouth, her best weapon, even against herself.

Val drummed pale, painted nails, waiting. Sylvie sucked in a breath and forced a subject change. "So, if he's been grabbed, what's your explanation for the spell still chugging away?"

Question and answer, Sylvie thought, watching Val's expression shift from peeved to contemplative. Val's weakness: She couldn't resist the urge to lecture, to describe the ways of the world to all those less intelligent, less aware. Most of the time that tendency drove Sylvie to eye rolling and backchat. Sylvie hated not being in the know as much as she hated being the object of condescension. But the tendency to lecture was also the reason that Sylvie, who thought all magic-users should be labeled: *warning, contents unstable under pressure*, could trust Val.

"It's just too sloppy," Val said. "Even if someone wanted to try to open the oubliette again—which doesn't make sense—the spell just doesn't look right." She dragged Sylvie closer, gesturing with her free hand toward the first looping coil. "Look at this. That Greek there? It's the signifier—the identity card, the thing that kept this station from becoming a Bermuda Triangle. But it's not Wolf's name. It just says Love, and that's damn broad."

"Or it says a lot about *how* they saw him. No one in his own right, just an appendage to Dunne. Their weapon against him." Sylvie frowned, liking this less and less. How in hell a onetime mundane cop had made such serious occult enemies . . . ?

Well, that was it, wasn't it? A onetime mundane cop now bearing a god-quantity of stolen power. That had to make enemies. It sure as hell didn't make the kind of friends you could trust at your back. Maybe it wasn't that they wanted anything at all from Dunne. Maybe they just wanted to make him hurt, and Brandon was the tool at hand.

Just another innocent in the line of fire.

"It's still careless," Val said. "It's too open-ended. There's a physical descriptor here, which would narrow it down some." Val traced an elegant series of squiggles in the air. "Red hair, hazel eyes; sound like your boy?"

"Yeah," Sylvie said.

"Then you've got some bad news for your client," Val said. "And I'm done." She began tucking her tools away, pausing to look up at Sylvie. "If he wants the body, I want no part of it. I don't deal in necromancy."

"You think I do? Thanks, Val," Sylvie snapped. "Maybe all I meant was that there'd be closure for him if there was a body found. You've been hanging around bad magic too long. There are other things to do with a corpse than fuck it or use it for spellcraft."

"Uh-huh," Val said, "And *maybe* that's all bullshit."

"It doesn't matter," Sylvie said. "He's not dead, according to Dunne. Weren't you the one saying that Talents could feel these things?"

"Even Talents can fall into wishful thinking," Val said as she snapped her case shut. "A normal man could not survive—"

"Not all that sure he's normal," Sylvie said. Proximity to the *Magicus Mundi* changed things, changed people. Brandon Wolf lived with a *god*.

Val raised an eyebrow, tapped the spell circle with her foot. "Human. That's in the descriptor, too. You like to rub facts in people's faces. Here's one for you. Wolf is de—" A sound penetrated the bubble Val had sealed them in, the *click-clack* of impatient high heels.

"The hell?" Val said, attention diverted, face shifting from anger to wariness. "Someone's at the spell edge."

"Guess I'm not the only one who's a hard sell," Sylvie said, though her gut was churning. Silly to think she could recognize the quick steps up above. There was only one set of them anyway. Didn't they run as a pack? Of course, the other two hadn't worn high heels when she'd seen them that morning; they had moved soundlessly.

Val licked her lips as if they'd gone suddenly dry. The cobweb spell wavered; a place at the entrance showed the air rippling like a curtain stroked from behind. Sound increased; the previously silenced noise from the streets slipped downward, complaints that the station was out of order, passing vehicles, sirens in the distance. Then, two distinct voices came clear, not caught by the spell, but pushing through it. Sylvie stiffened.

Never deny the gut instinct, she thought.

"He didn't say to wait—"

"He didn't say not to—"

"Stop arguing."

The first two voices were regrettably familiar, the rasping, hungry contralto and the poison-sweet tones: the leather-clad Alekta and the punk one. The third voice, sounding surprisingly normal, if weary, had to be Magdala.

Alekta's heels clicked on the concrete, distinct bursts of sound that made Sylvie want to find a hiding place and disappear. Beside her, Val muttered frantically, trying to reinforce the spell or trying to dismantle it before it blew apart—Sylvie couldn't tell.

The Furies took the choice from her, pushing through the wavering shield as if it were nothing more than the cobweb it had come from. Val yelped, her hands flying to her head.

"Sylvie," the punk sister said, and skipped down the stairs toward her, pleated skirt flaring. "Were you hiding?"

"I'm working," Sylvie said. "And, hey! Don't step on the evidence, okay?" To her surprise, the Fury stopped in her approach, blinking down at the spell circle.

"What's that?" Alekta said. She slunk alongside her sister to split her glare evenly between Sylvie and the circle.

"Oubliette," Sylvie said. "Swallowed Bran. I was—"

"Kevin," Magdala said, "come here." She never raised her voice. "Your PI found something." Sylvie bristled at the surprise in the girl's voice.

"Sylvie," Val whispered, face pale, hands trembling where they clutched her bag. "What are they?"

"Client's *pets*," Sylvie said. Magdala shot her a disgusted glare that had real menace in it. Sylvie put a hand to her back, touching the gun, but their attention had turned again, their gazes all shifting to a point about mid-stairs.

Beside her, Val shuddered; Sylvie heard the faint jangle of her jewelry complain with her movement, but kept her eyes on the man who had appeared without any fanfare.

Since she'd seen Dunne that morning, she had accepted that he was a god, that he had power to spare, that his whims were physical laws the world wanted to obey; she'd forgotten how much like an ordinary man he looked. How tired. How scared.

He came down the stairs, hope flickering in his worried eyes. "You found something?" His voice was rough and quiet.

"Spell circle," Sylvie said, her own voice uneven, thinking of Val's conviction that Bran was dead, of the sisters waiting to see this scene play out.

Dunne reached the intersection of spell edge and stair and paused. "This it?"

"Yeah," Sylvie said. He stepped into the curve of spell, and it went wild.

The swirling greens and blues rose as if they were the water they resembled, winding around him like a whirl-pool. Cold winds blew through the station; Sylvie's ears popped and ached under the pressure.

Over the roar of the not-water, she could hear the Furies shouting. Through wind-stung eyes, she saw Dunne at the heart of a cyclone, and had time for a frantic thought that she was going to lose her client, and was that good or bad, when the spell collapsed in a rush of heat and a sound like tearing metal.

In the lingering silence, Val's whimpers became gasping breaths. The spell circle gleamed and cracked, its paint flaking and drifting upward into brightly hued mist and dispersing, leaving only faint hints of its presence behind.

Dead spell, Sylvie thought. *Very dead.* If the *Maudits* intended to trap Dunne with it, they'd failed. But if they hadn't—why had it opened at his feet?

"Oh God," Val gasped, and surged to her feet. "Oh— *God*—" Her eyes wide with shock and horror, she darted for the entrance.

It took two steps before the Furies were on her, slamming her up against the stained concrete walls. "Witch, why do you run?"

"Stop it!" Sylvie yelled. She grabbed the nearest sister, trying hard not to think about what she was doing, just reached out and grabbed, getting a handful of warmed leather, and yanking her away. Alekta hissed, tongue narrow, black, and pointed, her teeth going sharp.

"Get away from her," Sylvie said, putting herself between Val and Alekta.

The preppie sister growled, and Sylvie's gun was out before she had thought about it, out and unwavering in

Magdala's face, Sylvie's arm braced on Val's trembling shoulder. Sylvie got a wild-eyed view of the punk sister leaning back against the wall—laughing?

"Dunne, call them off."

"A trap," Dunne said, and *now* Sylvie had no problems seeing him as inhuman. There was an utter blankness to his eyes, warning that no humanity was at home.

"*Val* didn't do it," Sylvie said, talking fast, hoping to break past that alien barrier to the man beneath. "Val's my research witch. You know, like an informant? She identified the spell. Hell, she was going to tell me more about it, maybe how to undo it, except someone had to lose his almighty temper and blow up the only piece of evidence we had. Guess being a god doesn't rule out being an idiot."

Something touched the barrel of her gun, and Sylvie's gaze flickered back to Magdala, who was, *eww*, licking her gun, with an avidity out of place with her prim and proper wardrobe.

"Won't kill me," she said.

"Maybe not, but I bet there'd be splatter. Get your button-down all splotchy," Sylvie warned. "Dunne?"

"Magdala," he said, "Alekta. Erinya. Stop." The words seemed to be dragged out of his throat, as if it were an effort to remember how to talk. An effort to act human.

Sylvie shivered, remembering him saying that it was hard to be less than he was.

Val ducked beneath Sylvie's arm the minute Magdala relaxed, and headed for the street, yanking herself to a walk after a first rapid step that brought the sisters' attention right back to her. Running was definitely a no-no around those three.

"Excuse me for a moment," Sylvie said, holstering her gun and setting out after Val. She collected Val's bag on the way.

She caught up with Val halfway down the block, her pale clothes a beacon in the evening light. "Val—"

Val swung round on her, and Sylvie ducked, waiting

for the glimmer of spell casting, that telltale flicker between Val's fingers. Instead, Val dropped her hand to her side.

"We're through," Val said, voice quivering. "I owe you nothing after this. A fucking *god*, Sylvie. You exposed me to a god." She snatched her bag from Sylvie's fingers, hurled it into the street, watched one car swerve around it, and a second drive over it with a soft *thud-crunch*.

Still the drama queen.

"You done? 'Cause I still have some questions, including why the hell that oubliette tried to eat Dunne. I thought you said it was keyed to Bran?" Sylvie asked. She didn't have time for Val's histrionics. Her only lead was gone, and Dunne—she rather thought he was on the ragged edge. Val's dramatic fits could find a better time to come out and play. Luckily, they were usually short in duration.

Val's breath rasped in her throat. "Get another witch."

Usually. Sylvie wondered if this time Val was covering fear with temper. She softened her tone.

"Val, I know you're scared, but I need you, need your talents," Sylvie said. "Please."

Val closed her eyes, her face a pallid, shocky oval in the dark. Her lips trembled. "You don't have a clue. Do you know what happens to a witch when a god goes off? It's like being hurled headfirst into a nuclear reactor. I'm burned, Sylvie. Burned to bits. Find another witch. I'm not one anymore." She wrapped her arms tightly about herself, shuddering.

Sylvie let the shock of it wash over her, felt the rising sickness of guilt trying to claw into her belly. Maybe this wasn't just another of Val's melodramatic starts, a sneaky way to get out of a task she didn't want to do. "Val—"

"What?" Val said. She saw a cab up the street and gestured. Sylvie saw her moment dwindling, while behind her Dunne and the sisters waited. She imagined Alekta's heels tapping impatiently in the subway and the world suffering tiny seizures at each impact.

"You could still help," Sylvie said. "You can't use the magic, but you can still help me—"

"Like I'd want to," Val snapped, and it sparked Sylvie's quick temper in response.

"Fine. Don't help. Then give me the name of a witch who will."

"You're cold," Val whispered.

"No, I'm on the edge of disaster," Sylvie said. "My only real lead just went up in colored smoke, and while it was pretty, it doesn't make me happy. You're hurt, you're scared, you're going to split, fine. I can't blame you. If I could, I'd join you. I can't. You said it yourself. Dunne's gone nuclear, and there's only me between him and a really big flash."

Val's face was streaked and blotched with tears, all her cool poise stripped bare. A memory jolt fed Sylvie, the image of Val on a sixth-grade playground, sobbing, while Sylvie fisted her hands and rounded on the class bully who had made her cry.

"I'm sorry, Val. I wouldn't have called you if I'd known."

"Yes, you would have," Val said. The cab drew to the curb, and Val nodded at the driver, darted into the street to retrieve her misshapen briefcase, and climbed inside.

Sylvie put her hand on the cabbie's door, a wait-a-minute. "Val—" she said. "Your abilities are really truly gone? Don't abilities grow back, sometimes?"

"You think I'm making it up?"

"You did a lot of lying, in school."

"This is a little different than avoiding essays. Fuck off, Sylvie." Val scrawled a phone number on the spell fax and thrust it out the window at Sylvie. "Here's your new witch. Anna D. A local power. Arrogant as hell. You deserve each other."

The cab merged into traffic and disappeared, becoming one of many. Behind her, a faint shriek rose, as someone attempted to go down the station's stairs and ran right into a nightmare, emerged again, shaking and breathless. Sylvie's paralysis broke as the man ran by. She would apologize later. At the moment, there was simply too much at stake to worry about the damage already done.

Sylvie turned her back on the streets, and rejoined the monsters waiting below.

9

Finding Trouble

IN THE COOL DIMNESS OF THE STATION, THE SCENE HADN'T changed. Dunne stared at the destroyed oubliette, the greasy reminders of paint and malign intent, his expression as blank as a dropped doll's.

Sylvie thought about that perfect, inhuman stillness and shuddered. People had thoughts; the thoughts reflected themselves on their skins. But Dunne, at the moment, seemed empty. Waiting for something, anything to wake him to movement and purpose.

Before him, Alekta and Magdala walked the oubliette, eyes closed, tracking something intangible to mortal senses.

Erinya winked into sight on the stairs, a punk mirage turning real, startling a shamed yelp out of Sylvie. It echoed the sound she'd heard earlier, the scared man who'd fled down the street.

Alekta raised her head to look at Sylvie, eyes reflecting silver-blue in the sputtering fluorescent light. She lunged forward like a Doberman, all the power in her shoulders, and vanished before she landed.

Erinya brushed past Sylvie and leaned into Dunne's side.

Dunne blinked at her touch, but made no further movement, never moving his gaze from the stairs, as if he could draw Bran out by sheer attentiveness.

Maybe he could have, Sylvie thought, catching a glimmer of something behind the set stone of his jaw. Some tinge of guilt, self-condemnation. Maybe, if the spell had stayed active, he could have worked his way through whatever it was that shielded Bran from him. If Bran were—

"He's not dead," Dunne said.

"What?" Sylvie said.

"The witch thinks he's dead. He's not. Don't let her plant doubts."

"What, you're a mind reader, now?" Sylvie said. She felt flicked on the raw. She'd cautioned herself before about assuming it was too late.

He turned his head and looked at her. Blank eyes. Inhuman eyes. Eyes that saw her as nothing more than a faulty collection of molecule and meat. A god's eyes.

"Shit," Sylvie said, under her breath. Mind reader, check. Probably went with the whole omniscient thing. Well, might as well hang for a sheep— "You sure 'bout that not-dead thing? Really sure?"

"If he were dead," Dunne said, each word precise and cold. "If he were dead, the results would be unmistakable. If he were dead, I'd have a name and a face to blame." His voice rose to a ragged shout; his jaw clenched until Sylvie imagined tooth enamel cracking. Beside him, Erinya whimpered and dug her head into his ribs, pushing hard enough to hurt.

Sylvie licked dry lips, twitching when Magdala vanished as Alekta had.

"Don't doubt me, Sylvie."

"Wouldn't dream of it," Sylvie said.

Dunne's hand rose, ruffled through Erinya's spiky crest of dark hair. "Wrong trails," she whispered.

"Is that what they're doing?" Sylvie asked. "Trying to find the sorcerer who laid the spell?"

"As you said," Dunne said. "I destroyed your lead. The sisters are trying to salvage it, but this is a busy station, and the feel of souls fades." He tightened his mouth.

Hunting souls? Sylvie said nothing, not wanting to think about the damage that could lead to.

"I'm sorry," Erinya whispered. "I can't track as well as the others."

He tangled his fingers back into her hair. "Not your fault," he murmured. "I know you're trying."

Trying means you go down fighting, that's all. Trying doesn't mean you win. Sylvie paced a circle of her own, tired of waiting, sick of that voice in her mind, preaching bile and pragmatism in equal measure.

"We're running short on time, Sylvie. In my search, I've played fast and loose with the rules, and it's been noticed. They won't let it stand much longer."

"They? Other gods?" Sylvie said. Just what this whole mess needed. More powerful looky-loos.

Dunne nodded. "Zeus. Ostensibly, he commands me."

"I know how that goes," Sylvie said. "It's amazing how underrated free will is."

Erinya stutter-growled deep in her throat, an oddly warm sound. Was she laughing? It almost sounded like it. Erinya eeled out of Dunne's grip. "I'm going hunting." She smiled at Sylvie and disappeared.

Sylvie didn't even recoil when Alekta reappeared at a jog, ducked her head over the circle, and vanished again.

Instead, she said, "What about time? You reversed it this morning. Why not just unwind the moment when he vanished? Or when you blew up our only lead a moment ago?"

"I should have done it when Bran vanished," Dunne said. "But each hour that passed made it less of an option. Time is heavy and fragile. Rewriting that moment in your office was nothing, a heartbeat of time disrupted. Even so, more changed than you know. You never fired the bullet. It was the simplest way to convince you I meant business. But others had their moments rewound, their lives changed, too. There was a cop on Alligator Alley, pulling a car over for speeding. He was shot for his pains. I rewound your moment, and he went to the car with his gun in his hand. He shot first. His career is over."

"His life isn't," Sylvie said. "Sounds like a win. Where's the problem?"

"The driver wasn't mine," Dunne said. "Don't know that he was anybody's, but if he was, I've committed an act of contempt toward a fellow deity. In a millisecond of time, I made an enemy. To change two weeks' worth of seconds—it would make the world unrecognizable, pit god against god, change everything. Even twenty minutes reversed would create a tidal wave of change, and for what? To show us the spell again with no guarantee of learning from it?"

Sylvie sat down on the concrete. Of course, it couldn't be that easy. "Never is," she muttered, and then said, "Couldn't you just—choose a future?"

"I'd have to be able to see the future first," Dunne said.

"You can't? What, there's a limit? Mind reading or pre-cognition? No combos allowed?"

Magdala and Erinya arrived back at the same time and began to confer quietly. Magdala, Sylvie noticed, had a spatter of blood on her khakis. It couldn't have been the sorcerer, or she'd have dragged him back to Dunne. No, some other fool had crossed paths with the Fury and come out the worse for wear.

"It's very rare, even among gods." A smile curved Dunne's mouth, something small, rueful, and rather sweet, giving Sylvie a glimpse of the man who was Tish Carmichael's friend, Brandon's lover. "Bran calls it checks and balances on a vast scale. Says otherwise all we'd ever do is jockey for position. A few monotheist systems have foresight to some extent, your Christian god, for example, and some gods have pieces of it. I don't."

A tiny spark drifted through the air, leftover, Sylvie assumed, from the destruction of the oubliette. She followed its will-o'-the-wisp path for a few moments, finding it as soothing as drifting soap bubbles.

"Kronos and the Fates," Sylvie said. "That's two, or whatever, in your own pantheon. You *really* can't see the future?"

"I really can't," Dunne said. "As for Kronos, they ate him after they deposed him," Dunne said. The pale spark brushed against his shoulder and disappeared. Dunne brushed his hand over his shoulder as if it had stung. "Kronos's power, split into so many pieces, lessened. We can use it to grant immortality. That's about it."

A second spark, blue-white, drifted toward him.

"Immortality," Sylvie said. Shock touched her. "That's why you know he's not dead. You gave Bran immortality."

Dunne twitched again, touched a hand to his forearm as the spark made contact, clasping it. He closed his eyes, and a wave of heat moved through the station. In its wake, more sparks appeared.

Not the oubliette then: Its sparks would grow fewer, not multiply. Maybe they were visible bits of Dunne's shedding power. They seemed to be drawn to him.

"Bran's mortal," he said. "And don't expect me to ask the Fates. They don't know where he is, either. The Fates can't see the future. At least not more than the span of a man's life. Shorter if Atropos gets pissy and cuts the thread.

"Truthfully, there are more humans who are visionaries than gods. It's a cruel thing. Checks and balances. Give them the ability to see, and no power to change what they see, while we hold the power, but are blind."

"I knew a visionary," Magdala spoke. She licked a finger, rubbed at the bloodstain on her knee. "Hera sent me after her, but I needed to do nothing to punish her. She did it all to herself. She was pathetic. Every moment of joy was soured by the recognition of upcoming pain. Even pain was meaningless when she knew that grief was transitory, that people forget. Ultimately, all she saw of existence was futility. She cut her wrists and bled to death."

"Like Bran tried to do," Sylvie said.

Dunne's attention whipped around like he had taken on the Fury's predatory instincts. "Tish . . ." he said. Taking the source from her mind.

"*You* sure didn't tell me," Sylvie said. "Why not?"

The sparks hovered around him like fireflies, a ghostly set of flares that glimmered and faded. After a long moment, Dunne said, "I didn't want you to hold his life cheap." He curled his hands around his forearms, rubbing at them.

"Does he?" Sylvie said, hating that he made her ask, when he had to hear it burning in her thoughts. "Am I going to ride to the rescue, only to find that he's decided not to wait?"

Dunne twitched again, a full-body convulsion this time. He shifted his grip from his forearms to his torso, muttered, "No."

The sparks nipped at his skin, and Sylvie said, "I thought they were yours. But they're hurting you?"

"Not hurting. Pulling. They're Zeus's summoning motes. Zeus must have found me. I made flares when I changed time, when I destroyed the oubliette. And now, he's trying to take me back to Olympus," Dunne said, through gritted teeth. "I'm fighting it."

"O-kay," Sylvie said slowly. "Problem?"

"I'm *losing*," he said.

The sharp, clean scent of lightning began to fill the station. Sylvie stepped back from Dunne, from ground zero. Ball lightning crackled into existence, spinning around his chest in a liquid-plasma tumble of blue-white light and sound. It stretched over him like a living net, adapting itself to his shape.

Dunne took a breath, closed his eyes, seemingly unaware of his clothes singeing under the lightning's touch. Then he dropped his hands from his defensive posture, and said, "No."

His eyes, opened, were no longer human at all, no contrasting shine of white and pupil, but the featureless grey of a distant storm cloud. The grey sky effect bled outward, a slow dissolution of his cheekbones, his temples, his forehead. *Pretending to flesh*, Sylvie thought. Was this what he was, underneath?

He grasped the lightning, plasma curling violently between his closed fingers, licking at his arms, thrashing like a living thing. "No," he repeated, and flung it away.

It splattered against the concrete, sinking into it and disappearing. It left a puddled slag of concrete and rebar on the floor.

"I don't have time," he said, relaxed in the face of calamity. "He'll try again, harder, and I'll be stolen from the mortal plane, perhaps broken down. And I've got other problems. I've used power indiscriminately, had too much bleed off. I've got backtracking to do, prevent any of my leftovers from being used by sorcerers and witches, hungry for a taste of real power. Find him, Sylvie."

He vanished like a cutoff screenshot. She wished he'd make sound effects to go with it, just so her movie-trained mind could accept the vanishing as real.

"Crap," she said, slumping down to a weary crouch. She still had questions, important ones; she still had no leads, and no way of reaching him. When Alekta crawled out of the floor beside her, Sylvie's nerves were too shot to allow for anything more than a soft rock backward to fall on her butt.

"How do I call him?" she said. Alekta paused in her perusal of the station and its overlaid soul traces. She wrinkled her nose and sneezed at the slag on the floor.

"Yeah, yeah," Sylvie said. "Zeus threw lightning at him. Though myth always said it was a *bolt* of lightning, not that shiny little net. The things you learn." She rested against the wall, letting the cool concrete soothe her aching neck. "So?"

"Pray," Alekta said.

"Pray," Sylvie echoed. "Well, that makes sense. But I gotta tell you—I'm not real good at prayer."

Sylvie kicked a sneakered foot against a lone piece of

litter, watched it drift into the tracks. "So, d'you know why the oubliette tried to swallow Dunne, when it was keyed for Bran?"

Alekta walked away, climbed the stairs, and stood looking out into the night, tension rippling through her shoulders.

Out of leads, Sylvie thought.

She wondered how many of the "leads" the sisters had found ended with blood. Magdala, at least, had found one person guilty of something. Even if they hadn't been hunting for anyone other than the sorcerer responsible for the trap, she couldn't imagine the other two, with their snap judgments and hunger for retribution, passing on the chance to mete out their brand of punishment.

"Some of him in him," Alekta said, finally, and faded from sight. Sylvie frowned.

"Cryptic," she said. Some of him in him. Some of Bran in Dunne. The spell didn't differentiate enough. *Sloppy,* Val said. Sylvie was inclined to agree.

Some of what? Sylvie teased at the thought, knowing she was missing something. Skin cells maybe, she thought. Shared living, shared scents, or maybe it was some romantic thing? A piece of his heart and all that jazz? Given that the sloppy sorcerer had defined Bran by his relationship, perhaps he had drawn Dunne into the spell, too.

The rush of air from the passing train sent her to her feet, heart racing. After all the spells, the sisters, after Dunne, the station had begun to feel like a no-man's-land. The world reflected his desire, she thought. He wanted us alone, and he hadn't needed a spell to make it so.

She made her way through the first stragglers on the stairs and headed back into the night. Nearly midnight and nothing to show for her day; time to retreat and think. She touched the crumpled paper in her pocket. Maybe give the local witch a call if she wanted to risk pissing off a spell caster by calling at this hour.

Her mind full of questions, she managed to get nearly

fifteen blocks, passing by darkened storefronts and deserted alleys, when it dawned on her that the throbbing at her spine wasn't merely protest at her long day but the gun reacting to the rapid steps behind her.

She turned, half-expecting it to be an ISI agent whose skill at shadowing had been made clumsy by Dunne-itis, or even Demalion, giving her fair warning of his approach.

Not ISI, she thought, as the binding spell lanced from his outstretched palm and pinned her in place as neatly as if she had been flash-frozen.

Sylvie had just found herself a sorcerer, and judging from the scowl on his thin-boned, dark-browed face, one in no mood for playing civil.

10

Luck and the Ladies

CARELESS, THAT VOICE IN HER MIND CHASTISED, FULL OF SELF-contempt. Sylvie snarled and wiggled the fingers of her right hand by sheer force of will. She had been reaching for the gun when the spell took; she could feel its warmth yearning toward her hand. An inch, no more. She had been so close.

Careless, the voice said again, this time in a purr. Sylvie agreed; the sorcerer hadn't followed his binding spell with anything more permanent. He closed the distance between them, moving with an unearned confidence, and stood before her frowning. Like he had any right to frown, she thought. He wasn't much to look at, either. Skinny, squinty; no great shakes in the fashion department, black T-shirt and dirty-wash Levi's under an army-surplus jacket.

Was this her *Maudit* sorcerer? He looked . . . rather more scruffy than she was used to from their kind. But the binding spell was a spell that took finesse. Not one of the common ones. Entrapment never was. Couple that with the oubliette—he had to be *Maudits.*

Sylvie forced her hand to move, though fighting the

spell chafed her skin like steel wool. Her fingertips walked the gun barrel, traveling until she found its butt.

She curled her fingers around it, let the spell lock them back into place, and turned her concentration to her arm muscles. Pull the weapon. Shoot. A simple plan, with a lot of problematic variables. He might catch on, the spell might tighten, she might shoot herself— She met his eyes as if she hadn't a worry in the world.

"You destroyed my spell," he said. "Why?"

"I look like a witch to you?" Sylvie said. For a moment, she was glad of the spell's constriction—it masked the urge to grin as the gun rose in her hand. "No wonder your work's so sloppy. You don't take the time to observe."

His face, young and more revealing than he probably liked, moved between offense and concern. "You were there—" Another thought passed his face, wrinkling that too-young, too-smug brow. A word hovered on his lips, finally made it free. Recognition. *"Shadows."*

Maudits, for sure, if he knew of her. Her reputation really hadn't spread that far.

"You're not a witch," he said. "You're nothing. Just a woman. How did you do it?" And oh, that easy contempt in his voice was textbook. The *Maudits* were utterly convinced of their superiority. It was one of the things that made it so much fun to fuck them over. The gun warmed her hand; she curled her finger on the trigger.

"Arrogance should be earned," Sylvie said, pressing the trigger home, and bedamned to a bad angle. The crack of the bullet never came. Instead, the gun made a distressingly hungry sound like a fervent gulping and purr, and the spell holding her disappeared.

Devoured? Not that she had time to wonder about what had happened, not when she still had the *Maudit* to deal with, not when his eyes were going wide with shock and rage.

The *Maudit* stepped back, flung up a hand. Light coalesced in his palm, and Sylvie took her own step back,

sighting down the gun—catch her twice; shame on her—
and firing.

The gun twitched in her hand and spat the binding
spell back out. Sylvie smiled as she watched the sorcerer
stiffen and grow still. Not exactly as she had intended, but
she could work with this.

She circled his body, posed like some war statue, arm
raised, all pissy attitude, and found a smile. She could
definitely work with this.

Maybe a god-touched gun wasn't all bad. The second
spell steamed like frost vapor in the *Maudit's* cupped
hand, still active. Careful not to come in contact with it
herself, Sylvie forced one reluctant finger to fold after
another and snuffed the spell, ignoring his tremors of
rage.

"I have some questions for you. I know you can break
that spell—it's yours after all. But I'm faster than you are.
I'm meaner than you are, and I'm on deadline. You heard
what happened the last time the *Maudits* went against me
when I was against a clock?"

She waited a moment, watching his eyes change, a
slow shift from anger to the beginnings of concern. She
smiled. "Cat got your tongue? Blink once for yes. . . . You
know, *I* fought your spell faster than you're managing.
Pretty sad. Hard to imagine you created the oubliette. Impossible to imagine you did it just for kicks. I want to
know *all* about it, but let's start with the big one. Brandon
Wolf—how do I get him out?"

"You closed the door," he grated out.

"Yeah, yeah, mea culpa, sort of," Sylvie said, impa-
tience sparking. "Can we move on, or should I see what
fun games I can devise with you as a stiff? There isn't
much traffic around here. But I bet there's enough. If I
pushed you into the street—you think you could break the
spell before you turned into roadkill?"

A passing taxi sailed by, slowing a little at the sorcerer's upraised arm, but picked up speed when Sylvie
waved him on.

"He doesn't come out," the sorcerer said. "That's not the purpose of an oubliette."

He's working his way free, Sylvie thought. The sneer was back. No one had ever taught these boys to play poker.

"Then why get so pissy over a closed door—or were you thinking to bargain with hope? I don't think Dunne's someone who likes bargains like that. I know I don't. It's crap, and everyone knows it. Like promising salvation to a damned man. A lie spread by gods to make us docile."

Sylvie found her breath coming fast, her anger resurfacing, thinking of Dunne and Suarez. Of hopes destroyed, and bargains struck when choice was only pretend. That black edge crept through her mind and into her voice. *"I don't do docile."*

His eyes widened; he licked his lips. Little nervous tells that told her more than his state of mind, told her the spell was fading fast.

She seized his shirt collar, tangling the fabric in one clenched fist, the gun's barrel jabbing into the soft flesh of his throat. Shaking with rage, she dragged him away from the street, into the shadows of closed storefronts, and threw him against a wall.

He oofed with the impact, legs giving out until he landed, slumped, on the sidewalk. She followed him, crouched over him, gun in his face. "Just tell me how to get him back and we can get on with our lives. You do want to get on with yours, don't you?"

Vigilante, Dunne's voice accused.

"Stop, stop," he panted, pushing away from the gun, composure shaken.

"The slightest hint of a spell, and we'll see what this gun spits out next," she said. Two women passing by in a flurry of heels and chatter froze midstep, gaping. "Not your business," Sylvie said. They gasped and looked away, picking up their pace.

Still, they were nice women, Sylvie could tell, the kind

who would worry and stop at the first open storefront to call the police. Nice women had faith in the police.

"I don't understand," he said. He sounded confused. "You—you're *hers*. I can tell—it's in your voice. We're on the same side here."

"Like that could happen," Sylvie said. "Stop babbling. Focus. Brandon Wolf. Free. Make it happen."

"It's not supposed to let him out. I swear—"

"You left it open, left a back door into the spell—"

"So we could *find* it," he said. "Keep track of the oubliette. Not bring a body out."

Body. "Is he dead?" She grabbed his collar again so tightly her short-trimmed nails dug into flesh.

"No," he gasped.

"You sure?"

"I'd know."

"Then open it up again."

"I can't!"

Sylvie sucked in a breath, grappling with anger, with the need to be calm, the need to think. "For a sorcerer who rearranges the natural world at will, you're awfully fond of *can* and *can't*."

He breathed harshly, then said, "It's the spell. It makes a pocket of Elsewhere. There are millions of them, as many of them as there are of . . . of . . . of stars. Otherwise, what good would they be? If every time we opened them, the previous stuff came back, we wouldn't use them. You can't open the same oubliette twice."

"It might surprise you what you could do if you were sufficiently motivated," Sylvie said. He shivered a little, and she grinned, taking care to show as many teeth as possible. God help her, but she loved it when the bad guys were afraid of her.

"I can't," he whispered. "I just don't have the will for it."

"Suggest you find it fast or, hey, call one of your friends to help. Maybe your *we* who decided to keep track of the oubliette in the first place. There's someone I want to meet. The man with the plan."

He tore his gaze from hers, searching the street. Sylvie tapped him on the chin with the gun barrel. "Trust me, a big city like this, there's no one looking to help you. Unless . . . You expecting your boss?"

"She wouldn't—"

"She," Sylvie said. The word pinged her mind like something unexpected on her radar screen, pushing past the simmering adrenaline and rage. "Thought you guys weren't much for the distaff side of things. Guess I really need to meet the woman who can change your mind."

"You—" Perplexity touched his face again. "But you have met her, you must have, I can hear it in your voice. You're human, but you belong to her." His eyes widened the same way they had when he named her Shadows. Recognition. *"Dieu,"* he whispered. *"L'enfant du meurtrier."*

"I belong to no one," Sylvie said. "Never have, never will. Do you understand me? I am the cat who walks by her goddamned self, and if you speak one more word in a language I don't understand, I will kill you."

He shook his head, laughter in his eyes, pushed past fear into bravery born of desperation. "You belong to her, and what she's going to say when she finds out you're opposing her . . . She admires willfulness, but this—oh, you're going to be in such trouble. You're working on the wrong side, Shadows!" He laughed in her face. "She'll bring you to heel. Show you the error of your ways. She'll make you *crawl.*"

Rage washed over her, distracted her, and she nearly paid the price for it. He turned a single hand in her direction, the clawed gesture familiar, as were the snarled words. *"Votre coeur . . ."*

Sylvie shot him, the close-range blast heating her hand and spattering her with blowback and blood. He slammed into the wall as if the bullet had pinned him there.

Sylvie looked at the concavity in his shirt, a perfect chest shot again, for a long, blank moment. She touched his neck, still warm with sweat, but free of anything resembling a pulse. He'd died hard and fast. Best way to deal with an inimical sorcerer who had been about to rip out her heart with a single phrase and a crooked finger, but still—

"Shit," she whispered, casting a wary glance back at the street, at the few cars passing by. It was one thing to threaten someone on a big-city street, another still to murder him. The gun felt treacherous in her shaking hand. Why not the paralytic spell again? Why the bullet? She hadn't wanted him dead.

Especially when he hadn't told her anything. She'd chewed Dunne a new one for reacting on instinct, but she'd made the same mistake he had: She'd destroyed a lead.

Soft footsteps approached, and Sylvie ducked into the nearest shadowed doorway, waiting.

The rubber-soled boots and torn plaid pleats were familiar, so she stepped out to meet the punk Fury's gaze, knowing that she couldn't hide successfully anyway.

"Nice," Erinya said, dropping to get a closer look. "Finally found someone to kill, huh. Feel better? I always feel better." The girl tugged the body forward, examined the exit wound, and the ragged hole in the mortared brick behind him. "Good ammo."

"What are you doing here?" Sylvie demanded. It couldn't be good to feel relieved at the presence of a Fury, but concentrating on her inappropriate relief was preferable to dwelling on the dead. She slipped the gun back into its holster.

The punk girl smiled up at her from where she was crouched. "I'm supposed to help you. He said. Since you could be relied on to think." There were layers of delicate amusement in her voice that made Sylvie flush.

"Fine. You want to help? Make that disappear."

"I can't undo that. I'm a small god, and he's dead."

"Didn't ask you to. He tried to kill me. Dead is good. Dead, *here*, though . . ." Sylvie said. "Just make the body go away. I can't help Dunne from inside a cell. Take him wherever you take your kills."

The girl smirked. "Why not take him where you left yours?"

"'Cause the damn Atlantic's a couple hundred miles away." Never admit anything, Sylvie reminded herself, but there was no point in hiding from Erinya's knowing gaze. "Just do it."

The girl stood in a quick, offended movement, crossing her arms over her chest. Sylvie couldn't tell if it was a put-on or not, a deliberate mockery of humanity or genuine feeling. "For someone who touts freedom, you're sure bossy. I get bossed around enough."

"Dunne?" Sylvie said.

"He's all right," the girl said, relaxing a little, toeing the corpse with her boot with the fidgety, destructive curiosity of a monkey. "He mostly tells me *not* to do stuff, and that's different than telling me what to do all the time. Alekta and Magdala—they make me mad. Just 'cause I'm the youngest doesn't mean I'm young, you know. But they're always biting my wings, putting me in my place. Even now, when Bran's in such trouble."

It was like listening to her little sister, calling up to vent about curfew, Sylvie thought, not some mythological creature. The more the girl spoke, the more she picked up the cadence of human speech. But for all that Erinya's speech was approaching normal, her actions—

Sylvie blinked, her analytical thoughts interrupted by the Fury kicking the body forcefully. Bones crunched, and the sorcerer's carcass left a glistening trail on the pavement as it inched away under the impetus of her kicks.

"Stop it," Sylvie said, tacked on a "please," when the girl's dark eyes swung round toward her, feral and red-black and not like a sulking teenager's at all.

A siren's wail turned the distant street corner, showing a faraway flash of blue and red, like a warning aurora. She was running out of time; even if that siren had nothing to do with her, each passing moment meant the exponential danger of a motorist with a cell phone calling the cops, of those women reporting her.

Sylvie bent over the body again, fumbled in pockets gone sticky; between the gunshot and Erinya's boots, the sorcerer's chest cavity was little more than a shattered mess, soft and splintered. Sylvie wiped her fingers on her jacket after she'd finished the search.

Nothing. No ID, no keys, no wallet. He'd come out just to pick a fight. Sylvie scowled. It was never that easy.

"Well?" she said to Erinya. So she'd shot her best lead; even dead, he could yield information, if she could figure out who he was. If she wasn't arrested at any moment.

"Oh, yeah," the girl said. "Get rid of it, right."

"If you don't mind," Sylvie said.

The girl hoisted the corpse into her arms, cradling it like a dead child, and stared down at it. She raised it a little higher and licked at the wound. "Mmm," she said. The sight stopped the words in Sylvie's throat. She coughed and forced them out, anyway.

"Stop that," she said, stripping off her Windbreaker and draping it over his torso, hiding the wound, the blood. "Dispose of him, don't eat him. Come right back, but remember his scent. You can help me track him back to wherever he's been staying."

"Sure thing, boss," the girl said, that poison-sweet petulance in her voice again. "Want I should bring you a latte as well?"

Sylvie laughed, the sound unexpected even to her. The Fury eyed her warily, shifted the sorcerer's deadweight in her arms, and vanished. Sylvie walked a block down the street, a block away from a bloodstain she didn't want to have to explain to anyone, and sat on the curb.

In one irritable gesture, she waved off a cab that veered toward her. Her phone buzzed in her pocket, and she pulled it out, angling it toward the streetlamp to see the number.

Alex.

Down the block, Sylvie saw the Fury reappear. Sylvie

looked at her spattered hands and shut the phone off. Blood on her hands, in her voice; there was no way she could talk to Alex like this. Alex might be a visitor to the dark side of the world on occasion, but she didn't need to know how comfortable Sylvie was in it.

11

Women on the Hunt

SYLVIE KEPT A CAREFUL EYE ON THE APARTMENT HALLWAY WHILE THE Fury put her hand to the latch. It opened without fuss or fanfare. "Slick," Sylvie said.

Erinya smiled, a wild-toothed expression that made Sylvie shiver even as she responded in kind. She and the Fury were getting along entirely too well. Really, what did that say about her—that these days she was more at ease working with a stone killer than talking to Alex? Sylvie slipped through the door behind the Fury and latched it.

A quick rush of controlled light ran along the door and frame, tracing an esoteric pattern burned into the wood. "You didn't tell me there was a spell on the door."

"It didn't matter," the girl said, sticking her tongue out at the voided spell. "No door can bar me."

"You and the Grim Reaper," Sylvie said. "Just goes to prove no good comes from unexpected guests."

"Don't compare us," Erinya said. "He uses tools. I use my hands. . . ." She flashed said hands in Sylvie's face, hands gone scaled and black, twisted from a human's five-fingered grip, to something more birdlike, something reptilian.

"Oh, and that makes all the difference," Sylvie said. "'Cause one is so much more dead than the other."

"It is if we eat the soul," Erinya said, licking her lips with a snake's tongue.

Sylvie refused to flinch at either claws or tongue. Erinya had been testing her nerve all the way to the sorcerer's apartment, leaping at her suddenly, shifting shape halfway, then grinning around a toothed beak.

Sylvie figured she was as safe at the moment as she would ever be from the Furies. Not only had Dunne sent Erinya to aid her, a clear sign of his intent, the Furies themselves wanted her to succeed. Erinya's rage at the *Maudit's* body had proved that.

Still, she shouldn't get cocky—their tempers were as bad as hers, and she had just killed a man she had meant to question.

Sylvie paused in the apartment's tiny entryway and took puzzled stock while Erinya prowled the room. The interior matched the exterior of the building; on the small side, a little run-down.

The *Maudits* were usually big on pomp and panoply, preferring five-star-hotel suites and the best of everything, no matter the splash it made. This apartment, with its tangled clutter of dropped clothing, of candle ends and piled DVDs, of Salvation Army furniture and velvet blackout curtains, looked more like a D&D geek's idea of a sorcerer's lair, minus only a tattered copy of the *Necronomicon*.

Of course, unlike a D&D geek, the resident really did have magical abilities, and the books lying casually on the coffee table, between half-empty soda cans, incense sticks, mortars and pestles, were honest-to-god-or-the-devil grimoires. The kinds too often made from human skin or written in blood. Sylvie tucked her hands into her jeans pockets and wandered inward, noting the TV screen and its hissing snow.

SINS & SHADOWS 109

"Any other spells lying around?" Sylvie asked. "'Cause I'm so not in the mood to go up in smoke. Or be turned into a toad."

"That'd be bad," Erinya said. "I'd eat you up if you were a toad."

Erinya's gaze was predatory, just that little bit sharper than a moment before, and fixed on her. Upping the bluff? "Back off, I'm not a toad, yet," Sylvie said. "Besides, if I were a toad, I'm sure I'd be poisonous. . . ." The girl's gaze didn't falter. Sylvie stuffed her nervousness behind a quick scowl.

"You're all over blood," Erinya said. "Didn't see it so much outside, in the dark."

"I'll wash up," Sylvie said, her mouth dry.

"You don't have to. I like it."

"I'll wash up," Sylvie repeated. There was a small kitchenette in sight, and she aimed herself at it, pushing past Erinya when the Fury didn't get out of her way. The brief contact made her shudder, a reflexive reaction to touching flesh that had only a cursory resemblance to human; it was like reaching out to touch a fallen branch and finding the lively suppleness of a snake.

She leaned over the kitchen sink, splashing her hands clean, using enough of the *Maudit's* soap that her hands were slimy instead of lathered and took forever to rinse, giving her an excuse to linger.

Don't forget what she is. She hunts killers. She destroys them down to their souls. The only thing keeping you safe is Dunne's need.

Sylvie couldn't argue with any of that, but she also couldn't deny the sense of camaraderie that had risen between them.

Part of it, she knew, was Erinya's situation. Once out of the reach of the sullen sisters, out of Dunne's brooding misery, the Fury had proved to be both chatty and profane, spewing bile that struck chords deep within Sylvie. Erinya, the afterthought sister, created only because three could corner prey better than two. For the worst offenders, the ones who deserved more than simple death, the Furies worked as a team. Two to flank their prey and one up ahead to devour the soul.

"I didn't even get a name," Erinya had said, vaulting over a mailbox in the sidewalk, kicking it on her gymnastic way down and knocking it over with a shuddering clang and a burst of broken concrete. "*We're* the Erinyes. I'm a thing, not an individual. *Alekta* got a name. Not a mind, though. She's all orders and rank, kowtowing to them all. Magdala plays their games, nipping and nudging them into listening to what she wants. We're gods, too, but fuck if they act like it. We're just the punishers. And if we forget our place—" Erinya shook her head; black wings shook around her and disappeared. "It's like a prison, Olympus. I was glad, glad"—she tilted her head back to shout at the dark sky above—"*glad* when Kevin took our reins from Hera."

Sylvie stifled the urge to ask how—it couldn't matter. "What can they do to you? You're gods."

Erinya paused in midstride and snarled. "You don't know anything."

"So tell me," Sylvie said, watching the girl's shape shift, pushing her into a canine crouch.

Fangs sprouted, a muzzle shifted to a beak, and still the words were clear, as if they bypassed such things as vocal cords or physical structure. "We're not bodied. We're just power. We make bodies, build immortal dolls strong enough to contain our Selves. The big gods, they break those doll-shells if we anger them. It's—unpleasant. If we can't put our shells back together fast enough, we disperse and die. And if we get help—well, better to have no help at all than be altered at their whims. Once, I had a name. Once I was Tisiphone. Now, I'm just one of a type. We're all vulnerable when we're just power. Hera learned the hard way. Zeus broke her shell at the wrong moment; now she's nearly the weakest of us all."

"The wrong moment," Sylvie echoed. She knew it involved Dunne somehow. It didn't make sense. None of it made sense. A man could become a god if he stole a god's power. Could he steal it by accident?

Hera got weak; Hera had owned the Furies. Dunne got strong; Dunne took the Furies' leashes in hand. Cause and effect. Obvious. But how had he done it? How could a man contain such stolen power and not be consumed by it? She'd seen sorcerers burn up tapping too much magic from another human. What would it feel like to be mortal and tap into a god?

Beside her, Erinya shifted full out, losing all human shape, embodying a creature that Sylvie had never seen before and never wanted to see again. A hooked beak full of teeth, a mane that writhed and tangled along an out-stretched neck, eyes that ran bloody tears. Sylvie looked away so fast her neck spasmed. Furies drove men mad. She bet it was after they'd revealed themselves, or given what Erinya had just said, what they saw as themselves.

"Put the scary away, huh?" she said. She stared up at the night sky, stars occluded by streetlights streaming upward. "No need for panic in the streets."

"There's no one to watch," Erinya said.

"There's me," Sylvie said. "Don't want me to go all hysterical on you, do you?" She made her voice light, as if the possibility were laughable; she wondered if her scent would give the game away. She heard the god stretching, the rasp of feathers and fur giving way to the more normal sounds of fabric and metal.

"So you took the out that Dunne provided and came to earth," Sylvie said. "You live in the mortal realm."

Erinya nodded. "With Dunne. With Bran. We watch over him, when Dunne can't." She stopped dead, hands fisting at her side. "We were hunting when Bran was trapped. It shouldn't have happened. We were hunting *mortals*. All four of us, when Dunne alone could have done it. It's our fault. We shouldn't have trusted that Bran was safe."

Sylvie raised a brow. She wasn't going to try patting the girl on the shoulder, or even mumbling a "there,

there," no matter how mournful she sounded. Sylvie valued her skin too highly for that. Besides, the dark voice chimed in, they had been fools to think Dunne could escape the other gods by running to earth. Someone had to pay for the theft. Brandon Wolf was vulnerable.

In the apartment kitchen, rubbing the last suds from between her fingers, Sylvie paused in her memory. Maybe that was it—the connection Erinya and she had: They both knew what it was like to have innocents hurt while under their protection.

She scrubbed her hand across her face, wiping a few stealthy tears from her lashes. Her hands came away red-tinged, and she shuddered, wildly.

God, more of it? She bent back to the sink, cupped water in her hands, and splashed her face, the stickiness at her neck, the crusting tangle in the hair by her left ear. The water pattered down, rust colored. She did it again until her shirt was sopped and clammy around the collar, and only the steel sink showed through the water drops.

No paper towels to hand, she spotted a worn shirt, crumpled on the Formica counter, and she used it to blot her hair and neck, soak up any lingering blood that might have evaded the water. Black, she thought, so good for hiding stains. It wasn't like the *Maudit* was in any position to object, and the cotton was soft, even if it smelled of sulfur and smoke. A slogan on the shirt scratched her skin and put an end to her grooming.

Habit made her drape the shirt neatly over the back of the single kitchen chair to dry. In Miami, everything mildewed given half a chance. The apartment refrigerator was going to be bad enough by the time the landlord realized that the sorcerer wasn't coming back, why add mold to his or her problem?

Absently, she read the broken, charcoal-colored letters, *NDNM*, wondering philosophy, rock band, or other.

Erinya was a series of soft scuffles in the other room, and Sylvie rejoined her. "Anything?" Sylvie asked.

"It all smells like magic," the Fury complained, frustration evident in her voice, and in the scales sliding along her skin. Sylvie was amazed that Erinya could even pass as human the way she shuffled guises. Either the stress was getting to her, eroding her self-control, or—scary thought—Erinya felt as peculiarly comfortable in the strange duo they formed as Sylvie did.

Erinya walked into the small bedroom, yanked the first drawer out of the dresser, ripping the cheap laminate, and dumped the contents to the floor. She rooted around in the mass of clothes with her foot.

"All right then," Sylvie said. "You check out the bed-room." *Since you're going to do it anyway,* she thought. Sylvie watched the Fury yank another drawer out, and sighed before turning to more organized searching.

The dead *Maudit* had had a partner, a woman, but she didn't live here. One chair in the kitchen. One pillow on the bed. One dirty plate at the edge of the futon was still half-full of cooling chow mein. Sylvie's stomach roiled. When was the last time she'd eaten? Ten, twelve hours ago? That cruller in the bakery.

She picked up the plate, unwilling to look at it, more unwilling to admit the urge to tuck into it. Hell, she'd eaten out of garbage cans more than once, back in the bad times. A sorcerer's recent leftovers didn't look too bad, and she liked chow mein. Still, eating your victim's last meal—Sylvie thought psychologists might find that deeply symptomatic of some regrettable pathology. She set the plate down on the TV, felt a tingly zip and zing in her fingers like the quick dance of current, and jumped back, thinking, *Spell!*

Two breaths later, she let out a slow sigh and forced herself to relax. Just faulty wiring. She leaned over to check and stared at the plug lying next to the baseboard, six inches or more from the outlet. The TV hissed quietly.

Sylvie backed up to take another look at the screen. Snow. Bad reception. Amazing reception, actually, con-sidering the lack of electricity to the set. But what had he been watching?

She squinted, seeing blurry shapes behind the static, dark, light, a long rush of steady movement that struck a chord of memory. She absently reached up for a nonexistent rabbit ear, then yanked her hand back at the tingle. Duh, Sylvie. Magic. Still, when in doubt. Gingerly, she reached out and thumped the side of the set, prepared this time for the little nonshock sensation. Her eyes stayed glued to the screen.

For a bare second, the screen grew clear, the signal noise twitched and lifted. Sylvie got a fast glimpse of the scene, and recognized it. Why wouldn't she? She'd been there. The screen was an "I spy" scrying spell keyed to the El station and the oubliette. Sylvie bet that the screen had been nice and clear before Dunne made things go boom.

Sylvie glanced at the noodles again, and grinned. Bet the *Maudit* had nearly choked when he spied, with his own little eye, Dunne making oubliette hash. No wonder he'd come running.

She turned her attention to the spooky stuff—the mess of chalks and candles, parchments and books—on the coffee table. She fished out that day's *Tribune*, folded open to the comics, then the various soda cans, grimacing as some of them sloshed and splashed. Slob, she judged, but sat down before the low table and the space she'd cleared.

Sitting down was a mistake. Weariness swept over her, turning the cheap futon at her back into near-impossible-to-resist comfort. She tilted her head back and closed her eyes.

Erinya broke a lamp in the bedroom, and Sylvie jerked awake. "Later," she said. "Finish this case, and I can either sleep for a week, or I'll be dead." Her body didn't want to listen. She raised herself to her feet and hit the kitchenette again. Eating a dead man's food was wrong somehow; fine, she could accept that, but surely the taboo didn't extend to his caffeine. She draped herself over the fridge door and selected a Mountain Dew. Good for that little jolt. Crap for taste. She drank it anyway, gulping it on the way back to the living room and dropping the empty on the floor. One more wouldn't matter.

As for fingerprints, well, it wasn't like his body was ever going to be found, no criminal investigation spurred by the bullet wound and broken bones. He might be listed as missing after some time, but even if someone reported his absence, the odds were good that he'd simply be presumed another feckless young man, drifting out of town. Safest murder she'd ever committed. Sylvie shuddered a little. It shouldn't have been so easy. It should disturb her more than it did.

She began sorting papers. A lot of them had scraps and sections of the oubliette spell written on them, different colors, different tilts to the Greek.

These were his practice runs, she thought, touching a shaky rendering of the Greek letters that read "love," and spelled nothing but pain for Brandon Wolf. Another sheet revealed row after row of paint stripes, some rough, some globbed, some runny. Getting the medium just right. Nothing was uglier than a spell going all to hell because the paint dripped and obscured a vital symbol.

Sylvie leaned against the futon again, twisting herself and curling into it, resting her head for just one more moment. Her unfocused gaze picked up something shining on the floor near the end of the table. She reached out and collected it. A pendant on a long, heavy chain, meant to disappear beneath clothing. The pendant slithered down the chain, snagging at the clasp. Sylvie raised it closer, frowning. She'd seen that half bat wing before in South Beach, back when she and Val had thought the *Maudits* might be allies instead of enemies.

It was an apprentice's badge.

"A goddamned apprentice," Sylvie said. In the other room, Erinya stirred. "A talented runaway with something to prove." Easy prey for the first charismatic leader to come along with a grand plan and an eye for talent. Even if that leader was a woman. Of course, Sylvie wasn't any closer to finding out who the woman was, but she was beginning to get a tentative feel for her. A woman who used the *Maudit* instead of being used by them. Sylvie could admire that.

Another piece of paper, sorted through, revealed not the stiff formal writing of the trained *Maudits*, but a new hand. Stark, confident, elegant, in a language Sylvie recognized but couldn't read; the bastard mix of Latin and archaic French that filled the *Maudits* grimoires. So his lady boss knew his language in more ways than one. But if she had helped him compose the oubliette spell—why bother with him at all?

The simplest answer was, like so many of those who hired sorcerers, the lady lacked talent herself. Strange, though, to find that kind of detailed knowledge in a non-Talent. What kind of person went to the effort to learn something she could never use herself?

She sifted through papers faster, looking for that strange, elegant handwriting, and found only one more scrap. A single sentence in English that could be construed as threat, support, or reminder, depending on their relationship.

"You know I'll be watching."

Sylvie wasn't sure which one it had been to the *Maudit*, but to her it meant nothing but threat. If she truly was watching the *Maudit*, then she had seen Sylvie kill him. While Sylvie hadn't felt the creepy certainty that came of being the object of unwanted attention, that lack didn't rule out less mundane means of watching.

Sylvie glanced again at the snowy TV and grimaced. The odds were good she had blundered into two "I spys" tonight, the *Maudit's* station spell and one focused on him. The fact that there had been no attempted intervention in her brief struggle with the *Maudit* argued for remote viewing.

The question was, had the *Maudit's* death woken the woman to outrage?

Ripping fabric in the bedroom caught her attention. Erinya lay sprawled on the bed, tearing a T-shirt into thirds with her teeth and talons. When she felt Sylvie's eyes on her, Erinya re-formed her muzzle to human lips, and muttered, "I'm bored. I liked you better earlier."

Covered in blood, gun drawn, with a dead man at her feet. Sylvie thought a scathing reply but was halted by recognition of the shirt—the one she'd used in the kitchen.

It made her skin crawl; she crossed the room in two adrenaline-filled strides and yanked it from Erinya's talons. No way in hell was Erinya going to be tasting her sweat along with the sorcerer's blood. That kind of thing could lead to a friendly fire she didn't even want to consider. But the shirt felt different in her hands; the cloth stiffer, newer, thicker, even dampened with Erinya's saliva.

Sylvie shook it out. *NDNM,* the shirt said. A newer twin to the one in the kitchen. Sylvie threw it back to Erinya, who shrugged and dropped it. Sylvie went down on her knees, rooting through the mess Erinya had made, pulling black cloth free from jeans, from colored tees and khakis, from the finger-nipping bits of broken lamp bulb.

Two of the same shirts, Sylvie thought, almost meant something. One shirt was nothing, a freebie, a promo, an impulse buy or gift. Sylvie dug up another matching shirt, tossed it toward Erinya, and found one more. Further excavations revealed a fifth, inside out and tangled with dirty socks.

Sylvie sat back on her haunches and grinned, looking at the charcoal script stretched between her fingers. *NDNM*, and beneath it, in nearly invisible, black-on-black script, a local address. NDNM was a *place*.

While one shirt meant nothing . . . five shirts . . . five shirts meant their sorcerer had worked there. A workplace meant coworkers who might very well know the *Maudit's* lady-boss. If she were really lucky, lady-boss was also his real-world employer, and she'd find her new guide to Bran's recovery at NDNM. Of course, there was the chance that the woman was waiting for her, ready to retaliate for the death of her lackey.

Sylvie knee-walked through the clutter, winced as a shard of glass bit through her jeans, and ignored the small pain in favor of reaching for the bedside table. Phone book? Yes. She dived into it and found a number. She dialed, got a blast of music and raised voices before a man said, "NDNM."

Sylvie disconnected. Only one type of place had that kind of background noise, and would still be open at this late hour. She grinned. Eager to get moving, Erinya crawled over the bed and, in a half crouch, stared down at her.

Sylvie rose, exhaustion pushed back. "C'mon, Erinya, we're going clubbing."

12

Ni Dieux, Ni Maîtres

THE CLUB WAS HIDDEN ON THE OUTSKIRTS OF THE CITY, IN THE no-man's-land where the airport gave way to near-empty space. NDNM was a small, freestanding building sandwiched between a gas station and a run-down strip mall on the top of a weedy slope. At this late hour, just past 1:00 a.m., the only lights came from the neon above the gas station, the flickering yellow light of the late-night noodle shop, and the blue glow seeping through NDNM's narrow, mirrored windows. They reminded Sylvie of gun slits, and her hands tightened on the steering wheel.

She drove past the building once, trying to get a feel for the club's layout. Front door, narrow windows, back door, no windows, delivery door. A basic box. In the passenger seat, Erinya grumbled. "Scaredy-cat."

"Reconnaissance is never a bad idea," Sylvie said. "Some of us are not immortal."

Erinya sank back against the fake leopard-print seat cover and sulked into silence, picking at a stiff stain in the ratty plush. Sylvie eyed the stain, then decided not to overthink it. They'd needed a car to get to the club; Erinya had gotten one, and made no mention of what its owner had thought about the appropriation of the vehicle.

There was no reason for Erinya to have killed for it; in Chicago, old cars were as common as concrete. Besides, that stain didn't look like blood. At least, not a lot like blood.

Sylvie drew into the lot, counting cars by row, six here, ten there, two dozen there, trying to estimate how many people might be within. She parked at the edge of the lot and paused, a little at a loss. Erinya had started the car for her; it lacked its key, and she didn't think the Fury had done anything as real-world as cross wires to jump-start it. Sylvie finally got out of the car with a shrug, the motor still running.

She touched the gun at her back for reassurance and headed toward the door, Erinya trotting eagerly at her heels.

The front door opened, and a young couple came out into the night air on a wave of cigarette smoke, dressed with dark European flair, and speaking in rapid and colloquial French. They passed Sylvie, and the woman turned back to look, her lips twisting slightly.

Sylvie paused; she'd seen Val look at her like that a thousand times. She didn't pass muster. Sylvie glanced at her reflection in the mirrored windows and groaned.

"Give me your jacket," she said. Erinya peered over her shoulder, studying Sylvie's reflection also, as if she could see what Sylvie was seeing more clearly that way.

It might be true, Sylvie thought. Erinya might see insides as opposed to outsides, a person's soul, rather than the flesh cloaking it.

Sylvie's grey T-shirt, thrown on that morning in anticipation of a day spent moving boxes, was ready for the ragman. Small dark spots freckled the collar; leftover droplets of blood had washed down from her face and hair, and the fabric was fraying beneath the stains.

Sylvie prodded a dark spot with a fingernail, and the cotton popped beneath her touch with the nasty sensation of a blister giving way. Sorcerer's blood, she thought. Some type of lingering power gnawing away at his killer. Good thing she'd gotten the blood off her skin.

Erinya handed her jacket over without objection. Black leather, heavily laden with zippers, and with a tattered Union Jack on its reverse. Not Sylvie's style, but better than nothing. She slipped one arm in and shivered. It felt weirdly alive, vibrating to that strange, nonhuman frequency that surrounded Dunne and the sisters. She hesitated.

"Don't be such a wuss. It's just clothes," Erinya said. She stuck out her tongue. "Bran bought it last time he was in London. A present for being such a good girl." She stepped closer and stroked the scarred leather, her face as wistful as a born predator's could get. The entire jacket shivered toward her, like a pet yearning toward its owner. Sylvie jerked away.

Gods and power. She finally understood, in a visceral way, what Dunne was fighting, his worries about the trails he left, the power he shed the way humans dropped skin cells and hair. Erinya's jacket radiated the same kind of weight a spell did and could probably serve as a tiny little battery for those who were magically talented.

Gritting her teeth, she pulled it on the rest of the way, shuddering as the gun purred against it. The dark spots on her T-shirt bleached white and slowly dissolved in vaporous wisps. "Wonderful," Sylvie muttered, zipping the jacket closed. She took a last look in the mirror, straightened her hair, checked that the gun was sufficiently hidden, leaving no revelatory bulge beneath the heavy leather hem. Good enough.

She tugged one-half of the double doors open, finding it surprisingly heavy, and Erinya flowed through into the dimness beyond and disappeared. Sylvie followed, slowing immediately and blinking in the low light.

The room was long, running the length of the storefront, but too shallow to be all there was. The light confounded her, being not only dim, but moving, flashing, alive with shadows. Muttered words reached her ears, a garble that she took for foreign before catching a word here and there, and understanding that it was several people speaking at once, not in conversation but in monologues. The light flickered again, blue-white, off to either side of her, and Sylvie's eyes adjusted.

Television screens. The light that had seeped through the windows, the flickering that teased her eyes now was the familiar glow of television in a dark room. On either side of her, the televisions were stacked in columns ringed by chairs. The screens shifted at different speeds, showing multiple channels. To her left, the seats were mostly full, young men and women leaning forward or lounging back, watching the screens with varying shades of attention. To her right, the seats were mostly empty. Sylvie leaned right, turned her head, caught a brief snatch of words— one television broadcasting into a lull on the others.

". . . each according to need is the standard we should strive to . . ."

"Tear it all down! The world without authority cannot be worse than the world we have now." An agitated orator from the left found an echo in a viewer. A man whose stubble gleamed in the reflected light spat the words back at the screen with the fervor of a fanatic. "Tear it all down." His hands clenched on his knees.

Sylvie, scenting trouble, listened harder and got a trace of a passionate voice tinnily exhorting through muffled speakers: "The government doesn't serve you. It doesn't serve me. It serves itself, and forces us to serve it, at the expense of individualization. I say better by far to have no government at all—"

"Ten dollars," a gruff voice spoke, startling her. She hadn't seen him approach at all, which amazed her, given his size.

"Ten dollars," he repeated. "No looky-loos. You want to stay, you pay." She eyed the stretched-out T-shirt across his broad chest, the palm as big as a dinner plate extended before her, and looked up, then up some more.

Gentle giant? she thought. *Let's not find out.* She fumbled through her pockets and pulled out two crumpled fives. "That cover my friend also?" She gestured toward Erinya, now crouched before the lowermost screen, watching the movement within, like a cat fascinated by a fish tank. No one seemed to object that she was blocking the view. It didn't require any sensitivity to the *Magicus Mundi* to see that Erinya was best left unprovoked. Even her human-shaped shell suggested that she was the kind of girl who might knock you down in a mosh pit, then kick you in the head if you complained. Kick back, and she'd grab a bottle and brain you.

The giant doorman looked at Erinya for a moment, thoughtful; as she felt his eyes on her, she turned and stared back. "Her? Twenty dollars for the trouble she's gonna make."

Sylvie forked over a twenty. He folded his hand around her arm and stamped her inner wrist with a crimson A in a circle. In the dim light, with those jagged lines, it looked more like a botched suicide than anything else.

"C'mere, girly," the bouncer said, gesturing to Erinya.

Erinya's eyes were full of "me?" Sylvie watched Erinya's nose wrinkle in distaste, then watched her expression slide toward baffled offense once Sylvie nodded, confirming that yes, the bouncer did in fact mean the Fury.

Erinya surged to her feet, feral even in the low light, muscles shifting under her fishnet shirt. Her eyes sparked like phosphorus, gleaming white, then green. "I don't want a stamp."

He shrugged. "Then you can't go in."

Prudently, Sylvie distanced herself. The bouncer was on his own. After all, either his soul, conscience, memories—whatever it was that the Furies tested—was clean or not. If it was clean, then Erinya's hands were supposedly tied by her own nature. Soiled—Sylvie had had enough of jostling with the Furies.

Sylvie slipped past the giant, into the cubicle he had

appeared from, and opened the door hidden in its depths. A hallway greeted her, a mural on either side of her. Oil painting, living colors, not what she expected at all, not after the grimy tech of the anteroom. NDNM grew more interesting by the moment.

The mural on her left was of a naked giant, handing a blazing box to a group of men huddled before caves. In the gold-shot sky, vultures circled a mountain peak. Sylvie leaned closer. There were words mixed in with the blaze of light, created purely by paint layered deeper in sections than others, words made out of shape rather than color. Sylvie touched it, tracing the elaborate curls—something about fire and gifts and gods and freedom.

The door at the far end of the hall opened on a wave of sound, and Sylvie stepped aside for a sweaty, chattering group of clubbers.

She looked to the other side. Eden, the temptation of Eve, instantly recognizable. Eve lingered in a smothering verdant world of tangled vines and roots and dangling branches laden with overripe fruit. It made Sylvie claustrophobic looking at it.

Beside Eve, the serpent waited, silvery in the dark earth; its tail coiled about a tiny sapling with one delicate fruit gracing its branches. Only then did Sylvie see Eve's hand outstretched beneath it, fingers straining against the pressing vines, pushing back the intrusive greenery, reaching for the tiny fruit that shone like starlight. Eden as a prison. Serpent as savior.

Sylvie spotted one more tiny piece of brightness in the mural, near the floor, and bent to look at it. A wolf in profile, standing on a pair of crossed arrows, the whole thing small enough to fit in the palm of her hand. *Wolf,* she thought. She touched the arrow shaft, and felt more of the tricky bas-relief painting. Tiny letters fought her fingertips, fought deciphering, insisted on being merely texture, but she persisted and found an r, an o.

A signature. Brandon Wolf. He'd been here, working

among his enemies. No wonder the *Maudit* had conde-
scended to work in a club.

Wolf's abduction looked worse and worse all the time.
The oubliette argued planning, but this type of planning
was another level up. This was the careful infiltration that
swamped its victim in lies and betrayal.

The inner door opened again, and a young man in a
staff tee came through, a pack of cigarettes in his hand.
"It's not that scary, you know," he said, grinning at whatever expression had frozen on her face. "You'll like it in
there."

He sauntered on by and headed outside. Sylvie opened
the inner door, stepped into the club proper, and was
numbed by sudden sensation. She shifted to the side, put
her back to the wall and rode the moment out.

After the silent hallway, the club seemed a riot of sen-
sory overload. Alcohol scenting the air, iced drinks chim-
ing against glass, the pounding drive of the rock music—
My Chemical Romance, Sylvie identified absently, Alex's
current favorite—dozens of people talking, breathing,
dancing, moving, and the chaotic visuals of a room divided into sections, not by walls, but chain curtains and
raised or lowered floors: All of it made her pause to catch
her breath.

Slowly, more details kicked in: The bar was situated to
her left, running the length of a cracked, mirrored wall.
Men and women leaned on the bar in small groups, talking and gesturing. Directly before her, two steps down led
to a dance floor that wound its way through raised sections for seating.

She took the steps down to the floor, heading toward
the bar, watching herself approach in the faceted glass, a
tired woman with a troubled face. She looked past the
weary lines in her skin and focused on the mirror itself.
Though she had thought the glass cracked on first glance,
now she saw the joins and seams, and realized that it was
deliberately done. The pattern eluded her, and she traded
that small mystery for that of the bartender, filling glass

after glass with a hasty hand, though the club was far from full. A staff member in the NDNM black tee took a tray from the bartender and vanished toward a swinging door. Backroom meeting?

Sylvie pushed past a chain curtain and climbed the three steps to the bar. Once on the same level, the cracks in the glass made words, scratchy, sketchy words, but easily readable. *Ni Dieux, Ni Maîtres.* NDNM.

While Sylvie had only menu-literacy in French, that phrase she knew. *No gods, no masters.* The rallying call of anarchists, and a sentiment that Sylvie endorsed wholeheartedly. Most of the misery she'd seen came from people thinking they could tell others how to live or think. She smiled, thinking if she weren't here for work, this might be a nice place to play.

The bartender barely glanced up, still tapping drinks that were 90 percent foam, tattoos shifting on his forearms, and Sylvie nodded. New carbonation. Mystery solved.

"Be right with you, Lily," he said, raising his voice to compete with the music, the four-foot space between them, and the constant hiss of the tap.

Sylvie twitched, hearing her own name at first. Then she realized that the sibilance came from the tap, and he had mistaken her for one of the regulars.

His eyes slewed around—hunting black shirts, Sylvie decided, as he hailed one, a girl with frizzed-out hair. "Mickey, come dump these for me."

The girl sighed but grabbed the tray. "Where's JK?"

"On break."

"I thought Auguste—"

"He didn't come in," the bartender said, "It happens." The cool was put on, Sylvie could tell. He was ticked and refusing to show it, refusing to let the girl show it; she wondered why. Maybe Auguste was the owner's golden boy. Auguste—Sylvie remembered the dark tee the *Maudit* had been wearing, before she blew a hole in it. Auguste, she thought, might not come in ever again.

"He's such a shit," Mickey said. The bartender twitched a shoulder toward Sylvie. The movement had a distinct "shut up, teacher's watching," feel about it.

"Vent all you want. I don't care," Sylvie said, inserting herself into the conversation. She took a few steps closer, hooked a stool, and sat, putting her between the bartender and a raised table with three young women. They paused in their debate over the merits of a pair of star-shaped sunglasses to stare at her. One of the women caught Sylvie's expression and stuck her tongue out before snatching the glasses and resting them in her curly hair.

The bartender looked over at Sylvie, startled. "I'm sorry. I thought you were . . . Never mind, can I get you something?"

Mickey took the opportunity to vanish, leaving the laden tray behind.

"Regular Coke," Sylvie said, "no additions." The sugar and caffeine would do her energy level a world of good. She sucked half of it down all at once, then turned to look around, pretending she hadn't scoped the place already.

Her order caused a furrow to start in his pierced brow, a wariness in his expression. "You gonna want anything else?"

"Another Coke, for sure," Sylvie said. "Maybe a little info. I'm looking for a friend of Auguste's." Go with the gamble. Really, in a club this size, how many staffers with French names could suddenly not show up for work?

"Cop," the curly-haired woman said, with a dismissive sniff and hair toss. The glasses in her hair caught the light and sparked. "Pay up." She held out a hand to her table mates, a Paris Hilton wannabe and a sulky brunette, and they forked over dollar bills.

The bartender shook his head. "Sorry. Drinks I can help you with. Anything else, try the Internet."

"Hold that thought," Sylvie said. "Do I really look like a cop?" She split her glance between the table and the bartender.

The woman who'd declared her a cop spoke up. "You

look nosy, and that's just as bad. People deserve their privacy. No matter what the government would have you believe." She tossed her head again, a flash of dark glass in her hair. Sylvie imagined her doing it one time too many and breaking her own neck.

"Some people forfeit it through their actions," Sylvie said. She took another long sip of her Coke, crunched ice. They wanted to argue; she could do that.

"Typical authority viewpoint," the woman said.

"You don't like it, don't eavesdrop," Sylvie said. "I'll just chat with the bartender instead. He's paid to serve, after all."

The bartender's lips tightened.

"Kinda ironic, considering the slogan at your back. But there's always going to be someone like you, just trying to make a living, working under someone else. I'm not trying to hurt you, or anyone like you. I'm looking for one of the alpha types, someone who *uses* people like you. A woman, a friend of Auguste's."

"Auguste doesn't have friends." The bartender walked down the bar to an emptied glass and waved hand, but had to come back for the refill. He refused to meet Sylvie's eyes.

"Don't you tell her anything," the woman said, with another aggressive nod. "Next thing you know, she'll be demanding names and making threats. Her kind always does."

"Look, chickie," Sylvie said. "Didn't your mother ever tell you about the golden rule? If you don't have anything useful to say, butt out." From the corner of her eye, she saw the bartender slipping away again.

"Watch yourself," the girl said. "You don't know who you're dealing with." She raised a hand and wispy flames began to sprout from her palm. Paris and Sulky shared *take-that* smiles with each other.

Sylvie swallowed a piece of ice wrong, then laughed until she was breathless.

"Oh God," she gasped. "The only way fancy fire-starting could scare me, after the day I've had, is if you lit a cigarette with it. Secondhand smoke's a killer." She dropped away from the bar and pulled up a seat at the table, unasked. Paris and Sulky screeched their seats aside. "But, hey, if you can do that, you have to know Auguste, right? Two magic-users and all that."

Though magic-user was a stretch—what the girl had shown her was akin to a toddler getting to its feet. All show, prone to collapsing at a single touch. The *Maudit* had undoubtedly scorned her, not only an amateur, but a female. That didn't mean, though, that the girl had no interest in Auguste.

The flame wavered in the girl's hand, and Sylvie said, "Do I need to spell it out? I'm not impressed. Put it out before I put it out for you." Sylvie slapped the table, and all three girls jumped; the flame went out as if Sylvie had snuffed it. "Thanks," Sylvie said. "All friends now?"

"Why don't you just wait and talk to him?" the Paris wannabe said. Sylvie bit back a grimace. Like *that* was possible.

"I'm impatient," Sylvie said. "It's a character flaw."

The chain curtains parted with a slithering clink just as one song drew to a close on the speakers. In the hush, the squeaks from the girls at the table rang out. Erinya stalked toward Sylvie with murder in her eye.

"Got stamped?" Sylvie asked, catching sight of a reddish smear on Erinya's inner wrist. Guess the bouncer was a righteous man, after all.

Erinya growled. Nothing human at all in the sound, deeper than a human throat could even voice. Sylvie flipped the Fury her wallet. "Guess that means you can drink. If you're so inclined. Then you can come chat with our new friends."

Erinya growled, human this time, complete with a "fuck you," but turned toward the bar. In the mirror, her reflection swirled, as if it wanted to reveal the monster beneath the skin.

The pyrokinetic girl leaned forward, capturing Sylvie's

attention, and said, "Auguste has a wand up his ass, but he's tough enough to take you down."

"Unlikely," Sylvie said. "But Auguste isn't my interest. I want the name of his friend. You know—the only woman he listens to." Present tense, she thought, keep it present tense. No need for them to remember that you spoke of him as dead when he turns up missing.

Pyro hesitated; her friends' eyes rested on her, and Sylvie said, "Don't balk now."

"Lily," the Paris wannabe said. "What? Like you wouldn't have told her?" Pyro humphed in exasperation, and Paris ignored her. "Lily. That's all I know. She comes around here a lot. She's a bitch. Kinda like you, actually."

"She here tonight?" Sylvie asked. She ignored the girl's insult. It wasn't anything she hadn't heard before. "Answers, anyone?"

"Haven't seen her tonight," Pyro said. "She doesn't come every night."

"Describe her for me." Sylvie's tension leaked through; Erinya was suddenly at her side, crouched, staring at the girls with predatory intent. Sylvie touched Erinya's mesh sleeve, a request for self-restraint. The fabric shivered beneath her fingers, and Sylvie took her hand away, nerves tingling as if a current had passed through them.

"Ordinary," Pyro said, and Sylvie's heart sank. Ordinary. That was not a hopeful word; a woman who could manipulate a sorcerer, who could plan and execute a kidnapping beneath the nose of a god, was hardly ordinary.

"You might be hot stuff, Helen, but you're blind as a bat. Lily's creepy as sin," Sulky said, speaking for the first time. She turned to Sylvie. "I mean, yeah, she *looks* normal, unlike your freak-friend there . . ." The girl's voice trailed off as Erinya's eyes turned to meet hers. A faint whimper came out of her throat; her muscles locked up, her hands clenched each other beneath the table.

Flames burst from Helen's palms; Sylvie caught Helen's wrists before she could interfere. Helen's bones and tendons trembled under Sylvie's tight-knuckled grasp.

Fire licked at Sylvie's skin, dry heat promising pain as it stretched and grew even closer.

One flamelet touched the leather of Erinya's jacket and turned a virulent green, stretching tall under the sudden influx of god-touched leather, coiling back toward Helen like a serpent.

"Erinya's just taking a look-see, that's all. You interfere, and there'll be trouble. More trouble than any of us wants."

"I can't stop it," Helen said, eyes wide on the flames encircling her fingers.

"You can. You will," Sylvie said, implacable. "Or you'll burn. Take control or lose it. It's your choice. But if you combust, don't expect me to put you out."

Helen shivered, but the flames began to die back as she pulled in her fingers, one by one. Sylvie relaxed her hold, and when Helen's flame had become puddles of ash in her hands, she said, "Now, tell me what you consider ordinary."

Beside her, Sulky began to drool. Paris sat frozen, head down, shoulders shaking.

Helen said, "Dark hair, brown eyes. Ordinary. Not too tall. Not a lot of anything. Wears designer clothes. That's all I know."

Sylvie studied the marks of distress in her face, blotchy cheeks, quivering lips, the blisters rising in her palms. "You should learn to be more observant of the world around you. Save you no end of trouble in the long run. You done yet, Eri? 'Cause her mind's going to pop any moment now, and that'll be messy."

The Fury turned to look at her. "Eri?" she questioned, offense hovering in her voice.

"You wanted a name that wasn't a thing," Sylvie said, watching Sulky collapse now that eye contact was broken. Helen and Paris grabbed her shoulders and dragged her toward the door.

Sylvie watched them go, sighing. *Ordinary. In a creepy way.* Not exactly enough to build an APB on. "You get anything useful?"

"Alekta's better at mind-tracking," Erinya muttered.

"That's not a yes," Sylvie said. "You climbed inside that girl's soul, scared her into catatonia, and I didn't stop you. *Tell* me you got a scent."

"I got it," Erinya snapped. "Mostly. She smells a little like every human. Even you smell like her."

Sylvie groaned. "So no bloodhound act. Did you get enough to recognize her if we run into her?"

"Yes."

"That's something," Sylvie said. She picked up her Coke, gone tepid and flat from nearness to the flames, and gulped the rest of it. Her mouth was dry. "Any visual?"

"Ordinary," Erinya said.

Erinya headed toward the door with the determined stalk of a lioness. Sylvie squawked and went after her. She took three running steps and snagged Erinya's wrist, heart thumping. No way was she letting Erinya out to hunt, not with a flawed scent that smelled like general humanity.

Under her hands, Erinya's skin shifted and stung. Sylvie forced herself to hold on. It never seemed to get easier, touching one of the gods. She wondered how Bran had stood it and stayed sane.

"No, no, no, Eri," Sylvie said. She leaned her weight back, trying to stop Erinya, and having as little success as if she were trying to hold back a bull. Erinya's mass seemed far more than her human shape allowed.

Sylvie gritted her teeth and dug her nails into Erinya's skin, jolted at the increase in sensation. Erinya stopped; her lips peeled back from her teeth, but she paused.

"Let's not go haring off into the dark. We know she's been here before. Maybe she'll be back to check on—"

Maybe, Sylvie decided, was the wrong word to use. The Fury batted her away with a single hand, slamming her backward. Sylvie's spine impacted painfully with the edge of a table; a chair screeched across the floor.

"I'll find her if I have to wade through the blood of every human in the world." The sweet-voiced, slangy

punk was gone; in Erinya's voice, in her eyes, all that
showed was rage. Sylvie lost the battle with her self-
control. Her skin burst into goose bumps, giving way to a
convulsive shudder.

The Fury's pupils swelled, feeling Sylvie's fear. She
leaned closer, nearly nose to nose with Sylvie, and said,
"Will you dare stop me? When you know so many humans deserve the pain I visit on them?"

Sylvie sucked in a shaking breath, trying for calm, and
losing. She gave up trying to control her body and focused
only on meeting Erinya's glare head-on, watching as
the engorged pupils slowly turned phosphorescent. She
counted her own heartbeat in the tiny sparks of crimson
that danced in the Fury's sclera, in the small scales that
began to dot the false delicacy of her temple and eyelids.

"Get off me, or I will make you comprehend mortality."
It wasn't her voice, not really. That dark inner core had
stepped to the front, spewing its determination not to be
beaten.

Erinya barked a laugh. "How?"

Sylvie smiled, letting the expression spread across her
face, displacing fear. "You said yourself, your shells can
die. I'm *good* at killing things."

Erinya frowned, her gaze clouding; Sylvie felt the in-
trusion in her mind, a brief kaleidoscope of bloody imagery. Cassavetes, Hellhound, sorcerers, succubi, an angel
with buckshot wings . . . Her greatest hits, replayed. Sylvie pushed Erinya out of her mind, put her hands on
Erinya's shoulders, and shoved.

Erinya stepped back; Sylvie ignored the sensation that
sparks leaped between her fingers, crackled against her
hands. She pressed harder. Erinya staggered, and Sylvie
advanced.

"I think. *You* help. Isn't that what Dunne sent you to
do? To act as I tell you? We stay here. Lily might, yes
might, come back. Even if she doesn't, we can get a better
description of her. A definitive one. Then you can hunt to
your heart's content. In the meantime, *stay.*"

Sylvie spun on her heel and strode into the crowd, past the few dancers who had stopped to stare at Erinya and herself.

Sylvie fetched up near the stage before the shaking found her again. She leaned up against its support, her legs trembling and her throat dry.

A drink drifted into her vision, held toward her in a nicotine-stained hand. "Coke, right? On the house." Sylvie shot him a glance, identifying him as the staff member she had seen in the hallway, heading for a smoke break. Sylvie took the glass, her hands so chilled that, for a moment, the cold sweat on the glass felt warm.

She held the glass, loving the heavy tangibility of the crystal, something natural, something normal, something that didn't fizz and burn like a god's power. She shifted uncomfortably as the leather jacket buzzed against her neck and back.

"You lied, you know," Sylvie said. "This place is plenty scary."

"Ah, you brought the scary with you," he said, as easy and casual as he had been in the hallway. "JK."

"Sylvie," she said. She eyed the Coke, contemplating the addition of more caffeine to a nervous system jazzed with adrenaline.

"It's fine," he said. "Promise. I owe you one."

"Yeah?" Sylvie said. She took a sip; sweetness exploded on her tongue and reminded her how parched fear made her throat. She took a larger draught and set the glass down on the stage.

"Well, you and your scary friend chased off my ex and her psycho Barbie accessory pack. Helen thinks it's funny to come here every night and make me serve her. I," he said, a scowl crossing his good-natured face, "don't."

"She's a bitch," Sylvie agreed.

"I've got better taste now," JK said. He hopped up and took a seat on the edge of the stage, swinging lanky legs.

"Yeah?" she said.

"Yeah," he said. "You want to prove it by giving me your phone number?"

Sylvie finagled a card out of her jeans pocket, held it before him. "If you answer a couple of questions first."

"Shoot," he said. "I give good answers. You should see me with parents. I can even make them overlook the tats." He presented his arm to her; the words *Live Your Own Way* blazed around the forearm.

Sylvie traced the final flare of the y, curling around his wrist. "My parents didn't object to my ink."

"Can I see it?" he said. "Is it someplace . . . interesting?"

Sylvie smiled, luring him in. It didn't hurt that he was cute as all get-out. For the second time, she thought this club had a lot to recommend it.

"Tell me about Lily," she said.

He blinked. "I was thinking it was going to be fave food, music, STDs."

She handed him the card, tapped the front of it. "I'm working."

"Working. Like a cop?"

"Not like a cop," Sylvie said, smoothly but quickly. Something had to have drawn him to Helen in the first place; she didn't want it to be a shared aversion to authority.

"PI?"

"Inquiry agent," Sylvie corrected. "See, Shadows Inquiries."

"What's that when it's at home?" he said. Laughter lurked in his eyes, daring her to answer truthfully.

"PI," she said. "But without rules."

"Cool," he said. "Didn't figure you for a 'draws within the lines' kind of woman. So, Lily?"

Sylvie said, "Anything you can tell me."

"Lily," he said, picking up her glass, stroking the condensation off it, and letting the drips fall from his fingertips. "Sweet Lily . . . though she isn't."

Sylvie made a go-on gesture.

"Lily—don't know if that's her real name. Doesn't fit her much. Toil not, neither does she spin—well, I don't know what she does for kicks, but she's just not the idle sort.

"She's got money. Rumor has it, she has a share in the club. But I think her real job's in art somehow. She found the artist for the murals here. You might check galleries if you're hunting her. It wouldn't surprise me to find she owned one, ran one, patronized one."

Sylvie sighed. "That's specific," she said. "She might be named Lily, or not. She's got money, or access to it. She likes art—"

"Some art," JK interrupted. "Do *not* get her started on traditional religious iconography. That woman can seriously hate."

"And she might own, work in, or hang out at one of the hundreds of galleries in and around Chicago," Sylvie finished.

"She travels, too," JK said.

Sylvie threw her hands up, giving him the reaction he was teasing for, but she didn't find it funny at all. JK, while being helpful, had told her nothing immediately useful. Some of that leaked into her voice despite her efforts. Inside her head, a clock kept a countdown, and she felt like it was heading fast to single digits. Part of it was Erinya; the Fury stalked the bar, back and forth, back and forth, like a caged animal.

"Look, JK, it's really important that I find her. Anyone else who might know more?"

"You might ask Wolf," JK said. "She hung out with him a lot."

Shock hit Sylvie. Of *course* Lily had hung out with Brandon. What better way to learn about your victim than to befriend him?

"Eye candy, I thought, when she first brought him in. Thought it'd be awful. Some no-talent hack with a line of bull and a pretty face, but turned out he could really paint. And she backed off some once his boyfriend showed up."

"Yeah?" Sylvie asked, and if JK thought her accepting the shift in focus was strange, he didn't say so. Truth was, Sylvie felt safer not saying Lily's name aloud. There could be more scrying-glass televisions, charmed to a mention of Lily's name. Sylvie shivered at the weight of unseen eyes on her skin, reminded herself that paranoia was a dangerous friend.

If Lily had seen her kill Auguste, or was watching Sylvie question her acquaintances, surely she would have already acted on it.

"Big guy. Quiet. Older. Dropped him off once or twice; I bet just to prove Wolf was taken." JK fidgeted, dragged out his cigarettes, tapped one out, stuck it in his mouth.

"So, what did Wolf think about her?"

JK lipped his cigarette as if it were lit, then let it drop into his lap. He chased it, studied it, avoiding her eyes.

"What?" Sylvie said. "You can't tell me you didn't get a chance to talk to him. I saw those murals. He was here for a month, minimum. And you were around enough to see Lily and him together."

"That doesn't mean I talked to him," JK said, picking up her Coke, melting ice and all, and taking a drink as if his throat hurt.

"JK, you always talk," Sylvie said. "I've only known you for minutes, and strangely, I'm sure of that."

"Look," he said. His voice dropped; his cheeks reddened. "I don't have anything against fags, I really don't, it's just that I couldn't—"

"Talk to one?" Sylvie finished in irritation.

"Couldn't deal with the fact that I wanted him, okay?" he snapped, then blushed again. "God. I watched him, you know, more entertaining than mopping up last night's stale beer. He just—there was just something. His hands were covered in paint, green, blue, gold, and I saw him forget, push his hair out of his way. He got paint on his face, in his hair, and he looked so surprised. Like he couldn't figure out how it got there, and then he just laughed. I wanted him so bad. . . . I stayed the hell away from him."

Sylvie let the silence lie while JK picked up the cigarette, and with a furtive glance at the bar, lit it.

"So," Sylvie said, "confession being good for the soul and all that, you feel better?"

"If by better, you mean mortified, sure," JK said, stubbing out the cigarette after two quick, deep puffs. He put it out on her business card. "I just—I don't swing that way. It freaked me out. So, really, I don't have a clue what he thought about Lily. I mean, she disappeared after his boyfriend came in, so maybe Wolf was annoyed with her hanging around and asked him to discourage her. I didn't see much of her after that."

He wouldn't, Sylvie thought. If Lily had gone after Bran to punish Dunne, she had to have some connection with Dunne, maybe even a history—though in that case, Sylvie would have expected Dunne to put her at the top of the suspect list. He didn't seem to have anyone there at all. Or maybe he hadn't shared.

"Look, I'm glad to talk to you. Mostly," he said, with a wry twist to his mouth for his confession. "But the person you really need to talk to is Auguste or Wolf. I can give you Auguste's address."

"Thanks," Sylvie said. "Would you do one thing for me?"

"Maybe," he said. A little wary now.

"Call me if you see her."

He hesitated; Sylvie stifled familiar exasperation. Always the sudden withdrawal. Talking was okay, just gossip, ultimately harmless. People could always reassure themselves that they weren't the only ones who would talk, finding both anonymity and absolution in the thought. But calling her? That brought them right into the picture, and worse, lobbed a bit of the responsibility directly their way. No one wanted that.

"Call me," Sylvie said, laying out a new card beside the scorched one.

A massive crunch cut the air, followed by a patter of falling glass. Sylvie whirled. Erinya crouched on the bar top, the bartender back against the mirrored wall, at the center of a new starburst of cracks.

Erinya reached for him, hefting his weight with inhuman ease. Along her back, muscles shifted and spikes snagged and stretched out Erinya's mesh shirt like a porcupine-quill coat.

"Shit," Sylvie swore, taking off at a run.

"Erinya," Sylvie snapped, even as the bartender's face went slack with terror. "Stop it!"

Erinya backhanded her, hitting her jaw with stunning force. Sylvie went down to the taste of rust, seeing stars. She crouched on the floor and shook long bangs out of her face.

Get up, the voice told her. *Make her pay.*

Sylvie drew the gun; a man near her yelped in surprise, and Sylvie whirled. JK gaped at her.

"Back off," she growled. Without waiting to see that he did, she jammed the gun barrel into Erinya's rib cage, snugging it in amidst the wide-spaced mesh of her shirt, nestling it into quills that pricked at her skin, and said, "Let him down."

"He wants her dead. . . . Wants to kill his mother—for her house . . ."

"Wanting isn't doing," Sylvie said. "One more warning, Erinya."

"Fuck you," Erinya said. "I'm doing my job—"

"You're interfering with mine." Sylvie fired, once, twice, and again.

Blood splashed her hands, more rust scent in the air, beginning to compete with the sting of shattered glass and high-proof alcohol. Erinya stiffened; then she lashed out, one-handed again. Sylvie managed to duck, warned by the tiny adjustment of muscles along Erinya's neck. Erinya's nails tore strands of her hair from her temple with a distinct and delicate sting.

The knit mesh of Erinya's shirt shifted to scale and covered the burned and cored flesh, the bloody gouges that the bullets had torn.

"You dare shoot a god?" Erinya said, shoving the bartender away. He dropped and scuttled for the front door. Erinya hissed, and he froze. "Not done with you yet, matricide."

Sylvie grinned, her own temper shining as bright and as sharp as diamond. "I've been stupid. I started to *believe*, to see gods everywhere. Dunne may be what he claims to be, but you—you and your sisters are no gods. You're nothing more than shaped power. Like angels. Like demons. I can destroy you." She raised the gun again, peered through her bangs, her narrowed vision like a gunsight.

"It might take some careful doing, I admit."

The screaming behind her was beginning to get on her nerves. Sylvie wondered how many shots she had in the gun now that it had been magicked. Would it make its own? Enough to take down the Fury? Enough to shut up the shrieking crowd?

What the hell *are you thinking?* For once it wasn't the dark voice that crawled out of her mind, but her own. She shuddered all over, cold, sick, and utterly horrified. She fed all the fear into rage, her specialty, and the talent that kept her alive.

Erinya leaped, and Sylvie fired. Three more shots, all into Erinya's torso. Erinya tumbled forward, somersaulting, and came up in a crouch. She hissed, a snakelike tongue lashing out from between sharpening teeth. Her wounds healed.

Sylvie, trying to assess the next move, met Erinya's furious eyes and fell into them. Her head pounded, sweat slicked her face, her neck, and her vision exploded into a thousand images.

Her gun, and the people who fell beneath it. Strangers. Enemies. Allies. Innocents. Michael Demalion. Val. Alex. Even her sister Zoe. Sylvie stood in a world turned abattoir and laughed as she made her will felt; when there was no one left, she turned the gun toward the heavens.

Not real. Not going to happen. Try again. The dark

voice spat it directly into Erinya's mind, refusing the madness, refusing to be influenced by something external.

The hallucinations fled. Erinya knelt before her, looking for all the world like a pup who'd been unexpectedly smacked. "Get up," Sylvie said, sheathing the gun. "Put your face back on."

Erinya rose to two feet, shook all her little monster bits—teeth, clawed hands, snaky tongue—into human shape once more. "I owe you pain."

"Collect it later, if you can," Sylvie said. "We've made ourselves unwelcome. Let's go."

She turned and froze, looking out over the club attendees—why hadn't they fled? They looked ready to bolt at a whispered "boo," and yet they still stood, shaking and watching. Her eyes flickered to the entrance and widened.

A woman stood there, leaning against the doorjamb, entirely at her ease. She wasn't much to look at, not quite as tall as Sylvie, judging by the space she took up in the door frame, on the whipcord side of slender, with hair a shade darker than Sylvie's, sleeked into a twist, held up with what looked like chopsticks. She straightened once she had Sylvie's attention and met her eyes.

"You," she said, her voice pitched low and very clear, almost familiar. "You are an interesting girl. Pity."

She was blocking the door, Sylvie realized abruptly. One rather ordinary woman holding a frightened mob of people at bay with only her presence. Lily reached up and fiddled with her hair, a nervous tell that spoke nothing of nervousness. Sylvie's eyes narrowed.

Erinya snarled and disappeared, reappearing across the room, claws arcing out before her.

Lily tugged a chopstick free, and snapped the stick between her fingers; a brittle crack that created a group moan from the nerve-shattered crowd.

"*Brûlez,*" she cried, and Erinya, a bare scale width away from sinking her talons into Lily's flesh, tumbled backward on a wave of scalding white light. The bartender went up like flash paper, flesh wicking the heat and raising a curtain of white flame.

Sylvie was already covering her stinging eyes. Dear God, no. Not this. She had thought Erinya's monster act had filled the room with terror, but that was nothing compared to this. The screams now were of pure, primal dread, as vision led to flame led to spontaneous combustion.

Sylvie pressed her hands tighter, screwed her eyes shut harder, still getting bleed-through, like flashbulbs all around her, strobing through the vulnerable skin of her eyelids. She felt feverish, on the edge of burning.

A hard hand gripped her hair; Sylvie forced herself to keep her vision blocked instead of fighting back. The only defense against balefire was not to look. It fed on flesh and spread by vision. It only burned out when there was no one left to see.

The hand tugged, claws scratching at her skin, and Sylvie gasped. Erinya had survived the blast. The Fury yanked, guiding her out of the club, while Sylvie stumbled and choked on the stink of scorched bone and charred meat.

"Don't look," Erinya said.

"Won't," Sylvie said. "Don't you look, either."

"Won't," Erinya responded in kind. "No eyes right now."

A trickle of fresh air reached her, and Sylvie picked up her pace, staggering over the asphalt of the parking lot and going down when Erinya released her.

She felt cold metal at her back, the smell of car oil, and a tire pushed up against her shoulder. She cracked an eye open, looking toward the ground just in case. The first hint of balefire, and she'd gouge out her eyes rather than turn herself into a firework.

Reassuring darkness soothed her nerves, the cracked yellow border of the parking spot barely visible. Sylvie opened both eyes and raised them toward the warmth before her.

No eyes, she thought, staring at Erinya's blind, blank face, only a smooth expanse of skin above the nose and mouth. Shape-shifting was a handy thing, she mused, and giggled a little wildly.

"Did you get her scent this time?" she asked, voice cracking.

"I got balefire in my face," Erinya said. "I'm scent-blind until I'm healed."

"Anyone else get out?" Sylvie said.

"No."

Sylvie pulled her knees up to her chest, rested her face on them. JK. Gone, just like that. The *Magicus Mundi* had a lot to answer for. She steadied her breathing and tried to listen to the night beyond her racing heartbeat. No fire alarm. Unsurprising since balefire had no interest in anything beyond flesh, but that was to the good. A fireman coming in too soon could catch it and pass the conflagration on.

"Don't shift your eyes back yet," Sylvie said. "I want that stick she was holding."

"Get it yourself. It's not like it's useful."

Sylvie leaned forward and tightened her hand on the Fury's shoulder. "That had to have been Lily, the big winner in our suspect lottery. I assumed she couldn't do magic. 'Cause she used Auguste as her hands. But balefire . . ."

"I don't know how she did it. The best clue to finding out is that stick. I want it. I need to know what resources she has."

"Enough power to kill everyone just to get to you," Erinya said.

"No," Sylvie denied. "She killed everyone to destroy her memory scent. I think she's been watching us. And she came armed with something that could put off a Fury, Erinya. You were her target. I was a surprise. An *interesting* one."

13

Art Appreciation

SYLVIE ROLLED OVER WITH A GROAN SHE TRIED TO STIFLE OUT OF courtesy for Tish, but dammit, she *hurt*. Wrestling with a Fury was definitely an all-pain, no-gain sort of endeavor. She shifted enough to ease the spasm in her back and cracked an eye.

Tish slept on, drooling a little, her dark hair a tangled cloud against her polka-dotted pillowcase. Sylvie found a tiny smile. Had to love those party girls. They tended to be up at all hours and were oddly blasé about strangers coming to their door, soot-streaked, battered, and begging for a bed.

Tish hadn't hesitated at all, dragging Sylvie in, seeing her showered, pj'd, and tucked in before she had so much as asked the question that had been trembling on her lips all that time—had Sylvie found any leads to Bran.

Nearly dead on her feet, Sylvie had confined herself to slurred syllables and half answers, concentrating more on dialing Alex's number correctly. Sylvie had pieces of a puzzle but no picture. Alex could give her that. But Alex didn't answer, undoubtedly tucked into bed like a good girl, not like Sylvie, staggering into a stranger's home, smelling of char and burned blood. . . . Sylvie left a message on Alex's voice mail, a raspy, coughing, muttering monologue about the art world, a woman called Lily, about NDNM.

Tish, listening with her ears cat-pricked, had chipped in the moment Sylvie disconnected. "Is that the same Lily Bran painted?"

Sylvie's exhaustion cleared long enough to collect facts. Brandon had painted a portrait of a woman called Lily, two months ago. A portrait he had worked on feverishly, then turned to the wall and forgotten. Tish thought it was still there, leaning up against other discards in his cluttered studio.

Go get it, Sylvie thought, staring at the clock, at the hour glowing 4:00 a.m. *Get up. Get the painting.* Her body betrayed her. Her attempt at sitting up had set her head to spinning, her vision to blurring, and Tish had pushed her back into the futon.

Finally it was morning—eight o'clock—and enough with the lounging about. She groaned deep in her throat, thought longingly of a vacation spent drowsing on the beach, and rolled over. Tried to. Tish's arm dragged her back, pulled her against warmth. "G'back t'sleep," she muttered, without ever really waking.

Party girls, Sylvie thought, not so fondly this time. She pinched at Tish's arm until the sleeping girl let go, pulling her arm away from the sting.

Sylvie made her escape and dragged herself into Tish's kitchenette. Coffee, now.

She found the coffeemaker, ladled in an extra scoop of grounds on principle, and the world began to smell promising. Behind her, Tish left the futon in a stumbling slide of sheets and blankets.

A moment later, a white flash filled the room, and Sylvie spun, heart pounding, thinking of balefire. Tish lowered her camera and yawned. "S'rry. Couldn't resist."

Sylvie turned back to the counter, rested her shaking hands on it, concentrating on stilling her breath. Coffee?

Who needed caffeine when you could have an adrenaline jolt straight to the heart?

Sleep-warmed fingers traced a pattern on her back, a delicate scratch of nails between the spaghetti straps of the loaner tank top. "I wanted a picture of your tattoo. It's Latin, right? What's it mean?" Tish said. Her touch made Sylvie's skin prickle.

"Cedo Nulli," Sylvie said. "I do not yield."

"Mm. Hostile," Tish decided, and snagged the first cup of coffee for herself.

Sylvie filled another cup and after the first scalding mouthful, turned to the next pressing problem. Wardrobe. Hers was smoked. Her jacket gone with the *Maudit*, her T-shirt a tattered mess, her jeans sticky with spilled beer, and all of it reeking of charred human flesh.

Tish curled up in a tiny, tidy bundle on the futon, tucking her feet under her, and Sylvie sighed. Five feet tops. No way in hell was she fitting into any of Tish's clothes.

"Closet's upstairs," Tish said. "Got some party left-overs that might fit."

Sylvie wandered upstairs, stiff and sore, to rummage through Tish's collection of clothes.

She hit the jackpot at one end of the walk-in closet, finding a tidy grouping of party stragglers and one-night leftovers. She pulled out a pair of men's khakis that looked about right, and a red T-shirt that extolled a brand of firecrackers with a truly offensive logo. She flipped the tee inside out and put it on rather than waste time looking for something better. It'd be under Erinya's jacket anyway.

A small shelf near the door yielded a giant bottle of ibuprofen, the dancer's faithful friend, and Sylvie snagged three, taking them dry before heading back down toward the scent of brewed coffee.

She found Tish looking much more awake and un-happy about it. "You didn't have to get up," Sylvie said.

"I'm going with you," Tish said. "I've got the key. I called, and Kevin's not home. He should be. I mean,

Bran's missing." Tish wouldn't look at her, and her voice held an edge that Sylvie couldn't decipher.

"All right," Sylvie said. "But hurry." Dunne's absence wasn't unexpected; he'd be out hunting, the sisters in tow. It did worry her a little. Sylvie had expected him to descend on her last night after she'd sent Erinya to update him. He hadn't. And Zeus had been pulling at him. . . .

Lily herself made Sylvie antsy, generated more questions than answers. Sylvie had assumed the woman couldn't do magic; she still found her logic sound. People who *had* power did not dragoon apprentice sorcerers to do their spell wetwork for them—that was like giving trade secrets to your competitors. But magic had definitely been done last night. Sylvie shuddered and chased the chill from her nerves with bitter, black coffee. Still slurping, scalding her lips and tongue, she rose to paw through her discarded clothes.

"Did you see something that looks like a broken chopstick?"

Tish said, "Maybe it's under that *gun*." The edge was stronger now, and identifiable. Fear. Sylvie dropped her eyes: The holster was there, bound up in Erinya's jacket, but the seal had been unsnapped, the gun pulled partially free. *Clumsy,* Sylvie thought, remembering her exhaustion, remembering shedding clothes without any concern for the weapon, just letting it slip free with her jeans.

"This is why you don't mess with other people's things," Sylvie said. She bent, tucked the gun back into the holster, and fastened the whole thing about her waist. It vibrated briefly, as soothing as a purr. "I'm sorry if it startled you—"

"That gun is not normal. It looks normal, but it's . . . It felt like skin," Tish said. Her voice shook, craving reassurance. Sylvie could see that fragile innocence crumbling in Tish's eyes, the bewilderment and betrayal that the world kept secrets of its own.

Bran and Dunne had managed to hide the *Magicus*

Mundi with its glories and its horrors from her, even with the Furies around. Sylvie, through carelessness, had betrayed the larger world.

"No," Sylvie said. "It's not."

"What is it? How—"

"Give me the keys. Stay here," Sylvie said. *Stay safe.*

"No," Tish said. She passed Sylvie on the way up the stairs, and said, "I have the keys, and I know their security code, so don't bother trying to go without me."

Sylvie sighed and let it go. She sorted through the rest of the clothes, ducked her head under the futon, and found the stick.

In the morning light, with caffeine sharpening her brain, the broken chopstick still looked ordinary as dirt— the kind distributed with every fast-food Chinese meal in the country, still splintery where it had been torn from its other side.

Sylvie handled it gingerly. When Lily halved the stick, balefire had appeared. Sylvie didn't want to find out it worked just the same if it were quartered.

She turned it over again in her hands, hoping for inspiration, but it was just a stick, inert in her hands. Nothing to say it was anything important at all, much less the trigger to a murder spell. If it was. Maybe Lily was the queen of misdirection and the stick was some type of in-joke, some game to send Sylvie chasing her own tail.

Sylvie groaned. She hated to do it, but she needed information. Chasing Lily was going to keep her busy enough; she didn't have time to figure out how the woman did what she did.

Usually, with a question on magic matters, she dragged Val to the hot seat. That was no longer an option, at least not without a bigger fight than Sylvie needed at the moment. Sylvie's options narrowed to two. Either throw herself on the mercy of this unknown Anna D, or try to winkle information out of the ISI. Neither thought appealed.

Tish thundered down the stairs and disappeared into

the bathroom; the crash of water running against tile followed in seconds.

Sylvie looked at the closed door in disbelief. "Hurry, and she needs a shower."

She took another preventative dose of caffeine and dialed, wondering what it said about her psyche and faulty memory that *this* number she could recall after one sneak peek.

"Sylvie," Demalion said, picking up on the second ring. "You're still with us."

"Barely," she said.

"So how was the club? It's been on my list of places to go."

"You had me followed," she said. Not surprised, but chilled nonetheless. She'd *killed* a man last night.

"Nah," he said. "Not once your witchy friend pushed Burke onto the tracks. He was thrilled to miss the rest. Thirty-one cases of spontaneous human combustion. Special even for you."

"Not my fault," Sylvie said. Her free hand found a box of raw-sugar cubes, and she started feeding them into her coffee.

"Didn't say it was," he said. "You okay?"

"I'm talking to you, aren't I? There's no in-between with balefire."

"Good to hear it," he said, and damn if she didn't almost believe him. "Is there a reason for the call, or can I just think you were worried that I might be worried and wanted to ease my mind."

Sylvie growled, borrowing wordless irritation from Erinya. "You talk too much," she said.

"Coming from you?"

A retort hovered on her lips, along with a smile, and she stopped. They weren't friends. "What do you know about magic sticks?"

"Aren't they usually referred to as wands? Or is this some new slang I'm missing out on?" Demalion asked. "I can never tell."

"Wands don't require you to break them to make the spell work," Sylvie said. "This did."

"Broken," he said. "Check. I'll see what we've got in the files. Anything else?"

"Lily, no last name offered," Sylvie said. "Connected with art, Brandon Wolf, and bad magic. Not a nice woman."

"Our firestarter?" Demalion asked, his voice growing distant. Sylvie imagined him frowning, sorting his own thoughts for information, imagined him rolling that little crystal ball between his hands, fidgeting as he thought.

"Yeah," Sylvie said. "She killed them all to keep her trail clouded. Lily's cold-blooded and dangerous. I can't believe she doesn't have a rep."

"This is related to Dunne, right?" Demalion said. "He's the problem we're trying to solve—"

"Typical bureaucracy. Focusing on the wrong thing. Lily is the problem. Lily started it," Sylvie said. "Lily kidnapped a god's lover. Forget about Dunne. You can't do anything about him anyway."

"I don't particularly feel like playing forgive and forget with him. He's dangerous. I don't know how much you're following the news, but he needs to be dealt with."

"Then *you* step up to the plate," Sylvie said. "Instead of pushing me to do it. Look, just let me know what you can find on stick magic. Or on Lily, won't turn that down, either."

"What are you up to?" Demalion said. "Save me the trouble of spying and just tell me."

The shower stopped, and Sylvie said, "What, deprive you of your special-agent fun?" and cut the connection. She'd shaken Tish's trust with the meat gun; she didn't want to be caught talking to the government. Especially not to the government man who'd been in disguise and present the night Brandon disappeared. It might be a little difficult to explain. To Tish and, God, to Dunne. Sylvie made a note. *Do not let Dunne catch you thinking about Demalion,* especially since Sylvie still wasn't sure what she thought about Demalion. Help or hindrance. Ally or enemy. Trust or—a belated thought touched her.

Forgive and forget, Demalion had said. What did he have to forgive Dunne for? Something more personal than the ISI teams' lack of success?

"Ready," Tish said. Sylvie finished tucking her cell phone into a pocket before turning.

Hmmm. Combat ballerina. Spandex as body armor beneath cutoff jeans and Doc Martens overlaid with leg warmers.

Sylvie snagged Erinya's jacket, making sure it covered the gun. A whiff of charred flesh touched her senses as she settled the jacket over her shoulders, but she judged it nearly unnoticeable. No worse than having lingered at a barbecue.

Outside, they both paused and stared up at the sky as one. "Wow," Tish said. "Look at that."

"I'm looking," Sylvie said. She was. She didn't like what she saw. The morning skies were sullen, cloud-heavy, and tinged green. And so still—the clouds looked carved in place, like some elaborate bas-relief. A white-backed gull fought its way through the sky, but there was no other movement. Even the planters at street level, laden with ivy and petunias, were motionless. A good Floridian, Sylvie thought it looked like nothing so much as a hurricane building up offshore. Only this was Chicago, and far from the sea.

"Cab?" she asked. She waved down a shiny new cab that was conveniently approaching, conveniently empty of fares. "Great timing," she said to the driver. Suspiciously good timing. How long had she talked to Demalion? While he was a talker, he'd rambled more than usual. Buying time? How long did it take the ISI to locate a cell phone within a city?

Not long, apparently.

The cab driver barely grunted an acknowledgment of the address Tish gave. Maybe more concerned with the discomfort of his shoulder holster beneath the strap of his seat belt. The bulge beneath his sweatshirt could be nothing less.

The cabbie turned on the news to fill the silence and first thing Sylvie heard was the local morning DJ laughing. "Weird world out there today. A section of I-90 was reported struck by lightning and turned to glass. Don't believe everything you hear, folks, but you still might plan an alternate way to work. And for those of you who work lakefront—massive fish kill last night. The surface is covered with dead fish and birds. So skip the picnic lunch.

"Forecast for today—rain. Tornadoes maybe. Hell, they don't know. When do they ever? Either way, O'Hare's grounding all morning flights."

Are you following the news, Demalion had asked.

Cataclysms and monsters, Val had said, *when gods walk the earth.*

Sylvie leaned back to stare at the gloomy sky, listening to callers reporting their own run-ins with weirdness. Beside her, Tish got more and more withdrawn, until she finally whispered, "Shut that off."

The agent did, but his eyes reached for Sylvie's in the back. Careless with his cover, too eager to see what she made of this mess. Sylvie blanked her face and gave him nothing.

At Dunne's apartment, Sylvie got out without even a glance at the tab. Tish hesitated, hand on her wallet. Sylvie said, "Don't worry about it. He can expense it."

The driver said, "Hey!" and Sylvie leaned back in and, before he could react, unzipped his sweatshirt.

"I can see the holster, Agent," she said. "Your cover sucks. Real cabbies like to talk. Sociability equals tip. Real cabbies are never there *just* when you need them."

"Demalion lets you run on a long leash," he said. "Too damn long."

Sylvie said, "Let me make this clear to you. I've never worn a leash. If there's a dog in this relationship, it's Demalion."

He laughed, a quick, harsh sound. "God, I'd love to see his face if you said that to him."

"He'll hear the recording," Sylvie said. "You get back soon enough, you might catch it."

"I think I'll stick around. Hell, I might even help you if you tell me why you're here."

"Don't tell him!" Tish snapped, voice tight with stress.

"Jeez, Tish," Sylvie said. "How 'bout a little faith." She grinned at the agent. "Run along home, now."

"Nah," he said. "Don't mind me. I'll give you a ride to HQ when you're through. Just don't expect me to play backup. I know what Dunne did to Demalion." He switched off his light, pushed the seat back, and closed his eyes.

Sylvie bit back the question that leaped to her tongue—a simple, one-word query—Demalion? To ask would break two of her personal rules: Try not to parrot questions like an idiot, and never ask information of an enemy. She wasn't thrilled with the idea of him waiting here either, ready to pounce on any information she managed to dig up.

Sylvie pondered the odds of foisting Tish off on him, serving up triple benefit points for herself. Get Tish out of her way; keep Bran's friend someplace safe; keep agent occupied. . . . Tish stomped up the stairs toward the brownstone, and said, "Coming?"

Win some, lose some, Sylvie thought, and headed after her. Besides, if Dunne came back, all bad mood and thunderweather, maybe Tish's presence could knock him back into human mode. Maybe.

Tish opened the door, and Sylvie twitched. A quick wave of *something* sheeted over her skin and vanished, a sensation that Sylvie had always attributed to haunted houses—that elusive sense that the air was more alive than in other homes, charged, ionized, full of potential, waiting for its spark.

Tish either didn't feel it or was used to it. Tish went in

with the ease of long practice, punching the code into the alarm pad, and flipping the switch by the door, bringing light into the dim foyer.

Sylvie fought the urge to whistle. What could be done with access to money— Tish's place was pricey because of its desirable location, but bare inside. This house was nothing much outside, a small, well-kept brownstone, but inside it was all about warmth and luxury.

Sylvie crossed from slate tiles to carpet so plush she found herself thinking maybe she should take her sneakers off. Then she recalled the Furies, their habits, and decided Dunne had a good cleaner on call. After all, carpet the color of *dulce leche* would show blood so easily.

Sylvie gave the rest of the main room a glance, seeing upscale bachelor furniture—a leather couch, dark rugs, state-of-the-art sound system, television, lighting, and nearly more artwork than wall space. *Bran's paintings mostly,* she thought, the vibrant colors vivid against the deep chocolate walls. Landscapes. She wondered which of them had decided not to hang anything more distressing in their home. Having seen the murals at NDNM, Sylvie knew Bran was capable of distressing art.

Tish slid a heavy wooden door to the side, revealing a shallow kitchen. "Voice mail's full," she said, studying the flashing light on the phone. "I don't understand. Shouldn't Kevin be here? What if the kidnappers call?" It was a quavering wail. Her fingers hovered over the phone.

"It's not money they want," Sylvie said.

"Then what?" Tish wrapped her arms around herself.

"To hurt Dunne."

Tish sucked in a breath, her eyes widening and darkening with pain. "Then, they don't really need to—"

Keep Bran alive. Sylvie finished the thought, but left it silent, letting Tish read it on her face.

"Oh God," Tish moaned. "God. Poor Kevin. You've got to get Bran back. Kevin won't be able to stand it. He seems so tough, but he *worships* Bran, you know. If Bran . . . I don't know if Kevin can take it—"

"Show me the studio," Sylvie said, thinking Tish was more right to fear than she knew. "Show me his paintings."

Show me Lily.

"Upstairs," Tish said, opening another door, a foldaway set that Sylvie would have taken for nothing more than pantry access. Instead, it revealed a narrow and steep set of stairs.

"Studio access only," Tish said. "Bran calls it his servant's stairs. Says it reminds him that art is his master." A brief smile touched her lips, stilling the tremor they wanted to stay in. "If Kevin's around when Bran says it, Kevin teases him, says love is a much better master than art, and he can prove it. Usually, the sisters and I go have an awkward lunch at that point."

Sylvie wanted to tell her to stop. Stop talking about Bran and Kevin, stop painting images that let her see glimpses of the two of them in this cozy niche of a kitchen. Stop showing her glimmers of a life that was now in ruins.

She pushed by Tish and headed up the stairs, feeling the burn as she forced stiff muscles to the task. *Fucking Fury,* she thought. *Remind me to kick her tail feathers if I see her again.*

The studio was dim and reeked of old paint. A narrow window fed in some morning sunlight, and she used it to track down the light switch. She hit it, and said, "Crap," right after. What had she thought? Tish mentioned a portrait, and Sylvie had expected to sail in, snatch it, and use it—a sort of police sketch for Demalion, a scent trail for Dunne, a reminder to herself. Lily's image was already fuzzy in her mind. She remembered the voice, the force of will, but the face—

"What's wrong?" Tish said.

"He's *productive,*" Sylvie said. It wasn't a compliment. Paintings were stacked everywhere, faces leaning against the walls or slotted into narrow racks; there were cloth-covered heaps, slightly squared, that held still more paintings under their depths. "A little compulsive maybe?"

"He doesn't like paper," Tish said. "He goes right to canvas. If he doesn't like it, he drops it."

"Expensive habit," Sylvie said. "I don't suppose there's a filing system."

Tish laughed. "I told him he needed one."

"Fine," Sylvie said. "You start on that side of the room. Any portrait of a woman that you don't know put aside for me." She was counting on the fact that she would recognize that ordinary face when she saw it again.

Her phone rang and she brought it to her cheek. "Yeah."

"Syl?"

"Yeah," she said again, turning slightly away from Tish's inquisitive gaze. She made a go-on gesture at Tish, telling her to get started. Sylvie tucked the phone against her chin and shoulder, and said, "You got my message? Sorry for the late-night call, but I need info on a woman—"

"Lily Black," Alex said. "And if that's her real name, Val's nose is the original model."

Sylvie paused. She wasn't often off balance, but Alex was always the one to make it happen. "What?"

"Lily Black, art appraiser, part-time art agent. I backtracked through *Ni Dieux, Ni Maîtres'* ownership deeds, hit art news sites, added Brandon Wolf as a data point. His murals are on the Net—including a little note about upcoming ones at NDNM funded by a Lily Black."

"Fast work," Sylvie said.

Across the room, Tish's attention sharpened. Irritably, Sylvie pointed back to the paintings. A name wasn't enough.

"Like I could sleep with you out gallivanting 'round Chicago with Furies for backup." Behind the snark and bravado, Sylvie read an entire other conversation. Despite an unsteady past spent shuttling between foster families, stepparents, and juvie, Alex had never seen anyone die. Traumatic enough, but when that first death had been Suarez, whom she considered a part of her chosen family— well, it was no wonder Alex stayed awake to worry.

Sylvie's part in this unspoken conversation was to ignore it. To that end, she said, "Ah, they're not so tough." Implying, of course, that *she* was. "Did you get an address?"

Sylvie flipped through the nearest stack of paintings. No portraits. Still life, still life, landscape, mythical animals.

"Embarrassment of riches, really," Alex said. "She supplements her income with land. I found her name on seven separate sites, one a condemned church in a neighborhood pending rezoning, two galleries, and four apartment complexes around Chicago. Lily's only got a PO box listed as her own address, but I bet if you check the complexes for unrented apartments—"

"We might find her," Sylvie said. "I'm impressed, Alex."

"You should be," Alex said. "If I billed you for that amount of computer time, I'd bankrupt you."

"Just tell me you aren't going to bring computer crimes down on me, and I'll be content."

Tish held up a gold-framed painting. Sylvie shook her head, shifted her mouth away from the receiver. The portrait showed an elegant blonde, clad only in an ornate set of emeralds. "Brunette," Sylvie said. "Ordinary is the key word here, Tish."

"Please," Alex said. "I cover my tracks. Oh, speaking of—tell me you're taking wolf clients again?"

"Why?" Sylvie said, aware of Tish listening in.

"Present on the store stoop," Alex said. "Rat skulls, bones, tied up in a bow of snakeskin. The front-desk bell says it's inert, though. Not some type of spell. Thought it might be an offering."

"Yuck," Sylvie said. "Maybe the sisters left it. They don't really seem to like me much."

"I think there's a club for people like that," Alex said. "Membership's climbing."

"Funny girl."

Sylvie flipped another painting and forgot the small

mystery. Portrait. Not Lily, but Dunne. The last of her doubts as to their uneven relationship died. She couldn't think Bran feared Dunne, not with this in her hands. Dunne, depicted as an angel: weary, shirtless, scarred; his wings, all hawk dun and beige, were drooping and chafed by a holster and a gun. In the shadow of his wings, Bran leaned against him and was sheltered.

"Syl?"

"Yeah, e-mail me the addresses," Sylvie said.

"Syl . . ." Alex said, held her to the line. "What if the satanists left the bones?" Her voice went tight and a little small.

Sylvie flipped another half dozen paintings face front, without looking at them, just getting them into the light. "Be very careful, or just get out of town. If you think it's them, call the cops. The satanists carried guns instead of power; they'll shoot first, curse later."

"Not comforting," Alex said.

"You came back," Sylvie snapped. Her fingers were white on the phone. Wasn't this what she had tried to prevent? She took a steadying breath, and said, "I doubt it's them. We're one for one, right now. They'll need to back off and reconnoiter."

"One for . . . What did you do, Sylvie? They killed Suarez. Did you kill—"

"What the hell are you talking about?" Sylvie said. Tish frowned at her, a weird look of disapproval in her eyes, as if Sylvie were cursing in church.

"I've seen the files," Alex said, still soft. "The cases where the problem just . . . goes away. Cases where you go it alone. Do you kill people to make the problems go away?"

Things, not people, she thought, stifling that retort before it reached her lips. "Christ, Alex, are you listening to yourself? No, okay. No." She glanced over at Tish and ruthlessly shifted the conversation. "It's fine, it'll be fine. Just be smart and call the cops if anything looks weird. Call Val if anything looks weirder. Her home's loaded

with protective spells. I gotta go." Without waiting for a
response, she disconnected.

Mask's slipping, the little dark voice said.

"Find anything?" Sylvie asked.

Tish shook her head. "I sort of remember the painting.
It had a lot of grey. So I was going to pull those—"

"Great, do it, don't tell me about it," Sylvie said. She
dragged her attention to her own row of paintings and
found her own worries blasted away by the first one in
the row.

So small to pack so much of a punch. It was barely a
foot square, but just touching it made her skin crawl. No
placid landscape, no pretty portrait. A flayed chest, skin
pulled back, revealed a glistening, tattered heart beneath a
worn rib cage. Fingers squirmed within the bone cage,
hooking into the heart, tugging it farther apart. The whole
thing bled at her in tones of rust and sepia.

Tish's footsteps headed her way, and Sylvie flipped
the painting to face the wall. No need to upset the girl
any further. Sylvie stared at the ruddy scrawl on the
back of the canvas and shuddered. *Devoured Heart,* self-
portrait.

Tish spread out three portraits, all rainy-day greys with
women.

Sylvie grabbed the last one and brought it toward her.

"That it?" Tish said, excited.

"Oh yeah," Sylvie said. She recognized the expression
in the eyes more than anything else, that confident stare.
Bran Wolf, she decided then and there, was one hell of a
talent. And, she thought, as she studied it more closely, he
should pay more attention to his subconscious. Lily stood
on the edge of the lake, hair whipping in the wind like live
wires. A drab brown woman on a drab grey background,
and yet . . . Sylvie took it over toward the window where
the sunlight streamed.

In the sunlight, the lake waves grew shadows beneath
lines of paint scraped into place, and showed animal teeth,
showed crosses burned and broken, showed red tinges

beneath the grey, like blood in the water. All of it spiraling out from Lily's shadow over the water.

"Let's go," she said. "We got what we came for."

"But the agent outside—"

"He brought us here, he can take us back," Sylvie said. She knew it wasn't going to be as easy as that. Nothing with the ISI ever was, but she had a portrait of Lily in her hand, addresses incoming, and felt that she had a grip on things for the first time since she'd taken this case. One ISI agent seemed a simple obstacle.

She clattered down the stairs, Tish following, protesting with the fervor of a good girl unused to making waves.

Sylvie opened the front door and balked. She put her hand back, stopping Tish from joining her. Outside, on the hood of the cab, the little firestarter from the bar sat dribbling sparks from one hand to the next.

"Come on out, Shadows," Helen said. "I have a bone to pick with you."

14

Burn, Lady, Burn

"SHIT," SYLVIE MUTTERED. "STAY BACK, TISH."

Tish, like the innocent she was, took a giant step forward to get a better look. "Did he call his team? What are we—" She trailed off at the sight of Helen, and eeped a little when Helen built a fireball in her bare hands.

"Hey, Helen," Sylvie said. "Don't remember doing anything to upset you. Well, anything worth this kind of effort."

Tish squeaked as Helen tossed the fireball at them underhand, a flaming softball that fell short. Sylvie watched it sputter out against the concrete and settled her gun comfortably in her hand before the fire vanished. Armed, ready, she hesitated. Shoot now? Helen had caved quickly enough last night.

In the cab, the agent just sat gaping at the fireworks, probably taking notes. Typical ISI.

"Lily told me where to find you."

"Yeah?" Sylvie said. "You want to reverse the favor? I'm dying to talk to her."

Helen paid no attention, her eyes fixed on Tish. "Where's your freaky friend? That's not her," Helen said.

"If I'm going to burn you up, I want to get her, too. Lily told me you burned the bar. Burned JK alive." With each sentence, fire rose from Helen's skin, first in smoky yellow flamelets, then in a rushing red halo.

Sylvie licked sweat from her lips, tasting salt and a trace of fear. Helen hadn't had that kind of heat last night.

"What? Nothing to say? No begging? You should," Helen said, and giggled, high and wild. "'Cause I am *on* today. Just ask your cabbie."

Sylvie flicked another glance at the still-staring agent, and realized not all the smoke scent came from Helen, the char of flesh not just a lingering remnant from NDNM.

"I put a hole right through him, with my own little hand," Helen said, giggled again. Half-mad with power, and half-frightened of what she'd done. Probably not frightened enough to stop. Sylvie's hand tightened on the gun. Every moment that passed, Helen was forfeiting the right to be human.

A wave of flame rolled toward them, a lava tide smoking over the concrete sidewalk, splashing over the curb. Sylvie said, "Run."

"Where?" Tish whispered.

"Away," Sylvie said. Tish tried to retreat into the house, but Helen let loose a blast worthy of a flame-thrower and Tish screamed, changed angle, and leaped from the stoop. Helen turned to track her with burning eyes; Sylvie dropped the painting, ignored the blistering heat as Dunne's front door smoldered, and redirected Helen's attention with a warning shot that embedded itself in the hood of the cab.

"Leave her out of this."

"Like you left JK? Lily said—"

"Lily's using you," Sylvie said. Tish was three houses away and accelerating, running flat out.

Good sense that, Sylvie thought, and lunged over the railing with far less grace than Tish, rolling, stumbling, as the flames rushed her heels, flashed up her legs and her back.

Sylvie rolled and beat at sparks. Her skin stung in a dozen places, screaming for attention, but she managed to keep focused. If she could get inside the cab, she'd run the bitch down and be gone, before Helen got up.

Sylvie dodged Helen's burning grasp, had almost made it when a sudden change in the air warned her, and she scrambled under the cab. A lash of fire blistered paint and raised dark smoke.

Fuck, Sylvie thought again, scooting backward, knees and elbows going raw against heated asphalt. Helen knelt, the better to aim, and Sylvie rolled out the other side, gun ready. Human or not, Helen had to be stopped.

She didn't want to kill Helen; she might be spoiled, mean, and dangerous, but she was also Lily's dupe, as well as Sylvie's best chance yet for finding Lily.

Sylvie raised her head in time to see another flame rushing her, and cold pragmatism took over—*her or me*—sighting along the gun and firing, sending Helen flying back under the force of a bullet. *Winged only,* Sylvie thought, and congratulated herself on avoiding the kill. Helen groaned, traced a fiery fingertip over the gash at her collarbone, and cauterized the wound.

"Sylvie!"

She pointed the same finger at Sylvie, and the flames wrapping her body rolled up her arm, as deadly as a line of belt-fed bullets.

"Sylvie," the voice cried her name again; an engine throbbed. "Sylvie, get in the damn car!" Demalion yelled, and Sylvie turned. He leaned half-out of the open passenger door, and behind the wheel, Tish. Sylvie lunged for the car, pulled herself in, and Tish took off. Helen darted before them and Tish, eyes wide with terror, didn't even slow. Helen burned as she bounced away.

"Are you all right?" Demalion said, voice too close for her comfort.

She twitched, realized she was sprawled in his lap, and said, "Do I look all right? What the hell did you bring Tish for?" She tried not to squirm, aware of the fit of her body against his.

"I didn't have a choice, not this close to Dunne's," he said. His hands fisted, one fist bigger than the other. Tish swerved, hit a curb, and Demalion's hands flew open. His little crystal ball bounced free and smacked Sylvie's shin.

"Ow," she whimpered. As if the admission was all her body had been waiting for, suddenly "ow" was all she could say. Her arm burned and stung, the flesh furrowed, her knees smarted, and if Erinya hadn't cracked her ribs last night, Sylvie had when she hit the pavement. She looked down to see the khakis shredded at the knees from flinging herself beneath the cab. "Ow," she said again, feeling sorry for herself.

Tish rebounded off another curb, narrowly avoided swerving into oncoming traffic, and Sylvie said, "Slow down. We're safe now."

"Safe?" Tish asked. Her voice was thin and lost, a child's; she leaked tears.

"Yeah, it's all okay, now," Sylvie said. Tish's speed slowed, but her hands shook.

"Safe?" Tish asked, going shrill. "How is this safe? She shot fire at us. With her hands! She tried to kill us." She gaped at Demalion, maybe only now taking the time to really look at the "us" involved, and the car swerved again.

Sylvie grabbed the wheel. Demalion cursed and began fumbling in the depths of the car, squishing Sylvie in the process, forcing her hands from the wheel. "Get off me," she said, crushed beneath him. Tish got the car back under marginal control, but her breath was ragged.

"I need my crystal," Demalion said.

"Right now?"

He nodded, mouth thinned.

"Then get off me," she said, "and let me get it."

He leaned back, and she bent to chase it around the seat well.

"Fire?" he asked.

"You were there. You saw it. Oh, and Helen killed your guy," Sylvie said abruptly.

"Helen?" Demalion turned to look at her, eyes wide. Their usual dark brown seemed peculiarly shiny, but then again, Sylvie's head throbbed, and her vision was keeping pace.

Tish braked hard for a red light, the first one she'd stopped for in a mile, and the little crystal ball rolled up against Sylvie's sneaker. She put her foot on it, reached down, and handed it back to Demalion.

"The firestarter at the bar," she said.

"Lily," Demalion said. "Got some info on her for you. I was coming to meet you."

"*Not* Lily," Sylvie said. "Though Lily sicced her on me. Helen wasn't anything much last night, sparks and flint. But today, she was rolling out the fire like a dragon."

"What the hell is going on?" Tish cried, ignoring the car honking behind her. "What's all this got to do with Bran?"

"Nothing," Sylvie said. "It's all about Dunne."

The driver behind them got out of his car and tapped on the driver's side window. Tish shrieked and stepped on the gas. Sylvie rocked back into Demalion and winced. "Ow," she whispered.

He touched her forearm, the blistering burn. "This was close."

"It's been closer," she said, and hated that it was true. She was going to quit, find herself a spot in the sand, lie out like a lizard, and snarf drinks under a tropical sun. There would be no witches, sorcerers, succubi, monsters, gods, or girls who blew fire.

Tish ran a red light; cars honked, and Sylvie said in unison with Demalion, "Pull over!"

"I'll drive," Demalion said, beating Sylvie to it. She

smothered her usual knee-jerk contrariness to anything Demalion said and nodded.

"How can a blind man drive a car?" Tish said. "You were at the intersection, in the car, alone. How'd you get there?"

"Drove," Demalion said. He prodded Sylvie's sore arm. "Who's Helen?" Demalion said.

"Bastard," she muttered, willing to ignore Tish for the moment. "Helen was at the bar last night; she left before the big finale. She got up this morning supercharged and superpissed. . . . Oh, hell," Sylvie said. "It's the damn gods!"

Tish pulled the car to a halt, and as soon as the way was clear, swung the driver's door open and scrambled out. A passing truck buffeted them, but Tish was clear of it, pacing on the shoulder. They watched her shaking, arms clasped around herself. When Sylvie was sure Tish wasn't going to fall into traffic, she turned back to Demalion. He tucked his crystal into his pocket and slid behind the wheel. "How does Helen fit—"

"Lily manipulated her," Sylvie said. "We've got bigger problems. Dunne's shedding pure power. Helen's a scavenger. I saw a little of that last night; when Helen touched Erinya's jacket, it flared. But at Dunne's, where he's been living, breathing, shedding—it's like throwing chum in the water. Only this chum turns shrimp into sharks. And anyone with a hint of talent can feed on it. . . ."

Helen's flaming hands, the insanity in her eyes, the death and damage she had done crossed Sylvie's mind again, but this time she imagined it happening in a hundred different homes as people woke up and smelled the possibilities. Dunne had been *everywhere* looking for Bran. Even Miami. At its best, South Miami was a city of predators. With blood in the water—Sylvie thinned her lips, biting at the lower one until a nerve spasmed in protest.

"Not good," Demalion said. "Let's get Tish and get back. The ISI needs to know about this." He leaned out of the car, calling to the dancer.

"I'm not going anywhere with you," Tish said. Her face was pale, a small welt rising on her brow, and her eyes were shocky and dark-ringed. "Something's really wrong, and it's your fault!"

"No, it's not," Demalion said. "Don't confuse the cure with the symptoms. We're trying to make things right—"

"By sneaking and prying? I don't trust you. I don't like you, and Bran was scared to death of you. I only helped 'cause I had to. Go to hell." Her eyes flickered over Sylvie's for a second; her face crumpled into tears. "Both of you." She raised her hand, dashed tears from her eyes, and waved frantically at oncoming traffic.

Demalion cursed under his breath and got out to corral her. Sylvie shook her head. Both of them idiots. Nothing good could ever come from a grown man chasing a screaming young woman around a major highway. Sylvie hit the horn and stuck her head out. "Demalion, get back here. Call her a damn cab if you're worried."

He got back into the car and dialed a number. "It's Demalion. I need a cab pickup. . . ."

Sylvie snatched the phone from his grasp. "A real cab. Not the ISI!"

"She needs to tell us what she saw," Demalion said.

"She needs to go stick her head in the sand and pretend *nothing* happened."

"You think that's okay?"

It was what Dunne wanted, Sylvie thought. She didn't want him angry at her. "Leave her *alone*, Demalion."

Lips tight, he recovered his phone, and dialed Airport Cabs, holding the phone out so that Sylvie could hear the dispatcher.

Then he put the car into gear and pulled them back into traffic. "Well, you saw what happened better anyway. Saw and understood . . ."

"I'm not going to talk to the ISI, either," she said. "I should be hunting Bran. Hell, I should be at home," she said, still mulling over that increase of ability that Helen had shown. "Dunne was in Miami. Talents will be ramping up there, too."

"Best to find Wolf and be done with this. What could you do in Miami, anyway?"

"Whatever I had to, to protect it," she said. "But maybe that concept's alien to a government drone who thinks every problem can be handled with the appropriate paperwork."

"Maybe your track record's not the best at protection," he snapped back. "Or was Suarez one of your success stories?"

She punched him, lost in rage, ignoring the common-sense rule that hitting the driver was a bad idea. Close quarters, but he managed to hunch a shoulder up to take the blow and keep the car from swerving. Much. A horn blared beside them.

"You're reckless," he said, his own temper burned out. "You're dangerous. You used to *think*, Sylvie. What changed? Keep going the way you're going, and you'll be no different than the people you fight against."

"Fuck you," she muttered. She slumped against the passenger door, as far from him as she could manage. "Just drive."

Traffic slowed and snarled as they approached orange cones on the street. Sylvie thought *road work* with minimal interest, more caught up in wondering what Dunne would do if she did pick up and run home. He'd send the Furies to retrieve me, she thought. But I could kill them if I laid a trap, made plans. They're monsters. Fair game.

But she didn't want to kill them, not Erinya with her quick tempers and childish ways, not elegant Alekta, or Magdala, who proved even deadly creatures could be dull. She was sick of killing things.

"We need to do something, or Wolf will die," Demalion said, in uncanny echo of her thoughts. "You don't want the ISI, then what?"

"Consensus is he's already dead. Dunne's the only holdout," Sylvie said. She gritted her teeth as the car came to a dead stop. Becalmed in the asphalt sea, she thought. She hated this city.

"He's a god," Demalion said. "You don't think he might know something you don't?"

"You sure jumped on the bandwagon easily," Sylvie said, "and you haven't even seen him in action." She blinked. That wasn't right. The cab/agent had said something. *I know what Dunne did to Demalion.*

"Seen more 'n enough," Demalion said. She met his steady gaze, and he reached out slowly, touched her chin, turned her head toward the street before them.

"Oh," Sylvie said. No wonder the traffic had stopped. The worn lane markings on the roadway were peeling away, winding upward like airborne ribbons and spilling backward, touching down and gluing cars into place, creating a spiderweb that slowly sucked vehicles into the asphalt. A busload of tourists had gotten out and were snapping pics as drivers crawled out of windows of trapped cars.

"It's been happening all day," he said. "Not this. But things. You say Dunne's shedding? I say, tell me something I couldn't have guessed."

"All day?" she said, staring at the webbing with more creeping terror than fascination.

"Transformations have happened all over town," Demalion said. "People have died. But you don't want the ISI to help. You want to go it alone.

"We really could help, Sylvie. You want to go home, worried about what? Your family, your friends? I could have the ISI pick them up—"

Wrong thing to say, Sylvie thought. *So terribly wrong.* She went cold all the way through. "If you do, I'll dig around, Demalion, find *your* family—you said they're local—drag them into this," Sylvie said. "Do they know what kind of job you have?"

"Point made," Demalion said. His jaw tightened. "I don't like threats, Shadows."

"You started it."

"It wasn't meant as a threat."

Sylvie stopped further explanation by drawing out the meat gun, setting it in her lap. "Stay away from my people. Or you'll find out how dangerous I really am." Even she was unnerved at the quiet fury in her tone.

Demalion raised an eyebrow like an aristocrat being abused by a peasant. But, and Sylvie had to admit it, Demalion had always had common sense as well as smarts. He merely nodded.

Sylvie continued in the same quiet tone, "We've come to a truce, you and I, am I right? Let's not jeopardize it."

"I'd call it a detente, myself, and one-sided at that," Demalion said.

"I gave you Lily's name. I gave you Dunne's identity."

"You didn't," he said. "You didn't say *which* god."

"Does it matter?" Sylvie felt the exasperation seep in and, even as she bridled with annoyance, admired the technique. Demalion backed her away from the killing edge, transforming shouting to bickering.

"I'd just like to know what pantheon I should convert to," Demalion said.

"Not funny," she said. "He's the Greek god of Justice, and it's a new position, so don't give me grief about there being no such god."

"Wouldn't dream of it," he said. "You'd be surprised at how little I want to make you unhappy."

"This is trying to make me happy?" She slipped the gun back into the holster. "You're right, as much as I hate to admit it. I find Wolf, I get Dunne to clean up his mess. Without Wolf, it only gets worse."

She reluctantly added, "Alex sent me some addresses. Stop by an Internet cafe, I'll print the list. They're places she thought Lily might be living in. We . . ." The word felt strange on her lips. Good, in a way she didn't want to think about. "We could check them out."

He took his eyes from the road for a long moment, looking at her. Then he nodded once, and said, "Lead the way."

15

Trails and Dead Ends

"SHE'S NOT HERE," SYLVIE SAID. SHE HADN'T EVEN GOTTEN OUT OF the car, and she knew, just *knew*, they were on the wrong track.

Demalion, hand paused on the ignition key, said, "Why?" Not another direct start to an argument but a definite call against her instinct.

Sylvie looked again at the apartment buildings, a series of interconnected town houses, at the children playing in the park across the street, the casual everydayness of the area, and shook her head. "Not a chance in hell."

"She owns the place; there are empty units," Demalion said. "I need more reason than that."

"I saw her," Sylvie said. She wasn't used to explaining herself. But she and Demalion *had* agreed to a detente, so she should try to cooperate. "Lily pretends to be ordinary," Sylvie said. "Everyone I talked to described her as ordinary. I saw her, though, and she's not ordinary at all. She's just good at masking herself. If you were like that, if you wore a mask all the time, would you want to live in an ordinary place? Would you want to have to worry about blending in, even in your home?

You'd find someplace else. Someplace you could be yourself in comfort."

"All that from one look across a crowded room?" Demalion said. "You don't think your impression came from her burning everyone alive a moment later?"

Sylvie shrugged. "You said it yourself. Even the ISI uses my instincts as Cliff's Notes."

She didn't want to share more than she had to, really didn't want to get into what she had felt when Lily's eyes had met hers: instant recognition, so strong that it might as well have been a physical shock. Logic be damned; Sylvie knew her, and more, knew what they were up against. A woman as determined as Sylvie herself. And deadlier.

"Let me see that list," she said, fishing it out of the space between the driver's seat and the gearshift.

"Where to, then, guru?" Demalion asked.

Sylvie dropped her eyes to the paper, edges crumpling in her hand. "Um, Bucktown apartments, no, too normal. MTV Real World trendy. Wicker Park—"

"A lot of artists, which is likely given her tastes, but there are also a lot of businessmen and loft living, which would make it a no by your criterion. Too normal."

Sylvie skimmed the list; only a few addresses were left, and if she hadn't felt so pressed for time, she'd have simply continued as they'd begun. Go down the list one by one. But she did feel harried by an unseen clock, by the fact that the children in the park were gasping, laughing, and the sand below their swing set was swirling and lapping at the grass in wavelets. Sharks would be next, she thought. Didn't little kids always see sharks in water? And one of those children, latently talented, obviously saw the sand as water.

"Shit," she muttered, as a sharp fin rose, and the children's shrieking laughter just turned to shrieks. "Go get them off—" But Demalion was already on the way out of the car. He ignored the screamers and focused on the little girl with the fixed stare and the incredulous horror in her eyes. He snatched her up, pressed her face into his shoulder, and as parents came out to investigate the crying, handed her off. Behind them, the fin collapsed to falling sand.

Demalion lingered outside once the mother left, cell phone in hand, and Sylvie's mood soured. Her great ally, reporting a nine-year-old to the government.

"What will you do with children like that?" Sylvie said. "You can't charge them with anything, even if you join those who want to try kids as adults."

Demalion said. "It's a flaw in our justice system. They don't recognize the supernatural, therefore—"

"There are no charges, no trials, no prison," Sylvie said.

"We're working on it," Demalion said. "ISI's got a ten-year plan. Five for concentrated study of the supernatural. Three for making and testing a security plan. Two for convincing the rest of the world—"

"You're behind then," Sylvie said. "I haven't seen any hints of understanding on the news."

Demalion laughed. "We've only been active for four years, Sylvie. We're still newbies. Before 9-11, the ISI was only a maniacal gleam in some bureaucrat's eye. After that, there were a lot more people willing to throw money at even the most undefined problems."

"It's the church," she said. "Gotta be." Changing the subject, and fast, before he saw that he'd shaken her.

Two years of tangling with the ISI, two years of running them in circles, and she thought she'd been winning. Too tough and too smart for the government. To find out they were still in a larval stage, that perhaps her success against them had more to do with their fumbling first steps into a bigger world, made her reassess. Just how much had she overrated her skills?

"The church?" Demalion parroted. He flipped through the list for the more-detailed reports. "That was condemned after a fire nearly twenty years ago. You think she's living there? She's got money. We know that. Rich women like their amenities."

"Regardless," Sylvie said. "It's *Sesame Street* training. One of these things is not like the others. The church is the odd man out, and anomalies are always worth a look."

"Your point," Demalion said with a smile. He restarted the car, pulled them smoothly back into the traffic. "I'll have the ISI check out the apartments anyway."

Sylvie bit back protest. The apartments were meaningless. The church dangled before her like the brass ring on a carousel.

She stifled her doubts, even when the neighborhood they drove through grew progressively run-down. The church was a hulking shadow on the street, a reminder that nothing evaded entropy. Its spire crumbled near the top, the bell long gone for scrap, and its gargoyles had worn to near-featureless stone.

They approached the church cautiously, noting boarded-up windows, a chain across the great double doors, and, with a glance at each other, turned and went around the side, hunting a door out of sight of the street.

All the way around the back, there was a narrow door, cast in shadows by the stone around it. "Prep room, I bet," Demalion said.

"Altar boy?" Sylvie asked.

"Yup," he agreed. He knelt, eyed the lock, and nodded once. From a pocket, he pulled a key ring dangling with filed-down keys. He forced one into the lock, thumped it once, and popped the latch open.

"Somewhere, a priest just cried," Sylvie said.

"Never said I was a particularly devout altar boy," he said. "After you?"

Sylvie kicked at the door. It flew open, and she watched for a moment, waiting for Lily to come at them, for any other esoteric security to make itself known.

"She's not home," Sylvie said.

"I could have told you that," Demalion said. He put away a gun she hadn't seen him draw and ducked inside. "I'm more than just a pretty face, you know."

"Yeah?" she challenged. He merely smirked and gestured her in.

"It's all about the eyes," he said, tapping just above the bridge of his nose.

"Whatever," she muttered. She was more concerned with the security measures Lily might have in place. No magical wards, Sylvie noted, as she stepped over the sill. If Lily were arcanely talented, there would have been wards.

The room was dark and empty; the linoleum beneath their feet cracked with each footstep. Sylvie opened cupboards meant to hold vestments, the unconsecrated host and wine, and found them restocked with secular items. Jeans, leather jackets, stocking caps, makeup. A woman's wardrobe. "Definitely my point," she murmured.

Demalion moved into the main body of the church, black with shadows. Automatically, Sylvie fumbled for a switch in the doorway, ignoring the fact that this was a church and not a home. A string brushed her fingers; she caught it and tugged. A work light, hung where a crucifix should have been, illuminated the altar and made valiant inroads into the congregational shadows that filled the rest of the building. Two pews had been turned to face each other, suspending a mattress between them. The sheets shimmered with a subdued luster that whispered silk. *There* were some of Demalion's amenities.

"Oh, she's so going to hell," Demalion said. He pointed at the holy-water font, and said, "Toothbrush and toothpaste stains. She's been spitting in the well."

"Creepy," Sylvie said aloud.

"But not normal," Demalion said. His voice echoed against the marble, the vast empty space.

"This is true."

It looked like Lily had concentrated her living space around and on the altar. A small generator hummed behind the altar, and a long tangle of extension cords led off that, anchoring a tiny fridge and a desktop computer that gave her a password prompt when Sylvie started it up.

Papers tacked up along a wall, fluttering in shadow and the wake of their movement, turned out to be photographs of Bran, Dunne, the sisters, and their house. Sylvie shivered when she noticed that every one of the Furies' images showed them red-eyed, and not in the usual flash-flare way, but in a burning, empty-eye-socket, red-flame fashion. The Furies weren't as good as Dunne at hiding what they were. Dunne's photographs showed a man. Nothing more.

Another picture showed Bran, bright head bent to speak to a man in a sleek, black sedan, just down the block from their house. The man in the suit looked blank, almost mindless, and in the bare periphery of the photo, Dunne lurked. *Team one,* Sylvie thought. Getting brainwashed. Two-step trick. Bran distracts them, and Dunne lays on the whammy. Sylvie couldn't blame the agent. Who wouldn't be distracted by his target coming up to talk to him, and smiling that smile?

Even in a photograph, Bran's smile promised all sorts of delight.

She moved deeper into the church, studying the stained-glass windows. Most of them had been slathered over with black paint, the color as thick and uneven as if Lily had climbed a ladder and simply poured the paint downward.

Other images were spared the black-paint bath, but none had been left alone. A few had been broken, and others altered in strange, telling ways. Sylvie looked up at a white-robed God whose beard had been spray-painted blue.

JK had been right. Lily was not fond of religious art. Even Sylvie, who considered her religious meter to hover around zero, felt a little uneasy at such concentrated venom.

Bluebeard, she thought, and in a flash of understanding that almost seemed to come from outside, got the bitter joke.

"Some churches changed the Lord's Prayer," Sylvie said. "Didn't they?"

"I guess," Demalion said.

"*Lead us not into temptation.* The PC crew took it out, because God wouldn't do something like that."

"Do you have a point?" Demalion asked.

"Not really," Sylvie said. She headed back up to the altar desk and took another look at the computer. Password-protected. Demalion would take it when they left. The ISI would hack it open, and Sylvie would get dribs and drabs of the contents, doled out in increments as they decided what was safe to let loose.

Sylvie traced the pattern around the altar, the Latin that read out "this is my body, this is my blood," following it around the back, where Lily had marked over the rest of it with more black paint. *My body, my blood, my soul are mine, and I yield them to none.*

It gave Sylvie a jolt, an uncomfortable spasm; the skin of her back itched and prickled as if Tish's nails were tracing the tattoo again. Oh yes, Sylvie understood Lily.

Sylvie finished her walk around the altar, thinking of Bran painting Eden at Lily's behest. Paradise as prison. God as Bluebeard. Lily's desire to steal a god's power. *Ni Dieux, Ni Maîtres.* No gods, no masters, save yourself.

Without conscious desire, her fingers stroked the keys, and she tapped in a familiar phrase. *Cedo Nulli.* I yield to none.

The computer welcomed her in with a chime that Sylvie moved to stifle even as it started. Demalion raised his head. "Shadows? What are you doing?"

"Seeing if I can guess the password," she said. She surfed Lily's desktop folders, headed for e-mail, and called it up. French again, she thought, and started skimming, hunting for words she could understand. She found one e-mail that fulfilled that, and made her growl. *Maudits. Sylvie Shadows.* A communiqué sent late last night.

Footsteps behind her; she started to close the program, but Demalion's hand caught hers.

He frowned at the screen, cast her a wary glance.

"How did you—" And he went back to reading, her hand still caged in his. "Do you understand French?"

"No," she said. "But I don't like that combination."

"Lily's inviting the *Maudits* to come get you. She says she knows they have been waiting for a chance. That if they weren't feeling energetic enough, that you . . . killed the boy they sent to her."

"Focus on the important thing," Sylvie said. "Are they taking her up on it?"

"Did you kill the boy?"

She shrugged. The deed was done, and dead was dead. Demalion needed her too much to get picky. "Like you wouldn't have done the same thing in the same situation. Anything else interesting?" Sylvie said.

Demalion read another few aloud, e-mails between Lily and the *Maudits* bickering over prices for an assortment of insta-spell sticks and a single pair of magic spectacles. Sylvie had divided the world into talented and not, had assigned Lily to the latter capacity, when she'd forgotten there were such things as gadget witches. Stored spells used by anyone and everyone. And supplied, at a hefty price, by unscrupulous sorcerers like the *Maudits*. At least Lily haggled with them, made it that much less profitable for them.

That disagreement, Sylvie thought, was all to the good, made it that much less likely the *Maudits* would get off their luxury couches to come hunting her.

She left Demalion to his muttering and skimming of Lily's mail and went back to the photographs. Lily had been stalking Dunne for several seasons; pictures of Dunne wrapped up in winter wools, Bran's hair a splash of color against the dull blues of Dunne's sweater, both of their faces bright with cold and amusement, looking straight at the camera.

Looking straight at the photographer. Sylvie peeled the photo from the wall, flipped it, already knowing what she was going to see. Two initials: TC. Tish Carmichael.

If Lily hadn't taken the photographs, then the wall

wasn't so much a record of her surveillance as a collage of her intent. Bran smiled at the ISI again and started a new row of photos, less-candid moments and more stalk-eresque. Dark, grainy shots taken at night with special lenses that washed all color away. Dunne's bedroom, their dining room, the two of them coming home, trailed by the sisters.

These were professional surveillance shots, her dark voice whispered, and how did Lily get them from the ISI?

Sylvie flicked a glance downward and shied back in reflexive concern. A pile of chopsticks bound with a scarlet ribbon lay next to a similarly bound collection of wooden matchsticks. Wood and brittle, the perfect things to contain a borrowed spell. Guess Lily had come to an agreement with the *Maudits*.

She dropped her gaze to the bottom of the wall and hissed out a breath. Maybe she'd come to an agreement with others as well.

The bottom level was comprised of reports, not photographs, reports on where Dunne and Bran banked, Dunne's past career highlights, Bran's psychologist's notes. And all the reports had e-mail headers ending in isius.org.

Can't trust anyone but yourself.

Demalion said, "Sylvie, what was the password? There are some other protected—"

"Earn your own damn paycheck."

"Hey," he objected, but Sylvie was already heading for the back of the church and out. Guess a government group didn't have to be around very long before corruption got to it. Lily had bought someone in the ISI.

The reasonable side of her brain popped up. Hadn't she already called Lily a thief? Maybe it wasn't betrayal, but hacking.

"Sylvie," Demalion said. He caught up, grabbed her arm, and said, "What's wrong?"

"You tell me. You're not hunting Lily, you all might as well be working for her."

She shook him off when his grip went tight.

"That's why I want the password. I need to know who's selling—"

"It doesn't matter," Sylvie said, sick at heart. She couldn't trust him. He might want the password so he could present his superiors with proof of a leak. Or he might be wanting to cover his own tracks.

He reached for her again, and she threw the information at him like bait. "Password? Try the big fat hint on the altar." He turned to look, helpless not to, and she was gone.

16

Riddled Through

SYLVIE GRIMACED AS SHE PAID THE CABBIE, FORKING OVER HER LAST twenty and a ten. She should have had Dunne magic her wallet after he'd magicked her gun. Cab fare had wiped her out, but there was no help for it. Sylvie had thought about taking Demalion's ISI sedan but figured it was either traceable or LoJacked. She had better things to do than wait for him to track her down.

If she couldn't trust Demalion to help her gain information, it was down to the wild card. Anna D, Val's local Power. Sylvie was already regretting it. Anna D, witch extraordinaire, didn't live near anything so plebeian as a bus or train route. In fact, she lived about as far from the city as she could get and still fit within the zip codes.

Away from the historic downtown area, the buildings were more modern, less prone to sneaking in bits of gothic frippery, or art deco details. Anna D's condominium glittered like an icicle in full sun. All that glass . . . It made Sylvie shiver, imagining what use a witch could have for that many reflective surfaces.

Did she really need Anna D's help, unknown quality that it was? The plate-glass exterior suggested a scrying witch at the very least, which could pinpoint Lily's current whereabouts for her if she were lucky.

The ISI would have secured the church by now, and Lily would get another e-mail, warning her to stay away from home. Sylvie had nothing left to learn from that site.

If Sylvie were unlucky, the building was glass because Anna D had a thing for modern architecture; she might be a nothing talent, no matter what Val had said.

Besides, Sylvie could ruin Anna D's life; after all, Lily was on Sylvie's tail—or Sylvie on hers, it was hard to tell—and balefire didn't care where it burned. Even if Lily wasn't a threat, Dunne was. What if he came seeking Sylvie and burned Anna D out as thoroughly as he had Val? Hell, even the ISI might pose a threat to a witch who aided Sylvie.

Her phone buzzed from her jacket pocket, and she fielded it absently. "Yeah."

"Stop dithering in my parking lot. Go away. Or, if you must, come see me." A sharp click marked disconnection, as crisp and as final as the woman's voice itself.

Fine, Sylvie thought. *Make it easy for me. I already don't like you; guess I won't cry if I put you in harm's way.* She stalked into the lobby, a ragtag figure in the middle of bland eggshell and marble luxury. The lobby receptionist didn't bother to look up, obviously forewarned, and Sylvie headed for the elevator. It dinged open as she approached it.

When Sylvie got in, she saw a floor had already been selected. *What, too much trouble to just* tell *me the apartment number?* Sylvie groused. Anna D was going to be difficult with a capital D. Sylvie only liked difficult if she was the one being that way. Other people just irritated her. Anna D was the type who played *games* while people died.

The elevator slid silently upward, releasing Sylvie onto the penthouse floor and a long hallway where the carpet was as gold as the beach at sunset. Sylvie stepped off, heard movement, and saw a woman walking away from her. Sylvie would have to jog to catch up. *Games.*

She growled and followed at her own speed, studying the stiff elegance of the woman's walk, the formal suit, the low-heeled shoes. An older woman, with a crisp style to match the voice she'd heard on the phone. Guess Anna D didn't have a servant, Sylvie thought, just as the woman reached the doorway to the penthouse, opened it, then, without turning, closed it in Sylvie's face.

Kill it, the dark voice snarled. *No,* Sylvie thought, taking her hand from the gun. But Anna D had better be a font of useful information.

Sylvie expressed her feelings by ignoring the brass doorbell and pounding on the door.

It opened immediately. *Games,* Sylvie thought again, bit back the growl, and blamed Erinya's jacket for bringing out the Fury in her.

The woman blocked the doorway and studied Sylvie, an eyebrow arched, the lips just slightly curled enough to express dismay and contempt. Sylvie stared back just as rudely. Society woman. An aging movie starlet in the gracious style: Hepburn and Garbo rather than Cher. Anna D was old-school elegance personified. Her sleek dark hair, untouched with grey, swept back into a tidy bob. Her eyes were the color of sandstone, her skin firm and deeply olive and oddly, she reminded Sylvie of someone she knew.

She dared another glance at those sunset-colored eyes and felt suspicion prickle. *Kill it,* her dark voice had said. Anna D wasn't just a witch. Anna D probably wasn't even human. The woman's mouth shifted, and she spoke, clipped, precise, clinical.

I bring joy and pain in equal measure,
yet men dream on me with naught but pleasure.
I make strong men weak, and weak men strong.
I am the heart of every song.

I can ne'er be touched, but only felt.
Once forced to flight by candle melt.
If I am caught, I die if neglected,
but, like hope, may be resurrected.
Who am I?

Sylvie banged her head on the doorjamb, unutterably
sick of this. "I knew you were the type to play games. Let
me guess. You're not going to let me in, or answer any of
my questions until I answer yours."

"Worse," Anna D said, a touch of condescension sliding into that blank voice. "I will neither allow you to en-
ter, nor aid you, until you answer my riddle *correctly*."

"You do know people are dying."

"It's the human condition."

"Repeat it," Sylvie said.

"You don't listen very well," Anna D said. "Tell me—
what did the sorcerer name you—do you remember? If
you repeat his words, I will repeat mine."

Sylvie blinked. The sorcerer? The *Maudit* she'd shot?
How could Anna know about—

"I grow bored."

"It was French," Sylvie said. "I don't speak French.
Enfant. Le Enfant Meurtrier, something like that."

"Yes," Anna said. "*L'enfant du meurtrier.* He recognized you. As I do."

"Maybe you've got the wrong idea," Sylvie said. "I
know who I am. I need to know who Lily—"

"*L'enfant du meurtrier,*" Anna D said. "The Murderer's
Child."

After a moment, Sylvie said, "I've heard worse," refusing to show that the name-calling rocked something deep
inside her. Not Murderer, but Murderer's *Child. The* murderer, like she should know what or who that meant. She
realized Anna D, that bitch, had taken advantage of her
silent abstraction to recite her riddle again, and she'd
nearly missed it.

Anna D's lips tilted up at the corners, a feline smile of

triumph and pleasure. Sylvie watched it grow, become more purely about victory, watched the door begin to close. At the last moment, Sylvie put her hand out, slapped the door back, and solved the riddle. "Love."

She grinned her own nasty triumph at the witch, and said, "I can play games, too."

Anna D stalked away from the door, ceding this round; Sylvie had a mental image of a ticked-off cat, lashing its tail, and smiled again.

"At least you recognize it," Anna D said, dropping into a velveteen-covered chair. "Enough to answer the question, and that's something." She sounded as if she were reassuring herself. She stroked the chair arms where the beige velvet tucked itself beneath brass nailheads.

Sylvie wandered around the sunken living room, with the focus not a television or entertainment system, but the floor-to-ceiling glass windows. Looked like she was right; Anna D was a scryer.

"It's like multiple-choice tests, really. When in doubt, choose B. Riddles always end in love or death." She detoured over to a knickknack table covered in crystal globes of varying size; she picked one up and warmed it in her hand. "So many things do."

"You guessed?" Anna D said.

"Correctly," Sylvie said. "Isn't that what matters?"

Anna sank back into her seat; her expression, never warm, faded to an icy hauteur. "You are a fool, Ms. Lightner. A dangerous one. You pick up shards of fact, hoard them like a magpie, pushing shiny things this way and that, and cackle over your own cleverness. You lack vision. Love, Ms. Lightner, is more than the answer to my riddle. It's the source of the problems you face."

"I get it already," Sylvie said. Her ears burned. She set the little crystal down before she hurled it at something. Or someone.

"Let me be precise. Love made Dunne a god. The dissolution of love will reset the world, and both the mortal realm and the divine will be forever altered."

"How about you shut up about me and start talking about Lily?" Sylvie said.

Anna D drew herself up in the chair; her hands flexed over the curved arms and stretched like claws. "I cannot discuss one without the other. You and the woman you misname are thrice linked, by blood, by circumstance, by purpose."

"Like my own evil twin," Sylvie said, pushing away another touch of chill with empty rejoinder. She sat down on the coffee table, hunched into the jacket for warmth, and tried to enjoy the way Anna bristled at the casual misuse of her furniture.

"Tell me about her then, if you know so much. Tell me how I have anything to do with her, other than being the one sent to make her give back what she's taken."

Anna D bridled again at Sylvie's challenge but finally said, "There were humans even before the gods turned their interest to the mortal realm. The gods began to watch, to shape themselves to interact with the humans, and the humans reacted accordingly. Millennia passed with each of us shaping the other. Then several of the gods chose to create their own peoples—"

"Start at the *very* beginning, why don't you?" Sylvie muttered, leaned forward, and put her head in her hands. She could smell the leather of Erinya's coat, lingering smoke, and a lingering wisp of Demalion's cologne. *Damn, he smells good.*

"I am not talking for my own edification, Ms. Lightner," Anna D said, in a schoolteacher-prissy tone of voice, and wasn't Sylvie going to kick someone's ass for telling the witch her real name. . . .

"I get it," Sylvie said, when the silence continued, when she realized she was going to have to listen *actively*, like some remedial student. "So which creation myth are we talking?"

"Can't you guess?"

"I don't think you like it when I guess."

"Her name's not Lily," Anna D said. "It's Lilith, and

she is an immortal creature of immense will, frustration, and rage."

"Lilith," Sylvie said, thought she said, though no sound came from her mouth. Her lips felt cold. It wasn't surprise; it felt like fate. After all, it was the succubi, Lilith's daughters, that had brought Sylvie into awareness of the *Magicus Mundi* all that time ago, Lilith's influence that had seen Sylvie's innocence shattered. Lilith's touch tainted everything. Her fingers curled tightly into fists, stretching the jacket's pockets taut.

"Your conflict was inevitable—"

"I made some of her daughters dead," Sylvie said. "In retrospect, not the smartest move ever." She picked up one of the little crystals and juggled it hand to hand. No wonder Demalion had taken to carrying one; they were as smoothly soothing as meditation balls minus the annoying chime.

"She has other offspring," Anna D said. "What's a double handful of them gone to a woman like her? To a woman of enormous will and obsessive focus? They could not help her; she dismissed them from her mind. But you, Ms. Lightner, are fated to face her."

"Fate's just an easy word for not trying," Sylvie said. "I make my own choices, make my own fate."

"Perhaps fate was the wrong word," Anna said, shifting in her seat to gaze at the sheet glass. Sylvie doubted that she and Anna D were seeing the same sky beyond it. "There are patterns. Cause and effect, choices so small they're meaningless until the accumulation is clear. Do you like to look in mirrors, Ms. Shadows? Do you like what you see?"

"We were talking about Lilith," Sylvie said.

"We still are," Anna D said. "Answer me."

"I always wanted green eyes," Sylvie said.

"Do not be pert," Anna D snapped, lips drawing into a snarl; her teeth seemed rather long and very white. "I have put up with enough of your foolishness. What do you see in the mirror?"

"Myself," Sylvie said, intimidated despite herself. The Furies were always enraged; their sudden bursts of temper were expected. This feral distortion of an elegant woman just plain scared her. *Kill it,* the dark voice hissed again.

"Tell me," Anna D said. "Is it the same face you used to show? Back when you first chose to protect? Or is it the face of a Fury, driven to punish?" Cat-quick, she reached out and flicked Sylvie's sleeve, leaving a long, rough scratch in the leather. "You smell of blood and death."

Sylvie slipped out of the woman's reach and rose. She leaned up against the cool glass and closed her eyes. "I know who I am," she said. "Tell me about Lilith."

She opened her eyes and watched Anna D sink back in the chair, almost seeming to dwindle. The woman's lips parted, the barest sigh soughed out. "You *don't* know," she said. "But we'll come at it another way. Lilith hates her God. Do you know that?"

"He told her to obey Adam."

Anna D made a chuffing sound, flicked her fingers open, dispersing nothing. "That for Adam. It was always about her God. She was created to be perfect, proud and intelligent, caring—why wouldn't she be all those things?—she was designed by a god, after all."

"You make her sound good," Sylvie said. "Not a demon."

"Lilith is as human as you, though considerably more long-lived," Anna D said. "She walked paradise and looked outside, at the other peoples, the ones her God meant to improve upon. They suffered fear, pain, death. Lilith asked why they should suffer, when she did not? Why were they forbidden the garden, when there was abundance within that never abated? She finally began to ask why God deserved her worship at all. What made Him worthy of devotion? What separated Him from the flock outside but a happenstance of power?

"She watched as he brought Eve into existence, the serpent, the tree. Soon after that, he punished them both, casting them out."

"Bluebeard," Sylvie murmured. "A planned punishment. An unfair test. Death."

"Lilith deciphered His plan. Eden was limited, even with his handmade followers. To that end, He sent Adam and Eve into exile, frightened, pathetic, hurting, so that their heartbroken, homesick wails could stir envy and longing in the hearts of other peoples. Stirring the desire to bow down, if only to earn a chance at the beautiful garden for themselves. After all, heaven is only a heaven in comparison to a hell.

"The more Lilith learned, the more she swore to depose Him. She created an army to storm his realm, an army she birthed herself. But her children were as earthbound as she, and so she turned to slaughtering men, in hopes of luring Him down to her level.

"Through every war she waged, every death she laid at His door, her God never responded, stayed remote and unconcerned with the world below. It drove her mad."

"She kidnapped Bran to get a god's power," Sylvie said. "To confront God in His own realm." She closed her eyes, finding a smile on her lips at the pure simplicity of the plan. If the mountain won't come to you—she almost wished Lilith well. Except, of course, it was Dunne's power, and Dunne's lover, her client and Sylvie's own life at risk.

"Such a god, too," Anna D said. "One whose powers could rally multitudes of other powers behind it. She plans well."

Justice? Sylvie thought, skeptical. Justice was a cold and abstract thing for most people, nothing to fire the blood.

"You sympathize," Anna D said. "You agree with her choice to make things right?"

"Right?" Sylvie said, "Right rarely involves burning people to death in a nightclub. Yes, I sympathize. But I will stop her."

"What cost are you willing to pay?" Anna D said, and waved a hand at the glass, her eyes distant, pupils narrowing.

Sylvie turned and blinked. Scrying without spell casting was an inborn talent, and didn't allow anyone but the talented to see—but the images rippled over the glass, visible even to her.

Sylvie's mother sat at a hotel desk, phone hunched between her shoulder and ear, one hand on her laptop keyboard, the other holding a cup of coffee, probably far from her first or last. Her father read at a table strewn with paper, red pen tucked between his fingers, sighing as he brought it into use. The usual vacation for them, in other words. Her sister crawled halfway out of the academy's restroom window to sneak a smoke without setting off the smoke detectors. Sylvie made a note: kick Zoe's butt when I get back.

Alex appeared in Sylvie's office, on the phone, spinning in the chair with a look of utter frustration on her face. She tossed the cell on the desk and jumped to her feet at some sound Sylvie couldn't hear. Alex had raided Sylvie's closet again, wore her 'Canes Windbreaker, and the gag belt buckle Zoe had given Sylvie, the fist-sized steel plate that spelled out *Sylvie* in rhinestone glitter. Sylvie wondered if Alex had ever gone home, or if she, like the loyal dog, intended to camp out and pine for her mistress.

The image blurred, swirling, as the silver warning bell gyrated in its bowl. Alex slumped into the seat then, and crumpled, not frustrated but scared, crying, and Sylvie wasn't there. . . .

The window glass cracked, spiderwebbing with impact and dispersing the vision. For a brief moment, the glass showed blowing sand, the jagged teeth of a broken pyramid. The small crystal ball, chipped now, fell to the carpet with a *thunk* and rolled back down the steps to Sylvie's feet. She picked it up again, barely remembering loosing it in the first place, though her shoulder ached with the force of her throw. "Don't bring my family into this."

Anna D gasped, sounding pained as if the crack of the

glass had found an echo in her bones. Anna D looked older suddenly, her bones etched clearly beneath tight skin.

"Your family is already a part of it. The Murderer's Child. Lilith loved once, loved a man who she believed had been manipulated and wronged. Cain, his name. Cain, the murderer. His line continues through you. Lilith is your ultimate dam, and you are the first one of her human children to be truly awake for centuries. Do you still think you know who you are?"

It blindsided Sylvie; the crystal left her hand again, dropped from numbed fingers.

"You can't trust yourself; Lilith is in your blood. Her strength keeps you from bowing before power, but it taints as much as it protects. All Lilith would have to do is call to you, and you'd join her—"

"No," Sylvie said, then more fiercely. "*No*. You've obviously never seen two alpha bitches meet. Why should I believe you? You're not even human. For all I know, you could be Lilith's hireling, meant to keep me distracted, meant to confuse me. You sure as hell don't like me. I can't see any reason on earth why you'd help me, and yet, here you sit, dispensing your wisdom with a cryptic hand. And really, you've told me nothing."

"I've told you *everything*."

"You've told me what *was*. I live in the present. I have to deal with the now. It's good to know who I face, but it'd be better to know *where* she is."

"You're right," Anna D said. "I don't like you. You're dangerous. But it could be worse. *You* could be worse, could become a dark creature to rival your dam. Do you want to travel that path?"

"I hate backtracking," Sylvie said flatly. "If I'm on a path, there's only one way to go, and that's forward. No matter where it takes me."

"Whoever said there are no branches?" Anna D said. "You're very near a fork in your path. Do not pass it by, unseeing."

"I think I liked it better when you were spitting insults," Sylvie said. "At least, that was sincere. New-age metaphors are not your thing."

Claws *shkk*ed out; the chair arms shredded beneath her tense fingers, and Anna D sighed, contemplating the foam stuffing beneath her nails. "I haven't lost my temper in years. Congratulations, Ms. Lightner."

"It's a talent," Sylvie said. "Apparently inborn." She turned and headed for the door. Enough was enough.

"Lilith's chosen future promises a bloody revolution that will damn generations to agony and pit god against god. Inhuman, I may be, and old with it, but there are those whose futures I would guard, those whom I love," Anna D said. Her voice was tired. "You seem to be the vanguard to stop it, much as it pains me. You, Ms. Lightner, are every mother's nightmare. To know that my son's future hinges on your actions—can you blame me for my concern? You are reckless when cornered. You trample others on your path. Worst of all, you are willfully blind to things that should be readily visible."

"You don't know when to quit," Sylvie said. "I almost felt sympathy for you—before you decided to go for the free-for-all into my flaws. Look, no one's dying today. Keep your son out of my way, and there's no problem. I don't put people between me and my enemies."

"Even when they volunteer?" Anna D looked up at her, her eyes summer-sand hot, blazing with fury. "You don't even recognize it. You truly believe my son dislikes you, distrusts you. Sometime you should ask him, what *wouldn't* he do for you. The answer might shock you. It should shame you."

Sylvie swallowed. Oh. Maybe she had been narrowsighted too long, to miss this one. Anna D's son wasn't just some stranger at risk in a changing world. Anna D's son was Michael Demalion. Sylvie walked back into the living room and took a seat, landing suddenly in a chair as her knees failed. "Demalion's your—"

"I thought it obvious," Anna D said.

"He's human."

"As was his father."

"He works for the ISI. He studies ways to drive things like you out of this world, or at least make them uncomfortable enough to move abroad. He . . . he doesn't know what you are." Sylvie studied the proud lines of the woman's face, the regal set of her neck, and laughed. "And you think I have denial issues."

"Your opinion is irrelevant." Anna D shifted in her seat.

Oh, Anna D regretted opening her mouth, Sylvie thought. She recognized the twitchiness, as if the discomfort were something physical that could be relieved. "What are you, anyway?" Sylvie asked.

What lies in desert sands
with a hiss?
Long-tailed,
smooth-shaled,
not a serpent,
yet deadly in her kiss?

Back to that again, Sylvie thought; to her surprise, the answer sprang up, unprompted, when she had expected Anna D to win this round. Maybe it was the sum of small things, piling up like a snowdrift, her mind working overtime to prove Anna D wrong. "Sphinx," she said. "You're the Sphinx." And still speaking in riddles, still testing men. Belatedly, she wondered what would have happened if she'd guessed wrong. Historically, death had been the result. A kiss? That was one way to describe having your head bitten off, she supposed.

Anna D nodded.

"Put those pieces together right, didn't I?" Sylvie rose. "You've told me everything about Lilith that you can, am I right? You don't know where she is."

"Lilith can veil herself, an inverse use of her self-will. As she makes herself charismatic, she can also make herself a will-o'-the-wisp."

"Just like school." Sylvie sighed. "All theory. No real-world application."

"You'll find your flippancy will mean nothing against her. You cannot win. The best you will do is delay her victory, prevent her from usurping the god's power."

"Sounds like defeat to me," Sylvie said. "You've accused me of missing or misinterpreting facts and decided I'll fail in my job. Let me tell you what you've misunderstood. Immortality is a *weakness*. There's nothing Lilith can want as fiercely as I can. She has all the time in the world, after all. If she loses now, there's always later, always a backup plan for another time. But humans know we only get a lifetime, a bare handful of years. So little time to redeem our mistakes—" She cut herself off, and shook her head, shook the thoughts away. She stood, rolled the little crystal ball back into its holder. "Never underestimate the will of a creature who begins to die at birth."

17

Back to the Basics

BACK OUTSIDE, SYLVIE PACED THE PARKING LOT, KICKING AT LOOSE landscaping gravel and bark chips. Her entire brain felt locked up, grinding between aggravation, fear, and yes— she'd cop to it, even if only in her own head—a little, treacherous pleasure when she thought of Demalion.

Still, the frustration, the thought that she should be doing something, anything, rolled pleasure under and drowned it as effortlessly as a riptide. To go through that interview and come out no further ahead was infuriating. So much so that she considered going back upstairs and taking it out on Anna D rather than the landscaping, but a faint glimmer of sense held her back. Anna D, sphinx, had *teeth*, and Sylvie still ached from fighting with Erinya.

As if on cue, all of her sundry pains sat up and cried for attention. From one breath to the next, Sylvie went from furious avenger to whimpering mortal. She staggered to the front steps and settled herself as gingerly as an old woman. Damn, she really thought at least one of her ribs was cracked.

What now? It was something to know who had snagged Bran and why, the confirmation of her theory that

Lily was after Dunne's power. Ultimately, that information did her little practical good.

Eventually, Lilith would have to deal with Dunne, if she wanted to trade Bran for power, though how she expected to accomplish that was a mystery Sylvie couldn't even begin to grasp. Unless, Sylvie shuddered, there wasn't going to be a trade, or even the lure of one. Maybe Bran was as good as dead. Maybe Dunne, weakened by grief and guilt, would make easy prey for a clever and willful immortal.

Sylvie wished she could think otherwise, but it seemed plausible. It wasn't like Lilith had any scruples about killing innocents. A nightclub turned crematorium proved that.

Sylvie had two real options as she saw it. Recover Bran herself or force Lilith to do it for her. Neither prospect pleased. Sylvie was no witch, had estranged the only one she trusted, and if a god couldn't force Lilith to obey Him, what chances did Sylvie have?

Tears stung her eyes, and she blinked them back. Weakness wouldn't accomplish anything. She needed a goal, even a little one.

Her cell phone chirped, a reminder that she had a message. She tugged it out of her pocket, frowning. Witch. She gestured rudely at the glass above and flipped the phone open. Three calls missed in the last hour. Maddening, since she hadn't shut it off. Guess Val wasn't the only witch to weave leave-me-alones into her house.

Sylvie tucked the phone up to her ear and listened. Alex had called first, and Sylvie flashed to the vision Anna D had shown her of Alex throwing down the phone.

Alex's voice tried for casual and failed. "You know how you said the satanists weren't magic? I think they got some real power. The bell went off, Syl. That curse went active. Call me! Tell me where to go. Val turned me down for sanctuary—you must really have hacked her off this time, Syl. Good riddance, anyway. She makes me nervous, and her mansion—bleah." Alex's panic faded under her familiar ranting about Val Cassavetes.

Sylvie grinned even through her worry. Yeah, a one-time juvenile delinquent, Alex never did make happies with the conspicuously consumptive. Still, Val had some nerve. It was one thing to turn on Sylvie, another to risk an innocent—where were her morals now?

"Look for me tonight," a woman said in the next message. Sylvie blinked. That was it? The voice wasn't familiar, and the number was blocked. Sylvie shrugged and went on.

Alex again, and more stressed. "I'm getting out of here. Hitting the hotels. Call me."

Sylvie hit memory, called Alex, and got nothing but her voice mail. "Hotels sound good, Alex," Sylvie said. "Stay tucked away. Stay safe. I hope you took my spare gun when you raided my closet. You know how to use it. Don't hesitate."

She swallowed hard. That wasn't going to make Alex relax any in her theory that Sylvie killed people, but Alex alive and horrified was a fair price to pay for Alex's safety.

She tucked the phone into the jacket and sighed. She really hadn't planned this day well. Coming to see Anna D left her stranded, no cab fare, no transit, and she felt itchy, fidgety, needing to move.

"Where's a hot-wiring Fury when you need her," Sylvie said, and sighed again, worry shifting. Erinya had been sullen and silent after Lilith's attack, slinking away as Sylvie approached Tish's, which, in retrospect, made little sense. Erinya knew Tish, and if Tish were willing to take in a perfect stranger, surely she would have accepted the Fury.

Sylvie wondered if maybe Erinya wasn't hurt more deeply than she'd let on. After all, Lilith had shown up soon after Sylvie had shot Erinya. Bullets followed up with balefire; even a Fury might hurt, and like an animal, might head for solitude to lick her wounds.

Pray, Dunne had said, and she would reach him. She wondered if transportation issues and a vague concern for one of his creatures was enough to rouse him from his troubles.

Approaching footsteps rounded the edge of the walk and faltered, probably at the sight of her. A dirty beggar at the gates of heaven. A conspicuous have-not at the doors of plenty. She'd be lucky if they didn't call the cops Of course, then she'd have a ride out of here. If the cops responded at all. If they weren't still absorbed in hunting Bran Wolf.

"What are you doing here?" he asked.

She raised her head, startled. "Demalion." He didn't sound angry, and Anna D's words were echoing in her ear. Apparently, he liked her. She licked her lips. "*Are* you selling information to Lil—"

"No," he said. "I'm not sure who is. It's different addresses every time. Like someone who doesn't belong is accessing any computer they can." He settled beside her on the stairs, giving the cement a quick glance to make sure his pristine suit would stay that way.

"Don't you all have passwords? Private terminals? Locked doors?"

"Temps, cleaning people, rookie agents, random politicians," Demalion said. "You didn't answer, though. What are you doing here?" he repeated.

"Suffering for all my sins," she said.

"Those sins include thinking I'd sell government information to a psychopath?"

"Yeah," she said.

"Forgiven," he said. "Go in peace, my child." He sketched a cross over her head, and she found herself smiling.

"You like to make the priests cry, don't you?" she said. "You were a bad altar boy. Drank the sacramental wine. Nibbled on the host when you got munchy."

"What, and bring shame on my mother? She's not much for religion but a big believer in manners. She lives here, you know," he said. It was a quiet explanation for his presence and a polite demand for hers.

"I know," she said. She watched his eyes darken. "She's a right bitch."

"After all you said about your family—you dragged mine into this?" He surged to his feet again, frustrated rage, and collapsed back against the stair railing. His mouth worked over things he couldn't get out.

"Huh," Sylvie said. "And rumor has it you don't hate me half so much as I thought."

"What did—"

"Give me a break. She was a source, Demalion, not a means for petty vengeance. I didn't know who she was until she told me."

"Hardly a *source*," he said. "She scries a little. A talent that she indulges just so she can decorate with shiny crystals. Who gave you her name?"

"Val Cassavetes. Anna D, she said. A local power. Capital P. It's way past time for someone to have a heart-to-heart with his mother." She grabbed his pant leg and pulled him back down beside her.

"Cassavetes," he said, tonelessly. He tugged the little crystal out of his pocket, rolling it, then stilled and stared down at it.

He knew Val, of course, knew her reputation, and right now, Sylvie thought, he was reassessing his own family history.

"Your family's occult," she said. "Deal with it."

"Easy for you to say." The crystal began its nervous migration over his fingers again.

"I just found out who my primogenitors are, and I'm not a happy camper, so don't expect sympathy." She stilled his hands with her own, enjoying the human warmth of them, nothing unearthly here, just human flesh and bone, no matter what his mother was. The crystals he carried, though, hinted otherwise. Maybe he had inherited some of Anna D's talents. Or maybe he just found crystals comforting, having grown up surrounded by them. She didn't have enough clues to guess. "What did Dunne do to you?"

"I thought you'd have figured it out by now," he said.

"God, the attitude runs in the family," she said. Then, as it crossed her mind, "Were you born with a tail?"

"What?"

"Ah, never mind," she said. "Keep your secrets."

"Dunne blinded me," Demalion said. The crystal shifted, dropped to the cement with a tiny *crack* as he turned his hands to clasp hers.

"You see me," she said. "You drove here." Even while she contradicted him, she was tabulating. He had talked about a third team spying on Dunne, spies who would never watch them again, a team of two field agents and a clairvoyant.

"As long as I'm not within five miles of Dunne, Wolf, or the things he considers his, I'm fine. The minute I overstep—" He swallowed hard. "It takes longer each time to come back," he said.

"Lovely," she said. "Perfect fate for a spy."

"I'm glad you admire his sense of irony. It makes it all so much easier to take." He detached his hands from hers and stood.

"Hey, Demalion," she said. "Where're you going?"

"Didn't you say I should have a talk with my mother?"

"Jesus, not *today*," Sylvie said. "She'd slaughter me for sure."

Demalion frowned but hesitated.

"So . . . I'm sorry for yelling at you earlier." If she'd thought she could manage it, she would have tried for a winsome smile. But tiredness made it an impossible effort.

"What do you want?" he asked. Noncommittal, still looking toward the condominium, still ruffled by her amusement at Dunne's justice.

"A ride," she said. "Suburbia's not my thing."

"Where to?"

"Haven't decided yet."

"Your hotel?"

"Cash-flow problems. Stayed with Tish last night. Not an option tonight."

"Fine," he said, held out his hand. She let him pull her up, wincing as her ribs shifted.

"Doctor?" he asked.

"Some strapping might be nice," she said. He slid an arm around her waist, and she let him, leaned her aching head on his shoulder. She wondered if his mother was watching from above, clawing at the walls. She tried not to smirk.

"You need to be more careful," he said, as they made their way across the lot to his car.

"I'm always careful."

"Yeah, in a way that would make a drunk stuntman blanch."

She pulled away from him, climbed into the car. "Just shut up and drive," she said, sinking into the passenger seat and sulking.

"It's a good thing I like you," he said.

"A very good thing," she agreed. After all, she was in no shape for another fight. She closed her eyes for a minute, then said, "You want to upgrade that detente of ours to a truce?"

"Depends. You going to run out on me again?"

"No," she said.

"Then very much," he said. "Not only for our sakes. I think this mess may take both of us. I think I've followed your path. Brandon Wolf was kidnapped to get to Dunne's power and immortality. And immortality's a powerful lure."

"Not for her," Sylvie said. "She's already immortal. Lilith, not Lily. The Lilith." *My blood kin . . .* That part she left unsaid; truce or no, there were some things she just wouldn't share with the ISI.

"Just the power, then," he said.

"Just," she agreed. "Don't you think Lilith would make a nice addition to the pantheons? Spreading balefire with a thought instead of a borrowed spell?"

"What's the plan?" he said.

Sylvie fidgeted. Trust Demalion to hit her weak spot. "See if we can find any other address for Lilith. See if Dunne will come check up on our progress. Maybe we can get him to hunt her."

"That's not much of a plan—"

"More 'n you have," Sylvie snapped. "I might be stalled for a moment, but that's ISI modus operandi."

He glanced away from the road, frowning. "Truce?"

"Mea culpa, just frustrated," Sylvie said. She shrank in her seat; they were just crossing back into the city proper, and the traffic was getting interesting. "Eyes on the road, blind man."

"So we're looking for her less likely hangouts, and continuing to watch the ones we know about," Demalion said. "The ISI could put out a bulletin, get the cops in on it."

"Most of the cops are either hunting Bran or dealing with the *Magicus Mundi*; the last thing they need is to be sent after a woman who throws balefire party favors around." She wasn't going to put people between herself and Lilith. She licked dry lips, said, "You know, you don't have to help me."

"I'm going to," he said.

"Fine," she said. *Take that, Anna D.* She'd tried. No one could say she hadn't.

Demalion pulled the car to a stop, and she followed him into his apartment building, workaholically close to the ISI base. She bit back a comment, at least until he opened the door to the tiny apartment and revealed piles of labeled cardboard boxes that showed clear signs of being lived out of. She looked at him again, all crisp and clean in his charcoal grey suit, and said, "Good call on getting the suits out first. Not like you'll ever want to eat on plates or anything."

"Hey," he said. "Hosting you, remember? Play nice."

"If I were nice," she said, "I'd offer to help unpack." She sat on the couch, admiring his forethought in keeping it, at least, clear of the clutter.

"I'm pretty sure my heart would stop," he said, dropping down at the other end of the couch with a woof of displaced air and dust.

"That better not be some oblique comment about my housekeeping skills, 'cause I'm not really in the mood to remember my apartment is on the ISI daily tour."

"Too tired to get mad?" he asked. "That's a first." He tugged out the little quartz globe, cracked now, and rolled it between his palms.

Sylvie pounced, grabbing for it. He jerked back, startled, and slid to evade her. She snarled one hand in his shirt, caught his wrist; they grappled for a moment until he fell from the couch. Sylvie grinned, crouched over him, crystal in her hand. "So, how does this thing work? And how often have you used it on me?"

"I haven't," he said. At her raised brow, he repeated himself. "I haven't." No excuses, no proof, just a statement. She was annoyed that she believed him.

"So, how *does* it work?" she said. "Do you need a new one, now that this one's chipped?"

"No," he said, relaxing from his cautious tension. He lay back, watched the crystal sparkle between her fingers. "It's only a focus. I'm clairvoyant. I see the images inside my head. It's not like real vision. It's color-reversed, or black and white. Sometimes it's blurry."

"Like satellite TV for the brain," she said. She dropped the crystal onto his stomach, rested her weight on his thighs. The crystal rolled with his breathing, and she put her fingers on it, pushing it along his rib cage, then chasing it down his belly and catching it in his navel. She pushed up his shirt to admire the gloss of glass against his warm skin, the way his flesh goose-bumped and shivered at her touch. "The talent's innate in you, and it never occurred to you to wonder why?"

"We have psychics on staff. They're human." There was unease in his voice. He rolled his head to the side, avoiding her gaze.

"Maybe they just think they are," she said. At the quick

wash of pain that crossed his face, she regretted saying it. After all, as far as her honed senses could tell, he read human. She opened her mouth to say so. "You really never wondered about your mother?"

He squirmed beneath her, and she answered for him. "You took her being human for granted. Like most of the normals out there who don't recognize the *Magicus Mundi* until it waves hello up close and personal." She rose and reseated herself beside him, braced comfortably between his hip and the low-fronted couch.

She poked the crystal into movement again. "Do you want to know what she is? What's lurking in your genes?"

"I'll ask her myself."

Sylvie studied the reflection of her fingertips in the glass and slid it between two ribs, using his tie as a net when the orb slipped away from her. He sucked in a breath. "Sylvie, not that this isn't . . . pleasant—what are you doing?"

"Do you think she's looking at you right now? Or when you're looking in the glass, does she look back? How do you manage to feel unwatched?"

"I try not to think about it," he said, breath catching as she pushed his shirt farther up to chase the rib all the way to his sternum, letting the orb slip and slither over his nipple. "We're talking about this now?" He licked his lips, laughed, but his eyes were wary. "I don't think this is the time to talk about my mother."

Sylvie said, "I don't think anytime is that time. I really didn't like her."

"I'm sure it was mutual."

"You say the sweetest things." She let the crystal roll away like a bead of water. She wanted to taste his skin, see if the crystal, like water, had left a trail. "But you're right. This is not the time." The ache in her chest told her that, the weariness in her bones, the brittle edge to her mood. She felt lazy now, but the rage still simmered, waiting to be woken to life again.

He leaned up, leaned close, and said, "Answer a question?"

She shrugged. "Maybe."

"What's up with the clothes? How bad did you piss off Cassavetes?"

She blinked at him, flashing back to six months on the run, learning that all the monsters of her childhood nightmares were real, before realizing he meant *Val*, not her dead husband. "Did cracking that crystal crack your head? What *about* the clothes? Yeah, they're kinda wrecked but—"

He tugged on the collar of Erinya's jacket, pushed it back, touched the lumpy seam of the inside-out T-shirt. "That jacket belongs to one of Dunne's bodyguards, the punk one. The T-shirt isn't yours either, unless you have some tastes the ISI isn't aware of, and is inside out, besides. The pants are cut for a man. Supernaturally speaking, you're running under a stealth shield."

"Like that would work," she said, then paused. "Would it?"

"Traditionally," he said. "I don't believe we've ever tested it."

"All talk," she said. "Here I thought the ISI was going to be a good resource for a moment. But no, you were picking my brain." She lifted herself off the floor just enough to slide herself onto the couch; the hard floor was beginning to create new aches. "Besides, maybe this *is* my T-shirt, and the ISI doesn't know all about me. Not all of us can have a formal sense of style, you know."

"Don't dis the suits," he said. "If you want fresh clothes, you'll be wearing pieces of them tomorrow."

Sylvie sighed. "This one's too small, this one's too large. I'm living in a Goldilocks world."

She eased herself up from her not-so-comfortable slouch, finding her ribs bothered her more now that she wasn't enjoying herself. "Aspirin?"

"Bathroom," he said. "There's Tylenol 4, Percocet, and

Vicodin." At her raised brow, he said, "The ISI believes in a fully stocked first-aid kit. Not so much in insurance benefits."

"Figures," she said. "Guess a bunch of people with unusual injuries all in the same insurance group might attract attention."

"I think that's their justification," Demalion said. "But it bites when you're getting stitched up by a student veterinarian in the backwoods who's freaking out about putting needle to nonfurry flesh."

"Life's tough all over." Sylvie wandered off to find the promised land of painkillers. Running her finger over the selection, she chose a handful of ibuprofen. Other painkillers might slow her down too much. She shucked the shirt, admired the bruises that had come up, stuck her tongue out at the dirt that had ground itself into her skin, and gave in. The world could wait while she showered. The hollow-eyed woman reflecting back at her agreed.

"Sylvie!" Demalion said. There was controlled panic in his voice, strong enough to bleed through a shut door.

Maybe not.

Sylvie pulled her shirt back on, and went out, gun in hand, though she doubted it was needed urgently. She might not trust Demalion all the way from heart to head, but he wouldn't call her out to face a deadly foe with only that bare warning.

She found him standing in his kitchenette, bent over the counter as if he'd been injured, one hand compressing a Chinese take-out container, the other white-tensed against the laminate.

"Sylvie?" he said, turning, seeming oddly off balance, as if the world had shifted beneath his feet. As if he'd suddenly been deprived of a sense.

"Blind?" she asked. She didn't need confirmation; the way he jerked and tracked her voice was enough.

"My crystal?"

"All right," she said, and went to fetch it. "I thought this only happened when you spied on them."

"At first I did, too. I mean, that's what we were doing when it all blew up in our faces. Sylvie . . ."

"I'm hurrying," she said.

"Lilith was there," he said. "It must have been her. A dark, angry force, watching us, watching them. We knew there was something else, but we never saw it. Just felt it."

"You'd know it again?" she asked, casting her gaze about the floor. Amazing how something so shiny-glossy could become invisible when you wanted it. She knelt, set her gun on the nearest cardboard box, and peered beneath the sofa. There it was. Sylvie forced her hand under the couch, stretching. "You said, at first? What's blinding you now?"

"It's nearness to something Dunne considers his. His lover, his house, his car. Took me a week to learn where Dunne parked and avoid passing by that garage."

So was this Dunne on the move? Coming back to check in at long last? Sylvie doubted life would be that easy.

Sylvie closed her fingers over the glass, scraping her arm against the sofa frame, and wincing.

"Hurry, Sylvie," Demalion said.

"What?" she said. She found herself in a crouch, waiting, gun in hand.

"It's getting closer. It's like pressure in my head." He cocked his head, listening to something inside it, and she tensed.

"Demalion, incoming, twelve o'clock," she said, and chucked the crystal at him. His hand closed on it as she bolted for the door. Even if it were Dunne, he and the ISI weren't a good combination.

"Sylvie," Demalion called, but she was already gone. She took the first flight of stairs down at a near gallop but drew up short with the agonizing pinch of ribs grating. She took the second flight more gingerly, slow enough, dammit, that Demalion, even blind, had found the elevator and caught up.

"Go back," she snapped. "Or at least, stay *put*."

Through the lobby glass, the night sky seethed with sheets of color. The aurora borealis ran loose in the streets of Chicago like the risen tide, a shimmer of blue and gold and deepest purples that made her scalp tingle. It parted the air with the sound of distant bells.

The hairs on the back of her neck stood up, a prickling warning. She didn't think this was Dunne's work, despite Demalion's blindness. Dunne was all storm cloud behind his eyes, leashed thunder, and this gaudy display—

A figure breached the stream, like a drowning victim making one last flailing attempt at breath and air and life. There was a flash of teeth, a choked-off growling, then the tide crashed down on her again, dragging her under as inexorably as a riptide.

"What is it?" Demalion asked. The light reflected off the shiny silver of his eyes, got caught in dancing sparks in his crystal.

"A god," Sylvie said. "It's eating Erinya."

"Dunne's bodyguard—"

Sylvie nodded. The gun was a weight in her hand, but Sylvie knew when a gun was outclassed. Even a magical one. She gritted her teeth; she wanted Erinya out of the lethal tide. For all she knew, Erinya had the linchpin piece of information Sylvie would need to save Bran.

A breath of superchilled air touched her, dropping down fast like ice water. She went from cold-scared to cold-frozen in half a moment. The icy air brought the scent of salt with it, the tang of a winter sea, and as it hit the sidewalk, the asphalt, and buildings heated by the day's sun, small tornadoes formed, wisping upward, taking glass in its wake, taking small stones, then bigger ones.

Sylvie drew back into the doorway of the apartment building, pushing Demalion ahead of her.

"Amazing," he said. A breath hidden in the howl of wind.

"What do you see?" she asked.

"A man's hand pulling a woman's long hair," he said,

staring at his crystal, "pulling her away, and an animal tangled in the hair."

The aurora swept upward, spiraling as it went, twisted into the storm, leaving a shape hunched and growling, on buckled tarmac.

Sylvie kept her gun out and cautiously approached. The Fury's head snapped up, teeth bared, eyes full of phosphorescent heat. Her short, punk bob stood out as stiffly as a porcupine's quills.

"Erinya," Sylvie said. "Eri." The Fury let her hackles settle.

"Is the attack done?" First thing first. If the gods were going to start brawling again, she wanted to be elsewhere.

"Not an attack," Erinya muttered, breathy gasps of explanation. "Just a squabble. Hera took a chance. Kevin found out."

Demalion followed Sylvie into the street, and Erinya's calm disappeared. Her eyes went hollow and dark, bloody gaps beneath tangled lashes. "Why are you with him?" she growled. "Traitor—"

She eased to a low crouch, veering between shapes, and Sylvie said, "Don't start a fight, Eri. You're beat. Demalion's going to help us."

"I'll kill him—"

"You'll have to heal first," Sylvie said. She holstered the gun and crossed to Erinya's side, ready to help though her ribs winced at the thought. Erinya got to her feet, unaided, slunk after them into the elevator.

In the light, Sylvie grimaced. Erinya looked worse for wear, and nothing much of human. If Sylvie were grading on human disguises, Erinya would get a C minus. And that was on a curve. The Fury had always looked lanky; now she looked like a puppet about to come apart at the joints.

"It's all his fault," Erinya said, and the petulant little-girl whine did nothing to belie the menace in her presence. "He doesn't want to help."

Demalion, wisely, stayed silent, though he turned a betrayed look on Sylvie when she said, "You don't trust him? Go on, then. Look for yourself; read him. Judge his sincerity."

It was a risk, but one Sylvie found worth taking. If Demalion couldn't be trusted, better to know now, and if he was found wanting—Sylvie wouldn't have to do anything about it. Not with Erinya's shape rippling through cloudy spikes of scale and claw.

"Don't feel like it," Erinya said. She didn't check; Demalion, still standing mutely before her, hand raised with his crystal "eye," was proof enough of that. Sylvie remembered the rigor tension of the girl in the bar, her own collapse in Miami. Being read took something from you.

The elevator dinged open, and Erinya slumped with the jolt. Sylvie reached out, wrapping an arm around the Fury's waist. Pins and needles, a shocking cold/heat confusion, and nerves firing in overload—Sylvie nearly jerked away. Demalion reached out and steadied her, fumbling only a little.

Together they manhandled the quietly growling Fury to his apartment, with only one gaping eyewitness.

Sylvie just shook her head. Normally, she'd worry about it, but with all that was going on in the city? A single, bleeding, mythological monster wasn't much of a secret.

They dropped Erinya on the couch, Demalion fidgeting, the crystal going hand to hand, until Sylvie stopped it with her own. "You should go elsewhere," she suggested. "Erinya's presence is causing the blindness."

"It's my apartment," he said. "End of discussion."

"At least go into the bedroom, shut the door." Like that would even slow the Fury down if she lost it. Sylvie wasn't going to endanger Demalion; wasn't that what she had told Anna D?

"No," he said. "I'll be watching." He tapped the crystal meaningfully.

"Fine," Sylvie said. "We'll be getting cleaned up in the bathroom. Eri—you ever had oxycodone?"

18

Playing Doctor

"I'LL HEAL," ERINYA SAID. "DON'T NEED YOUR HELP."

Sylvie stared at the strange, smoky stain leaking through the Fury's skin and mesh shirt, staining Demalion's pale couch. "Then get up," she said.

Erinya raised herself a bit, fell back panting. Sylvie helped her up, ignoring the growl. Hell, Eri's growl was becoming an almost familiar sound track to her life.

"Before we get cozy patching you up, is Hera gonna come back for you?"

"No."

Demalion made a quiet scoffing sound. Sylvie was on the same page. Nothing was so untrustworthy as a flat denial.

She asked again. Erinya snarled, made a sudden sharp whine as she stumbled over one of Demalion's boxes, and nearly fell.

Sylvie got closer, put an arm around her waist again, and was bombarded once more by the sensation she'd just grabbed hold of a live wire. She gritted her teeth. *Bran* lived with the Furies, and he was human; he could stand their touch. Loved a god, and invited him into his bed. Sylvie could walk a Fury to the bathroom and the first-aid kit.

"As long as I'm not trying to get to Kevin, they don't care," Erinya said. "You told me to tell him about Lily. I haven't been able to."

"I thought Hera lost power. You couldn't beat her?"

"She made me," Erinya said. "I can't raise my hand to her. But she could destroy us at will. Once. Now, she can only hamper."

"Some hampering," Sylvie said. "You look half-dead."

Erinya growled beneath her shaking hands. Supporting the Fury was not doing Sylvie's ribs any good; the Fury was surprisingly heavy, as if magic weighed more densely than flesh and bone.

"First aid and triage, coming right up," Sylvie said. "Get out of the way, Demalion."

"She's a monster," Demalion said. He leaned up against the wall to the tiny bathroom, his blind eyes disapproving.

"So don't watch," Sylvie said, and with a last grunt of effort, dragged Erinya around Demalion and into the bathroom. She kicked the door shut in Demalion's face and sank to the floor, Erinya landing atop her. "Ow, ow, ow," Sylvie said, and pretended that was release enough from the pain, that the tears on her face were from exertion, not hurt.

Erinya nuzzled her throat, and Sylvie managed to still her instinctive reaction to jerk away. If she torqued her ribs once more today, she'd probably faint. If she passed out, the Fury might eat her; right now, Erinya had the teeth for it, curving needles the color of ancient ivory. Bony stubs protruded from her shoulder joints, flared back and ended abruptly, like stripped bat wings, broken off.

"You smell like that old cat," Erinya complained. "That's where you were? Hidden beneath her time? Smothered in her memories of sand?"

Old cat, Sylvie thought, mind dragging away from pain

into rational thought. Old cat. Anna D. "How old is she?" Irrelevant really, to everything else, but—she cast a furtive glance at the closed door, at the man behind it—she wanted to know.

"Forever," Erinya said. "The only one. The oldest thing ever."

The oldest thing—well then, maybe, Sylvie would allow that Anna D might know what she was talking about. Maybe. Still didn't excuse playing games with the information.

Sylvie knelt up with a wince and reached for the first-aid kit. She scored another Advil or two for herself and dry-swallowed, then pulled out gauze, sutures, the curved needle.

"Take off your shirt," Sylvie said. Erinya grinned wolfishly, and the spiderwebbed, torn mesh of her shirt began to sink into her skin, first, like dark veins moving beneath pale flesh, then like a shadow sinking into deep water, vanishing.

"That'll work," Sylvie said, and tried not to wonder about the jacket she had borrowed. Surely the Fury wouldn't have let her wander off with a chunk of her skin? No, Erinya had said Bran had bought it for her.

Sylvie shook the thoughts away and stopped her hands from trembling. Erinya seemed minded to allow her to play doctor; still, best not flaunt an unsteady hand.

The wound was worse than she had thought—the mesh of the not-shirt had tangled shadows over it, disguising its depth, its breadth. A raw slash ran from just above Eri's hipbone, across her muscled belly, up under her scant breast, going deeper. Sylvie put her hand out and leaned Erinya forward, looking at her back. Exit wound there, a triangular tear where the spine should be.

"Spear?" Sylvie asked.

"She was pushing me all over this city," Erinya said. "Wrought-iron fence."

They bled, for lack of a better word, but nothing so ordinary as blood. Sylvie touched the wound with a cautious hand, drew the loose flap of skin upward. Dark fluid leaked over her fingertips like ether, cold, slippery, not quite weighty, and drizzled up her palm. It was like the ghost of blood, and her hand buzzed and shook with the touch. *Inhuman,* Sylvie thought again. On the surface and within.

Sylvie's mouth dried. The skin, pulled away from the wound, revealed nothing human at all beneath. There should have been outraged tissue, carmine and gory, the creamy slick shine of exposed bone, the smell strong and foul. If Erinya had been human, the makeshift spear would have shish kebabbed the lung, liver, stomach, and severed the spinal column.

Erinya wasn't human, and there was nothing within her flesh but the roiling ghostly blood.

"You healed fast enough when I shot you," Sylvie said, and didn't Erinya bridle at that reminder.

"It's bigger than a bullet hole," Erinya said. "And I'm . . . tired. But I'd heal, even without your help." She cupped her hand beneath the thickest stream; the blood stained her hand, then faded inward like the shirt had done, reclaimed by her body.

"Such gratitude," Sylvie said. It wasn't blood; it was power. The core that *was* Erinya. The soul her shell was meant to contain. Soul, blood, power; for a creature like the Fury, it was all the same.

Sylvie threaded the needle, trying not to broadcast that her skills were all theory, no practice. She put the first stitch in; Erinya didn't bother to flinch. What every med school needed, Sylvie thought, feeling a little light-headed, a practice dummy that bled but didn't feel.

The soul-blood clung to Sylvie's fingers, trickled upward, and coated her palms and wrists like rising smoke; she reached a point where the shaking of her hands could grow no worse, then she was done.

"Turn around," she whispered. Erinya twisted front to back, baring the smaller wound.

"You're pale," Sylvie said, touching the white-mottled skin, the color of a blanched corpse. "Is it shock? Can you suffer—"

"No," Erinya said. "Finish."

Sylvie dragged the needle back to work. She ran her fingers along the ridged line of blue thread, testing for leakage, for wisps of ethereal blood and power. Erinya sighed, and her skin grew dark, glossy. A new shirt appeared out of flesh—this time, a scaled, leather tunic, more warlike than fashion-goth.

"If you shift shape, will the stitches—"

Erinya knocked her over in a single fluid movement. Sylvie's back impacted against the tub, sparking white-hot pain and driving the breath from her lungs in a pained yelp.

Even before the black spots could clear from her vision, she grated out, "I kicked your ass when you *weren't* injured. Do you really want a rematch—" Her bluff broke off in a gasp as Erinya licked a long swath across her defensively raised hand. Hot, damp heat licked around her wrist, diving into her palm, and sucked her first two fingers into the Fury's mouth.

"Sylvie?" Demalion asked. "Are you all right?" The doorknob rattled and Erinya spun a leg out and kicked the door shut again.

"Mine. Taking it back," Erinya growled through another mouthful of Sylvie's flesh.

Taking it back? Oh. Sylvie relaxed. This wasn't hostility, it was cleanup; Erinya was reabsorbing that spilled power, the smoky blood that stained Sylvie's hands.

"Okay," Sylvie said. Response enough for both of them, and all her brain could cope with at the moment.

Erinya chased the spilled power up Sylvie's wrist, and her eyes gleamed at Sylvie's hammering pulse. "I scared you."

"Not even close," Sylvie said. Never show weakness.

"Breathless," Erinya said.

"Pain," Sylvie said. "Broken ribs. Mishandled. Next time, ask."

"Next time?" Erinya said, and grinned as she licked a section of skin that was completely bare of blood, a section that had never had blood on it—the tender juncture of Sylvie's elbow. Erinya nipped at it, a tiny pinch of needle-sharp teeth that sent shock waves through Sylvie's nerves. "Would you say yes?" Suddenly, this wasn't about spilled power anymore, but something far more intimate.

"No," Sylvie said. She'd played rough-and-tumble with a monster before. She didn't repeat her mistakes. Sylvie tugged her arm away; Erinya let it go.

"I like you. You're savage. Like me."

Sylvie looked at Erinya's shape, human-shaped, but not human at all, remembered the emptiness inside— Erinya was a shell, no more. At her core, all she was was hunger.

"Not in the mood," Sylvie said. "Broken ribs, remember?"

Erinya's predatory look became something thoughtful. She shuffled closer and tore Sylvie's shirt open.

"I said no, Erinya."

Erinya eyed the red scraps of T-shirt clinging to Sylvie's skin, and pushed them off.

"Ribs," Erinya said. She touched the bruised area with a surprisingly cautious hand. "I kill people. I trap them in the certainty of their guilt. I rip them apart with claws and teeth, because I crave the struggle. But"—she put a finger to Sylvie's mouth—"I can kill with a thought. Crumble bone to dust, boil blood, liquefy minds."

Sylvie's attention never wavered. Erinya's fingers dropped back down, traced the contours of the swollen ribs, and she said, "It's just reversal. How hard can it be?"

"What?" Sylvie asked. Then her body jerked as pain lanced through her, a scorching supple line that zoomed up her spine, and slid out along her rib cage, winding, compressing, burning the air from her lungs like a python. She gasped, and Erinya smiled.

"It's not so different," Erinya said. She leaned back and licked her lips. "Feels good on this end."

"Fuck you," Sylvie said, when her breath returned. She pushed Erinya back and scrambled to her feet. Her hand was on the doorknob when she realized none of the movements had hurt.

Erinya stretched tall, the sudden force of her presence looming in the small room, and Sylvie said, "You fixed my ribs?"

"Cure, kill, not so different," she repeated. Erinya reached out, stroked a talon over the raw burn that snaked up Sylvie's arm. The flesh sealed tight, scabbed over, then scarred in a matter of seconds. This time the pain was distant. Erinya shrugged, "Killing's better."

"Yeah," Sylvie said. "Now that's cleared up, and you're reaffirmed in your career choice, let me ask you this. You couldn't get to Dunne."

"Said so," Erinya said.

"We have to find a way," Sylvie said. "Things have changed. Lily's not . . . She's human, but only barely. She's Lilith."

Erinya cocked her head. "The deserter from Eden?"

"Yeah; we're not facing a mortal. She's lived this long, and she's learned a lot along the way."

Erinya shrugged. "Kevin will reach for you if I don't come back. He'll find you."

"When? When he's done getting Zeus off his back? I don't think we have that kind of time."

"Kevin's smart," Erinya said. "He'll think of something." She yawned hugely, all lion-teeth and curling predator's tongue, and stretched out on the bathroom tiles. Her eyes closed.

"Not if he's sucked into heavenly infighting," Sylvie said. "This is serious, Eri. Lilith's planning to take his power."

Erinya chuffed. She didn't even open her eyes. "She can't claw her way to Olympus, and she can't catch him on the fly. Kevin's safe from her."

"Bran's not," Sylvie said. Erinya started paying attention again. "If we can tell Dunne about Lilith—well, he can't find Bran, but he might have a shot at Lilith."

"Maybe," Erinya said. "I saw Lilith and didn't recognize her as immortal. She's slippery. Tracking her will be like—"

"Tracking a snake through a rock pile," Sylvie said. "It's always one rock away from the one you've just lifted."

"Yes," Erinya said. She yawned. "'m going home. I'll watch for a chance to get to Kevin."

Erinya vanished, and Sylvie blinked. *Guess she's feeling better.* "Demalion? You can see again?"

"Cloudy, but clearing," he said. "She gone? You all right?"

"Yeah," Sylvie said. He opened the door, and Sylvie tugged the largest scrap of T-shirt up to play propriety.

"What is she? Besides Dunne's bodyguard. We knew they weren't human. Labeled them chimeras of some kind."

"Right language, wrong beast. She's a Fury, one of three. Sad to say, probably the most sane one—though admittedly, I don't know Magdala at all. Still, you just can't trust someone who wears J. Crew as a fashion choice."

"Furies? The Furies. And you had to help her." Demalion fell back against the door.

"Hey, worked out all right. Just like in the stories. I aided a mythical creature—I got a favor."

"I don't like this, Sylvie."

"And I do? Get out, let me shower in peace."

"You're worried about a blind man scoping you out?" he said.

She looked into his dark eyes; only a faint hint of luminosity lingered as the curse faded. "Yeah, go play with your crystals, blind man." He laughed, but left.

Sylvie climbed into the shower with one thought in her mind. *Finally.* She ran the water hot, admired the water pressure, and sank into the cascade with a moan. She closed her eyes and something red and sinuous snaked across her mind's eye, like a rapid ripple of blood. She twitched awake.

She scrubbed shampoo into her hair, squeaked it out until there were no leftover traces of char or blood, nothing but the dark fragrance of sandalwood. Cooler water slithered down her back, and she shuddered, repulsed by the feel, and gave up on lingering in the shower.

She stepped out, found Demalion had been back in; her clothes were gone and a clean pile of cotton beckoned from beside the sink. White, she thought, as she shrugged into the dress shirt. He really needed color in his life. A pair of boxer shorts, still in plastic, and Sylvie thought, boring, but put them on. Slim-hipped Demalion liked pale blue. Not even basic plaid.

"I need pants," she said, coming out into the apartment. "I need—"

"To rest," he said. "Get some food, some sleep. Start fresh in the morning. The world's holding. It'll hold 'til morning."

Anxiety churned in her stomach; morning was too late, she thought, but didn't know why. She shook her head, wordless but still defiant. He took her shoulders, and said, "Sylvie—please." He turned her toward the table, to food set out, and she sat down.

She lifted a forkful of rice noodles, watched them pour off the fork like something alive, and shivered. "Can I use your laptop?"

"Yeah," he said.

She gratefully pushed the coiled nest of noodles away, called up e-mail, and looked for Alex's username online. This hour most nights, the girl was online.

Nothing, but there was an e-mail from her. Sylvie opened it. "Look at this," she said, turned the laptop so he could see it. It was a list of businesses in Chicago that Alex thought Lilith might be associated with.

Demalion stopped chewing for a moment and scrolled

through the information. "This will save us some time. You hire her out?"

"Get your own," Sylvie said. "Alex is mine, all mine."

"Can I—" He forwarded the information to himself, then on to the ISI, while Sylvie watched. High-handed, she thought, but right now it was simpler just to let Demalion have the info.

"This'll help. I'll start them looking, then the night won't be a waste, even if you sleep right through it."

Sylvie bit her lip. She was exhausted. But something nagged at her, raised the hair on her nape, left her coldly zero at the bone. She'd never sleep feeling like this, tangled in anxiety and stress. She put her head down on her arms; her hair, mostly damp, snaked down her neck and left wet trails on the paper napkins. She shut her eyes, and drifted, listening to the distant susurrus in her head.

"There you ar—"

Sylvie jerked awake as Demalion said, "Up you go," and his hands came down on her shoulders like brands. She spun to face him, hand sliding behind her back, but the gun was—

"Easy," he said. "Sorry, I didn't realize you were sleeping."

"Wasn't," she said, looking around. Where in hell had she put it—

Careless, the dark voice said. Insanely so, she agreed. She should know where her gun was. At all times.

"Okay," he said agreeably. It made her edgy—but suddenly everything was making her edgy—the shadows undulating along the walls, the laptop's hissing drone, her discarded meal.

"Gun's on the couch," he said. "If that's what you're looking for."

"Isn't," she said. Knowing where it was eased some of the dread from her stomach.

"Contrary," he said.

"Am not," she said, and found a small smile for him.

"Remind me not to wake you suddenly again," he said. "Slow and easy, some coffee, maybe croissants . . ."

Her smile wavered. He took a step closer. "If I give you my bed, are you going to make me sleep on the couch? It's not as comfortable as it looks."

"We're adults," Sylvie said, thinking, *This could work.* Something to keep the anxiety at bay, something to warm that chill from her belly. "Surely we can behave like adults."

He took another step, reached out, and tugged the button placket of his dress shirt, hers now. His fingers were dark against the pale fabric, and it drew her attention like a magnet. "But what kind of adults?"

"I don't follow," she said. Who could blame her, with that single fingertip leaving the top of the shirt and trading cotton for skin. He snaked his fingers down to where the buttons fastened, popped the first one open, and chased the new path.

"Civilized adults," he said. "Professional, how're you, nice weather we're having, job well done or—"

"Or," she echoed, prolonging the tease. Enjoying it.

"Consenting adults," he said, "Friendly, postwork drinks, a little dancing, low lights, a lot less clothing."

"Hmm," she murmured. She closed her eyes, the better to feel that single, moving point of contact. "Oh, consenting all the way," she said, and was gratified by the wash of heat in his eyes. She kissed him, and when his lips parted against hers, she licked into him, tasting coffee, tasting spice.

Yes, she thought, now she could do this. Now, she could trust him not to use this against her, trust him not to inform the ISI. After all, now she knew something, too—something the ISI would love to know. Anna D wasn't human.

She folded her fingers into his hair as he bent to taste her throat. That quick ripple of red crawled behind her eyelids again, too quick to really catch, but she stiffened, nerves firing, then lost that tension in a more pleasant one that coiled low in her stomach. Demalion's hands, inside the shirt now, slipped it off her shoulders.

Stepping back, she let it fall, a white drift in the room, like the slow fade and flare of a buckshot angel's wing. She put that thought back where it belonged, locked its door tight. The borrowed boxers came off with no association at all save anticipation.

She dragged his mouth back to hers, nipped at his lower lip, and he said, "Bedroom," on a breath.

She followed him into the dimly lit room, her eyes on the sleek line of his back, the curve of his butt in dress slacks. She might get to like suits after all.

He dropped his slacks, sprawled across sheets the color of goldenrod, and Sylvie's thoughts devolved into one simple *Yum*.

"Sylvie," he said, drawing her down, his skin animal warm against hers, the raw rough silk of his hair between her clutching fingers again. She slid against him, rubbing, caressing, and his heartbeat rushed into her ear, racing hers, her name whispered on every outborne breath, a sibilant snake hiss of pleasure. "Shadows, Shadows, Shadows."

She seized his hands, dragged them from her body, pinned them above his head, and shuddered at the sight. Black hair, yellow sheets, and her nails, oddly rust red and shiny—some of the Fury's power staining them still. She turned her gaze away, caught her own shadow on the wall, hair wet-snarled and wavy, alive with her movements, like Medusa's mane. Back to the bed, his hair, the sheets, her nails. Red touch yellow touch—

"Turn out the light," she said. "Put it *out*." The three colors—red, yellow, black—pulsed in her vision like the beginnings of a migraine.

"Let go, and I will," he said, licking his lips.

She slid back, skin rubbing skin, eliciting a pleased groan from both of them. He fumbled over and snapped off the lamp.

"Condom?" she asked. His mouth sealed to hers for a brief moment, then pulled away.

"Foreplay?" he asked.

"Who wants to wait that long?"

He flicked the light back on—red-enamel, yellow light, the dark sweep of his hair—and fished a foiled square from his nightstand. She took it from him, unrolled it over him, stroked it down with her fingertips, loving the way he strained into her touch. Then she turned out the lamp once again.

She fitted herself to him, and slid down, gasping at the slow, sweet breach; his hands clutched her hips, her thighs protested the incremental pace, and she let herself fall. She rode him, muscles tensing, flexing, her breath coming faster—she lost the rhythm when the streetlamps flickered, sulfur colored, drifting through his blinds, reaching snaky fingers out toward the red-glowing LED of his clock.

His hands tightened on her hips, nails dragging against her skin, drawing her attention back to the juncture of heat between them, that heartbeat pulse between them, their ragged breath. He pressed upward, and she let her head fall back, eyes fall closed. So good; his fingers tracing flesh, a hand wrapping about her arm, and the slow sweep of his tongue licking the bullet scar, making it as glossy as a newly molted snake . . .

She jerked; he groaned; the anxiety took on a fever pitch within her. The streetlamp kept creeping, licking at the red numbers, *red touch yellow*, her head chanted to their rhythm, to his stroking hands, getting frantic, *red touch yellow*, and he leaned up all at once, wrapping about her, his black shadow falling like a bar between the LED and the streetlights, and Sylvie shuddered once, twice, and came on a crest of relief and pleasure. *Red touch black. It's okay*—

He pulsed within her, groaning, and she stroked his back, watching the walls, the shadows undulating in the streetlight, hearing the hiss of cars passing by on rainy streets. Demalion slid back down to the sheets, and said, after a moment, "So where was I in all that?"

Sylvie swallowed, her throat dry from panting. "Yeah, sorry. A little distracted about saving the world, here. But you seemed to enjoy yourself."

Demalion slid her off him, tugged the sheets up to cover damp skin. "I'm easy. This time."

Sylvie sat up, coiled her legs beneath her, stared at the sheets, at the hidden depths beneath. "You hear snakes hissing?"

Demalion laughed. "Sylvie, Freud would have a field day."

"Shut up," she said, and slapped his shoulder. "I'm serious." She crawled out of the bed, checking beneath the bedframe, peering into the closets. "You don't hear that?" The slither of scale seemed as evident as the air conditioner's rattle and hum. She grabbed her shirt from the floor, shook it out, and put it on. "Where are my shoes?"

"In the other room," Demalion said. The amusement left his eyes. He grabbed her hands, stopped her restless movement. "Sylvie, you need to—"

"Let go," she said, nerves jangling. She needed her hands free.

"You're hallucinating," he said. "You've got to calm—"

"Don't tell me what to do," she said.

He growled. "Why the hell not? You've been slinging orders all day. Maybe it's my turn."

"News flash," she said, snatching up the discarded boxers and yanking them on. "I'm not one of your ISI flunkies, and one round in the sheets doesn't mean you're in charge."

"Goddammit, Sylvie. . . ."

She studied his face, watching for intent. Movement to her left, and she sidled away from what turned out to be a lamp cord running along the wall.

He ran his hands through his hair, much as she had done, and it seemed to ease his temper. "You think we'll ever stop fighting?"

"You're the clairvoyant," Sylvie said. She sank back down beside him, into his warmth.

He rubbed her back, kissed the nape of her neck.

"You really don't hear anything?"

To his credit, he paused, head cocked, listening. "No," he said. "Not a thing. How long have you been awake now?"

"I slept," she said. Curled next to Tish, smelling of charred flesh, and drowning in dreams of flame.

"But not well," he said. He stroked a tendril of hair back from her face.

"Comes with the territory," she said. She closed her eyes, felt the exhaustion lurking, that snake-flash of movement again, and a sudden, silent blue sky. She twitched awake. *Gun,* she thought, and slipped out of Demalion's grasp to get it.

He sat up and watched her, professional wariness on his face. *Wondering how many monsters came through his door today,* her dark voice said. Wondering if Erinya was only the obvious one.

Sylvie stepped into the dark living room, shied as something cool, muscular, and slick slithered past her ankle. She slapped on the light, and there was nothing there. Didn't keep her heart from racing. Maybe Demalion was right, she thought. Maybe she was sleep-deprived, hallucinating, delusional.

She looked back; he patted the sheets, and they looked warm, inviting, safe.

Faint hissing, the scent of must and mice—Sylvie backed toward the couch, collected her gun with one hand, and tucked herself into the cushions, sweeping the room with her gaze.

"Sylvie?" Demalion padded into the room, bare all over, and she tore her eyes away.

"I'll take first watch," she said. She spotted her sneakers, set down the gun long enough to drag them onto her feet, and curled up against the couch's arm again, gun in hand. "It's just midnight. I'll wake you in—"

"The door's locked. The alarm's on. The apartment's secure. Come back to bed, Sylvie."

"There are things out there that scoff at locks," Sylvie said. "You know it. I've seen it. Never let your guard down."

"You need sleep," he said.

"Sleep when you're dead," Sylvie said. She stared hard at the crack beneath the apartment door, at the pale line of light seeping through from the hallway beyond. Anything that crept through there would be seen. She needed to worry about the less overt entry points.

"What will it help anyone if you're too tired to think straight?" He shook his head and closed the bedroom door behind him.

It was the ISI, she thought, that weakened him, made him rely on external safety precautions, like alarms, like backup and calls for help being answered. A bureaucrat's world. He didn't understand the dangers here, not down deep in the bone the way she did.

Sleep? No, she couldn't risk it. Not when her nerves felt as shaken as a rattlesnake's tail. But she didn't need all of herself to keep watch. Only her senses, the gun in her hand, like an animal lying in wait. Her world degenerated into fragments. Sit still, shift in the darkness, aim the gun, assess. Relax. Repeat.

The shadows gave way all at once to daylight, a blue sky washing her dreamscape, and she jerked awake. Even she had limits. Three in the morning, and she couldn't stay awake another minute. She ghosted toward the bedroom; Demalion slept through the faint creak of the door opening, through her path to the bed. He roused when she touched his shoulder, coming awake with an alacrity that pleased her.

"Your turn," she said, gesturing to the living room.

"What am I guarding against?" he asked. His voice was delicious with sleep, a low rumble in his chest. She wanted to shuck off the clothes, drop the gun, crawl into his arms, and listen to his voice from up close. She didn't.

"Anything," she said.

"Something," he corrected. "You're afraid of something specific."

"Snakes," she said. "I see them, hear them. They're not there. Not yet. Maybe it's some warning."

She waited for him to give her grief, to play the paranoia card, the exhaustion, the hallucinations; instead, he touched her cheek and slid out of bed.

"Put the gun on the nightstand, huh?" he said. "Not beneath the pillow. Be stupid to shoot yourself by accident."

He stood over her until she laid it down, the soft *thunk* of it leaving her hand, and kissed her hair, still shower-matted and sex-tangled. "Go to sleep, Sylvie."

The bed beckoned; she slid into his warm spot and nearly moaned at how good it felt, the smooth cotton, the lazy heat lingering, and his scent, sandalwood and lime, steeped in it. Sleep dragged her down like a sinkhole opening beneath her.

"It's about time," a woman said. "Stubborn creature."

Blue skies arched above Sylvie, a blue so pure and deep that the heavens looked hot to the touch, and shot through with veins of gold fire. Lapis lazuli, she thought, but freed from cold stone; lapis lazuli, alive.

Her eyes watered; she blinked but couldn't check the tears. She raised her arms before her to block it out and nearly fell from her seat when it proved to be backless.

"Too much, hmm?"

The world shifted. The sky fell in and darkened, turned teak netted with fishermen's floats in worn and pitted glass. Sylvie's stone cup of a chair turned to leather and grew a back and arms. The walls shifted from white marble to plaster, and Sylvie smiled. She knew this place, the Mucky Duck, a vacation restaurant she used to go with her family, when she was still young enough to giggle over the waiter's bottles of string ketchup that they pretended to squirt on customers.

"A dream. This is all a dream. But *you're* not," she said

to the voice. Familiar voice. It hadn't been a wrong number after all. And Erinya had said that Kevin was smart, that he'd find a way to contact her. Guess this was it.

"Quick," the woman said, making her appearance. A tiny woman wearing something out of Sylvie's onetime art-history book approached. A toga, Sylvie thought, the woman's arms bared from fingertip to shoulder bone, showing multiple semicircular scars. No, chiton. But as soon as she identified it, the fabric changed, adjusting itself to the setting. The woman, now sundressed and sandaled, sank onto a stool next to her. "I'm Mnemosyne. Kevin Dunne sent me."

19

All Gone to Hell

SYLVIE SAID, "DOESN'T HE GET AROUND," BUT HER ATTENTION WAS gone. Outside the plate-glass windows, beyond the scrubby parking lot, two girls played on the narrow shell-strewn beach, one all gawky legs and windblown hair, racing into her teens, the other a toddler, chasing after her sister so fast that she fell. The older girl turned, dusted the child off, and comforted her with a hug and a smile.

"Things change," Mnemosyne said, and waved her hand irritably. The window closed over, turned into another netted wall. "You cannot go back. That is the nature of history, that it is in the past. All that can be done is study it, to see the seeds that were planted and anticipate the growth coming."

"Shut up," Sylvie said. "I've had a long day, and this might be a dream, but I bet it's not helping my sleep deficit."

Ignoring her, Mnemosyne continued, "I do not usually involve myself in these matters, but I owe Dunne a great debt."

"Yeah?" Sylvie said. "Save your life did he? Like a god's life is worth it. You've all lived your share and more." Sylvie bit her lip and made a note to herself: Dreamworld equaled no rein on her mouth.

"He did," Mnemosyne said, still placid, which, perversely, Sylvie found more irritating than a relief. "Do you know how we are created, what we are?"

"Power, flesh shell, broken or unmade, big puff of stealable stuff, got the gist." Sylvie squinted into the dark corners of the empty restaurant and sighed. She was hungry. She was in a restaurant. Didn't seem right. A waiter loomed out of nowhere, green duck on his white shirt, and asked for her order.

Mnemosyne squeaked and made the moment sweeter. Guess she hadn't expected the dream to be more Sylvie's than hers. But just because she set the stage didn't mean Sylvie couldn't control it.

The waiter turned around, her food instantly ready; Sylvie sank her teeth gratefully into the French dip, but it tasted nothing of food and everything of memory. Of sandy days, of salty air, of skin gone sticky with seawater, and the ever-present scent of coconut oil and rubber flip-flops. It exploded in her mind like a little bomb, and she set the sandwich down, near tears. Innocence tasted strange on her palate now. Inedible.

"I apologize," Mnemosyne said. "History lives around me. It is my task to keep it, to record it, to watch it. I am the Muse of history, and I see all." The bare skin of her arms rippled, and what Sylvie had taken for dozens of tiny scars blinked open into eyes. In each of them, in the heart of the pupils, Sylvie saw bits of her past.

"Stop it," Sylvie said. Mnemosyne turned her palms up, showing two moments that Sylvie could only identify as Before and After, Then and Now. In Mnemosyne's right palm, Sylvie saw herself striding across campus, determined, head held high, and anger in her eyes. Portrait of Girl with a Cause.

In the left palm, Sylvie saw a woman with a gun, eyes blacked by shadows and rage, but a curling smile on her mouth. The face of a murderer. *L'enfant du meurtrier.*

Do you like what you see when you look in the mirror?

"Stop it," Sylvie repeated, and Mnemosyne closed her hands. Sylvie felt heat in her own palms and realized she'd brought the gun into her dreams, had it pointed at the Muse. "Dunne sent you. Let's leave the psych tests and parlor tricks behind and get down to business. I've found out who's behind this. Lilith, *the* Lilith. If he wants to lend a hand, maybe prove his ability to find anyone he's laid eyes on, he could drop by."

"Dunne's busy," Mnemosyne said.

"I've reached a dead end," Sylvie said. "I need his help. If you're all about history, you know I don't say that often or easily." Her hand tightened on the table edge; a crack ran from side to side, widening. Sylvie tucked her hands in her lap, like a chastened child. Her dream. Her temper.

"Dunne is trusting you to do what he cannot, while he defends your world and himself. Dunne is not a loved god."

"No one loves a cop," Sylvie said. Some of her temper faded. History, huh. Mnemosyne might be able to give her some of the answers that eluded her, questions about Dunne.

"Especially not petty-minded greater gods," Mnemosyne said. "Whose wives were turned inside out and drained to fuel Dunne. Zeus hates him, and he has never been the most rational of gods. When Dunne first came to power, Zeus had to be coaxed into accepting him, and he laid in a caveat: As it was love that allowed Dunne's ascension, it was love that kept him there. Should love ever leave Dunne, then he was fair game to be destroyed, the power reclaimed, Hera restored."

"And now his love's left him, not by choice, but gone all the same," Sylvie said. "I don't suppose Zeus had a hand in arranging that with Lilith."

"No," Mnemosyne said. "Zeus would rather concentrate on their rivalry than admit any threat could be poised by a human. It's shortsighted. If Lilith gains power because Dunne is weakened fighting Zeus, the results will be wars across the multiple heavens."

"Better than on earth," Sylvie said. "Look, I'm doing my job. Don't expect me to care or cry for gods. I like Dunne—sort of—but it's the man he was, the glimpse I get of that, that I like. Not his opinionated justice-freak god act. And I'm hunting Bran because he's an innocent, and I'm hunting Lilith because I—"

Beneath her hand, the crack in the table widened, and scales rose to touch her fingers, the faint flicker of a tongue. "Fuck!" She threw herself back and watched the snake slip free, a beautiful, deadly swath of red, gold, and black that poured itself over the edge of the table and vanished.

"Do you see that?" she cried.

"It's a curse come searching," Mnemosyne said. "You do make enemies, don't you?" She reached down and collected the serpent. The coral snake coiled and thrashed in her grip. The eyes along her arm opened to better look at it.

Another sleek head began to protrude from the table crack, and Sylvie said, "So what do I do?"

"Nothing," Mnemosyne said, and dropped the snake. It curled and hissed, tongue flickering. Sylvie aimed the gun, but hesitated; Mnemosyne didn't seem concerned, and while gods couldn't be trusted to care about human lives, they needed her.

"Nothing?"

"It's questing. It can't see you. Not cloaked as you are in the scents of others, splashed with inhumanity, and dreaming under my aegis. It'll vanish with the dawn. A limited sort of curse, all spite and petty arrogance. Borrowed power fuels it."

Sylvie watched the snakes slipping around her ankles and growled. "A curse on me." The satanists, she thought, scavenging Dunne's bleed-off in Miami. The curse alert going active, and Alex on the run. "Can I shoot them?"

"They're not real to you, as you're not real to them."

"I *want* to hurt them," she said. They'd made a mistake. Their being human had kept Sylvie from her guns, but now, by stealing power, they'd forfeited that status. She *killed* monsters.

Mnemosyne shook her head. "Better to elude—"

"No," Sylvie said. "I'm not going to wait around for them to try again. I want them to see me, feel me, *fear me*." At her feet, the coral snakes merged and melded, doubling, tripling, growing in size, until it rivaled the mass of an alligator. Her heart pounded in her ears, panic and rage mingled together.

"Do as you will."

"I always do."

The snake suddenly rose and struck, and she dodged on pure nervous reaction. She leveled the gun, and the snake raised itself again like a cobra, and hissed her name, "Shadows."

"Go away. I'm too much for you to handle," she said, and pulled the trigger. The bullet blew its head into spatter, and it dissolved back into a dozen or more regular coral snakes, all retreating through the cracked table. "What, giving up so soon?"

Mnemosyne said, "Many people throughout history have taunted their enemies. Many learned to regret it."

"Shove off," Sylvie said. "You've delivered your message; I've given you mine. So the sooner you go, the sooner I can wake up and get back to work."

Mnemosyne raised her hands, and Sylvie turned her head. "No. No more pretty pictures. Just go. It's my dream. I don't want you in it."

When she looked back, the Muse was gone. Sylvie propped her feet up on the table and noticed that the window to the beach had returned, though the girls were long gone, and night had fallen. Phosphorescent waves curled lazily across the sea, and Sylvie leaned back and watched the sun rise over the water.

Maybe, when all this was done, she'd take a vacation. Make it a long weekend, and pull Zoe out of school. Take

Alex, too. They could lie out, watch the tourists burn, and count license plates from around the country. Alex could teach her to parasail, and Zoe could whine when Sylvie wouldn't let her trot off after cute lifeguards. Maybe it wouldn't be the carefree time of her childhood, but it wouldn't be bad at all. Hell, maybe she'd even invite De-malion, if he could be convinced to give up his suits for board shorts.

Sylvie woke to noise with the sensation of having been smiling in her sleep; before she could enjoy it, the ringing phone was answered, and Demalion's voice, first sharp, went quiet and furtive.

Maybe I won't *invite him,* Sylvie thought. *ISI, secretive, son of a bitch.* She never even considered that he might be keeping quiet out of basic courtesy; he knew the phone would have woken her, hair-triggered as she was.

She ghosted to the door, leaned into the dim hallway, and heard, ". . . condition?" He listened for a long moment, and the answer didn't please him. He swore into the phone, still at a whisper, then said, "I told you to watch her. What about the other?"

Watch *who*? Sylvie wondered, though the prickling heat of her resurgent anger suggested a name or two. *You trusted him,* the dark voice gloated. *You thought you and yours were safe with him.*

"No, no, there's no help for it. Bring her in. But discreetly! And be careful with her, she's an innocent. She'll be scared."

"Then maybe you shouldn't send men to scare her."

Demalion jerked; his eyes widened, and he looked away despite himself. Guilty, Sylvie judged. But of what?

"Got to go," Demalion said, and set the phone down.

"Why do I think that I'm involved in that conversation? Why do I know I'm not going to like it?" She crossed her arms across her chest, tucked her hands away when he reached for her.

"Sylvie," Demalion said. He licked his lips. "I—"

"What did you do?" Sylvie asked. "Bring her in. Who's *her*?"

"Zoe," Demalion said. "Your parents are on vacation, and she's not safe where she is. Her school was canceled on account of snakes in the lockers—"

"She's my sister. I'll protect her. Or I'll arrange protection for her. I thought we had an understanding—"

Demalion said, "Sylvie, please. I'm trying to help."

"I don't need your help," she said. Her hands fisted. She wanted to throw herself at him, but held back, a little uncertain whether angry grappling wouldn't lead back to the bedroom. And if he was going to betray her, she wanted it to be a point of pride that she walked away first—

"Alexandra Figueroa-Smith is dying."

Sylvie's entire body spasmed as if she'd been electrocuted. Cold traced her nerves, made her pant. Her brain locked, repeating those words. Not Alex.

"A curse of some kind. Or one hell of a freak accident. Her jeep overturned. They didn't find her right away, and when they did, she was covered in—"

"Coral snakes," Sylvie said through numb lips. She'd driven them off, feeling in control, feeling smug—it was her fault entirely.

Her breath seared her throat, and she realized distantly that she was hyperventilating. Her ankle complained, and Sylvie eased it out from under her, wondering when she'd hit the floor.

Beside her, Demalion crouched, still talking, empty words where one or two percolated through every so often. Paralysis. Neurotoxin. Ventilator. Antivenin. Hours. Sylvie's mind raced. Shorted out. Started again. Swerved to vengeance. They were going to pay and pay. . . . Dunne could save her. No, Dunne couldn't save himself at the moment. Mnemosyne had said as much. His attention elsewhere.

So get his attention. You know how. The one thing he

can't ignore. The one thing he'd die for. Sylvie closed her eyes. Impossible. But, if there were no other options, then the impossible had to be done. A scheme unfolded, bit by bit by impossible bit. Sylvie's breath steadied, her pulse slowed. She looked at her plan through a sniper's obsessive focus and found it acceptable.

". . . you on a private flight to Miami," Demalion said.

"What good would watching her die do?" She ignored the shock that lit his face. "I need clothes, I need your car. I need my phone and my gun."

"What are you planning?" he said, eyes growing less concerned and more wary. "You're upset, not thinking clearly."

"I'm *angry*," she said. "I find it clears the mind extraordinarily well."

20

Waking the Oubliette

SYLVIE ABANDONED THE ISI SEDAN ON A SIDE STREET. DEMALION would figure out where she had gone; he had all the pieces and had shown himself more than capable of putting them together. Abandoning the car was only a slowing device, but she wanted things played out before he hit the scene. Before he put himself between her and danger. He'd be furious, not only that she left him behind— *again*—but that she'd used a weakness he confided in her to do so.

She'd allowed his company as far as Dunne's apartment, Sylvie driving the last mile when proximity keyed the return of Demalion's blindness. They had changed places in a tension-ridden silence, and Demalion sank into the passenger seat, cradling his crystal "eye." Once there, Sylvie had taken ruthless advantage of his blindness, of the effort it took him to see through the crystal; she collected what she had come for in a rush, too fast for him to make any sense of it, and hightailed it out of the brownstone.

Her actions had blown the hell out of their truce and set the ISI back on her tail, but it was the only thing she could do. The curse on her had rebounded onto Alex, who had been—mostly—safely out of the way. At her side, Demalion was nothing more than a walking target.

Another wary glance at the storm-churned sky, and Sylvie thought, *Better hurry.* Chicago was a shadow of itself, a town lit by tempest light, its borders girdled by towering dark clouds, and its people hunkered down in growing panic.

Lightning flickered and licked the clouds, coming not from within them, but from elsewhere. Dunne was on the run, hiding his own storm-cloud core of power somewhere within the sky tumult, and Zeus—Sylvie winced as another sheet of lightning crackled across the face of the cloud, red-violet, bruising the sky—Zeus was hunting. A bird splatted into the concrete near her, a twisted thing half scale, half feather, all writhing movement, before a passing cab smeared it into the asphalt. The cabbie slowed, backed up alongside her. "Car trouble? Lady, you need a ride?"

Sylvie shook her head. "El," she said.

"It's not running. Power outage at the main line."

"Best news I've heard all day," she said.

He drove on, not bothering to waste more words on an obvious idiot. Sylvie had been serious, though. Doing what she planned to do was already in the impossible category; doing it with an audience? Might as well ask her to save the world. Her intentions were much smaller. One girl, one boy. Alex. Bran. The world would have to fend for itself.

She hefted the artist's satchel out of the backseat; she'd stolen it from Bran's attic studio, filled it while Demalion hovered sightlessly, if not quietly, at her side. She bit her lip. If he'd just stay out of this . . .

If you wanted him safe, the dark voice said, *you shouldn't have let him in.*

She shivered and forced those thoughts away. *Keep him safe,* she thought. It was a lie, or rather, a partial truth at best. She didn't want Demalion at her side. Demalion was her weakness because he offered her his strength, a shoulder to lean on, arms to shelter in. Right now, Sylvie needed to stand alone and tall, needed aggression and vitriol more than understanding. She needed to keep her rage, and she fueled it by knowing she was alone against the world. Demalion had no place in that.

She slung the satchel over her shoulder and headed for the El, ignoring the crackling, fulminating sky above her head.

The entryway to the El gaped, dark under cloud cover, without electric lights. Sylvie stumbled down the stairs in the dimness, let her eyes adjust. In the uncanny storm light that trickled through, the oubliette spell's greasy residue gleamed. Sylvie smiled at it and dropped the satchel.

"You can't do it, Sylvie," Val had said, when called for advice. Sylvie, still thinking of Val's sending Alex away, had no problems in riding roughshod over Val's objections and demanding answers. Rebuild the oubliette? Why not? No magic? When she was immersed in a city drowning in a god's despair? When she had a Fury's blood beneath her nails? And the will to refuse failure when so much depended on it.

Sylvie crouched and drew out the tubes of paint snagged from Bran's studio. Vermilion, cobalt, titanium white, cadmium yellow, malachite green, mars black. Val had warned it took special ingredients to build a spell circle, that ordinary paint was fit for nothing but decoration. Sylvie, having recently seen the way a god's sphere of influence could affect things, figured that these oil paints, stored and used in a god's house, were *soaked* in special.

She unfolded the sketch she'd made of the oubliette and stuck it to the cement with a glob of white paint. She wished she'd brought a flashlight.

The moment on her, she hesitated.

"It's not paint by numbers," Val said. *"It's magic. It's*

bending reality. It's more than will. It's know-how. Even if you can muster the tools, get any kind of result at all, it won't open the same door."

It had to. Sylvie closed her eyes, breathed steadily. If she had Bran in her custody, Dunne would have to deal with her. Dunne would save Alex.

"You are resourceful, aren't you?" the woman said, and Sylvie spun around. She had thought she was alone. At first she didn't recognize her, felt an instinctive liking and camaraderie for this woman, slouched lazily on the stairs, dressed in clothing that looked every bit as "found" as Sylvie's. Worn black denim, loose at the hips, bagging over cracking cowboy boots. A T-shirt that declared the wearer wanted Dead or Alive, a tangle of dark hair, and a bronze sheriff's star on a thong around her neck, like an old-Western gunslinger doing CSI. Her eyes seemed sheened with silver, and in this city, that made Sylvie wary.

"Sylvie Lightner, aka Shadows," she said. "I've been doing my homework. You have had a barrel of misfortune of late, haven't you——"

"Lilith," Sylvie said. Recognition swept over her all at once. The Old Cat was right: Lilith was able to blend in as well as stand out.

Lilith sat sideways on the stairs, fading in and out of shadow more deeply than her clothing could account for. She leaned back against the wall, stuck long, denim-clad legs along the riser, and inspected the dusty toes of her boots. "You're really going to give it a go, aren't you? The old college try. Well, more power to you," Lilith said. "I knew you were interesting when I first laid eyes on you, a girl with a Fury on a leash, but——"

Sylvie raised the gun to bear, and Lilith sighed. "But now, you're being dull. Go ahead. Fire. You want to, and I can tell there's no talking to you until it's out of your system. Just don't expect much. I'm immortal, not——"

Sylvie pulled the trigger. One shot, aimed directly at the star-shaped metal at Lilith's breast. The second shot was between Lilith's iridescent, unblinking gaze, the thunder crack of the first shot still reverberating in the cement confines. When the second roll of noise stopped, Lilith was unharmed.

"—stupid," Lilith finished. She fumbled in her jeans pocket and pulled out a pack of cigarettes. "You a smoker?"

Sylvie stepped closer, closer, and Lilith lit her cigarette, sucking it to red-tipped life.

Trembling—Sylvie couldn't miss from this range, no matter what—Sylvie put the barrel of the gun to Lilith's temple.

Lilith cast a sidelong glance up at Sylvie, eyes silvery-glossy under dark lashes, and said, "Go ahead. I admire perseverance. But remember—*I'm* not stupid. Immortal's not the same as invulnerable unless one takes steps to make it so. So try it again if you want, but I'll tell you true, I don't know where the bullets go. They don't stop in my flesh, but that's not to say they don't *find* flesh. After all, isn't that a bullet's *raison d'être*; to pierce and kill?"

Lilith took a long breath, let out the smoke, and said, "I know your bloodline. I know you're a killer—I watched you kill my *petit sorcier*. What a temper you have. But are you an indiscriminate killer? You've already sent two bullets into the world without a target. Will you send others?"

Sylvie let the gun barrel drop, her breath a loud rasp in the quiet. "You can't make me think you care. You burned people alive in the nightclub."

"You destroy everything and everyone you touch. And then you blame them for being weak."

"You pretended to be Bran's friend. You betrayed him."

"Your arrogance saw your associate killed—"

Sylvie's vision greyed. Was she already too late for Alex? She couldn't believe it, *wouldn't* believe it. "Are we done with the pissing contest? I'm bad, you're worse. Pretty sure the vote would swing my way." Her voice, though ragged, held its edge. Sylvie was perversely proud of that.

Lilith raised her head and smiled, serene. "It all depends on whom you ask. We're not painted in black and white, Sylvie. Just different shades of grey."

Sylvie closed her eyes, wished she could close her ears. "You can't stop me from doing what I have to do."

"I could. Of course I could. Just by snapping my fingers," Lilith said. "Or a stick. Balefire down here would be spectacular, I'd imagine." Like a stage magician, she folded her fingers closed, opened them again to reveal a wooden match. She pressed it between two fingers.

Sylvie's hand dropped to the gun, though it hadn't proved useful. She couldn't stop watching the matchstick rotating in Lilith's agile fingers. "You should listen better, Sylvie. There's no need for melodrama. I *could* stop you. I have no intention of doing so."

"I don't believe—"

"Well, it's not like he's doing me a lick of good all locked away like that, now is he? Auguste, my little prodigy, was quite a genius when it came to magical doors, locks, keys . . . oubliettes. Pity he slacked on his defensive skills. I expected him to be able to open it for me. Now, I've got you, willing to do the same."

"I'm not a talent," Sylvie said. "So there's no point in you hanging around, playing cat at the mousehole."

"Never a cat," Lilith said, making a moue. "Nasty, sly, self-indulgent creatures." She gestured broadly with her cigarette, tracing a pale, smoky path in the dim light. "The fun part is I don't think another sorcerer *could* reopen it. Too much power. They'd open *another* oubliette, maybe, and that wouldn't slice the bread for sandwiches, would it? But a nonwitch, a nonsorcerer, doesn't have power to open *anything.* . . . Such the conundrum. I was furious with you at first. I admit it. You made my simple, elegant plan into a locked-room mystery. But then you show up, carrying all the tools to redeem yourself."

Lilith finished her cigarette, fished out another, and dropped her hand to the cement, the matchstick reaching out. . . . Then she yanked it back, unstruck. Unbroken.

"Oops. Wouldn't *that* be overkill for lighting a cigarette?" She lit the new cigarette from the ashy tail of the first. "You want one?"

Sylvie shook her head, wordless. Lilith raised the fine hairs on her arms and nape. Her chatter couldn't mask the stink about her, the obsessive rage that betrayed itself in a hundred little tells in her false calm, in her ragged finger-nails, in the flick, flick, flick of those silvery eyes. If Sylvie were a dog, she'd have been laying her ears flat and growling low in her throat.

"No, suppose not," Lilith said, putting the cigarettes away in her hip pocket with a little pat, as if to make sure they made it there. It reminded her of Demalion with his little crystal and his constant check on it. A crutch. "Mortal after all, and who needs lung cancer? Though, Syl, I've got to say, you aren't going to live long enough for that kind of death." She spun her own cigarette away; Sylvie dodged the burning tip with a scowl.

"I'm not helping you."

"You *are* being painfully slow about it," Lilith said. "Is there anything I can do to speed matters?"

"Go away."

"If it's confidence you're lacking, don't," Lilith said. "You know what they say. There's not a safe that can't be cracked, given the right skill set and a good set of tools. And you're well prepared. Got your hands slicked with power I can smell from here."

"I'm not—"

"Tick, tick, Sylvie," Lilith said, voice dropping low and smooth as a snake. "Your friend's counting on you, isn't she? And your poor blinded lover boy—whom you left all alone. You may work alone. I don't. I'd get started if I were you. I'm really being very patient."

Sylvie shivered at the glimpse of the steel core beneath the persiflage. Her trembling increased until she felt it rattle her spine, felt the room vibrate with it. Rage. Fear. Stress. She wasn't sure what the driving emotion was, and her little dark voice seemed to have deserted her.

Tick, tick, she thought, and Lilith tapped her wrist as if she plucked the thought from Sylvie's mind.

Sylvie took a last look at those faintly luminous eyes, trying to decide if the moment she turned her back, Lilith would incinerate her. Lilith's gaze gave her nothing to go on, and finally Sylvie turned to the satchel.

Tick, tick. Sylvie clenched her jaw and knelt before the stained remnants of the first spell casting. Bending reality, she thought. Val had made it sound impossible for a non-Talent. But it seemed to Sylvie that doing it once was the hard thing, doing it twice—well, the world had bent already. It could bend again and would follow the path of least resistance, the path it had followed before.

Sylvie uncapped the cobalt paint and globbed it onto her fingertips. The dregs of Erinya's blood leached toward the oils, and Sylvie sucked in a breath. Once begun, she couldn't stop. She wasn't a magic-user, had never wanted to be one, but that didn't mean she hadn't picked up a few basics. She'd seen elaborate spell casting done before. Always build the circle first, Val had said, in full-out lecture mode.

A tiny crack behind her made her jump nearly out of her skin. She spun, hand full of blue paint, spattering the wall. Oddly dizzy, Sylvie forced her eyes closed.

"It's okay, you know," Lilith said. "It was a dud."

Sylvie opened her eyes, breath lodged in her throat, heart pounding, still half-expecting balefire to devour her. Instead, all there was was Lilith looking down at the broken matchstick in her hand and pouting. "*Maudits* bastards. I despise shoddy work."

"You burn me up, no chance in hell of getting Bran back," Sylvie snapped.

"True," Lilith said. "I didn't mean to snap it. I was getting bored, and it just . . . slipped. Don't bore me, Sylvie."

Tick, tick.

Lilith traded the most recent end of a cigarette for another fresh one, chain-smoking, staring blankly at the cement ceiling. *Dud, my ass,* Sylvie thought. Lilith was far too careful to set off any spell accidentally.

Gritting her teeth, Sylvie globbed more cobalt on her fingers and started following the first curve. *Build the circle first,* Val said. *That way, if the spell goes wrong, it's contained.* She couldn't let this one go wrong.

She tucked the tube of paint into her palm, nozzle down, squeezing, providing herself with a steady flow. Beneath her fingertips, the concrete felt as rough as sharkskin. She scuttled along the old curve in an uncomfortable half crouch, trying to keep an eye on Lilith even while she focused her will on the circle.

Halfway around, and Sylvie paused, knees cramping, fingers still connected to the concrete. It wasn't working, she thought, and despair made her fingers tremble. Shouldn't there be some sense of progress? She was learning nothing more than finger painting on a surface rougher than sandpaper sucked and that oil paints smelled like gassy swampland. An inane thought echoed in her head. *Art is pain.*

"Focus," Lilith said. "Keep moving."

Sylvie almost gave up then and there, wanting just to spite Lilith and half-convinced it was too late for Alex anyway.

"Listen to me. Focus your will. Get it done."

Sylvie bent back to the oubliette. Three-quarters around, and a tiny spark of *something* lanced upward, an electric tingle like touching a battery with wet hands. Then, a last knee-walk, sideways crab scuttle, and she closed the circle. The sting returned tenfold, ran up her arms in a jangling, nerve-strung firecracker series of tiny explosions. Her entire body felt sensitized, like she stood too close to a hot-wire-laced fence.

"*There* you go," Lilith said. "Do the signifiers next. Don't lose focus. The world doesn't like to bend. It'll fight back."

Sylvie bit her lip, needing to concentrate. That electric

feel increased, and her thoughts felt fuzzed out. She traded the squeezed-out blue tube for the green one, and when her hand left the diagram, a vaporous trail traced her movement, luminous in the dimness.

"What does it feel like?" Lilith asked. "It's always bothered me, that I lack that particular talent. It's ridiculous how important power is. It trumps everything, and that's not right. Look at Zeus, throwing petty fits just because his will was balked. Power shouldn't go to idiots. Or to those who see life as a source for experiment. Power shouldn't be used to prod and poke, deceive, blind, manipulate—but the gods reflect us, and we reflect them. Bound together in foolishness, venality, and greed."

Sylvie concentrated on smearing the malachite green with fingers that felt bee-stung and raw, shivering as she traced the looping Greek letters that read *love*. The station felt as if it had warmed at least ten degrees. Sweat beaded on her scalp, on her cramping thighs, behind her knees. Somewhere, she could hear someone trying to start an engine that resisted, grinding as it stuck between gears. It annoyed her, made her head buzz. Her eyes itched and burned; the template of the oubliette blurred in her vision, and she echoed Lilith's admonition to herself. *Focus.* You can do this. Never mind that she had never had a desire to touch magic. Distrusted it.

Tick, tick, her heartbeat said, pointing out that she no longer had the luxury of swearing off magic on principle. Too much depended on her successful use of it. Just this once. An exception to the rule.

Lilith said, "You've heard the truism a thousand times. Power corrupts. There are those who might wield it wisely, who would understand that power is best used sparingly. *You* understand. Don't you burn to do better? To take the power from those frivolous hands and hold it safe in yours?"

"That's you, seeing yourself mirrored in me," Sylvie muttered. Getting better at this. Sweating bullets, but her focus was refining itself; it left her breath enough to argue. "I don't want power over others, at least not magical power. It's a burden."

"I never said otherwise. But if it's needed— If you know you could do what was needed. Someone has to do it; someone might as well be you. Or me, of course." She grinned. "Preferably me."

Sylvie scowled; Lilith just kept talking, and her voice was insidious, slipping in past Sylvie's concentration, past the numb fuzziness of reality fighting her attempts to alter it. That engine sound wasn't real at all, she thought, as it shifted to a Doppler pulsing in time with her heartbeat. It was reality slipping, earthquake fashion, along a fault, a basso continuo protest.

Lilith's words were hard to ignore, trickling in like icy water on a rainy, winter day, snaking in beneath her collar, as relentless as a bore who held forth despite the blank, desperate expressions of his captive audience.

God, she thought, suddenly appalled. *It's in the blood.* The laser focus, the obsessive stubbornness, the inability to shut the fuck up. She whimpered low in her throat, tuned her senses to the oubliette spell, trying to block Lilith out.

"—of it is, if left alone, mankind would settle itself out, like the animal kingdom. There is no sin in nature. There is, instead, equilibrium. But gods, they have to poke and prod, make rules and pick fights—tell me about wars, Sylvie. Can you think of one that didn't have religion at its core?"

"It's water torture," Sylvie breathed. *Or subliminal programming,* she thought. Her fingers wavered; she forced her focus back on that machine-grinding, bone-humming, electric sensation of power coiling beneath her.

"The gods—"

"What about you?" Sylvie said, pausing for a moment as she came to the end of a curlicue she couldn't interpret. Her breath came in gasps; her belly growled, and her knees felt like they might reverse themselves at any moment. The Fury's borrowed power aside, the spell was eating through Sylvie's own energy. The way things were going, even if she managed to open the oubliette, she'd be as weak as an infant, easily brushed aside. Sylvie fought to distract Lilith with the only means left to her. Words. "*You* want power. You want to be worshipped."

"Never," Lilith said, her temper flaring in instant denial. "Worship's where—Sylvie, *watch out*. You almost missed a spot."

"Backseat spell casting?" Sylvie griped. It was more maddening that Lilith was right. She'd nearly skipped a tiny little symbol, and for all she knew, that could be a vital piece. It still burned that Lilith had spotted it before she did, when she was far enough across the room that she shouldn't be able to see anything.

"It's like perfect pitch," Lilith said. "I can hear it, still can't carry a tune. Be careful. Neither of us can afford a mistake. Where was I . . . ? *Worship* is where things go wrong. Worship means you've stopped seeing people as independent beings, infantilized them permanently. I don't want worship. I just want to make things right."

"Run for Congress," Sylvie said. "Hell, run for president."

"Worthless," Lilith said. "You aren't listening. We reflect the gods. What happens with them, happens with us. The gods are corrupt, petty, despotic—so are their followers. The worst, though—"

"Let me guess," Sylvie said. She gritted her teeth, pushed a last spurt of paint through the tube, stained the cement in a crimson swirl and shuddered as the entire diagram rang like a crystal goblet being struck. The tortured-machine hum smoothed out as reality bent and accepted its restructuring. Her bones vibrated to the new tune. "The whitebeard who booted you from Eden. Or should I call him Bluebeard."

"You saw my work?" Lilith said. "You are dogged. Can you say I'm wrong? The similarities are striking. Bluebeard gave each successive wife a key and demanded that she not use it. And He put the Tree in the midst of our garden. They both demanded implicit trust but were not worthy of it. Neither of them ever considered that trust was a two-way street."

Sylvie lifted her dizzy head and stared at Lilith. She panted, shivered, fought for breath. She felt cold and hot at once, as if the oubliette was a roaring fire in an arctic room. Everything she had learned only confirmed it for her: She *loathed* magic. All those sorcerers who did this kind of thing on purpose were morons.

When her breath had stabilized enough, when the buzzing in her limbs had faded, she said, "Does this really work for you? Talking people into submission? Did you just expect me to crumble and say *of course* you're right?"

"No," Lilith said. "I told you. I don't want worshippers, or witless obedience. I want—"

"Anarchy," Sylvie said. "Free will, free world, and you step in only if the whole shebang starts to go to hell. Lose your precious equilibrium."

"You do understand. Maybe even agree."

"Too general not to," Sylvie said. She stood, her legs shaking, and backed away from the spell circle. It hummed in her head, alive, but not open. "If, on reflection, I say you're full of shit?"

"I don't care," Lilith said. Abruptly the edge was back in her voice, the danger vibrant in the underground room. "Just be a good woodsman and bring me the little lover's heart to eat. Open the door, Sylvie. Where's your key?"

Sylvie hesitated, the moment upon her. There weren't a lot of options; she *had* brought a key, or something she hoped would pass for one. But she didn't want to use it with Lilith waiting. She had no intention of freeing Brandon just to have Lilith pounce on him; Sylvie's entire body still shook with the effort of rebuilding the oubliette, and the gun was useless. What was left? Her mind raced, searching possibilities. *A door has two sides,* her dark voice pointed out.

Sylvie licked dry lips. Not an option she really wanted to consider, but the alternative? She imagined Brandon

Wolf dead at Lilith's feet, at Dunne so grief-stricken that
he fell to Lilith's attack, or turned the world inside out,
trying to recover what was lost by time. In every scenario
Sylvie could imagine, innocents died, *Alex* died, suffering
for Sylvie's mistakes. Unless—

Sylvie picked up the remaining item in the satchel,
unwrapped it from the silk scarf she'd carried it in to protect it. Behind her, Lilith hissed something under her
breath.

Sylvie didn't pay attention, her eyes riveted on the
painting, the small, violent self-portrait of Brandon Wolf.
The flayed heart seemed to pulse. The oubliette throbbed
in sympathy.

Dunne had set off the oubliette. *Some of him in him,*
Alekta had said. The painting, crimson in spots, dull
brown and flaking in others—Sylvie thought it, too, had
some of Bran in it. She flaked a tiny little rusty chip off
and watched it stream toward the oubliette, a tiny object
caught in an eddy.

Disturbing, Sylvie had thought the first time she saw
the painting. A second viewing had clarified her visceral
response. It looked painted in blood, and it seemed that
looks weren't deceiving.

"What is that?" Lilith said.

"Can't you tell?" Sylvie said. "You were fast enough to
point out my errors in spell copying. You think this'll
work?"

"Yes," Lilith said, her voice husky, a little excited. "Do
it. Bring him up. Do it now." Her eyes were almost pure
silver now, gleaming and milky in the low light. Her gaze
was avid, was fierce, was . . . off. Something had changed.

Sylvie cradled the painting to her chest and shivered as
the oubliette seemed to yearn toward it. One choice left.
Sylvie shivered again. She didn't want to—God, she
didn't want—

She clutched the painting close, the image facing outward, as if the heart shown were her own, her rib cage
split asunder, and stepped back, one step, two, keeping an

eye on Lilith, whose face grew distantly puzzled, pallid eyes going narrow under frowning brows. "What are you doing, Sylvie? Open it, at once."

A third step, and Sylvie could feel the tug of the spell, like a magnet aligning, reaching out for its complement. Lilith stood, moving with the awkward, lanky haste of a marionette, and Sylvie laughed. "Jesus," she said, seeing it suddenly. "You're blind! Dunne's spell. *You were there* when he blinded Demalion and his team. You got caught in it. You were half-blind when I came in carrying supplies from Dunne's house, but the key's wrapped in silk. Inert, magically, until I unwrapped it. You can't see me at all."

"Don't need to," Lilith said. "I can feel the spell. I can—"

"Pity," Sylvie said, on an adrenaline high. "I would love to see your expression when you realize what I'm doing." She took that last step back, her heels clearing the sticky-wet, painted lines. Beneath her feet, the cement trembled like quicksand. "When I lock the door from the inside." Then the oubliette tasted her, tasted the painting in her hands, and found it a match, tugged it to itself. The world bent, and she plummeted into the spell.

21

Love Divine

WHEN SYLVIE WAS IN FOURTH GRADE AT PINECREST, THE READING curriculum had included *Alice in Wonderland*. Sylvie was one of the few who hadn't enjoyed the assignment. Even then, her core of practicality was set; she found Alice and her casual curiosity to be the acts of a dangerously careless girl. Now, at the mercy of the oubliette's undertow, Sylvie felt the first glimmer of sympathy for the girl, as she plunged on her own long fall.

She was surrounded by a colorless haze of motion that pulled and pried and tried to take her apart. The tough leather jacket creaked; seams popped like the breaking of tiny bones. Bran's self-portrait warped and wavered, trying to escape her hands. The gun fluttered feebly at her spine like a stunned bird. "No," she said, her voice swallowed by nothingness. "No." She would not loose her grip. She had no intention of coming out on the other side naked and defenseless, assuming she would finish the journey at all if the painting, the *key*, left her grasp.

The idea of spending eternity locked in nothingness—Sylvie reassessed her ideas of hell and growled under her breath. "I'm coming through, and I'm taking it all with me. *My* gun, *my* key, *my* clothes."

As if it had been a test, the oubliette spat her out, abruptly and painfully, into absolute darkness. Her knees ached from the impact; her free hand stung where she had flung it down to protect her face. Her breath sobbed in her throat. She dropped the painting, and dug her fingers into the surface, trying to guess what it was. Softer than concrete, harder than earth, all one piece, melting slightly away from her hand but warmer than ice. It reminded her of nothing so much as molten glass, drifting, stretching, minus the scalding heat.

She held her breath, listening, trying to hear someone else's presence, trying to guess how big the enclosure was. *He's dead,* Val had said. But the room didn't smell of decay. Her heartbeat pounded in her ears with the effort of not breathing, deafening to her and defeating the purpose. She sucked in a grateful gulp of air and froze. God, the *air*—how did it . . . ? Would it last?

A faint candlelight glimmer touched her eyes, a diffuse glow in the darkness, a splotch of color that could be wishful thinking.

"Hello?" she said. "Brandon?" Her voice wavered, but was, at least, audible. She didn't want to be alone in the dark, cut off from everything, dying in inches. She wanted to have made the right choice. She wanted her chance to save Brandon, to save Alex, to save innocents from the manipulations of the powerful.

The glow strengthened, then raced around the room, spreading outward in fiery streamers, delineating a circular enclosure about the size of a conference room. A whisper of breath touched her ears, then a sudden trickle of something that was distinctly running water. Sylvie, who hadn't realized how ringingly silent the oubliette was, began to relax. The glow increased.

The water became visible first. Of all the things she'd expected to find in a spell prison, a scaled-down Greco-Roman fountain, complete with fat cherubs dribbling water, was not one of them. The marble gleamed with a slick, soapy shine; the water smelled sharp and clear and cold.

The confines of the oubliette slowly came clear, a pinched-off teardrop of a room, a demented genie's bottle. The walls curved undulantly at their base, arched inward at the top, seemed made of some shifting, opaque material that roiled like chemical-laden toxic clouds.

Sylvie inched away from them. The floor . . . She shifted her gaze until the vertigo passed. She stood above the floor on some stretched-out pane of glassine material. The true floor belled beneath it, and Sylvie dared another glance down. It, too, burned with the chemical cloud-roil of the walls, made her think of planks laid over lava spills.

She was alone on one side of the fountain, but on the other? Squinting against the growing brightness, she walked around the curve of the fountain and stopped cold.

Brandon Wolf lay asleep—not dead—on the floor, naked as the day he was born. The dread she'd held tightly to her since the beginning of this case, from the moment Dunne had sworn Bran was alive against all reason, fled. Sprawled, asleep. As if the oubliette was nothing more than a time-out for a child.

She knelt suddenly, knees weak.

God, photographs did not do him justice. Sprawled, prone, head tucked on one outflung arm, he woke nothing so much in her as sheer animal want. His supple skin, the dark-flame tint of autumnal hair, the long eyelashes peeking out beneath longer bangs, his lips, slightly curved even in sleep, his shoulders broad and golden, his lean thighs, his—Sylvie's kaleidoscope thoughts derailed entirely, leaving her with nothing but a quickened pulse and the undeniable urge to pounce. She shivered. And she'd thought *succubi* were dangerously attractive.

The idea shocked her cold for a brief, brain-saving moment. Bran's attractiveness, even unconscious, more than a match for a succubus, for a preternatural creature of desire? Sylvie's breath caught. Her dark voice whispered.

Human? It sounded perplexed. The edge was gone from it, quiet wonder in its voice.

Sylvie caught a quick gleam of eye shine as he peeked through his lashes, and realized he was feigning sleep. "Brandon," she said.

He swung into a crouch, facing her. "What do you want?" Even his voice was delicious. Low, husky, as warm as a firelit room.

"To get you out," Sylvie said. She looked into amber eyes and forgot to breathe. "My name's Sylvie. Dunne sent me."

"Bullshit," he said, though his entire face washed with relief before closing off again. "You're one of Lilith's lackeys."

"I am no one's lackey," she snapped. He flinched, and she thought, *Great, scare the guy senseless.* "Really, I'm working for Kevin."

He flicked a glance at her, flicked it away. "You're wearing Erinya's jacket. I bought it for her in London."

"I am. You think she'd let just anyone borrow it?" He wanted to believe her, but he had the eyes of someone used to pain and disillusionment. It deepened the beauty of his too-pretty face.

He shivered, and she tracked the ripple of muscle and skin, sliding her gaze down the taut curves of his shoulders, down to the flat planes of his chest, the narrowing of his waist and hips. He dropped his hands to cover himself, flushing. Sylvie yanked her gaze away. God, what was wrong with her? The poor guy was scared, naked, and she gawked at him like he was nothing more than meat. She shucked the jacket and dropped it into his lap. "Sorry," she said.

"Used to it," he muttered, and she looked over in time to see the resignation on his face, and more—the old scars on his forearms.

He might be strong physically—his body attested to that—but there was a fragility in his eyes that she didn't like.

"It'll be okay," she said. Shit comfort, but the best she could manage.

He nodded, still not looking. His hands fisted in the coarse leather.

"You don't believe me."

"Lilith's clever. Erinya's not. I'm not. We're easy to fool." Bitterness laced his voice.

"She got you with the murals."

"She got me way before that," Bran said. "Years and years ago."

Years and years? Dunne had only become a god recently. Sylvie got that irritating prickle again, the one that said she hadn't been given all the information she needed.

Bran stood, put his back to her, and she tried to keep her eyes from wandering over the long line of exposed skin. Not the typical redhead, creamy pale with freckling. Brandon Wolf seemed to have been tapped by Midas instead. His skin laid claim to gold and held the silkiness of flower petals. It looked so—touchable.

She fisted her hands. *Human?* Her dark voice raised the question again. Sylvie still didn't have an answer for it. How much of this attraction was built into him by Dunne thinking of him as beautiful, the reflection of a god's desire? How much of it was intrinsic?

He lowered the jacket and stepped into the skinny, unzipped sleeve. Sylvie blinked. *What the hell—*

He tugged on it, and the jacket stretched, shifted, *grew*. Brandon Wolf drew the jacket on like a pair of pants, and it shaped itself to his need. He buttoned the front closed and sighed in obvious relief at being clothed, even partially. Sylvie, on the other hand, felt immeasurably worse. Perhaps she was the fool Anna D had called her.

She'd risked so much to rescue the human innocent, and he was neither; he was Power.

"You're not human," she said. The client *always* lied.

"I am," he said, hugging himself. He lowered his head to stare at his bare toes.

"Humans can't create matter. A sorcerer could transform the jacket, but he couldn't make more of it. That jacket should have gone as sheer as Saran Wrap as you stretched it. You *created* more of it." She shivered. Fool. The pieces all put together wrong. Anna D had told her straight out. It was love that made Dunne a god. Love made Dunne. *Love.* While she was unfamiliar with the pantheon, she could juggle a few pieces, pluck a name everyone knew out of the air, and create a new picture. "You're a *god*," she accused.

"That, too," he whispered.

How did an American cop end up a Greek god? He married in. How did a man built of Hera's power become a god of Justice and not simply her replacement? Some of him in him. Revenge tempered by love. Brandon Wolf, who would wake a corpse's senses, Brandon Wolf, the heart of Anna D's riddles, who signed his art with a pair of crossed arrows, who by all accounts drew admiration and desire wherever he went, even from pissy, violent godlets like the Furies—Brandon Wolf could be only one god.

"Eros," she said.

Dunne wasn't Lilith's target. Dunne was incidental. Lilith had already caged her god.

"Why are you alive?" Sylvie asked.

He tugged fitfully at the low waist of the leather pants, grew it up another few inches. "Killing a god isn't a simple thing." He raised his face to hers, as wary as a wild animal. "Kevin really sent you?"

"Yes," she said. "Look, he changed my gun. You can sense that right?" She held it out; he shied, but when she held the muzzle down, he reached out to touch it. He sighed, slumped back to the floor of the oubliette.

"He sent you in here to get me?"

"That was . . . not part of the original plan, no," Sylvie said. "It was a spur-of-the-moment decision. But hell, it's got to be easier to break out than break in."

He laughed, three hitched breaths, then gasped back what might have been a sob. "There's no way out."

"Have you tried?" Sylvie asked.

"Of *course*," he said. "Do you think I like sitting here, just waiting for Kevin to come rescue me like some pathetic infant?"

Sylvie was glad to see the anger, a hint that he wasn't broken.

"The oubliette was meant to see me dead. But I've managed to keep ahead of that, at least."

"Transformation and creation of matter," Sylvie said.

Bran nodded. "Air to water, hair to air—all small things."

"Dunne defeated the oubliette entrance without effort," Sylvie said.

"Kevin's a god," Bran said. Some color crept into his pale face. "I'm not. Or not much of one at the moment. Lilith—"

"Got you years ago," Sylvie remembered aloud. "Fill me in. You're human?"

Bran nodded, clutched his forearms again. "I am both. More human than god. I have power, but it's not easy to reach it."

"You made Dunne a god," she said.

"I didn't even think about it. We were out late. We got mugged. Kevin got shot. He was dying in my arms. I couldn't—" He choked down the waver in his voice. "I cheated. I asked him for his soul, and he gave it to me. I don't think he understood I meant it literally. All of us have access to ambrosia, the source of immortality. It's intrinsic to our being."

In his hands, a flower bloomed briefly, a flame-colored thing with seven petals that shifted from the shy, curled shape of rose petals to the spiky ylang-ylang. He folded his hands and it sank back into him, spreading a quick rosy glow through his skin and scenting the air.

"I called it up, fed it to him. But immortality without purpose is an exercise in frustration, so I started feeding him my power, what I could access of it."

"You *shared* it?" Sylvie said. She hadn't really thought any of the gods would do that.

"Surprised them, too," Bran said, mouth quirking a little in rueful humor. "Especially since . . . When you start an immortal feeding on power, it's like making a baby black hole. It pulls power like a magnet. Hera was disassembled. The first I knew of that was when her power started flooding into Kevin. He should have been a minor deity like the Furies, but mine, a cupid-type godlet. Enough to give him purpose. Instead, he became something new. Something *more*."

"Revenge, that's Hera's shtick, isn't it? And revenge tempered by love equals justice."

Bran nodded.

"All that's interesting," Sylvie said, "but not to the point. Why are *you* human? Dunne looks human, but he's not. That shell he wears is only an echo of who he used to be."

He looked up at her, and she sat down beside him, trying to make herself more approachable. The hesitation in his eyes, the way his glance kept sliding away from her, all of it bespoke reluctance and more—embarrassment of some kind.

"Lilith," he said. "I told you. I'm not clever. We've been friends for a long time, she and I. I *thought* we were friends." He slid down farther to lie supine, crossed his arm over his eyes.

Sylvie, unable to resist, put a hand to his bared belly. His skin was as touchable as it looked, velvet smooth and blood warm. He arched into her touch, recoiled a second later, and blushed.

"It's okay," she said.

He relaxed under her touch when she kept it clean, kept to the safe territory between his rib cage and hipbones. He laid his head back, letting her admire the long line of his throat. And she had teased *Demalion* about being her dog.

Brandon Wolf, despite being a god, was about as submissive as any creature could get. Dunne probably had his hands full finding the delicate line between protective and possessive.

"The other gods used me," he said, voice muffled by his skin. "It's my nature. I am Desire, and I am as much at its mercy as my worshippers. But I wanted to die for the weight of it. I was a god, and they treated me like a tool, with no mind or feelings of my own. I ran to earth. Lilith found me and suggested a better way to hide.

"She said she knew how I could mask myself in human flesh."

"She wanted you helpless," Sylvie said.

"I know that, *now*." Bran dropped his arm to frown up at her. She stroked a soothing line across his belly, and his frown shifted to a more content expression, a cat accepting its due.

"To gain a god's power, the shell must be destroyed," Sylvie mused, caught her fingers tracing the no-man's-land of the waistband, and removed them from temptation. He sighed and shifted his head to her lap, putting them back in contact. "Which is difficult for a human to do."

"Very difficult," Bran said.

"But flesh can be destroyed."

"Very easily."

"Why didn't she kill you outright? Why all this nonsense?"

"Coming at me directly would have been a mistake. Either I'd escape, or Kevin would stop her. Distance is nothing to him."

"She couldn't shoot you?" Her fingers disobeyed her and traveled through the thick silk of his hair. He turned his head, rubbed his cheek against her hip. Her temperature spiked.

"She could," he said. "But think of this flesh form as a plug in a drain. If it's knocked out, the power flows immediately. If she was some distance away—"

"She wouldn't get all of it."

Bran laughed, a rough unhappy sound. "It would be like throwing chum in shark waters. Lilith's not a shark. She only wants to be one. She'd have to fight her way to the front, and again, Kevin would be there soon after."

"So an oubliette to cage the power after you die," Sylvie said. "And a key to open it in her hands. No wonder she's been cranky. I killed her sorcerer."

He shivered, moved off her lap, sat upright. She wanted to drag his warmth back to her and quelled the urge. "All that's true. But there's more. To kill a god—it's an evil thing."

Sylvie rolled her eyes. "That sounds like self-serving propaganda to me."

Bran shrugged, obviously unwilling to fight with his rescuer.

"So that's the game. You were supposed to die down here. Then she opens the oubliette and drinks in your power, claiming it for herself. Replaces you, at the mercy of your peers?"

"Her will's stronger than mine," Bran said. He withdrew another inch or so from her. "And they wouldn't destroy her. Love's important," Bran said. "No matter how I feel about my fellow Olympians, I know that's true. I thought I could do my job from hiding."

"I haven't seen a whole lot of love in the world," Sylvie said. "Which begs the question, are humans so fucked up that nothing you do can help? Or are you shirking?"

He rose to his feet, padded silently toward the glowing walls. A nasty muttering hum rose to greet him, and Sylvie tensed, wanting him to stay away from it. He raised a hand and rested it a bare inch above the surface of the wall. The hum increased. It sounded . . . hungry.

"I made a mistake," he said, so subdued. She shifted to watch him more closely. His eyes were closed, expression turned inward, reliving it. "I made myself an infant, but such a small bit of flesh couldn't hold my power. For the first thirteen years of this existence, I was as wholly human as you even though I carried the thread that makes me Desire, Love."

"But you had no power."

"Couldn't reach it, couldn't contain it. Not even when it counted most."

"What happened?" Sylvie said. It was guilt pulling at his beauty, self-contempt lacing the pain.

"I taught humans it was possible to abuse Love," he said. "It's not coincidence that the number of child molesters has skyrocketed. I let it happen to me. And the world reflected it."

"Let it?" Sylvie said. "I thought you had no access to your power."

"I should have recognized the signs. But I didn't want to believe it." Bran sank back down to the miserable huddle she was beginning to recognize. Knees up, ankles crossed, arms tight around his legs, face buried in the cavity of shoulder and knee.

"Flesh is stubborn," he said, voice muffled. "I tried to end it, regain my godhood, but it wanted to live when I didn't. Eventually, as I got older, saw the results of what I'd let happen, I realized that I had to make amends."

"You can't make them from in here," Sylvie said. "It's time to leave."

Bran raised his head from the protective cradle of his arms, despair washed away, replaced by blatant disbelief.

"You think I haven't tried?"

"You seem pretty cozy," Sylvie said. "No signs you've been clawing at the walls."

"It's a death trap," Bran said. "The walls, the original floor, everything. When I fell through, the oubliette started eating away at my body. My hands were down to bone before I managed to get the floor in place."

"Destroys flesh, stores power," she said, grimacing. "Charming. Bet Auguste was the kind of boy who cut the tails off mice."

"Auguste?"

"Yeah, that's your lackey, the one who built this little

de Sade dream." Sylvie spared a moment to think that maybe she didn't need to carry a load of guilt for shooting Auguste. That kind of nastiness was inbred, not taught. "I refuse to believe a crappy sorcerer like Auguste could build something that defeats a god."

"Well, I can't get out," Bran said. His irritation faded into something approaching sulkiness. It all looked good on him.

"Can't is a ridiculous word in a god's mouth," Sylvie said. "If Dunne were in here, would it hold him?"

"No," Bran said, "but it's not the same thing. He's all power, all the time."

He played with the leather ankles of his pants, running the zippered cuffs up and down, all nervous fingers and hissing rasp. Sylvie tried not to find the tiny little bit of anklebone worthy of arousal, but something in the way he toyed with the zippers encouraged it. Sylvie reached out and stilled his hands.

He was dancing away from the topic, Sylvie thought. Distracting himself and her as well. He looked up at her from under dark lashes, and said, "We can't get out."

"Don't start that again," she snapped. "Of course we can. It's just going to take some thought. And some time." She bit out the last, thinking time was the thing they couldn't afford to waste.

She stretched sore muscles into some semblance of normalcy and assessed. What did they have going for them? Bran's power, which kept them alive long enough to escape; *hell,* Sylvie thought, *it should be instrumental in our escape. What kind of god lets himself get penned by a human?* A glance at Bran showed him curled back into his quasi-fetal tuck. A depressed god. A god who blamed himself for something he couldn't have fought. A god who would rather hide than fight back.

Sylvie made a tally mark in the "what did they have *against* them" column also for the same reason.

Sylvie paced around the fountain, thinking. Bran had enough power to fuel a spell; Sylvie had the will to make a spell obey. But the only spell she knew was the oubli- ette. She could draw it again—her map had blown in along with her—but that would just build a loop; from the oubliette to the oubliette.

Bran, however, might not need a spell. Not if he had more power. Sylvie looked over at Bran. "If you died, is that it? Game over? You said something earlier about re- gaining godhood. How?"

Bran raised his head, shrugged a shoulder. "Die. Re- lease my power and re-form as I was meant to be. Theo- retically."

"Wouldn't that give you full access to your power? You could blow this place to hell, be back home in time to catch the ninth inning of the apocalypse upstairs."

"If Lilith doesn't have some sort of shunt ready to pull the power—"

"She doesn't. Or she wouldn't have been so mad-keen for me to open the spell again."

Bran worried his lip. "It's not an easy process. The power wants to be free, and I have to corral it."

"Four walls," Sylvie gestured. "No one around, 'cept for me."

"It takes time," he said, back to playing with the zippers.

"You're the one who's got nothing but time," she said, her voice as quietly ominous as a viper's hiss. "You don't want to go back."

"I do," he said. "I want to go home."

"That's not what I meant," she said. "You don't want to be the god again. You want to stay *mortal*. That's why Dunne lives on earth, *endangers* the earth. Because you won't leave it."

"It hurts to die," Bran said.

"Fuck that," Sylvie said. "I've got a gun. A single round between the eyes isn't going to smart at all."

"I die, the air goes away," he said.

"You come back, so does it." It was a valid fear, one that sparked terror in her belly, but she wasn't going to let him get away with hiding from himself. "You don't want to."

"I . . ." He stilled completely, like a prey animal making itself invisible. "If I go back, I'm their tool again. Nothing but Love. On earth, I paint, I play basketball, I go to concerts, I have friends, I eat out, I even cook breakfast. I have a life."

"Dunne wouldn't let you be their tool," she said. "That's not what you're afraid of. You're afraid of something he won't protect you from. Your responsibilities."

"I stayed on earth to make amends," he said. He surged to his feet, actual temper showing in his eyes. "How is that avoiding my responsibilities?"

"Then why wasn't it on your list, alongside partying and painting? You *know* what happened to you wasn't your fault. You were a child, and an adult raped you. Not something you could control. Dunne would have told you that. He would have told it to you until you believed it. You're using it as an excuse to stay here."

Sylvie watched the angry flush mantling his cheeks white out, all at once. *Bull's-eye,* she thought, with a certain dark triumph.

"You know, I don't have to convince you to do anything," she said. "I have the gun."

She sighted along it to his too-pretty, shocked face. "I could end this argument just by pulling the trigger—"

The little dark voice said, *Why stop with killing him? You could take his power when it comes. Free yourself and turn to the world next.* The cadence was all too familiar. Lilith's quiet conversational tone, preaching better living through deicide, like a tune she couldn't be rid of, like a cult's brainwashing drone. She tried not to listen. What was it doing in her head?

"Sylvie—" Bran said, trying to sidle away from the muzzle of the gun.

She tracked him, all serpentine reflex. "You think you could access your power fast enough to transform a bullet?"

He flung up a hand in futile self-defense. Before Sylvie could even decide if she would pull the trigger or not, the gun surged in her hand, coming to a life beyond its simple animal warmth and heartbeat. It melted over her hands, oiling between her clutching fingers, and came back at her, some impossible snake creature, sprouting fangs and gunmetal scales.

Fail-safe, she thought, even as she flung it down. Dunne really didn't trust her. A tiny bit of his spirit playing watchdog; it let her kill the *Maudit*, let her shoot the Fury who could heal, but turn it on Brandon and—

Sylvie ducked the strike at her knee, dodged behind a stunned Brandon, and caught a quick breath. Dunne's spirit. Her flesh. She knew which to blame for the ugly shape the gun had taken.

The gun-snake coiled for a strike, forked tongue flickering. Sylvie forced Bran into playing living shield, ignoring his yelp. If she were right . . . The snake swayed, hesitating. Dunne's spirit ruled it, and Bran was sacrosanct. She, on the other hand, was a heretic. "Gonna stop it?" Sylvie asked.

"What?" Bran gasped. She rocked him back and forth, keeping herself behind him. Defensively, he was a great tool. Offensively? She'd be better off with a rock.

Sylvie took a breath, stepped away from Bran, and when it struck, she was ready. It lunged; she caught it behind the head.

"Kill it!"

Bran backed away, shaking his head. "I don't kill things. . . ."

Sylvie's triumph faded; the snake was strong and agile, it might work its way free. And then what? The question was never answered. Its dagger tail whipped around, grew a head, and sank needle fangs into her shoulder.

Pain blazed upward; her fingers on the other head spasmed, loosening, and the snake bit down, chewing a long line of punctures across her arm.

"Oh God," Sylvie muttered.

She yanked it away from herself, heedless of injury—it couldn't get worse, now—and tossed it toward the shifting, blazing walls that made up the oubliette. The dark shape flailed and hit the wall and stuck, slowly being eaten away into its component bits.

Pain racked her, sent her to her hands and knees, then to darkness.

22

If at First

SYLVIE WOKE CRADLED IN BRAN'S ARMS, HIM TAPPING HER CHEEK, using her name as a lure to wakefulness, her face pressed up against the drum of his heartbeat. His gentleness was surprising considering what she had just threatened to do. She liked to think she wouldn't really have done it— wiped out that generous concern and caring nature just to prove a point.

Not to prove a point. But if it were the only way—the dark voice said.

She raised her arms toward the ceiling, still sore, but her flesh admirably clear of serpent bites.

"Make house calls?" she whispered. "I know a girl who needs you."

Bran dumped her from his lap. "You tried to kill me; why on earth would I help you?"

"It was a bluff," she said. He relaxed, believing her at once. She thought, no wonder Lilith talked him in circles. He might be a god, but he was an innocent.

"If I had died, would you have resurrected me?" she asked. "Transformed me into something useful? I mean, you're pretty handy with that, right?"

"I suppose," he said. His eyes were wary, already seeking ways to deny whatever it was she wanted.

She gritted her teeth, forced temperance to her voice, and said, "What about transforming the oubliette walls—"

He was shaking his head before she could finish, and Sylvie sighed, exasperated but not surprised. "What?"

"I'd have to touch the spell to transform it."

"So?"

"So I don't think I could keep my focus while my hands burned away." In his lap, his hands fisted, the leather creaking beneath them. "Any other brilliant ideas?"

"I don't see you contributing," she said. She paced the room, ignoring the way heat and dizziness rushed her every time she pivoted. "You know, when I first met Dunne, I thought you might be hiding from him, afraid of your dominant, dangerous lover. Now, I see it right. He loves you way more than you love him."

"You don't know anything about us."

"I know that Dunne's up there, getting his ass handed to him by Zeus, running himself ragged trying to find you, and keep the world in one piece. And you—" Sylvie didn't even need to finish the sentence. One contemptuous eye sweep of the room, ending with him pinned beneath her gaze spoke volumes.

"I gave him immortality. I made him a god—"

"Things you don't value yourself. It's like regifting the ugly lamp. Doesn't count toward virtue points. You didn't save your lover's life; he's not your lover. He's your bodyguard. Your *servant*—"

"It's not like that," he said. His cheeks flushed.

"From what I see, it's exactly like that."

"Black and white. Just like Erinya." He changed seats to lounge on the fountain's edge and trailed his fingers in the water. "You see things as wrong or right. User and used. Powerful and powerless. It's not always about power. Yes, he's my protector. I love him for it. But that's hardly the only reason—" He dropped his head forward, hiding his face behind the flame of his hair.

"Did he even have a choice?" Sylvie said. Anger bloomed in her blood, the dark voice unfurling and crawling out through her mouth, whispering venom. "Did you *make* him love you? Just looked around and picked him up, a twofer kind of deal, bodyguard and fuck toy—"

"No," he said. His voice was hoarse, trembling along with his hands. The water took on little wavelets, transmissions of his distress.

Sylvie grinned. Hitting a little close to home, maybe? "No? No, what? No, you didn't pick him out? No, you didn't crush his free will for your convenience? To give yourself someone indelibly loyal to make sure you never had to do anything you didn't feel like doing."

"It's not like that," he repeated, telling the water his side of it. "It's not all one-way. I take care of him, too. When his duties are too much, I give comfort—"

"Duties that you made him responsible for. You made him the god. Gave him a hard job that never ends. Justice will never rest until the earth is scoured clean of human life. What kind of comfort can you offer that makes that bearable?"

He sucked in his breath, wrapped his arms tight about his ribs; his wet hands left streaks of water dribbling down his skin. "You think this is all my fault," he said. "Blame me for being kidnapped."

"No," Sylvie said. "I blame you for *staying* kidnapped."

"I can't do anything about it," he shouted. "I'm just human. Just like you. I don't see you walking out of here." He panted, cheeks flushed; she got a quick glimpse of feverish eyes, shining with a gloss of tears. Abruptly, he put his back to her.

"You're nothing like me," she said. "And nothing like a human. Humans are *animals*, subject to biology and primitive urges. Trap us, we'll gnaw off limbs to escape. You, on the other hand, just shrug and say, don't have access. . . ."

Sylvie blinked in the sudden silence. Her mind locked

on that word. They'd been spitting it at each other often enough. *Access?*

She turned it this way and that in her head, a tiny glimmer of possibility cooling some of the rage trapped in her skin.

He paced a tight two-step across the oubliette, obviously unwilling to get any closer. A god, she thought, and she'd been shouting at him like he was a disobedient teenager, like he couldn't turn her into Sylvie-jerky at a moment's notice. If he could access his power.

She licked her lips. "What do you mean when you say *access*. Exactly."

He twitched a shoulder at her, a half shrug, still sulking. She wanted to shake the answers out of him. "Tell me."

"It's in the dictionary," he said, voice rough.

"I swear I will knock you down and brain you against your own fountain if you don't take this seriously." Sylvie forced down the adrenaline rush and sank down to sit on the false floor.

"I'm human," he said. "Human flesh can't hold a god's power in its entirety. It would be like expecting a . . . a . . . *sponge* to dry up the ocean. My power is—"

"Elsewhere," Sylvie said. "Someplace that you can draw on it, in tiny bits, but keeps the majority of it stored."

"Yeah." He paced in the circles the oubliette encouraged. She watched his leather-encased legs go by, once, twice, snagged his ankle on the third go-round.

"You stored your magic. Exactly where? Why don't the other gods swoop in and eat up all the set-aside power?" Her heart gave a little lurch. Oh yes, she was onto something now. "Why can't Lilith simply help herself to it? Why all this rigmarole, when the greater part of your power is just sitting there, somewhere, waiting to be used?"

He shook his head as she spoke, confusion on his face. "They can't get to it. It's not a where. It's not a real place. Does this matter?"

"Oh, it matters. Immensely," she said. "I get it, now. You're a god, all intrinsic power. You compared it to the ocean, you're right. As a human, you could only carry so much of it within you. You hid the ocean, Bran, and you're carrying that sponge."

He opened his mouth, shut it again. "Ocean? Sponge?"

"Don't snark. Your analogy," she said. "You couldn't hide your power on earth. That much power, even contained, would make ripples; witches and sorcerers would figure it was there, in the same way astronomers find black holes by their effect. You didn't leave it on Olympus, either. A god's power, set aside, would be fair game, right? They'd be tearing Olympus apart looking for it."

He started to speak, one more objection or protest, and she talked over him, high on hope. "Neither heaven nor earth, not hades nor hell—" Sylvie smiled. "You stored it in an unreal place. Outside of the world. Just like us."

Awareness bloomed in his eyes, like the rosy heat of the immortal flower. "You think it's in an oubliette. You think *I* made an oubliette. I don't know how to make—"

"Magic's instinctive to gods, not learned. You secreted your power in a hidden place and pinched it off. Dunne couldn't find *you* in this oubliette, and he's your lover, a part of you, as well as a god. No one but you can open the safe full of goodies."

He shrugged a shoulder again, uncomfortable. "Maybe."

"So—look, the dilemma is that we can't get out of this oubliette. But you can. You still have access to your power. Even in here. We have an escape hatch, connected to your skin. All you have to do is open it."

She picked up the painting that had brought her here— torn heart, blood spray—and forced it into his hands. "I used it as a key to confound the spell. You can use it to find the path to the other oubliette. The one you control."

23

Just Passing Through

THE LIGHT IN THE OUBLIETTE DIMMED, MAKING SYLVIE REALIZE ANEW that this little cage was Bran's world at the moment, and like the world above, it resonated to the god. The shadows darkened around him, shielding him from her demand. The painting started to slide from his grip; he clutched it closer, like some perverse teddy bear. "I ca—"

"That better not be *can't*," she interrupted. "Of course you can. You did it before."

"I'm barely more powerful than a sorcerer now. How can I open a spell like that?"

"I managed just fine," Sylvie said. He didn't need to know about Erinya's inadvertent loan of power, of Lilith's guidance, of the paints taken from his studio. It would only give him grounds for doubt.

"I can't make an oubliette." His voice, the only thing she could sense clearly of him in the growing darkness, was desperate and quiet.

"I'm not asking you to *make* one. I'm asking you to open the door into the one you've *already* made. I'm asking you to help me help you escape. We open the door, we go through, and we're in an oubliette that you can leave of your own free will."

She grabbed his wrist and dragged him toward her. The painting bobbled, but he folded it closer still. She leaned in and said, directly into his ear, "Bran, you can do this. Stop hiding, and do it."

He shuddered; she felt the shivers move through his wrist, traveling his body like an animal's dying spasm. She said, "*Now*, Bran."

"I can't—"

"You don't have a choice," Sylvie said. "It's put-up-or-shut-up time. You claim you're staying human to atone for your mistakes—for letting Love be abused. Prove it. Get out of here and go fix things.

"You say you love Dunne, that you're not using him as a shield. Prove it. He's up there, about to set off the end times if Zeus doesn't devour him first. Rescue yourself. Save him."

Her hand wound around his wrist, his blood dampening the soft skin under her digging fingernails. His mouth was drawn with pain.

She shook him. "Bran, dammit. Do it. You say you love the life you've built. Prove it. You know what's happening up there. What the gods will do to the earth. You can stop it, just by getting out of here. Except you're too passive, too frightened, too selfish to try. . . ."

He shook his head. "I can't!" She shook again, and the painting's edge hit his lip, raised a bloody line that he licked away, eyes numbed and blank.

"Dunne . . . *Kevin* could be dying. His immortal shell cracked by Zeus, all that power drawn out and dispersed. I bet that hurts like hell. It makes me sick to think about it, and I barely know him. How does it make you, his *lover*, feel?"

"Shut up!" He flung her back, not with his hands, which kept the painting clutched tight, but with power. Sylvie landed on her tailbone, whooped for air, and just as she caught it, looked at Bran and lost her breath again.

The painting was gone. Absorbed. His bare chest gaped, a bloody mass of pulled-out bone and flesh; his flayed heart throbbed once, twice, effort-laden beats that spilled blood and paint over the rest of his skin like it was a canvas. He sobbed; his fingers sank into his own chest and touched that faltering heart.

"Oh God," Sylvie said, lunging forward to stop him from worsening the damage. She caught his bloody wrists, and they stood close, his breath sobbing and hot against her skin. The wound closed slowly, ribs pulling in, heart steadying, and then— He arched back in her arms.

His skin flashed gold, glowing with light; his veins darkened beneath the flesh and spread across his body like ink, drawing by-now-familiar shapes: loops, lines, and Greek letters last seen on the floor of a subway station. Bran's oubliette spell. Marked in agonized flesh and blood. She leaned into him, closed her eyes against the heat and light The sudden displacement was as dizzying and as distressing as a plane's plummeting.

His moans choked off in a gurgle, as if his mouth had filled with water, and Sylvie drowned after him. If the first oubliette journey had been a black hole, this one was a riptide, bubbles bursting along her skin, her breath gone, lungs crying out. Her hands spasmed on his shoulders, slipped free, and she fell, gasping, against a wall.

She opened her eyes to Bran's screaming, but couldn't find him, blind to anything but the light. *Fort Knox,* she thought muzzily, *it's all gold—* Then Bran cried out again, and Sylvie found him, tangled in gold, like predatory vines, crawling under his skin, matching the oubliette patterns, devouring him.

It was his power, she realized. Power trying to pour itself into a human form. But human flesh couldn't store it—it split and gave it back into the oubliette in a spray of blood and misty gold. Sylvie grabbed Bran's shoulder, and said, "Get us out!"

"Wh-where?" His eyes were wild and black with pain.

"Anywhere! It doesn't matter." Blood spattered her arm

where the power touched him, touched her, burning hot, raising blisters, and she said, "Hurr—"

The world blurred, gold gave way to darkness, and just as Sylvie took in a shuddering breath, a slap of salt water hit her squarely in the face.

The world was water, a tumult of oddly salty rain as if a hurricane had swept inland, bringing the ocean with it; she was sprawled in water, soaked to the skin, water lapping up around her hips, and beneath all that, the solid sense of concrete. Not a beach in a storm, then.

Lightning whited the sky, left livid purple afterimages and the brief glimpse of a landscape in her eyes. Bran choked nearby, and she fumbled over. Of course, he'd be facedown in the water. He was nothing but trouble. She dragged him up against her. "Where are we?" she shouted over the storm. Thunder obliterated any answer he could have made; the rain slashed sideways, welting her bare skin at hands and cheek. There were ice crystals at the heart of the drops, rain turning to hail. Another flash of lightning, and Sylvie caught a glimpse of a wall nearby.

She dragged Bran through shin-deep rushing water to the dubious safety of a wall with a tiny overhang. Sylvie put her hand to it, steadying herself, steadying him, and the wall felt rough, splintery, nearly chalky beneath her hand. She sniffed. Smoke. Char. A burned-out building. Wooden, not concrete. "Where the hell are we?"

Lightning, thunder, a god shaking himself to pieces against her were her only answers. Bran crumpled; she caught him, lowered them both. There were stairs beneath them, the wreckage of a decorative railing. They were huddled in what used to be someone's doorway, the overhang protecting them from most of the weather. In the inconstant light, Bran's face was shocky and wet. Sylvie brushed the rain out of it. The dampness on his face reappeared no matter how often she wiped her fingers across his cheeks.

Crying, she thought. She'd broken him. When government stalkers hadn't. When kidnapping hadn't. When abuse hadn't. One day with her, and she'd done this kind of damage. He felt boneless in her lap, given over completely to his misery. She'd done this to him. Sent him through pain and fire and heartache. "It had to be done," she whispered. "I'm sorry."

It was necessary, the dark voice echoed.

Sylvie had to agree. At least in theory. But the larger part of her was cringing. She had known to tread carefully, known he was fragile, and still . . . She had flung his fears in his face, dismissed his pain, belittled everything he said, forced him to confront things he had tried to forget.

Bran hiccuped in her arms, a shudder washing his entire body. His skin was cold beneath her fingers. She used to protect innocents. She rubbed his skin in hypocritical comfort, feeling uncomfortably like an abuser apologizing, swearing it would never happen again.

Sylvie wanted to cry alongside Bran, but her tears were gone. Crocodile tears, anyway, she thought bitterly. Maybe it had been necessary. But there might have been another way. One that didn't make her a monster.

The wind picked up, howled in her ears, pressure dropping. The rain curled in the sky, went from westerly to northern, and stung them both.

In her arms, Bran shuddered again, and his silent tears gave way to coughing. Blood speckled the back of her hand, brief spray of crimson washed away in the rain.

"Bran?" she said. Her heartbeat, already fast, sped up until she felt light-headed. She'd broken him. She knew that. But physically? He'd touched his own raw heart. He'd split himself apart under his own power; he'd dragged himself inside out to take them back to earth. Barely more powerful than a sorcerer—how fast could he heal from that? A sorcerer would be dead.

She put her hands to his throat; his pulse was shallow, fast, and uneven. He moaned.

Have to get out of this storm, she thought. *Have to assess the damage. Hospital would be best.* But where the hell— She squinted at the door behind them in the dim light. There was a number. She traced it with her fingertips, with her eyes.

Oh God. She pushed the door off its hinges just a little and looked into a burned-out shell of a house, still smoldering with blue fire under the rain.

Where would a scared and injured god go? Home, of course. They were in the wreckage of Bran and Dunne's home. And from the remainders of the uncanny fire, probably ground zero for one or more of Zeus's strikes. What now? Sylvie gnawed her lip. Somehow, she'd expected Dunne to appear the instant Bran had returned to earth, but it had been fifteen minutes at least. And no Dunne. No Furies. Nobody at all. A nagging thought crossed her mind. Bran in tears. Maybe—

She dropped down to her knees beside him. "Bran, c'mon, Bran. Is he alive?" Bran responded about as well as a catatonic. Sylvie wrapped her arms around herself, shivering in the cold and wet. Suddenly all she could imagine was that they'd missed it all. That the city was dead, that everyone in it was dead . . .

Bran had finally stopped crying; now that the misery had left, he just looked blank, as lifeless as a pretty mannequin. She rested her hand on his pulse, and was reassured. It actually felt stronger, his skin warmer. Maybe he wasn't in shock, but concentrating. Healing took effort.

Thunder rumbled, then continued long past the time it should have dispersed. Sylvie raised her head. *Vehicle. Big one.* Passing by. Military? She reached for her gun, but of course it was gone, burned up in the oubliette. She crouched, dragged Bran through the broken door with her. The rain poured in through the torn-out roof, but at least now she had a little shelter from whoever was out wandering the streets.

She should be glad. Evidence of life meant she wasn't too late, but she doubted people who were out in the storm were people she wanted to meet.

Sylvie maneuvered them closer to the still-burning rubble. The blue flames flickered and spat, and despite their icy appearance, raised the ambient temperature around them.

"My home," Bran said.

She nodded.

"Can't go back again," he murmured, sounding drugged, sounding dazed. Lost.

"Dunne?" she asked.

He closed his eyes. "Not sure—"

"Alive?"

"Yes," he said. "But gone one-track."

"Can you contact him?"

"If I said no, would you listen?"

She sucked in a breath. "If you promise to answer without your knee-jerk no. Be honest."

"I can't," he said. "I'm down to all but human at the moment, and I'm not even healed all the way."

"Shit," she muttered, and took a closer look. Still too pale, eyes too distant, too bruised. His body shivered in random bursts, spurred by pain, cold, or shock. "You going to be all right? You healed the big things first, right? Didn't leave your liver for last or something?"

He shook his head, shivering too hard to speak.

They had to get out of there; that wasn't in question. She hated to do it, but didn't see any other option. She huddled over her cell phone and dialed Demalion.

24

Shelter from the Storm

TWENTY INTERMINABLE MINUTES LATER, DEMALION ARRIVED. WITH company. She shouldn't have expected anything else. She'd run from him twice; now he was going to ensure she couldn't. It still hurt, still felt like betrayal. The ISI van forded its way through the water, its side door opening, discharging Demalion as well as another agent. A third agent, the driver, stared coldly at her and left the engine running, a low, angry sputter under the constant roar of approaching thunder.

Demalion dropped out of the van, splashing ankle deep, gun in one hand, a crystal glowing in the other.

Blind, she remembered. He couldn't have come here alone.

Wishful thinking, her more cynical self whispered. *The truce is over.*

Bran moaned at the sight of him approaching, and Sylvie felt like echoing it. Demalion raised his gun hand; all Sylvie could manage to do was slide herself in front of Bran.

"Dammit, Sylvie—take it already. I've got my hands

full, and I can't see for shit." He reversed his grip, flipped it so the butt was to her, and proffered it again.

She found a hopeless grin stretching her mouth. "You brought me your gun?"

"Yeah," he said. "Just in case." He dropped it into her eager grasp, then pulled another crystal globe out of his rain slicker, this one strung on a thong about his wrist. He cradled it and smiled. "Better. Seeing in stereoscopic again."

Sylvie turned the gun over in her hands. Just metal and engineering, and it worked like a shot of endorphins on her exhaustion and guilt, pushed her toward giddy relief. "Does this mean we're engaged?"

Bran shuddered against her and pushed away from Sylvie. Betrayal glossed his eyes. Demalion, she remembered, was no friend of Bran's. "I can't trust you—"

"I got you out of the oubli—"

"*I* got us out," Bran muttered. "*You* tried to kill me." He forced himself to his feet and nearly fell. He yanked away from Sylvie's lunge, from Demalion's blind grasping, and stumbled into another pair of arms.

"It's all right," the second agent said, propping Bran upright, then kneeling before him. He looked up at him like an adult would a scared child, calming. "You know I won't hurt you. We just want to get you someplace safe. Get you back to Dunne."

Some of her good feelings faded fast. Sylvie might be willing to work with Demalion, but the whole stinking ISI? Not a snowball's chance.

And this agent in particular was no friend to her. She still had bruises from his grip as he marched her toward the elevator. She curled her fingers around Demalion's loaned gun and wondered how she was set for bullets.

Gingerly, Bran rested his hand in the man's hair, like a man petting a dog he thought might bite.

"Rodrigo, he's all yours," Demalion said. "Let's go."

"Go where?" Sylvie demanded.

Demalion said, "You've done your job, Sylvie. You could go home, get out of this mess, be with Alex—"

"Alex is why I need to finish this. Dunne's going to pay me for some unexpected expenses. . . ." She wiped rain out of her eyes, shook her head. "I'm a burr, I'm a tick, I'm glue. Get used to it. Now, where're we taking my client?"

Bran settled into silence, and Sylvie was warmed to think he hadn't wanted to be left alone with the ISI. She didn't delude herself that meant he liked her whole bunches either, but it was something to be one up on them.

"ISI," Demalion said, and raised a hand, forestalling her mutiny. "Any port in a storm, Sylvie." His shoulders tensed, visible even through the weight of the rain slicker. His jaw clenched. He was ready to argue her down on this.

"Fine," she said. Right now, the ISI seemed the only choice. Bran was done in, she was off her turf and at the end of her endurance.

"What?" Water beaded over Demalion's arms, spouting over the crystals dangling in his grip.

"I said, fine," she said. "Fine. We'll go to your big ISI safe house, secret base, justice league hall of doom, whatever you call it." The surprise on his face and the wariness on Rodrigo's made her capitulation almost worth it. At least she was unpredictable.

Rodrigo scowled at her, and she marked it. Best not to turn her back on him. Rodrigo really didn't like her. Demalion got the scowl in turn, and Sylvie rephrased: Rodrigo really didn't like anyone.

"If you're both done jawing," he snapped. "Bran needs rest. Warmth." He jerked off his rain slicker, draping it around Bran's bare shoulders.

Team one, Sylvie remembered. Bespelled to worship and protect. Demalion's choice of ally suddenly made more sense.

"After you," she said.

"Finally," Rodrigo said. He swung round, shaking water from his back like a dog, and picked Bran up. Bran moaned, and Rodrigo nearly dropped him, bespelled not to harm.

Sylvie snapped, "Don't you dare—"

Rodrigo's grip firmed; Bran clenched Rodrigo's slicker with two fists, holding tight.

"Jesus," Sylvie muttered. "I don't care what kind of spell Bran put on your brain. Use some fucking common sense. A little hurt *now* is better than a world of hurt later." She strode away from the door, reached back, and tugged at Demalion's sleeve. "Stop gawking. Start walking. You were the one in a hurry."

Bran moaned again as Rodrigo stumbled into movement, heading through the soggy, smoldering wreckage of their living room. This time the whimper had more of laughter in it than pain. "I thought it was just me," Bran said. "You treat everyone like that. Even your lover."

Sylvie opened her mouth to protest, and a slap of salty rain whirled around and drenched her as if guided. She sputtered; her face stung under the impact. She shook her head, her ears ringing like a rock-concert attendee.

Demalion slid close to her, crystals held before him, glowing like avid eyes. They shone with the same ghostly light as the occult fires around them. Demalion was feeding on the god-power, she thought.

"*Bran* bespelled Rodrigo?"

"Bran, Dunne, same thing," Sylvie muttered, and clambered into the van. Careless, she chastened herself. Demalion wasn't stupid. The ISI would cream itself if it thought it could harness a god's power.

As if Bran had the same concerns about walking into the lion's den, he said, "Kevin knows where we're going. He's going to meet us there."

Sylvie winced. That might work as a threat, but it was sure to spark questions. A god knowing where his lover was, was one thing. The human lover able to account for the god's whereabouts was a little sketchier.

"You seem to know an awful lot about this," Demalion said.

Bran flushed and fidgeted. Rodrigo ushered Bran into the van, actually growling at Demalion.

"Dunne's not the only power here," Demalion said, joining Sylvie with only a minimum of fumbling with his crystal "eyes" and the van's door frame. "What's Bran's deal? He put the whammy on Rodrigo, not Dunne? Tell me, Sylvie. I need to know."

She put her arm around his waist, guided him whisper close, and gave up that last secret. It wouldn't take long for Dunne to add it up; this way she at least got cooperation credit for the info. "I've sung this song to you before. Bran's not just an artist, not just a pretty boy, not even just a human. He's a human that was and is a god."

25

Looking for a Way Home

BURKE, THE DRIVER, WAS THE HARD-EYED MAN SYLVIE HAD LAST seen leaping off a subway platform, but he took one look as they spilled onto the van's floor—wet, bedraggled, shivering—and cranked the heater to full.

"HQ?" Burke said.

Demalion nodded. "Full speed," he said.

Burke pulled the van into motion. Kneeling up, Sylvie saw the shell of Dunne's home vanishing behind them, her last glimpse of it the pale blue of St. Elmo's fires devouring its bones. The van turned onto higher ground, taking them into the heart of the city. It was a strange new world in this storm light. Chicago's tall buildings glimmered and developed uncanny life under the influence of the battling gods. Ornamental art deco fripperies swayed like anemones, took on luminous edges that gleamed through the darkness. In their phosphorescent glow, gargoyles left their moorings and skittered across facades of buildings, talons chinking into plate-glass windows and leaving little starburst fractures behind.

The city felt drowned in power. Two buildings, leaning

close, tangled their carved eaves in some slow undersea
waltz.

The sky was livid, bruised black and green; lightning
seared a white-hot line across Sylvie's retinas, and she
jerked back, slamming into the van's layers of hard plastic
and metal. Surveillance equipment, all useless now, unable to show what was truly happening. The LED colors
blinked idly, red, green, amber, taking the pulse of the
city, recording bits and pieces of mysteries that might
never be solved.

Right now, tired as she was, she'd have traded them all
for a single bench seat. Scuffling noises drew her attention
through the dimness. Rodrigo was rummaging through a
duffel.

Demalion leaned close, stroking his hand up her arm,
finding her shoulder, putting his mouth close to her ear.
She didn't think it was going to be for sweet nothings, and
his first words proved her right. "*Which* god?"

She sighed. Always something more with him.

"Sylvie," he murmured, and the heat of his breath
against her chilled skin made her shudder. "It's dangerous
not to know. I want to follow your lead, but you have to
share. Prove yourself worthy of trust."

"Eros," she whispered back into the curve of his neck.
The name seemed to have thundering weight in the world.
The rain, drumming on the roof, faltered for a bare second, as if the sky were listening also. She put her hand up
to stop him from blindly repeating it. "Don't."

Across the van, Bran watched her, unblinking, until
Rodrigo pushed a black sweater over his head. "Arms,"
Rodrigo said, and Sylvie grimaced at the god of Love
being fussed over like a toddler. Bran pushed the too-long
sleeves up afterward, looking insanely frail.

Playing to his audience, she thought. *Ensuring Rodrigo would stay protective. Good enough.* The more helpless the ISI thought him, the less likely they were to keep
him. More eyes on her, and she found that Burke kept
shooting looks back over his shoulder as he steered.

Sylvie followed his line of sight, and said, "Oh for God's sake. So the shirt's transparent. Get over it and drive before I push you out of the car."

Demalion broke into a laugh, muffled it in her shoulder, then drew back, studying her, unsmiling. "What are you looking at, blind man?"

He reached out and traced a pattern on the sopping back of her shirt, centering between her shoulder blades. "Tattoo," he said. "*Cedo Nulli.* The same phrase Lilith used for her password. Coincidence?"

Aware of Rodrigo's gaze sharpening, of Bran's recoil, Sylvie said abruptly, "Consanguinity."

He stiffened, and she said, "Don't give me that. At least I didn't inherit a tail."

"Is that supposed to mean something to me?"

"You're clever. Figure it out."

"Old Cat," Bran said.

"Hey," Sylvie objected. "He can figure it out. If you want to 'help' so much, how 'bout you unblind him. Cryst-o-vision might be nifty, but he can't hold a gun."

"I didn't say that," Demalion said.

"You gave me your gun," she said. "You didn't *need* to say anything." It warmed her heart, it really did. He trusted her to kill for him. "C'mon, Bran, even you have to see that having your point man blind isn't a good thing."

"I can't—" Bran said, and stopped. She wasn't surprised: She'd felt her expression change. Harden. Darken.

He licked his lips, dropped his gaze, and started again. "It's Kevin's will that did it."

"With your power threaded through his," Sylvie said. "Doesn't that give you an in? The oubliette, which was keyed to you, opened for him." She kept her voice conversational though she could feel Demalion bird-dog tense beside her, eager to be healed. She wanted to know if she could talk Bran into something rather than bully him into it.

Bran sighed. "I can try."

"That's better than can't," she said. "But how 'bout you just *do*?"

The van lurched, wheels slipping on wet asphalt, and Bran let himself fall forward into Demalion's lap.

From her vantage point, Sylvie twitched. Bran looked up into Demalion's blind face in an assessing way that made her want to yank him right off Demalion's lap and slap him. The worst part was she wasn't sure if it was jealousy driving it or sheer unabashed possessiveness. Demalion was *hers*, dammit. Or would be. If he proved himself trustworthy. If he didn't feed both her and Bran into the ISI mills.

She bit back the growl in her throat, kept it unvoiced. Demalion didn't need the ego stroke. Bran, though, he heard it, again showing the uncanny awareness of things relating to love. He smirked and stroked Demalion's arms beneath his wet sleeves. Demalion's breath hitched.

The van rocked again, and water splashed up alongside with such force that it sloshed over the high windows. Sylvie took the opportunity to escape Bran's game and crawled forward through the jolting van, collecting a bruise on her shoulder when she failed to adjust to a sudden swerve and clipped a computer console.

She crouched beside the driver's seat. "Bad roads?"

"Rain," he said. His hands were white on the steering wheel. "This is definitely not natural."

"The fact that it's coming down hard enough to flake asphalt didn't clue you in earlier?" Sylvie sniped. The road was degrading, turning to a crumbling, jagged mess that threatened their tires. She took another look, realized exactly how dense the rain was ahead of them, and winced. "It's been doing this all night? It *is* night, right?" It was hard to tell. She'd lost time in the oubliette, and the skies were apocalypse dark. She took a look at the speedometer and sighed. They were creeping along the roads, at a bare ten miles per hour, and as much as she mocked the ISI, she couldn't even blame him for it. Not in this weather. Not when strange shadows swept the night to either side of them. When behind all the dark windows, people's fears might be taking on a new life—all it took was a little talent and spillover from Dunne or Zeus. She wasn't going to tell him any of that, though.

"Acid rain, whatever. I don't care. It's been doing that for over twenty-four hours," he said. "But it wasn't *parting* for us before." Burke goosed the accelerator, pushing the van into the sheets of water before them; the wheels slipped a little. Rain pounded the roof of the van for a bare second and stopped, like a switch had been thrown. Now that Sylvie paid attention, she realized she'd been hearing that sound pretty much constantly, a low, intermittent drumming. He swerved hard to the right, erupted into rain. It ceased again.

"We're carrying valuable cargo," she said. She licked her dry lips again, felt a tiny pain, tasted salt. Somewhere in the evening, she'd bitten it, or had it hit hard enough to bleed. "Someone's paying attention." She ignored his questioning glance, not inclined to share more information than that with the ISI.

Behind her, she heard Bran murmuring, "You know, it's traditional to make an offering when asking a god for aid."

"*I* didn't ask," Demalion said, and his tone was so strained that Sylvie's attention swerved back. He held Bran close, protecting him from the jolting of the van, but his jaw was tight and tense. "*Sylvie* asked."

"Jesus," Sylvie said, rejoining them in the back, dropping to the floor with a thump that rattled her bones. "You haven't fixed him by now? What have you been doing?"

"Fixed is a bad word," Demalion said. "Fixed is what you do to your dog." He seized on the possibility of banter with such enthusiasm that Sylvie knew he was scared.

"Just making sure he understands what I'm going to do," Bran said. "I can't reverse the curse. I can alter it. But it doesn't absolve him of the sins that Kevin punished him for."

Rodrigo smiled in mindless agreement, nodding,

blissed out by Bran's presence. Sylvie slapped his shoulder speculatively, and he merely rocked back and forth. Bran's spell might have been too strong. This close to the object of his worship, for this long, Rodrigo had stopped functioning. She wondered what would happen if she slapped Bran, instead.

"I make no apologies," Demalion said. "I did my job to the best of my abilities." His breath was coming fast, a little panicked, and from the way he clutched at the crystals in his hands, Sylvie thought even his clairvoyance was being balked now.

"Bran," she warned. He ignored her completely.

Bran shifted closer in his lap, pressed his lips to Demalion's neck, and said, "That's been the excuse for countless acts of atrocity. Aren't you a thinking man?"

Demalion's eyes were pure silver now, as reflective as mirrors. Sylvie wondered if Anna D would be able to scry through her son's eyes, and slid to one side, just in case. She had enough problems already without getting the sphinx in a hissy fit.

Demalion regained his poise, and said, "Dunne was a source of unusual and unknown power. I owed it to my employers, my city, and my country, to assess the situation accurately, the better to protect my world. So, yes, I followed my orders. I judged them fair and worthy of being obeyed."

"You ruined everything," Bran said. "Everything." He put his head in his hands. "All I wanted was to live in peace. To be myself and happy with Kevin. And then you came, and Lilith—I want to hate you so much."

Demalion's stern face softened. He might not have been able to see Bran's beauty to be seduced by it, but the voice was powerful enough to have an effect, Sylvie thought.

"You can't," she said. "Can you? Not because you think Demalion has a point, *which he does*, mind you, but because you can't hate—"

"I lack that fire," Bran admitted.

"What burns hot but can't keep a body warm?" Sylvie said, under her breath. Demalion and Bran turned identical expressions of startlement on her; she shrugged. "Sorry. Thinking of the sphinx."

Bran made a moue. Apparently, the sphinx was unpopular all the way around, if even he wasn't a fan.

"Sphinx," Demalion said. "There's *another* monster in all this?"

Sylvie let out a breath. So not the time to get into *that*. "Bran, we're under the gun. Pick up the pace."

Bran leaned back against Demalion, and Demalion fended him off, one palm flat against Bran's chest, one fist holding a crystal with white-knuckled intensity. "Just the eyes," Demalion said. "*Nothing* else."

"I don't understand," Bran said.

"No Rodrigo specials," Sylvie said. She waved at him, flipped him off, and Rodrigo ignored her completely, still blissed out on Bran. "No 'love me, love me' force-fed into his veins. Rodrigo might as well be meat at this point. We need Demalion whole, sane, and sharp-witted."

"If I'm going to love someone," Demalion said, "I want it to be *my* choice."

"I understand," Bran whispered. "Didn't I choose my own life? My own lover?" He knelt up, blew a stream of air across Demalion's eyes. When Demalion's eyes blinked shut, Bran kissed the closed lids, right then left, and followed with a lingering kiss on Demalion's forehead above the third eye.

Wonder what that'll do to his clairvoyance, Sylvie thought.

Demalion's hands, fisted tight around the crystals, suddenly spasmed and collapsed inward. His arms twitched; veins popped as if something had blocked their flow. "Bran," Sylvie said. "Heal not hurt."

Demalion groaned deep in his throat, through clenched teeth. His body shivered through tiny seizures.

"Shh," Bran whispered, "'s tricky, this."

Demalion fell out of Bran's embrace, gasping, eyes

wide and strained. The distortion in his veins raced upward, bulging through his shoulder into his neck.

Demalion's eyes went blank and glassy, the eyes of a corpse, and his body fell limp. Sylvie shoved Bran out of the way, grabbed Demalion's collar, got her hands on his throat. His pulse was strong, as was her relief. He blinked, and his eyes—changed. First from mirror blind back to his usual dark espresso, but then, before Sylvie could let out her held breath, his eyes lost color, ending as gold and as glossy as heartless topaz. The pupils rounded, then slitted catlike, before rounding outward again.

"What did you *do*?" She let Demalion go and shook Bran. She got in two good shakes before Rodrigo lunged forward and stopped her— They all fell into a tangle of limbs; she elbowed him in the throat, and Rodrigo yelped hoarsely. She kicked again and hit something unyielding—the driver's seat. Burke snapped at them from the front. "Trying to concentrate! Keep it down back there!"

"I did what you asked," Bran said, extricating himself from beneath her and Rodrigo with a muttered curse. "Kevin remade his vision. I couldn't restore what had never changed as far as his body was concerned. That takes a full-powered god. I just . . ."

"What did you do?" she asked.

"He had two genetic choices," Bran said. "Kevin's spell blinded the man. I sort of . . . switched tracks on his genetic line, went the monster route?" Her hands fell away from his sweater, and he said, "Hey, he can see now. That's what you wanted. . . ."

"Demalion," she said. "You can see?"

His voice was rough, furred with pain and amazement when he finally woke from the abstracted trance he seemed to be in. "It's not like it used to be," Demalion said, blinking. He closed his right eye, looked through the left, then reversed it. The pupils slitted and flared. "It's—Sylvie—it's *more*. It's—there are patterns. I was a clairvoyant, could see things that happened out of my sight. But this . . . Now, I think I saw bits of my future." He rubbed at his head, and sighed, obviously at a loss for explanation.

"Old Cat," Bran muttered.

Demalion's attention swerved; his eyes flared. "Old Cat? What the hell are you—"

"Can you shoot straight?" she interrupted. Unmasking his genealogy in an ISI surveillance van was a capital-B-bad idea. Burke was casting disturbed glances back their way.

"You are a scary woman. But yes, I can shoot again. Hell, I might be able to shoot around corners at this point."

The van swerved again; rain splashed, ceased, and Sylvie snapped, "Stop playing with the rain, Burke, or I'm going to come up there and take my bad mood out on you."

"It's . . ." Burke said, the van slowing. His hands shook on the wheel. "It's not rain anymore. It's blood."

Sylvie beat Demalion to the front by a nose, and peered out. Her view was rapidly eclipsed by Bran, who lunged over her and jerked the window open. Blood spattered across his hands, his face. He brought his palms up to cover his eyes. His shoulders shook. He scrubbed at his face as if he could unsee it but only managed to smear the blood into his skin.

The rain's grey needles changed to a slippery darkness that ran the streets, foaming at the curbs. The rain-free zone over the van wavered and closed in, blood falling stickily and staining the windshield, obliterating even the minimal line of sight they'd had before.

Sylvie shuddered. If the storm cloud was Dunne, the rain sprang from his soul, his immortal body. That was why it had parted for them, Dunne instinctively easing his lover's path. Rain turned to blood—

"He's hurt, isn't he?" Sylvie said. "Zeus did him some real damage." She watched the wipers sheet blood from one side of the windshield to the other, catching in the small cracks that the heavy rain had created.

"Yes," Bran whispered, his face pale beneath the streaks of his lover's blood. His lips lost color.

Demalion leaned into Sylvie, and said, "You were counting on Dunne, weren't you?"

"We still are," she said. Lilith was still out there somewhere, awaiting her chance. Sylvie's skin prickled in waves of gooseflesh; she rubbed her arms fiercely, listening to her little dark voice growling a litany of warning. Lilith was smart. Too smart to waste time hunting them through the storm when she had to know how limited Sylvie's resources were. When the ISI were the only resource she had left. Lilith was sitting somewhere, warm and dry, waiting for her ISI lackeys to give her a call.

"Best to go on as we've begun," Sylvie said. "Not a lot of choice left. Dunne knows where we're heading; no injury short of death will stop him. And gods? They don't die easy."

Bran turned to look at her, eyes wet, but he nodded. "That's right. That's right." If he sounded like he was trying to convince himself, Sylvie chose to ignore it. ·

"That's fine, but we're not driving anywhere in this," Burke said. "I can't even see the road."

"It's the straight line in front of you," Sylvie said. "Just go slow."

"I can't see, Shadows!"

"I can," Demalion said. His pupils widened and shone. "Old Cat, right?" His expression was grim, beginning to piece it together. "Burke, move over."

"No way, Demalion. No way in hell." Burke put his hand on his gun butt. "I'm not letting you kill us all."

A particularly vivid line of lightning etched itself across the sky, a long, jagged whip that started out phosphorescent white and lasted long enough to turn blue and red as it burned the clouds. Sylvie's hair crackled and popped with all the power in the air. Something plummeted toward them, heard first, a whistle of tortured air, then a dark shape slammed into the roadway before them with an impact that shattered concrete and cracked all the windows in the van.

Burke put the van into reverse, fighting Demalion's hand on his, but before anything else could happen, a fistful of talons slammed through the remaining shreds of window glass and into Burke's chest. He shrieked, but only very briefly.

Alekta withdrew her hand, opened the door, and pushed Burke's body into the center aisle. "*I'll* drive." Her claws closed around the steering wheel, shifted back to human shape, though red to the wrist. Her human shape was considerably the worse for wear. Her leathers were scuffed, torn, and singed; her hair was matted dark with water or blood.

Sylvie's breath was gone. Bran was curled tight into Demalion's side, whimpering.

"He worked for her," Alekta said. "Waiting his chance to turn on you." She stretched out a hand; Demalion flinched back, but all she did was reach out to tug on Bran's hair. "Hey, baby. You okay?"

"He'd be better if he weren't underneath a corpse!" Sylvie snapped.

Alekta turned her eyes from the unseen road, grabbed Burke's body, and hurled it out the door. It bounced once, jolting the van as it rolled under its rear tires. The van slithered and slewed, but Alekta steered with complete confidence and worrying speed.

Demalion's jaw was clenched so tight, Sylvie thought he might splinter teeth. With a muttered, "Monster," he crawled into the back as far away from Alekta as he could get. Sylvie wanted to shake him. Monster or not, Alekta was a welcome ally; a better bodyguard than Sylvie could ever be. It wasn't for simple strength and power; Sylvie had seen Erinya beaten back *twice* by humans—Lilith and herself—and pounded by Hera, and there was no hint that Alekta was more powerful than her sister.

No, where Alekta beat Sylvie in the bodyguard stakes

was her motive. Sylvie wanted Bran alive, because a living Bran meant Sylvie got her job done, and more, Alex—healed or resurrected, she didn't care which. Let Val mutter about dark magic all she wanted; Sylvie knew how and when to look the other way when it came to getting results.

Alekta guarded Bran for more reason than duty. The little crooning encouragements she made as she stroked his hair argued genuine concern.

Sylvie, on the other hand, kept listening to the little dark voice murmuring, *He's not worth all this trouble.* Sylvie agreed silently. Bran had accused her of blaming him for his kidnapping. She'd denied it then, but there was truth to it. This was his fault. A runaway who brought trouble wherever he went.

Children ran away all the time, and Sylvie had always felt a sneaking sympathy for them, even when she was the one paid to find them and haul them back. They all ran for the same reason at the core—they felt powerless where they were. But a runaway god? Maybe there was a level of contempt in her view of Bran. If he'd been stronger, more able to use the power he held— Catch *her* ever being that weak-minded, and she didn't even have any power of her own.

Bran caught Sylvie watching him and reflexively smiled, then traded it for a warier gaze. Alekta growled and slammed the van to a halt.

"Sylvie," Demalion warned. "We're here."

The ISI building loomed ten stories above them, its marble facing traced in witchlight that gleamed like candle flame through the bloody, murky sky.

"You sure this is safe?" Sylvie asked.

Demalion dropped out of the van. "Do we have a choice?"

26

Reunion

IT WASN'T RAINING AT ALL ANYMORE. BLOOD, WATER, OTHERWISE. The sky above was a mass of swollen clouds with a heart coiled inward like a sky-pinned hurricane, roaring and howling at being kept from the earth. Centered, of course, directly above the ISI nest.

Lightning crackled around the ISI headquarters, weaving a net in the sky, illuminating the edges of the storm clouds, and tangling them in a fine, fiery mesh. Sylvie muttered curses. That net looked far too familiar. Dunne had blown it off once before, but could he do it again?

Bran emerged from the van, Alekta on his heels, and yelled something in Greek, throat taut with the effort, hands fisted by his sides. Words of encouragement to Dunne, or abuse heaped on Zeus. Sylvie hoped for the encouragement. If anything could aid Dunne, that would be—

The world flashed. Reversed itself in a quick strobe like a photographic negative. White/black, dark/light, and so bright that Sylvie's eyes burned even as the sight etched itself into her vision. Sylvie cried out, heard Bran and Alekta echo it. She knuckled tears from her face, green spots dancing, red lines flaring in her line of vision. But she could still see—she let out a gasp of relief.

"Sylvie," Demalion said, helping her to her feet. *Knocked down by a vision,* Sylvie thought. Gods played rough, but to what—

"Inside now," Demalion said. He made sure she was steady on her feet, and helped Alekta get Bran to his. No sign of strain on his face—but then again, now sighted like a sphinx, he might not have been affected by Dunne's flashbulb imitation. Or he might have seen it coming and closed his eyes.

Rodrigo stumbled out of the van and fell to his knees, gazing blindly upward at the skies. Demalion reached for him, and Sylvie said, "Let him be. He's no use to us like that."

Demalion nodded, though obviously reluctant, and took the lead again. Sylvie followed him through the deserted lobby, the marble floor sheeted with pink-tinged rainwater; her sneakers slid and turned her hasty advance into a near skid. ISI had its own troubles, obvious by the dimness. The lobby was lit only by emergency lighting, small amber pools in the murk. Where were the guards?

"That lightning net got sucked inside the clouds." Demalion asked Bran, "That's good, right?"

"Not *sucked* inside," Bran said. "In is out, out is in. He reversed himself. Like I did in the oubliette. Zeus bonded the net to Kevin's storm skin, trapping him. But when Kevin turned himself inside out—"

"He trapped Zeus instead," Sylvie intruded. "He learn that little trick from you? 'Cause I think he did it better. He didn't bleed. Demalion, where the hell's the staff?"

"Dead. I can smell it," Alekta said, sweeping by them both. Her feet made strange clicking noises on the floor, and when Sylvie looked down, she saw talons peeking out through boots that looked less worn than grown.

"Hurry, Bran." Alekta held open the doorway into a dark stairwell. More emergency lights, more concrete.

Demalion hesitated in the lobby, sweeping it with a golden gaze, seeing more than just the present.

"Something got here ahead of us," he said.

"Lilith?" Sylvie snarled. It made sense. She'd understand what the storm clouds meant, even if the general run of the ISI didn't. All her ISI contact would have needed to do was let her in. Her little dark voice whispered, *Tick tick*, gleeful about the coming confrontation. Sylvie fed on the anger, let it narrow her focus.

Demalion shook his head. "I don't know. I see it, like smoke in the air. Went up the stairs. Be careful, Sylvie."

"Smoke," Sylvie said. Her thoughts turned inexorably to balefire and the missing staff.

"Hurry," Alekta said again, a growl in her voice. She shoved Bran into the stairwell, then took point.

"Wait," Sylvie said. When had the situation gotten out of her control? But Bran moved on obediently.

He turned back to say, "If I can get to Kevin before Zeus wiggles free, it'll be all over." Hope was written across his face.

That made Sylvie oddly angry. She recognized the hope for what it was. Yes, two-thirds of it was relief that Dunne was alive, but one-third of it was that selfish desire to cling to stronger forces. "Zeus will stop, just like that?" Sylvie scoffed. "Because he's what? Scared of you? A god who ran to the mortal realm?"

He let his silence answer her, and Sylvie bit her lip. Not big with the confidence builders. "You joining us, Demalion? Your turf," she said.

He had balked at the base of the stairs, gazing at the walls. He pressed his hands to his temples, blinked a couple of times. "Yeah," he said. "Go up. It all happens on the roof."

She let him draw alongside her, and said, voice low, "Tell me Bran's fix is holding."

"Eyestrain," he said. His tone was flat. "This is going to take some getting used to. Tell me, Sylvie. Will my mother be able to train me?"

"She won't need to. We'll make Dunne put it back right," she said. "After. No monster for you."

He laughed, the pinched tension lines in his face easing. "Only you would think you could bully a god, Shadows."

"Someone has to do it," she said, not really in the mood to be mocked.

On the risers before her, Bran suddenly gagged, froze in his tracks. Alekta paused, one foot poised on either side of the charred corpse on the landing, inquiry in her face.

"Go on," Sylvie said. They had no time for squeamishness, not when she expected Lilith at any moment. "Just don't look."

Bran closed his eyes, face drawn and sick, and followed Alekta's quick hop over the corpse. Sylvie knelt by the body. Security guard, flash-fried, skin bubbled and crisped, eyes boiled out. It hadn't been balefire. Balefire would have left only a greasy, sooty smudge instead of this wreckage. She and Demalion traded a wary look.

Sylvie pushed past the fifth-floor landing, legs aching with weariness. Storm light seeped down from above, limning the edges of the stairs in silver, showing the clear shot to the top. Bran and Alekta seemed diffused in its gentler light, blurred shadows moving forward. The roof door was open already, she thought. Invitation? Or trap? A little surge of anticipation made her pick up her pace. Now. Lilith.

Sixth floor, seventh floor passed in a blur of drumming feet echoing back at her. Eighth floor and she saw the shadow of whoever waited for them. Her breath came quick, anticipation, excitement, fear, rage—Sylvie couldn't even tell what drove her on.

But the woman who stepped out of the shadows, grinned down at them with a mouthful of fire, wasn't Lilith, but Helen. Sylvie faltered, everything in her stammering with surprise. The little dark voice whispered into that void, *Kill her.*

Alekta, half a flight ahead of her, shoved Bran downward, sending him plunging toward Sylvie. Demalion halted his fall.

A white streamer of flame engulfed Alekta, pushed the Fury into the landing wall, and pinned her there, snarling, growling, shrieking pain and rage.

Sylvie's breath sucked out of her lungs; she covered her eyes, but the only burn in them was due to the wash of heat. Not balefire, then, but bad enough. The temperature skyrocketed in the close quarters. *Down,* she thought, but they needed to go up. Fight and flight warred. The cement walls turned ashy, soaking up heat like a kiln, preparing to bake them. Even the icy air from the storm was beaten back under the wash of flame.

Alekta was nothing but a writhing mass in the fire.

"Help her," Bran whispered. "Please." His forming tears dried instantly in the superheated air.

"She's a Fury," Demalion said. "She killed one of my men."

"She's my friend," Bran said. Demalion just shook his head, held Bran tighter.

"We wait," Demalion said.

"On the clock here," Sylvie said. "We've got two gods upstairs and somewhere there's a woman who wants to cut out Bran's heart."

Demalion smiled at her. His gemstone eyes slitted in the fire's light. "She's burning her borrowed power faster than she can replace it. We wait. Then we take her out."

Yes, the little dark voice agreed. *We don't run.* "Let's not give her the chance to recharge," Sylvie said. She slipped up the stairs, though her skin complained about getting closer to the heat, and Demalion bit back a protest. Alekta was silent now, struggling less. And Sylvie was going to stand by and wait for her attacker to run down, the better to kill her. Behind her, she heard Demalion's grunt of effort as he blocked Bran's sudden rush to aid Alekta. A quick glance downward showed Demalion holding Bran in an armlock.

The fire sputtered, and Sylvie rushed the landing, gun before her.

Demalion said, "Not yet," but Sylvie was in no mood to wait. Disappointment drove her, she realized. *This is it? My last obstacle?* When it came down to Lilith's endgame, she'd sent a mortal pyrokinetic to stop them? She hadn't thought Lilith such a coward.

The flaming Fury a torch at her back, Sylvie narrowed her eyes against residual dazzle and took stock of her opponent. "God," Sylvie said, "that can't be comfortable."

Helen was wreathed in her own fire; it cloaked her, shielded her, more—Sylvie squinted against the brightness—it held her together. Ropy stitches of fire covered the damage from their previous encounter, and her eyes were smoking in their sockets.

"Shadows," Helen said. Her voice was the dry crackle of kindling. Alekta dropped beside Sylvie, all seared meat and angry, making staccato attempts to stand, crawl, attack—but she was down. Helen rictus-grinned and threw her hand out toward Sylvie. The fire faded to a curtain of dry heat before it touched her.

Helen whimpered and tried again. A wild flame shot from her hand like out-of-control fireworks, palest blue and far hotter than anything they'd seen from her before, a vast wave of scalding air, pouring down the stairs toward Sylvie, toward Bran.

Alekta staggered up and embraced the flame, sucking it into herself, while Sylvie dodged.

Alekta . . . frizzled away, and as the fire faded, a rusty flood of loosed power streamed upward. Helen tried to seize it, reaching flaming hands for it, and Sylvie shot her, point-blank.

Helen's legs gave out. The fires that sealed her wounds faded, the injuries reopening, sending blood sizzling over her skin.

"Should have gone to a real doctor," Sylvie muttered. "Should have stayed out of my business." She raised the gun again. Her hand shook; exhaustion, she realized. Demalion said, "She's down, Sylvie. You don't have to—"

Helen opened her mouth; smoke and flames traced the outline of her lips, and Sylvie fired. The bullet, despite her tired hands, went where she wanted it to go. Helen's skull cracked, and the flame began to devour the body.

"I had to," she said. "She had a taste of real power. Even if it faded. She'd want it back. If I didn't kill her now—it'd be worse later."

"There are laws, Shadows," Demalion said.

"Oh, *those*," Sylvie said. Her voice cracked with exposure to the residual heat. She coughed for a moment, then said, "'Cause the ISI's success rate at dealing with the supernatural evil is so superb. . . . Oh wait. Your success rate depends on pushing them off onto people like me. I take it back, Demalion. This isn't your turf. It's mine. Will you follow my orders?"

"Will you kill people needlessly?" he shot back.

"No cells, remember," Sylvie snapped. Then, remembering Demalion had become her ally, she said more calmly, "Besides, did you really want to leave her at our backs?

"Come on," she said. "Not nice to keep a god waiting." She fought back a mad giggle, unsure what she found so funny. She wanted to chalk it and the strange distance she felt from her body to simple exhaustion and fear, but wasn't sure she believed it herself. Demalion's eyes, palest gold and slitted, rested on her, judging her. It didn't worry her much. When it came right down to it, Demalion was an ISI agent; he'd side with the safety and security of the human world. He'd side with her.

Tick, tick, the dark voice reminded her. She concentrated on what had to be done. "Bran, let's go. Up and at 'em."

Bran pressed himself away from the wall, nodded mutely, then said, "All right." He allowed Demalion to escort him upward.

When they stepped out onto the roof, Sylvie's attention went straight to the sky. Hard not to when the clouds were as close as they were outside an airplane window. Darker than night, they condensed themselves, boiling toward the ground.

"Demalion, thank God," a man said. "Do you know what's going on? We came up to see what was happening, then got stuck up here. There's some type of firestarter—"

"Not anymore," Sylvie said. She tore her eyes from the clouds to look at the scattering of ISI agents on the rooftop. One suited agent, two security types in army wear, and a single secretarial-type woman, clutching a pencil close, another behind her ear, her mouth unattractively open.

"Stairs are clear," Demalion echoed. "But stay here. We might need backup."

"But—but—" the secretary started to protest.

A paler spindle of cloud stretched down, touched the gravel; the entire substrate rippled, shivering beneath Sylvie's feet, like a horse about to buck under a fly's bite. It was not a soothing sensation.

"Stay here?" the suit said. "I don't think—"

"Stay put. That's an order," Demalion said.

Yes, Sylvie thought, let them witness it. See what they precipitated with their snooping and spying, their bureaucratic ideals and careful forms. They needed to know the world wasn't theirs alone. These were civilians on whom she wouldn't waste one iota of worry.

The roof surged again. Sylvie shifted her feet, trying to keep her balance, and the roof crackled with the sound of splintering ice. It froze her in her steps. The clouds wound themselves down the delicate tornado, masses of them spilling damply down to the roof.

Like water, the clouds poured faster and faster as they got closer to the last of the storm. The entire storm condensed as it came, flaunting a strange disregard for physics. It should miniaturize, or become blackly impenetrable. Instead, it stayed simultaneously vast and confined in a small space. A hurricane spinning and taking a vaguely human shape. In its slow movement, Sylvie could see distant gulls windswept and trapped. One winged close, a beady, desperate eye rolling at Sylvie, a flash of white-backed feathers against an ominous sky, then it was far distant, still in the cloud loop.

Sylvie's ears popped and rang. She saw Demalion's jaw working to relieve the same pressure, but his eyes never left Dunne. He stood like a man stunned, gaze flickering from cloud to empty sky and back again. How did this all look to him, to his new vision? Bran slipped away from Demalion, heading for Dunne, and Sylvie grabbed at him. "No," she said.

A sudden pulse thrummed out beneath her feet, a shivering, skin-crawling burst of power. Dunne was bleeding some of it off, Sylvie thought, to fit the man shape better. Power saturated the air and made such a presence of it that Sylvie found she could actually taste it: the sharp bitterness of ozone underlaid with something sweet and heady, darkly floral, and beneath that, the entirely mortal scent of gun oil and powder. The air reached some strange critical mass, and in a Fortean moment, everything changed.

Demalion's hands grew clawed and furred; a tail lashed behind him. His eyes widened; he turned his hands over, flexing the claws.

It wasn't just Demalion, either. The agents on the roof were affected in other ways. The suited ISI agent coughed, a hand to his throat, alarm on his face, and an abiding panic in his eyes. The camo-clad agents collapsed, their drawn guns foaming into water, and their skins following after. The secretary squeaked and darted behind the choking suit, putting him between her and Dunne. So much for backup.

Still, Dunne apparently had a chivalrous core; only she and the secretary remained unchanged.

Bran slipped free from Sylvie's restraining hand, heading toward Dunne and the heart of that altering power.

"It's dangerous!" she called.

"Not to me," Bran said.

Sylvie half expected Bran to be sucked in toward the cloud as brutally as if he were trying to embrace a black hole.

Instead, the clouds firmed, and a gusty sigh moistened the roof like the last salvo of a spring rain. Then it was Kevin Dunne again, yielding to flesh for the pleasure and need of touching his lover again.

He was barely recognizable as the man Sylvie had met three days ago. Wounded—his right arm ended at the elbow, and he tucked the stump against his side. Exhausted—his eyes kept closing, springing open to gaze down at the man in his arm, and closing again. All too human yet, at the same time, so completely not.

Lightning danced in his eyes; his mouth, parted to whisper Bran's name, showed storm-cloud core, but the clutch of his left arm around Bran's waist, the way he rested his cheek against Bran's bright hair, the open thankfulness on his face was all human love and relief. Bran twined himself around Dunne as if he meant never to let go.

Dunne arched back suddenly, spat out a crawling mass of lightning that, like the storm before, was too dense, too big, and too small all at once. It spat sparks and melted holes in the roof before it rose into the sky like a demented UFO and disappeared.

It made Sylvie shudder with her own relief. The right thing had happened. The rare thing. The happy ending.

"That was Zeus?" she said, into the lull. "What's the forecast?"

"Fleeing to Olympus and gnashing his teeth as he goes," Erinya said, appearing on the roof and slumping to a low, pained crouch. *One tired punk puppy,* Sylvie thought. *If the girl had ears and a tail, they'd be drooping.*

Magdala followed, cast a glance around, and said, "Where's Alekta?" Demalion gestured mutely toward the open door into the building. Magdala darted for the stairs.

Her voice rose from the stairwell. "Hera's furious. She wanted her power back. Zeus *promised* her her power back. But Dunne was too strong. We were too strong, and Zeus got nothing." She carried Alekta's body onto the roof, cradling it like a child, and Dunne moaned.

He released Bran reluctantly, their hands clasping to the very last, then came across the roof in strides that weren't quite human, taking too few steps and still making too much progress.

The secretary's nervous squeak took on a slightly desperate note as she realized she was between Dunne and Alekta's body. She backed up, hands fluttering. The pencil snapped between her fingers with a tiny crack, oddly distinct in the charged atmosphere. A broken half rolled down the roof, butted up against Sylvie's foot. She stared at the splintered edge for a moment, something clicking in her head. What was broken couldn't always be repaired.

"It's not over," Sylvie said, without conscious volition. The little dark voice growled out between her teeth, "It's not done yet. It's sweet you got your big reunion scene, but Bran has to die."

27

Broken World, Breaking Hearts

EVEN BEFORE THE LAST WORD LEFT HER LIPS, DUNNE PIVOTED, HEAD-
ing for her. Sylvie threw up her hands, projecting *Unarmed, unarmed!* as loudly as she could, though it went
against the grain.

Dunne halted, his hand on her throat, eyes black with
fury. This close, she could smell the ozone on his skin,
feel the prickling thunderweather hiding beneath his false
flesh, feel the tiny muscles in his fingers moving as he
failed to crush her windpipe. A warning. An effective one.
This close, with the echoes of what her voice had said still
jagged in the air, she couldn't see anything of the nice guy
in him at all.

Behind him, Bran wrapped his arms around himself,
shaking, turning his face away from her. She couldn't
blame him. The last time she'd held that note of determination in her voice, she'd run him through hell and back.
Demalion leaned in and offered support, putting a clawed
hand on Bran's shoulder, eyes resting on her, oddly un-
surprised.

It all happens on the roof, he had said.

She curled her fingers around Dunne's wrist, shifted

her gaze from the Furies creeping up behind Dunne, murder in every line of their bodies.

The little dark voice wound beneath her own, tangled in her breath, winding around her mind like a secret demanding to be told. *It's not done yet. You know what has to be done.*

"You know it's true," Sylvie said, obedient to its prompt. "This can't continue. I know you want to pretend nothing's changed, but that's not possible. Look at the damage that's been done." The ISI suit was frozen in place, perhaps literally, Sylvie thought, as a shift in the available light revealed a stony skin. *Man gone statue*—she thought. *There's a Greek god for you.* Tucked behind the shelter of his body, the young secretary huddled, hands clenched tight in her braided hair.

The wrist under her fingers twitched, and Sylvie swallowed hard. Distraction would be fatal now. "If that doesn't move you—look at Bran. He's wrung out, damn near dead several times over. And he's *still* a target. He's walking power, a scrumptious all-you-can-eat buffet, ready to be devoured by any starving sorcerer who comes across him. This will happen again and again and—"

"I won't let it—" A low growl in three-throated harmony: Dunne, Erinya, Magdala.

"Did you *let* Lilith take Bran? I didn't think so. She's just a human who can plan better than most. What will you do—what will Bran do, when a bigger threat comes hunting? When a god who wants to shake things up thinks Bran's just what the doctor ordered. But if Bran *dies*—"

Her weight dangling from Dunne's arm let her mind catch up with what her body knew—he'd transported them again. Not far, only a matter of feet, but enough that his grip on her throat and her grip on him, were the only things keeping her from plunging ten stories to the ground.

She wriggled the toes of her sneakers onto the roof edge, seeking purchase. An updraft climbed her spine, stirred her hair, and made her shudder.

"You brought him back to me," Dunne said. "Do not make me repay you this way."

"Make you?" Sylvie said, gagging a little as his hand tightened. "You're the fucking god, Dunne. Can I *make* you do anything?" She was bone-cold and not from the drop at her back. That drop was a problem, a tiny part of her acknowledged. The bigger problem, the one she couldn't understand, was her moving mouth.

They were her words, her throat, her thoughts, undeniably. It wasn't even that she didn't think she was right, it was simply that she had had no intention of starting this here and now. But the voice in her head was on its own time line and wouldn't be swerved. *Tick tick,* it reminded her.

"You were a cop, Dunne," she said. "You know the hard truths. If someone really wants to get to Bran, they will. Sooner or later, they will."

"No," Bran said. "I was careless." Taking the blame on himself, trying to defuse the situation between Dunne and Sylvie.

Demalion drew Bran back, wrapped him close, clawed hands crossed over Bran's chest, keeping him from worsening the confrontation.

Sylvie said, "Lilith used the *Maudits* and the ISI to flush Bran from hiding so she could net him. You couldn't stop *her*. You never even saw her coming. How could you fight another god?"

"It would be war," Dunne said. "They wouldn't—"

"Sure they would," Sylvie said. She coughed. The pressure around her neck hadn't tightened, but it hadn't slackened, either. "Zeus acted fast enough when he thought he could slaughter you. And as for war . . . The gods must love it, or humans wouldn't do so much of it."

"That doesn't make killing Bran the solution," Dunne growled. His grip increased, and Sylvie fought the urge to kick him. He wouldn't feel it, and she—she needed the fragile support of the rooftop ledge under her feet.

Magdala panted in mocking synchronicity with her. Erinya crouched, ready to leap into movement, but her eyes went from Sylvie to Dunne and back again, and her mouth turned down. Sylvie directed her next words to her.

"I don't want him dead. . . ." Pause to fight for a breath past those tightening fingers. "I want . . . regain godhood. It's not death . . . *transition*."

Staring up into Dunne's eyes, past the sheer horror of the inhuman storm-cloud gaze, she realized it wasn't only rage that drove him to choke the life from her; it was fear.

Dunne *agreed* with her: Bran *was* a target. All Dunne's training told him so, probably in ways more vivid than Sylvie could imagine. But, when it came down to it, he didn't believe Bran had personal strength or will enough to make the transition from human death to renewed godhood.

Dunne looked at his lover and saw the man who yielded rather than fought, who bent, and endured the unendurable until he broke. He didn't see, maybe didn't *know*, the man Sylvie had met, the one who could be pushed to action.

Over Dunne's shoulder, she saw Bran leaning into Demalion's arms, seeking external strength, hiding his face in Demalion's skin, hiding from an argument that was literally life and death for him.

She tried to lick her dry lips, but her teeth were locked, gritted against the strain on her neck. Maybe Dunne was right. Maybe she was.

Only one way to find out. She and the dark voice meshed, found perfect harmony. *"Kill him to set things right."*

Sylvie gibbered inside, all her calm a veneer. She was right. She knew she was right. Bran couldn't continue this life, not now that the clock had gone midnight and the masks had come off.

She knew she was right. Panic still scrabbled at her insides. *She* was right, but *something* wasn't.

"It has to happen," she said. The concrete beneath her feet crumbled a little as Magdala rested her weight on the ledge next to Sylvie's sneaker, nudging her that much closer to the drop.

"We won't let you," Magdala growled.

Behind them, Demalion pulled Bran closer, stroked the bright hair with a taloned hand, as if shielding Bran from the inevitable bloodshed. Demalion's eyes, as ever, rested on Sylvie. Waiting. *Her turf,* she had declared. *Her orders.* Whatever vision he had had earlier, he was willing to follow her now. She had a momentary jealousy that he knew how this played out. She had no idea at all.

Magdala nudged Sylvie's ankle again, playful as a shark, and Sylvie teetered backward. A breath tore from her lungs; if Dunne's hand hadn't held her throat so tightly, it would have been a scream.

The street, ten stories down, might as well have been miles below. All it promised was an inky abyss, the darkness of a city without power—she whimpered. It seemed an impossibly long way to fall.

"I won't allow you to hurt him," Dunne said. So calm, so reasonable, despite the hand pushing her toward her death.

Demalion stiffened, claws flexing, a query that she read across the roof. *Now?* he asked with his eyes. *Now?*

She nodded, a tiny jerky movement, constrained by Dunne's hand.

Demalion never hesitated. Hell, she thought briefly, he'd probably known what she was going to ask before she did. He'd had some time to come to grips with it.

We are both going to die for this, Sylvie thought.

So be it, the dark voice murmured in response.

A sudden flare of doubt struck her: The dark voice usually argued for survival at all costs. Scratchy panic flared again; she twisted in Dunne's grip. Something *was* wrong. With her.

Demalion's hand tightened on Bran's nape, and Bran raised his head in pained protest. Demalion stilled the movement with his second hand, an apologetic caress along Bran's jaw that the god of Love couldn't help but lean into, just before Demalion used the leverage to snap his neck.

The sound echoed, froze them all as if it had been the sound of giant shackles snapping open rather than a tiny section of bone and nerve being displaced. Bran folded in Demalion's arms.

Dunne threw back his head and howled. Sylvie clung to his arm like a limpet, shrieking over his wordless grief and rage. "Don't undo this, don't rewind it. Help him *regain*—"

Then he was gone from her grip, the Furies' betrayed howls joining his, but she had no space to care as gravity tugged her backward.

One foot fell forward, over the edge, planting her on the roof, but the other fell back, over the void, her weight following. Sylvie fell, scrabbling at the crumble of concrete ledge, at ashy remnants from the lightning's touch, and managed to hook one arm over the edge. She hung there, panting, muscles shrieking.

A stray, crazed thought raced her mind. So *this* is why the schools used to count pull-ups during health assessments. . . . She sobbed for breath, for strength, for control over the animal part of her brain, which whimpered in panic. Her feet kicked and dangled. Wetness splattered her face, traced her forehead and cheeks, dripped to the roof; rain, sweat, tears, blood—she had no idea and no time to investigate. A white fog rushed over her, drifting to the streets below, and making her hands slippery in passing.

She flailed, hooked her second arm up over the edge, and kicked madly for any type of footing beneath the overhang. Finally, she got a toehold planted on one of the ornate sculptural details so loved in Chicago, and kicked her weight upward, scratching her hips and belly and thighs, ignoring the pain, and pulling with all her might. She landed on the roof like a netted fish, graceless, flailing, but considerably more grateful.

Until she focused on the picture outside of her own pains and tribulations, on her near call with death. She had escaped her own death, but Demalion—hadn't. His blood painted the roof, sprayed wet and fine in a giant circle as if the two shape-changed Furies had hit him so hard and so fast from both sides that his skin exploded.

Blood ran black in the moonlight, sticky on Sylvie's face and hands as she frantically scrubbed it from her skin, and thick, gouting red where it ran from Erinya's muzzle as she ripped chunks from his chest and throat. His clawed hand spasmed as Erinya hit the long nerves in a body so recently destroyed, and his crystal globe erupted from the ruined flesh, glowing with dim ghostlight. Magdala made a long lunging slide at it, snapping her jaws, but missed. It rolled down the slant in the damaged roof, plummeted to the streets below.

Sylvie's breath caught in her chest, locked there. The guilt, the pain—it solidified in her lungs like iron. She couldn't breathe, couldn't breathe at all.

Dunne held Bran in his lap, face wild and strained. Bran's body was dissolving, flesh to motes of gold that shimmered in the air.

"You did it," the voice said.

Sylvie shuddered. She did it, and Dunne had listened to her—he wasn't rewinding the moment, wasn't undoing Bran's death, wasn't undoing *Demalion's.* . . .

"Please," she whispered, a thin thread of pain. The Furies' snarls were constant rumbles of sound as they continued to maul what was left of Demalion. Not content with simply killing, they were chewing him into scraps. Some crimes, Erinya had said, needed more punishment than a body could provide. Some crimes required destruction of a soul. . . . Sylvie gagged.

Demalion had killed Bran on her orders. He died for it, and Bran died for it. . . .

And for what? The motes that were Bran's essence kept spinning outward with no cohesion, no sense of sentience at all. She'd gambled her life, Demalion's life, Bran's life, and she had *lost.*

"I'm impressed," the voice said, and Sylvie realized it

wasn't internal any longer. An intense voice, so similar to her own, but not hers at all. Hadn't been hers . . . for how long? A *spell*. There had been a cracked stick in the subway, a broken pencil on the roof. A spell in two parts. Cocking the gun and pulling the trigger in two steps. Ready, aim, and fire.

Sylvie's words, her will, had been subsumed in a dangerous spell, insidious because it built on truth. Bran had had to die. But it shouldn't have been here. Shouldn't have been now. This could only benefit those who wanted Bran's resurrection to *fail*.

A few feet away, the secretary stood, shedding her false fright as easily as a lizard shed its tail. Lilith plucked two elaborately spiral sticks from her braid, tugged the glasses from her face, revealing two silver-blind eyes. She raised the glasses to her face again, winked at Sylvie, eyes dark and sighted behind the bespelled lenses.

"Oh, my dear. I gave you the command to kill, be my woodsman, and you . . . delegated. You are my daughter to the bone."

28

Grudge Match

LILITH HELD THE TWO SPELL STICKS IN HER FREE HAND. SHE TUCKED one over her ear, laid the other on her outstretched palm. Her eyes, even unfocused and blind, were intent. After a moment, the stick rose on point and began to spin in the palm of her hand. As it did, it created a tiny vortex. Bran's self, that misty shimmer of gold, began to flow toward Lilith, twining around the tips of the sinuously curved stick, feeding themselves through the larger eye at the top. Lilith grinned; the muscles in her forearm bunched as if the motes had a tangible weight to them.

She flipped the stick up, caught it, and brought it to her mouth, as greedy as a child with cotton candy, plucking tangled clouds free and dissolving them on her tongue.

At the first bite, she moaned, then flung the spelled glasses away from her. She licked her lips, and her eyes lost their blindness, shading back to their normal brown. "So much better," she murmured. She caught a last strand of gold on her lip with her thumbnail, sucked it clean. "A victory is so much sweeter when one can actually see it."

"Not a victory yet," Sylvie whispered, still on her hands and knees, still trying to surface above the grief that threatened to sink her. She'd been too confident in her resistance to spells even to imagine this trap.

Lilith set the spell sticks in either hand, setting both to spinning. "What's going to stop me?" Lilith said. "The Furies? Sorry, granddaughter, they're too busy hunting your man's soul. They've destroyed his flesh, but it's not enough for them. Not after what he did." She devoured another long streamer of Bran's power, then turned heavy-lidded eyes back to Sylvie.

"It'll take them a while. His soul's tricky. It's a little more than human. It's not merely a matter of rooting it out. It's a matter of chasing it down. They're rare beasts, you know. A sphinx cub can take a millennium to gestate. The man you delegated to die in your place might have been only thirty-some years old, but he was a thousand years in the making, a thousand years lying cradled beneath his mother's heart."

Sylvie whimpered under her breath; guilt surged up a higher notch. She hadn't thought it was possible. But there it was, scouring her from the inside out. Dry-mouthed, sick with revulsion of her own skin—she wanted to be someone else, anyone else, anyone but the monster.

Magdala snapped her jaws in the air near Sylvie, swallowing down some fluttering piece of light, silvery grey. A soul fragment? Another piece of Demalion eradicated completely.

"Dunne," she said, a breath of scratchy hope that he could make her pay for what she had done, and end this agony of guilt.

"Dunne has his own problems," Lilith said. "Some of which are mine, dammit."

Sylvie managed to raise her head. Anything that put that note of startled frustration into Lilith's voice had to be good.

She was wrong.

Dunne still knelt where he had cradled Bran's body, shoulders slumped, face racked by fear and longing. He was surrounded by a smeary gold shimmer like a veil. Sylvie's heart gave a tiny, hopeful leap; the gold mist was denser than it had been, less spread out, more focused. Bran was trying to re-form. . . . No, she realized, he wasn't.

All that was left of Bran was trying to get closer to Dunne, seeking a familiar shelter. In this state, it meant they would mingle together, meant that Bran would dissolve his soul into Dunne's, eradicating himself in a way Dunne could never repair.

A tiny wisp of gold darted in toward Dunne's parted lips, licked inside, and Dunne gasped, covering his mouth. "No, baby. No. Be yourself. Please, Bran, come back to me." A storm cloud pressed outward from Dunne's skin, pushing back the gold.

The shimmer, rejected, grew wispier.

Lilith's spindles still worked, collecting ingestible power, but with the power motes dispersing outward, she had to work harder to draw less.

"No," Sylvie muttered. God, no. Dunne's shell-shocked concentration was focused solely on keeping Bran and himself distinct entities, his own power trickling out through the stump of his right arm like mercury, thinning him down. While he worried about that, Lilith would keep picking off Bran nibbles here and there, until she had enough, or until Bran faded into the sky to be snagged by any passing collector. And it was all Sylvie's doing.

The Furies were gone from the roof, vanished after a tiny ghostlit will-o'-the-wisp, chasing an elusive piece of Demalion's soul; hell, Sylvie thought, they were probably mad enough to kill Anna D simply for birthing him. Then they'd be back for her.

The thought didn't upset her, and *that* realization shocked her out of the stupor shrouding her. Her despairing inertia was another spell, some fail-safe that Lilith had planned and implemented to keep Sylvie out of the way.

Lilith feared what she might do.

Given something to fight, Sylvie dived for the heart of

her stupor, rooting out the miasma that weighed her down, bringing back awareness of her body as more than a vehicle for numb despair. Her hands clenched tight in the softened roof tar.

She might be guilty. She might be damned. She probably wouldn't withstand the Furies' vengeance any better than Demalion had, but dammit, she'd go out better than *this*. Demalion deserved better. Bran deserved better. She reached inside herself and found that little dark core, the voice that spoke survival and spite. It sprang to life at her touch, shrieked in outrage at what Lilith had done to her.

Make her pay, the little dark voice commanded.

First things first, she answered back. There was more at stake here than avenging her pride.

She marshaled a savage edge to her voice, as intimidating as anything Erinya had voiced. "Bran! Stop it. You might solve your problems by melting away, but you'll screw everyone else. Every *thing* else." She broke off to pant. The acid rage felt raw in her throat, but it was a pain that was clean and good, familiar and strong.

"Leave him alone," Dunne snapped. "He just died. He's confused. Give him a moment."

"We don't have—"

"Then make some time," Dunne said. A command.

"Shut up," Lilith snapped through a mouthful of power. She raised a hand, and a smear of gold flame rose from her fingertips.

"Gonna waste that on me?" Sylvie said. "You aren't that juiced yet; hell, your firestarter had more oomph than that. She was nearly to balefire when I shot her down."

"Shut up!" Lilith repeated, but didn't release the flame.

Handicapped, Sylvie thought. Lilith couldn't fight and suck in power at the same time.

"Sorry. It's in the blood. I'll talk 'til I'm dead, and there's nothing you can do about it." Sylvie grinned as the smear of power in Lilith's hand sucked back into her skin, the spindle beginning to rotate again. She'd bought a little time.

"Bran, listen to me," Sylvie said. "There's no safe haven for you like this. Not even within Dunne." Across the roof, she saw Dunne's anger warring with a tiny spark of hope that she might be able to rouse Bran faster than he could. The grey shielding around him sparked and flared as gold motes rebounded from it. His damaged arm was unraveled nearly to the shoulder, and he made no attempt to repair it, concentrating instead on corralling Bran.

A tiny breath of a whisper, a voice made entirely of air, reached her. Bran wasn't thinking of his own safety. *I can heal him. If he lets me in. Tell him to let me in,* Bran said, muzzy-voiced, tenuous, and focused on the wrong thing entirely.

"Don't know that I trust your motives," Sylvie said. "You're greedy for protection. Heal *yourself* first."

Distracted by proof of Bran's existence, even so attenuated, Sylvie nearly missed the movement on her left. She dodged but too late. Lilith's foot caught her cheek, flung her back. Sylvie's head hit the edge of the roof, and the world greyed for a moment. When she came back, Lilith's foot was planted on her throat.

"Forgot for a moment that I didn't need to use my new power or even my hands," Lilith said. "Not for you. My little girl with no power of her own."

Sylvie kicked up, thumped Lilith weakly in the back of her thigh. The woman's face showed no pain—invulnerable to blunt force as well as bullets—but pushing someone off balance had nothing to do with injury and everything to do with leverage.

She gagged, shifted beneath Lilith's instep; the pump's narrow heel punched a tiny hole in her skin, and Sylvie kicked harder. Lilith staggered away, her hand flying wide to help her keep her balance, and the vortex spell faltered. Sylvie rolled to her knees, levered herself to a crouch, panting for breath.

"I didn't say you could fight back," Lilith said. "I don't have time for this, you stupid girl."

In the background, Dunne murmured quiet prayers to

the only god he still worshipped. Bran. Eros. Pleading in one breath for him to come back. For him to stay away in the next, as Bran persistently tried to merge his powers with Dunne.

If she could just distract Lilith long enough, it would all be over. Surely Dunne could make Bran see that restoration had to come before repair.

"Did you really think I'd just lie down and die?" Sylvie said. "It's not in my nature, any more 'n it's in yours."

"You overestimate yourself," Lilith said. "You're only mortal. You've done your task. Go home. Mourn your dead. Put another notch on your gun." The air around Lilith shivered; amber light glowed beneath her flesh as the power that had built up on the spindles overflowed and poured into her skin.

Tears started in Sylvie's eyes as Lilith's taunts flicked her on the fragile hurts beneath her rage; she forced them back. "Thing of it is," she said, voice ragged, "someone's got to stop you, to save what can be saved. And like it or not, someone always seems to be me."

"Pity them, then," Lilith said. "You'll help them into their graves. You think your snakebite girl is still alive? Or did she die with your name between her teeth, cursing you—"

Sylvie's hearing blacked out. She lunged out of her crouch like any linebacker and tackled Lilith around the knees, taking her to the roof. Or at least, that was her intent. Lilith's body was as unyielding as granite. Side effect of the invulnerability spell? Or evidence of Bran's power successfully integrated? Sylvie didn't stop to theorize.

Lilith stopped the vortices with a frustrated shout, fisting them in one hand. She dodged Sylvie's next lunge, but when Sylvie elbowed her in the throat, Lilith actually quailed. Sylvie noted it, but the neck jab had never been more than a feint. She had a more important target.

Sylvie's other arm snapped out, a knife-edged hand aimed at one thing only: the spell sticks clenched in Li-

lith's fist. She struck them straight on, yelped at the jolt
they gave her, as unpleasant and as startling as the den-
tist's drill. One of them slipped Lilith's grip, and the
golden glow stopped completely.

Sylvie made an attempt for the second stick, but Lilith
burned some of her stolen power to fling Sylvie away
without touching her. Sylvie, half-expecting it, rolled this
time and saved herself a concussion.

Sylvie panted, "No finesse, no points for style. Brute
force is so passe. Some god you'll be."

Lilith ignored her, scrabbling for the fallen stick, and
Sylvie pounced, this time, directly for the neck: She *liked*
it when Lilith flinched. She wanted to see it again.

Lilith's back was to her, her nape bared as she fumbled
the sticks back to her hands, back to spinning. Perfect for
Sylvie. She got both hands around Lilith's neck, but her
nails made no impression. Lilith sent her sprawling back,
without apparent effort.

But Sylvie had felt something beneath the bland
button-down collar, a serpent slide of leather under her
clawing fingers.

A flash of memory; Lilith in the subway, tricked out in
goth cowboy gear, complete with sheriff's star. It had
hung from a woven leather thong. Then, Sylvie had
thought it just wry fashion statement. But if Lilith wore it
still, wore it when every other part of her masqueraded as
a white-collar worker, from the crisp white blouse to the
navy pumps beneath dark slacks—it might be something
else. Something important.

A hailstorm of pebbles and gravel poured from the sky,
stinging Sylvie's bare hands, her neck, her head, increasing in size as the torrent continued. Sylvie huddled up,
protecting her face, wincing as a rock the size of a softball
pelted the roof inches from her, biting her lip as her back
stung and welted.

Lilith was getting the hang of her stolen power and had
found a way to keep Sylvie off her back from a distance.

Dunne was murmuring again; this time it wasn't in

any language Sylvie recognized, something liquid. She wondered briefly if it was aimed at helping her. She doubted it.

Sylvie rolled away, aiming for the shelter of the roof-top stairwell. Each step toward safety put Lilith farther from her reach.

The golden motes in the air swirled suddenly, blown as if in a sudden draft. A faint ripping sound reached her, and a sudden stink of arterial blood. Erinya emerged onto the roof in human form, sheeted in blood, with three livid claw marks across her face.

Magdala galloped into sight on Erinya's tail, four-legged, skeletal, bat-winged, and heading straight for Lilith.

Lilith threw up her hand defensively; fire leaped from her fingers, first ruddy, then white-hot, coiling around her palm. The fiery blast washed over both Furies, tumbling them over the edge of the roof. Sylvie clapped hands over her eyes before realizing it wasn't balefire, that she hadn't just bought herself a ticket to an ashy death. Lilith wasn't that strong yet, couldn't summon balefire by wishing it. *Yet.*

The glow that stippled Lilith's skin faded, as did the fire. The rocks pelting Sylvie shrank back to pea-sized, stinging, but mostly harmless. Lilith panted and forced the vortex spell back into action.

Don't let her get that strong, the dark voice said. *Stop her now.* With no further plan than that, Sylvie moved forward. She didn't even bother with stealth. Between the whine of the vortex spell, the rattle of falling gravel, and the Furies clawing their way back onto the roof, Lilith's attention was well and truly elsewhere.

Lilith wasn't a sorcerer, or hadn't been. Her invulnerability had nothing to do with her immortality; she'd implied as much in the El station. It might have everything to do with an amulet. Gadget witches did so love their trinkets.

Sylvie got her hands on the cord, and Lilith knocked

her back again, but it was too late. The thong whizzed through Sylvie's clawing hands, the sheriff's star thunked into her palm, and Sylvie *yanked*. The thong snapped, leaving a tiny red welt on Lilith's neck, already beading with blood.

Lilith clapped her hand to it, eyes wide and wild.

"Forgotten what pain feels like?" Sylvie asked. "I'll remind you." She drew her fist back and punched Lilith in the face.

Stupid, the dark voice said. *A wasteful blow.*

But so very satisfying, Sylvie told it. Between her fingers, the thong seethed with motion and repaired itself. Sylvie laughed, and slung it around her own neck. *Now,* this *is more like it.*

Sylvie had never been all that fond of hand-to-hand fighting. She much preferred her guns, which made variables of size and strength almost irrelevant.

But this—she was just as glad the guns were spent. She craved Lilith's skin shredding under her nails. Use *her,* would she? Sylvie didn't play pawn for anyone. She stepped out into the spray of gravel, pausing for a brief second to enjoy the fact that she couldn't feel its sting.

Erinya crouched low, ready to dive in, and Sylvie's attention swerved. "Mine," she growled.

Erinya dropped her eyes in surprising obedience. Lilith took the chance to murmur a spell under her breath and vanished. Magdala clambered over the roof's edge, fighting her own weight, and sniffed. "Still here," she growled. "Somewhere."

Sylvie swept the rooftop with her gaze. An eddy of gold shimmered near the other side of the roof, not spilling over, but disappearing steadily nonetheless.

There, Bran said, a thready whisper.

No shit, she thought, already in motion. If she misjudged, if Lilith dodged the right way, Sylvie would find herself over open air, but that thought only occurred in the tiny piece of space and time between motion and contact.

She slammed into Lilith hard, nearly had them both over the edge.

Doesn't matter, the dark voice crowed. *You can stick the landing.* Sylvie laughed again, an edge of mania in it. Lilith flared under her hands, bubbles of power rising, bursting against Sylvie's clutching hands.

"Burn," Lilith said. The illusion of invisibility broke with her voice.

Sylvie's shirt smoked.

Sylvie shook Lilith, even while slapping at her own skin, damping whatever blaze had started. The metal of the star felt warm against her skin.

Lilith jabbed at her eyes with the spell sticks, and Sylvie caught her wrist, pounded it against the edge of the roof. Lilith yelped. The sticks clattered free. Sylvie snatched them, ready to hurl them over the edge.

"Burn," she heard Lilith shout beneath her, and the sheriff's star on Sylvie's chest burst into white-hot flame under Lilith's touch. The star fell free; slagging as it went. Sylvie screamed as the molten metal wrapped around her arm for a brief caress before dripping to the ground. Her hands spasmed, and she dropped the spindles.

Beneath her, Lilith screamed also, as the effort she poured into breaking the invulnerability charm left her mostly human again. Sylvie wrapped a hand in Lilith's hair, attempted to pound her skull into the roof.

Lilith gouged at Sylvie's neck, reaching toward her eyes, and Sylvie rolled away, covering the spindles with her body. Lilith tried to get them, nails digging at Sylvie's side, and Sylvie fumbled a rock into her hand. She brought it up, crashing it into Lilith's temple. Lilith dodged in time to turn it into a scalp wound, nothing more serious, and Sylvie, in pure incandescent rage, rolled her over and struck down.

Squirming, Lilith caught the blow on her shoulder and managed to pinch the long nerve in Sylvie's arm. The rock in her grip trembled, but Sylvie refused to let go.

A sudden pulse, like a giant heartbeat, rocked the roof. A roll of grey fog passed over them, through them, and circled the roof, corralling all the drifting bits of Bran.

A small distant part of Sylvie wondered what that effort had cost Dunne, to use his own faltering power with such a finesse for borders, but most of her was fixated on wiping Lilith off the map. In the silence as the world was cut away from them, she heard a tiny word, a word weighted by Erinya's growl. *Matricide.*

Sylvie's hot blood cooled as if a glacier had breathed on her. Magdala met her eyes, licked away a bloody streak on her cheek with a long, inhuman tongue, and sat back, watching. *Any excuse,* her posture said. Yeah, Lilith wasn't her mother, but hadn't Anna D said it? That Sylvie was the first of her children to be awake? Maybe it was close enough to give them the excuse they wanted.

The rock in Sylvie's hand trembled and fell. The dark voice wailed as they fell out of concert with each other, but Sylvie shuddered. So close to a crime the Furies considered unforgivable. The dark voice snarled, *You're damned anyway. Dead anyway. Make her pay for it.*

Tentative hope sprang up in Sylvie's chest. Would Erinya bother to warn her if her life were already forfeit?

Lilith laughed, a sound hoarse and sore. "Cain's child, too. A rock in your fist. But you should never show mercy." A flick of her fingers, and a tiny stick dropped into her hand, a thin matchstick, brittle, breaking, a tiny ghost flare promising balefire. . . .

Sylvie scrabbled for something, anything, found a weapon, plunged it into Lilith's chest. Lilith's shriek broke off into a familiar whine. Sylvie glanced down, at the blood on her hands, at the spindle embedded in Lilith's rib cage. Glowing, spinning, dragging power directly into her heart.

Mistake, she thought. *Bad mistake.*

As if Bran had just been waiting for blood, the motes that made his soul poured toward Lilith, as if *she* were the black hole. Sylvie heard a protesting gasp from Bran, but it wasn't repeated. Instead, the gold began to shift and struggle. If Bran had been sleepwalking through the transformation before, now he was awake, aware, and very afraid. The more concentrated streamers of his power coiled tightly around Dunne for aid.

Lilith vanished from beneath Sylvie, reappeared closer to Dunne, closer to Bran's power.

Sylvie pushed herself to her feet. She didn't know what she could do, but she had to do something. Dunne was at the end of his strength.

She shook her head. Careless thinking. He wasn't at the end of his strength; he was at the limits of his ability to *control* that strength. In the storm-cloud core of him, Sylvie saw a sight as bleak as a nuclear winter. He could stop all this. Smite Lilith, force Bran into shape, but he couldn't do that and keep his strength confined. Working against himself was burning him to nothing. The raveling of his body was considerable. His torn arm was gone, and a large divot was eating out his rib cage.

"Erinya. Magdala." Dunne held out his good arm. There was pain in his voice. "I need you."

Magdala leaped forward. Dunne held her close, and she dissolved into him. Erinya looked at Sylvie, and said, "Save Bran."

"Eri—"

"I only kill things; sometimes you save them," Erinya said. She turned and burrowed into Dunne, fading. His body, torn and winnowed, arced. Light flashed once, and when it was done, he was whole again. But his right arm was a thing of scale and feather, with a hand that flashed talons.

Lilith glowed brightly against the grey shielding Dunne had surrounded them with. Sylvie gritted her teeth; she was going to get swatted like a bug buying Dunne some of his "moments."

She took a step forward, and Dunne's hand caught her,

pulled her back as he passed her. "I'll deal with her. You—" He licked his lips. She caught a pale glimpse of fangs on the right side of his mouth, the jut of animal muscle, before his words made it through. "Help Bran. Protect Bran. Whatever he needs to put himself back together."

29

Picking Up the Pieces

HELP BRAN. PROTECT BRAN. SO MUCH EASIER SAID THAN DONE, Sylvie thought, when she was overwhelmed by the idea. So much simpler to fight an enemy than aid an ally who had given up. Lilith wanted to be a god so desperately, and Bran—he had wanted to be human. And Sylvie had taken that away from him.

Sylvie had failed before, pulled defeat from victory. She had no intention of doing so again, not when Demalion had died to make this victory possible.

Across the roof, Lilith scrabbled at the shielding Dunne had ringed them round with, tearing bits free like curls of paper beneath a cat's claws. Under Dunne's influence, the curls only rewound and sealed themselves tighter. Lilith wasn't going to be able to run away.

Lilith doesn't need to, Sylvie thought. Not if she could absorb more of Bran. The power still flowed toward her, into her, like water running inexorably downhill. Dunne must have been thinking on the same lines; a strange construct swirled into place around Lilith, gleaming like a mirror and acting like a dam. Power still slipped in, under, and over it, but it was a bare trickle compared to what had been heading her way. The rest of it pooled up against the dam and glimmered, a wealth of power and potential just drifting.

"Bran," Sylvie said. It was a whisper, drowned in the sounds of Lilith cursing Dunne as she chipped at the dam, temporarily letting go her attempt to escape the shield. Made sense, Sylvie thought. If the shield fell, and Lilith escaped, the power would pour after her; with the dam up, though, she couldn't take the power with her.

Of course, if Sylvie could get Bran back together, Lilith could do nothing, either. Bran's mind was still around, somewhere—his occasional words reassured her that her task was at least theoretically possible.

A subtle vibration of rage, so low-pitched that Sylvie felt it in her bones before she heard it, came from Dunne, as Lilith continued to fight him. Dunne had taken more than the Furies' strength for his own, obviously, Sylvie thought as she watched him stalk Lilith with a predator's calculated patience. Unearned patience. Sylvie wanted to scream at him to hurry.

Do something, the little dark voice warned. *If you fail here, Dunne will take us apart. Or Lilith. The only way to win—*

"—is if Bran's whole," she said. Behind Dunne's rooftop shielding, strange bursts of white light flared and faded. Someone or something was working its way in. A wild card no one wanted or needed.

Sylvie spun, looking, hunting for some hint that Bran's consciousness was near and able to hear her. The gold spill of his power seemed massed in three places; one, the mindless juncture of Lilith and working spindle, two, the needy coils winding about Dunne, and—there—by the stairwell. A cloudy density hovered, heedless of the currents of struggle. It wasn't particularly big, but it was almost man-shaped.

Sylvie realized it was hovering over Alekta's corpse. Definite consciousness, she thought. Grief—an inevitable part of love.

"Bran," she said. She put a tentative hand out, stirring the nebulous cloud to shifting, sending a cold chill through her skin, as if a ghost had turned in its path to touch her in return.

She loved bad jokes, Bran whispered. *But she didn't know that until she came to be Kevin's. Until she followed him to the mortal world. This is my fault. But I thought—*

Hurry, hurry, the dark voice shrieked, but Sylvie tried a gentler approach.

"You thought you could get away with it," Sylvie said. Her lips were dry, and when she licked at them, one cracked and bled. "You thought you had it all under control. It hurts to find out you're wrong," she said. "But dying isn't going to make anything better."

That's not what you said earlier, Bran communicated, and, despite the sullenness, Sylvie was heartened by his anger. Anything was better than that pervasive grief and despair he'd been projecting a moment ago. Anger, she could live with. But grief—it drowned her, made her numb, thinking of a pair of gold-flecked eyes.

Behind her, Dunne said, "Hurry, Sylvie." followed by a low groan.

Aggravation mixed with a healthy dose of terror spiked her. "You think Alekta's death hurts you? Wait 'til Lilith gets smart and uses your power for something other than brute strength. Wait 'til she uses it as it wants to be used. Wait 'til she goes for Dunne's weak point. His *heart*."

She can't. . . .

"She can. She will. She's not stupid, Bran. Just frantic. Why did she choose you in the first place? Not simply for your availability. She plans long range. She wanted your power specifically. She'll be a new and different and deadly kind of Love. And Dunne, who already has a piece of you in his makeup . . . I'm betting he'll fall easy. You may not have forced him to love you. She will."

His protests fluttered against her mind, and she shook her head, ignoring him. "Imagine what she'll do to him.

He'll be her puppet as she makes war on heaven, and sends the *Magicus Mundi* into chaos."

"No." An actual word. A brief eruption of mouth and teeth and flesh. "Kevin's *mine*." There was a hint of body breaching out of the glitter-ghost.

"Then you'd better fight for him," Sylvie said. "But you can't do it like this—she'd eat you up like dessert."

"You do it—"

"No," she snapped. "Bran, I can't—"

"Thought you didn't believe in can't," he whispered in her ear, a cool breath, a ghost of something warmer.

"Just do it," she said. "It's not my battle. Live or die, the world rests on you." She coughed, suddenly bone-weary. She dropped to a crouch, as close to a state of readiness as she could manage. Her head rang, and her vision blurred and faded. Her arm burned steadily where the charm had melted, and she kept smelling scorched flesh, even over the blood.

"I'm no good at confrontation," he murmured. "I couldn't save myself. You think I can save Kevin? The world?"

Sylvie bit back her retorts. He might be protesting, but he was also doing it. Pulling himself together, making something solid and real out of a ghost image in a gleaming fog.

Like the artist he was, he made a sketch first, a thinned-out body delineating the borders where paint would lie were this anything so ordinary as a canvas. If she had to name the sketch, Sylvie would call it *Apprehension*, his fear evident in every line, the edge of a bitten lip, an arm that wrapped itself around the jut of a rib, the nervous twitch of a man expecting to be struck.

It called for an encouraging word, but Sylvie couldn't find anything to say that sounded more meaningful than a Hallmark platitude. Her brain had defaulted to a whisper of desire—*Please, please, please, let him do this. Let him succeed. Let him be real again.*

His gaze, eyes bare hollows in a shelter of cheekbone,

turned to hers. The bitten lip tugged free of white teeth, flushed to color, and curled slightly. "Don't pray *for* me," he said. "Pray *to* me."

Across the roof, Dunne's spine straightened, as if the sound of Bran's voice was enough to give him a surge of will, enough to push Lilith back, to dissolve the dam at his wish, instead of hers. He used it like a tidal wave, a collapse of weight pushing the power back toward Bran and Sylvie.

Lilith spat a curse, hard-edged words that smudged the air and ignited. Dunne threw up a hand and shielded himself. When the curse faded, his shield crumbled and flowed toward Lilith. She said, "I won't let you stop me. And I won't let him." The next spell ignored Dunne entirely and pinpointed Bran.

Bran's shell lost definition as the spell roiled forward, absorbing all power in its path. Dunne reached to stop it, and his power was rolled over and into it, increasing the spell's impetus like an avalanche. Sylvie blinked. Power. Lilith wanted to steal Bran's power. The curse swallowed power. Sylvie forced herself to her feet, hurled herself in the spell's path.

Better be right, the dark voice warned.

The blast knocked her backward, scraped some skin from her elbows and her forearms, made her head ring, and gave her the unpleasant sensation of a hungry pig rooting at her body, bruising, invasive. Ultimately, though, it left her unharmed. *She* didn't have anything it wanted.

"Want to try again?" Sylvie said. "'Cause Dunne's on your tail, and I think he won't be fooled again."

Dunne slapped the next spell out of Lilith's hand; her eyes went black with rage. Sylvie said, "Back to work, Bran."

"Yes," he said. The process quickened; ghostly shoulders firmed, knots of bared tawny skin and shifting muscle that ran and flexed downward, drawing in the spine and a strong, bare thigh.

It was a bizarre sort of striptease, watching Bran's

body appear in segments from behind the veil of his power. The more he recovered shape, the more the scattered power on the roof flowed toward him and rejoined him. A defined hand, elegant and purposeful, created a long line of naked belly and narrow hips. He grazed fingertips down his newly created skin, as if he were reacquainting himself with how it *felt*, how it *was* to be a god, a being of pure will and power.

Sylvie opened her mouth to say something scathing about the need to play with himself later, but got derailed. Bran might be sculpting flesh, but he was still a painter at heart. His tracing finger suddenly left a trail in its wake, a last homage to the art he had preferred for so long. Butterflies bloomed on his skin; lapis lazuli, sunset orange, and crimson, striped and spotted, following the path his touch took, starting from his navel and swirling outward.

"Oh," Sylvie found herself saying instead. The wings looked dusty, real, quivering with his breath. She wanted to cage them beneath her palms, feel his skin warm and flutter against hers, wanted to taste them and see if their scales would melt on her tongue like raw sugar.

Pray to him? At that moment, she'd worship him, just for a chance to touch him.

She swallowed hard, closed her eyes, thinking he might very well be as dangerous as balefire to look at. She'd thought his human shell built to bring out mindless want; by the time he finished rebuilding his immortal shell, she might be a pile of ashes, immolated by her own desire.

A gasp reached her, and for a moment she felt relieved. At least it wasn't just her. Then the pitch of the voice warned her. Dunne lost focus, turning toward Bran as devotedly as any human worshipper, his face blind with joy and want.

Lilith stepped up behind him, skin-close, and Dunne didn't pay any attention, all his eyes on Eros.

"Hurry, Bran," Sylvie said. Building the shell was only the first step, after all. It wasn't enough simply to regain immortality, regain some of his power. He had to get it *all* back, and at present, Lilith was scooping it up at an enormous rate. Her skin—

Sylvie blinked, and in that single moment, Lilith found the core of Bran's power, that hopeless desire that fueled men's dreams and made them try for the impossible. One moment, Lilith was the Lilith Sylvie had come to know and loathe. The next—she flickered, skin warming, going from a too-pale, sharp-boned, witchy woman, to a *goddess*.

Still knife-edge lean, still competence and will made wiry flesh, but Lilith now appeared as sleek and as elegant as a glass-bladed sword. She demanded respect and admiration, and created in her beholders a helpless urge to touch, even if, like a blade, yielding to that temptation would gain you nothing but bloody fingertips.

Sylvie closed her mind as best she could. Falling into worship of Bran was dangerous, but falling for Lilith was just plain suicidal. She whimpered; her skin buzzed, caught between the two gods of Love. If she could have, she'd have crawled away and hidden. Dunne didn't look much better. Lilith dropped a hand to his shoulder, and he shuddered, tilted his head back, baring the line of his throat. Her white hand crawled over it, cupped his chin.

"I want you to do something for me, lover," she said.

Dunne shook his head minutely. The Fury-influenced arm rose, clamped around her forearm, but the claws stayed lax.

"No," Bran said, but the kind of force Sylvie needed to hear in it was lacking. Lilith had lapped him on the field, taken the main bulk of his power into her. We, Sylvie thought bleakly, are *losing*.

"I need you to strengthen those lovely shields of yours," Lilith said to Dunne. "We've got visitors I'm not ready to deal with yet. Can you do that for me?"

Clever, Sylvie thought. Dunne couldn't really object to that, not when he wanted Bran's power corralled and kept safe. If Lilith had asked something else, he might have tried to fight her pull on his loyalty, but this . . . And having said yes to her once made it so much simpler to say yes again.

"Bran, do something," Sylvie said, even as Dunne slowly nodded to Lilith. The shielding around the building turned from the cloudy opacity of pebbled glass to the complete darkness of steel. The flashes of white light behind it disappeared, and the world within grew dim and close. Lilith and Bran glowed, and the loose power on the rooftop spiraled between them in a brilliant Mobius strip.

"Thank you," Lilith said. "Keep it strong for me."

Madness flashed in Dunne's eyes for a moment, trapped between her will and his own. "Not for you," he choked out. "For Bran. For the world."

"If that's what you need to tell yourself—"

"Thought you weren't big on obedience," Sylvie said. Her body might be down for the moment, but never her mouth. "Thought you wanted independence of thought. Guess you're not content with being the god of Love. Aiming for god of hypocrisy . . . ?"

"Dunne, get rid of her," Lilith said, and Sylvie, despite her terror, found herself laughing. That response proved it. Power corrupted, and all of Lilith's ideals had become empty words. If they had ever been anything more.

"Don't do it, Kevin," Bran said.

Dunne's face had relaxed as soon as Bran spoke, and Lilith, seeing her hold on him slipping, chuffed in an aggravation that Sylvie understood without words. *If you want something done,* her dark voice whispered, and Sylvie was sure that was exactly what Lilith was thinking.

Self-preservation uncoiled fangs in her belly, chasing away some of the hapless admiration and dread. Bran had Dunne locked in place; he couldn't attack Sylvie as Lilith had commanded, but Bran didn't have enough will to override Lilith completely, setting Dunne free. A very fragile stalemate, and Lilith was on her way to cut Sylvie out of the game.

Get up, her voice said. *Will you let her win? When you beat her once already? Will you lie still while she kills you? Will you yield?*

"Get up, then what?" Sylvie muttered, but the voice was not to be denied, even if it had no answer. She clambered to her feet, stiff, sore, her knees treacherous. She swayed.

"Hey, Grandma," Sylvie slurred. "Got something to tell you. About genetics. About our blood."

"I'll see anything your blood hides soon enough," Lilith said. "Spread out over the roof."

Sylvie shrugged. "Probably. Your point?"

"I'm not so sure you're mine after all," Lilith said. "If you had any survival sense at all, you'd be trying to crawl away." She smiled, thrust a casual hand out, and Sylvie's legs were swiped out from under her.

Sylvie whimpered as she hit the rooftop again, banged her head. Again. She staggered back up to her feet, and said to Lilith's back, "You're soft, Grandma. Your enemy's never fought back."

Lilith's spine went rigid. Sylvie laughed, high and strained. "But me . . . My enemies come at me from all directions, and I'm still standing. I've won. Every single time. *Cedo Nulli.* I will not yield. Not to you, not to anyone, not even to my own better instincts."

Lilith raised a hand, plucked the gleaming spindle from her breast, and aimed it like an arrow at Sylvie.

Light flared, brilliant in the demiglobe of their world, and Sylvie watched it burn toward her. There really wasn't any point in running. Even the dark voice, rabidly bent on survival, agreed that this was it, praised her for going out on her feet, going out without begging, then fell silent.

The sudden impact of warmth and weight, rolling her across the roof, left her gasping and stunned, even as the spell light shattered off the body shielding hers.

"Bran?" she said. Dunne groaned protest, outrage, and Lilith's attention turned back to keeping him docile. Dunne's features twisted, the absorbed Furies showing their touches. Lilith said, "Oh, lover, don't fight me now—" But her voice was brittle, a little scared. Dunne was contained partially by her, partially by Bran, and mostly for preservation of the world. The Furies wouldn't care about the world. Sylvie knew it. So did Lilith.

"Help me," Bran said, a breath in her ear. "I need something of yours." His arms cradled her head, his body nestled against hers; his skin was velvet heat beneath her clutching hands.

She'd wondered how Bran could stand to be held by a god, to feel that power thrumming against his skin. Now she knew. Being so close to a god, to *this* god, was . . . pleasant. Definitely pleasurable.

"*Anything,*" she said, all instinct and desire, then shrugged, a shred of rationality struggling through. "Though I haven't got anything left."

His hands stroked her neck, her nape, traveling down her back. "This," he said. "Give me *this*." She shuddered, feeling his touch reach far deeper than just her skin.

The dark voice within her purred uncertainly, stopping and starting like a faulty engine.

"Give me this," he repeated.

She hesitated—give him *what*? His touch was within her, but wanting what? She couldn't tell. Everything in her throbbed to his presence.

"Sylvie, now. . . ." The determination in his voice decided her. Anything he wanted that badly could only be a good thing.

Yes, she thought. She didn't have to say it aloud, not with him so close, within her skin. . . . He pulled, and Sylvie screamed as her entire soul woke to blazing pain.

If Sylvie had ever doubted the dark voice was hers, she didn't any longer: As Bran tugged on it, it felt like he ripped free a piece of her soul.

Panting for breath, her eyes stinging with tears, she could only stare up at his face. His pretty-boy looks hardened. Something dark touched his eyes, something unforgiving. Black bloomed along his collarbone, like the butterflies had along his belly, though it was her doing, her soul's design. A serpent coiled around his throat, tail to head, forked tongue flickering down from the divot in his collarbone.

The spell light from Lilith's casting sucked into his skin all at once, and he stood, graceful, beautiful, and newly deadly with Sylvie's borrowed strength of will.

Sylvie rolled to keep him in her sights. The sudden change raised the hairs on her neck. Lilith, grappling with Dunne, felt the change in the air as well and broke free of Dunne's grip. "What did you do?" she spat.

"Does it matter how you lost? Or just that you have," Bran said. "I trusted you, Lilith. I believed you were my friend. You're not capable of it. And if you can't even be a friend, you sure as hell aren't fit to be god of Love. As much as I hate the responsibility, you have to give it all back."

He didn't wait for her response, if she had any to give. Bran simply opened his arms to the world, and in a series of golden flashes, he *took* it all back. First the loose power, still coiling about the rooftop, then the power caught in Lilith's lure, and, finally, to the sound of Lilith shrieking, took back the power she had absorbed herself.

He collected the spindles with a single command, and snapped them between his fingers. "It's *all* mine. My power. My lover."

Dunne rose to his feet, all wordless, animal rage, and caught Lilith in a paralyzing grip, a hand on each arm as if he meant to rip her apart like a paper doll. The power he had absorbed from the Furies, Sylvie thought, tipped the balance. Gave him a taste of their insatiable hunger for vengeance. He fisted his clawed hand and angled it for the best blow to take Lilith's heart.

"Don't," Bran said. He wrapped his arms around Dunne's chest, leaned his head on Dunne's shoulder, rubbed his cheek, catlike, against him. "Don't." It wasn't a plea, but a command.

Dunne's voice was a wreck when he got a word out

finally, the sound of a man who'd buried language beneath rage. "She—"

"She's not ours to judge," Bran said. "Take down your shields; a verdict is waiting for her beyond it."

Held against the edge of the roof, bloodied at chest, and utterly human, Lilith still dredged up spite enough to say, "If you're waiting for Him to judge me, you're wasting your time. He's had eternity to do so, and so far, He ignores me. I rather think He has some purpose for me, and if it's all the same to you, I'd rather you tear out my heart than let Him have His way. Kill me; bring on your wars in heaven. . . . If I can't defeat Him, maybe you can."

Sylvie shivered, wondering if that was what she had looked like, defying Dunne, dangerous even while cornered. Deeply, rabidly unsafe. If Sylvie kept getting up, what could Lilith do if Dunne released her . . . ?

Well, she could think of one thing. Sylvie joined Bran's side, and said, "If you kill her, all you worked to save will be in jeopardy. Killing another god's favored subject. She's right about that. He's had millennia to stop her, to punish her. Take down your shield."

"It is not just," Dunne said. "Alekta died. Men died. The world was endangered. Bran was—"

"Kevin," Bran said. "Please."

And that was it. Dunne sighed; the shields came down. The riot of angels outside flared back, startlement in their bright, insectile eyes, their narrow faces.

"We return her to you," Bran said. "Bloodied but unbowed. The Olympians have no quarrel with your master."

The largest angel nodded once, perfectly still, silent as always; the rest spilled upward and faded from sight. Lilith turned to look at her captor, lips a thin line. "Still, He doesn't come for me, but sends His puppet. I suppose it doesn't matter. At least this time I got some of His attention. I'll try again."

"No," Sylvie said. "You won't." Dunne's head rose sharply from where he had been pressing a kiss to Bran's throat. With the last of her strength, Sylvie pushed.

Lilith clawed at Sylvie's arms, scoring bloody marks deep into the flesh, but it was too late.

"I may be your daughter. But I am also Cain's child," Sylvie whispered. Lilith's grip faltered, eyes widening in shock; she reached for something to throw back at Sylvie, but her stolen power was gone, her borrowed spells gone, her invulnerability gone, and she was just a woman with a ten-story drop rising to meet her.

Sylvie watched her fall until her body was swallowed by distance and darkness, while the angel bore witness with expressionless eyes.

30

Afterglow

SYLVIE BACKED AWAY FROM THE ROOF EDGE, CALM AND CONTENT, even over the worry that the angel might not be pleased with her. But really, what could it do? Angels were soldiers, nothing more, their lives wrapped in heavenly red tape and orders.

The angels had come to ensure that the Greek gods didn't tamper with His property. They hadn't. Sylvie had. Sylvie was only human when all was said and done, and if one human killed another, it was only business as usual.

The angel rose into the sky like a meteor defying gravity, streaks of white and gold and fire's-heart scarlet unfolding in its wings. It stopped before her, stood weightlessly in the sky, eyes like insects, glossy and black, looking into her mind and soul. "Sylvie, Daughter of Lilith and Cain. He knows thee," it said. It soared upward and disappeared in the rising sun.

Not good, she and the dark voice thought in unison. Always a momentous thing when an angel actually spoke. Much less spoke your name.

It wasn't the angel, though, whose eyes remained an uncomfortable weight on her skin, an itch along her nerves. Sylvie looked over her shoulder at the two silent gods behind her. "Oh, don't play that game. You wanted it done. I got it done. You outsourced the wetwork is all. The Furies did it for you before, and you can't tell me you're sorry I did it now."

Dunne stayed silent, the thinned line of his mouth disapproving, even as he drew Bran closer to him, stroked his skin.

Sylvie threw up her hands. "Do I need to remind you— she took Bran, kept him in a cage, and was waiting for him to die? Do I need to point out you were about to kill her yourself? What I did—"

"Matricide," Dunne said with the voice of the Furies.

"Enough," Bran said simultaneously. "You've made your point."

"Have I?" Sylvie said. "She twisted my mind. A man died for it. An innocent man."

Dunne's face stiffened; Demalion hadn't been innocent in his eyes. Sylvie shifted gears, hunted broader truths. "Lilith has manipulated, hurt, and killed people for millennia. She courted war in heaven. She endangered the world. What I did was justice, long overdue."

"No," Dunne said.

"Why not?" Sylvie said. It wasn't that she'd really thought they'd thank her—gloating over an enemy's death didn't seem the way to keep peace between pantheons—but she hadn't expected the lecture. "Is this some type of holier-than-thou god-thing, 'cause I have to tell you, humans are perfectly capable of correcting injustice on their own. Demalion did." She ran out of steam and dropped to crouch on the roof, saving her legs the strain of standing. Leaning against the roof lip gave her a distorted view of Dunne above her. He seemed enormous, a looming thunderhead.

She closed her eyes, rubbed the soreness out of them. "You thought it was just," she said, and knew she sounded petulant instead of persuasive. "*You* were going to do it."

"You enjoyed it," Dunne accused. "That makes you a murderer—"

"Am I smiling?" Sylvie said. "Am I dancing in triumph, asking for high fives all around? It had to be done. I *had* to do it—"

"And it satisfied you. Fed some hunger in your soul. To see her crushed for manipulating you. Vengeance for your lover. Your cry of justice is only your latest excuse. You will always have an excuse, Shadows, to give you a reason to pull the trigger, to vent your rage. In the end, that's all they are. Excuses."

Sylvie licked dry lips, let the shock of his words stop rattling her bones. "It's—irrelevant. An executioner doesn't have to hate her job." A wash of sickness touched her. Was she really thinking of herself as a killer?

She shook her head, shaking the thoughts out like dust from a rug. "It doesn't matter. The end result is the same. I did two things you couldn't do, only one of which I'm getting paid for. I saved Bran, and I punished his abductor. You owe me."

Bran whispered something in Dunne's ear, rising on his toes to do so. Sylvie held her breath.

"We don't owe you anything. The debt is cleared."

"Bullshit," Sylvie cried. She ached. Dry lips, dry tongue, sere heart, charred soul. "Demalion's still dead. Bring him back!"

"If Lilith deserved death for laying hands on Bran, for kidnapping him, do you think your Demalion deserved less for first stalking, then killing him? He killed a god," Dunne said. "That cannot be forgiven." He stroked the smooth expanse of Bran's back, each finger width a gloat that he had what she had lost.

"You're punishing him for my command, my decision. How is that fair?" She had to win this one; she couldn't bear it if she failed.

"It's in our bargain, don't you think? Intrinsic. The converse. If I earned a death for my enemies for saving Bran's life, then I earned a life for my ally for killing your enemy."

"No," Dunne said again. Flat, sure, uninterested. How

could she argue with a man who refused to be drawn into debate. With a god who might squash her if she pressed too hard. But Demalion's life—

"Punish me instead," she meant to say, but the words stuck in her throat as every instinct in her rebelled at that. She was a survivor.

Dunne was turning away already, his judgment rendered, his interest shifted to the man—the god—fitting himself into his arms.

Bran nuzzled into Dunne's neck, then looked back at Sylvie with eyes like clouded honey. "Your debt's been cleared. Don't push it further. You won't like it." He smiled at her, smug. Sylvie bit her lip as she recognized the expression as one she'd seen herself wear in the mirror.

He was making her pay for the hell she had put him through. No sweet gratitude—he'd tasted too much of her soul to allow that.

Even in her despair, she found some tiny vindictive satisfaction in that. The Greek gods, including Dunne, who'd dragged her into this, were getting a subtly changed god of Love back.

Bran bit Dunne's neck, a tiny lick after, slid arms around his waist. Dunne frowned; he tipped Bran's head up so as to look at his face, his eyes, then sighed and kissed him, slowly and deeply. Bran leaned into him.

Sylvie bit her lip hard enough to draw blood. Punishment, she thought, god of Love style, showing her what she had lost with Demalion's death.

Bran made a sudden gasp that sounded more like pain than pleasure, and a snake slithered out from between his fingers, coming out from under his skin. At his neck, the vibrant colors faded from the serpent markings, fading to a greyed shadow against his skin.

Their kiss broke, and Bran said, "This is yours. I don't need so much of it." He thrust his hand toward her. The snake riding it, all jeweled elegance and hidden fangs, hissed.

"I don't want it," Sylvie said. Tears were hot in her eyes. *"I don't want it."*

"Take it back," Dunne said. Sylvie scrabbled backward, to the limits of movement; the lip of the roof pressed into her back. Bran opened his hand, and the snake dropped into her lap, thrashing, hissing, biting. . . .

When the pain cleared, the sun was rising, and she was alone on the rooftop. Alone with the wreckage. Again. And hadn't she surpassed herself this time. In the merciless light of the sun, all she saw were moments that encapsulated pain or failure. There, a broken pile of rubble that had been a man, whose name she had never learned, whose only fault was being in the wrong place. There, the place where Lilith had lurked, seen but unrecognized until too late.

The roof was rent before her in the spot where Demalion had died; with a little effort, she could dangle her feet into the room below. The asphalt sheets dripped downward, collected water with a roseate hue. A brief shine of glass caught her eye, and she crawled toward it, found herself the possessor of a sharp curve of what had been a crystal ball. It gleamed faintly in the sunlight. She cupped it in her hands, shielded it from the sun, and peered again. It shone pearly grey in her fingers, like a tiny scrap of soul. She clenched her fist about it. *Demalion.*

She put her face in her hands and heard sirens in the distance like a mourning wail. The sound gave her the impetus to rise. She didn't want to be found here. Not with this mess. Not when the morning crew of the ISI arrived to see who'd knocked their sand castle down in the night. Somehow, she thought pointing a finger toward the heavens and saying, "gods' will," wasn't going to cut it.

She stiff-legged her way to the door, body aching in every joint, and into the stairwell. Alekta's body was gone, but Helen's charred body waited, a fetal curl of blackened agony in singed designer clubwear.

Sylvie stepped over the corpse, wincing as her back

protested, got halfway down to the first landing, then slowly, stiffly made her way up again as a thought occurred to her. All well and good to think, *Get out of here*, but it wasn't as easy as that.

She knelt beside Helen, fumbled through ruined fabric, grimacing, and found a key ring. Flipping through the keys yielded one that belonged to a car.

In the parking garage nearby, Sylvie found herself wandering row after row of shiny black sedans and matching SUVs. And in the third one, a red Beetle. She tried the key in the lock, and muttered, "We've got a winner."

She climbed in, cursed the stick shift when working the clutch hurt, and put off driving away for a quick sortie. Glove box: wallet, gas card, credit cards, cash, $150.

Sylvie took advantage of the early hour and the nearest gas station to fill up the Beetle, using Helen's card. The gas-station attendant, boarding up blown-out glass windows with a shell-shocked expression, never so much as looked at her. Judging his exhaustion level and his state of shock as "wouldn't recognize his mother at the moment," she also bought and filled three gas cans' worth of gas. Homeland Security was all well and good, but not when they were relying on traumatized wage slaves to make the reports. 'Sides, it was Helen's card. HomeSec could investigate Helen all they wanted.

Sylvie was more worried about the cops. No point in stealing the car and card of a murdered woman if you were going to lead the cops on a trail right to your front door. This was enough gas to get her halfway home, then there was the cash for the rest.

She had the car's nose turned toward the highway and home, but couldn't make the turn. One more stop. One job left to do.

She made the loop out toward the suburbs and headed toward Anna D's. Wreckage kept surprising her; one moment, it seemed like all the violence of the night before had been tidied away, or centered on her and the gods, the next, there were pinpoint places of utter destruction, as if a tornado had danced through the city. Or a god masquerading as a hurricane.

There were cars dented and abandoned at the side of the highway, scorched and sheared-off trees where lightning and wind had lashed out and made their mark. Water still lapped over the cracked asphalt in low sections of the road, and sometimes Sylvie caught glimpses of stranger destruction yet. Places where materials seemed to have undergone a sea change. Where retaining walls sagged like taffy and were marked as if exotic beasts had been slammed into them, leaving feathers and scale. Where broken glass had spun out of windows and made patterns like dragonbones in the ground.

Sylvie tried to imagine what things would look like if Dunne hadn't been so concerned about the world, but she didn't want to dwell on it. She hadn't forgiven him for refusing to bring Demalion back.

Anna D's apartment complex was one of the casualties. The tower looked like a skeleton of itself, taken back in time to when it was still being built. The glass facing had been blown out, and all was dark.

Sylvie parked, sat in the car, wondering if she had to do this. Anna D surely knew already. Erinya's scratches could have come from no one else. She hesitated, waiting for that little voice to advise her, but got nothing.

Eventually, she clambered out of the car and headed toward the apartment. She nearly gave up on the first flight of stairs, but by the third, the pain was bearable—constant, but bearable, and she went on.

The apartment door was open, and Sylvie inched in and came to a dead stop. Anna D was sphinxed out in the midst of massive wreckage. Glass glittered on every surface, studded the walls, the furniture, Anna D's russet fur.

The sphinx breathed in deep gasps, and there were bloody gashes along her sides, from the Furies on their soul hunt, from the glass explosions, Sylvie didn't know.

"Get out," Anna D said. Her tail lashed, tipping over an already precarious table. She didn't even look at Sylvie.

All her attention was on the tiny glass orb between her paws. It glowed faintly and showed a child in its depths, a boy with Demalion's tawny eyes and dark hair. "Leave."

"I had no choice," Sylvie said. "But I am sorry—"

Miserably inadequate, she knew. Sorry was for breaking a window, staining a borrowed blouse, losing a library book. Sorry had nothing to do with the sickness in her heart, the queasy pain of a blow she had dealt herself.

Anna D swung around too quickly for Sylvie's exhausted eyes even to follow. She ended flat on her back, glass nipping at her skin, while the sphinx loomed above her, growling.

"Sorry? Do you have any concept of the word? I should have your throat between my teeth."

"But you don't," Sylvie said.

Anna D looked away, closed her amber eyes, and slunk off of Sylvie. "I don't need to sully myself."

"Demalion knew," Sylvie said. "I had no choice. But he did. He didn't have to be my weapon. Of course, the world would have ended if he hadn't acted."

"It's for my son that I don't kill you," Anna D said. "Do not tempt me with platitudes. There is nothing you can utter to earn forgiveness from me. I will wait for the day to come when you die, in agony and alone. And I will be watching. I am eternal, and I am patient."

"Fine, see you then. I'll save you a front-row seat," Sylvie said, all in one breath. Her mouth was dry, and her chest hurt. She couldn't blame Anna D; her snark was just a way to keep the guilt from crushing her. She rose to leave.

"Do you understand what you have done, Shadows?" Anna D said, just as Sylvie moved to shut the door behind her.

Sylvie hesitated. Games again. She should have known it was too easy, but Anna D deserved her say. She eased the door back open. "I killed your son," she confessed.

"With Lilith, fool girl. Do you understand what you have done?"

"Obviously, you were watching," Sylvie said. "Why don't you tell me?"

"You haven't killed her," Anna D said.

"Beg to differ," Sylvie snapped. Adrenaline surged in her. God, what if Anna D had seen something different? What if Lilith had survived the fall . . . ? She wished, belatedly, that she'd taken the time to limp around to the front of the ISI building, never mind the incoming agents. She should have made sure there was a body.

"You haven't killed her," Anna D repeated steadily. "You've replaced her. One murderess for another. How long do you think it will take, Shadows, before you're pushing people into the path of danger instead of asking? Before you turn your friends into fodder, and lack even a shred of regret for it. Sorry? You'd do it again in a heartbeat."

Sylvie bridled, that inner core rising, the refusal to be cowed by anyone. "I'm human," she said. "I don't have cheat sheets to the future. I can only make choices as I come across them. I did nothing that I wouldn't do again, given the same information. Your son would still be dead, and while I wish it weren't so, I know it's true. But I can still grieve."

Anna D closed her eyes. "You will find no absolution here. And you're long past your welcome."

Sylvie pulled the door shut behind her, and this time, Anna D let her leave. Sylvie leaned against the hallway wall and fingered the small fragment of crystal in her pocket. She had been going to give it to Anna, but to what point? No, she'd keep it for herself, a reminder and a warning of where her choices could lead.

At last, nothing slowed her path out of Chicago, not the bad roads, not the slowly gathering police presence, not even the brief thought that she should tell Tish everything was all right. It wasn't, really. As far as Tish was concerned, Bran and Dunne might as well be dead. Sylvie couldn't really see them popping over to Tish's next party, two gods mingling with the mortals.

Sylvie drove on, stopping at the rest area on the Illinois border to clean the worst of the blood from her skin. She turned the stained black shirt inside out and covered up the rest that way. She did it all without ever once looking at the mirror directly. Anna D's condemnation lingered too loudly for that. *Do you like what you see?*

An hour later, she had to pull the car onto the shoulder while the events of the night tried to shake themselves from her bones. She laid her head against the steering wheel, shook and screamed and sobbed until she was empty and exhausted.

In Kentucky, hours later, the little dark voice muttered back to life. *Stupid Old Cat. If she hadn't hidden her own identity from Demalion, he might not have been in the line of fire at all. What kind of dutiful son would join an organization dedicated to corralling monsters, after all, when his beloved mother was one? The fault lies with her.*

Sylvie felt obscurely comforted and made the rest of the drive without having to pull the car off the road for any more hysterics. A few stealthy tears here and there hardly counted. She stopped instead for a big gulp of caffeine and nuclear-cheese nachos, a king-size Snickers bar, and a bag of beef jerky, scarfed them down somewhere in Georgia, and gave her body enough fuel to make it the rest of the way home.

Her brain was locked on autopilot, locked in cold anger at herself. Hadn't she vowed to change? She hadn't. Hadn't she promised not to put others in danger? She had.

Finally, she sat outside Baptist Hospital in South Miami, trying to gather one last burst of courage. Once more into the fire. One last chance to have her numbed heart pushed back into grief and pain.

Or she could just leave and never know. Leave it all. Alex's fate, the job, Miami. Start somewhere new.

She got out of the car instead. Nothing on that list was worth running from. And she couldn't run from herself. If she wanted a change, she'd have to make it herself. Starting now. Kinder, gentler Sylvie coming right up. If she stayed out of the *Magicus Mundi*, surely she could do it.

Sylvie strode into the hospital, hit the desk, and said, "My friend was checked in—" How long ago? One day? Two? Three? Sylvie shook her mind into order and said. "Wednesday. Alexandra Figueroa-Smith."

The receptionist typed for a second, then looked up, face still, and Sylvie braced herself. "ICU."

Alive. Sylvie nearly gasped with the relief. "ICU? Did I say friend? I meant sister. Which room was it?"

"Family only," the man said. Bored with the routine.

"She hasn't got family, not decent family anyway," Sylvie said. "Except for me. Look it up, bet there haven't been people beating down her door to visit."

"We can't give out that kind of—"

"Look, I've driven nonstop for twenty-four hours, I've been through hell, and seeing Alex is the only thing keeping me on my feet. Trust me, you don't want to get on my bad side."

"Or what?" he said. He flipped papers without ever looking up.

She reached across the desk, laid her hand over his. Smaller than his, but smeared with scratches from glass, bruising from hits she couldn't even recall, nails torn, blood pooled beneath the quicks. His gaze fixated on it. Sylvie said, "I've been through hell. And I'll share it with you."

So much for kinder and gentler, she thought. But who was she to argue with success?

He gave her the room number, and she smiled, though she was sure it looked more like a rictus than a thank-you.

She headed down the hall at a fast clip, in case he decided to call security after a second or third thought. Her speed faltered at the closed door. She'd seen snakebite victims before. Ugly business. Bruising, swelling, necrotic tissue, comas, machinery, and death.

She pushed open the door and blinked. Alex looked— asleep. Despite ICU and the machinery humming nearby, supposedly monitoring her vital functions, there were no tubes in her, no sensors, no needles. Sylvie blinked in cautious hope. A deep fragrance reached her as she closed the door behind her and sealed out the scent of bleach. *Orchids.*

Orchids massed in the ICU room, propped everywhere, potted and fragrant, impossibly out of place. But she supposed if anyone could leave flowers in an ICU, it would be a god paying his fee. Sylvie collapsed in the chair beside the bed, a half-choked cry leaving her lips. The whole room smelled like Fairchild Gardens, like the outdoors. Like life.

The debt's been cleared, Bran said. Not such a bastard after all, she thought, shaking again.

Alex's hand clenched, unclenched in the blanket; her eyes squeezed tighter shut, as if she was enjoying her sleep.

Sylvie licked her lips, said, "Hey, wakey-wakeys."

Alex's eyes fluttered open, turning first toward the sunlight, as if she'd never expected to see it again, then back toward Sylvie. She blinked at the orchids for a long moment, the riot of white-speckled pink, of violet and cream, of attenuated yellow. "They're not lilies," she whispered. "I guess I'm not dying. Am I going to prom?"

Sylvie laughed for the first time since Demalion had died. It was ragged and started up about as well as a cold engine on a winter's day. She folded her hand around Alex's cold fingers. "Do you feel like dancing?"

"I'm alive," Alex said. "You're alive. Yeah, I could dance."

"Club night, then, soon as you're out," Sylvie said. Her voice was roughened. She scrubbed at her eyes. "How you feeling?"

"Confused mostly," Alex said. She struggled to sit up, wiped bleariness from her eyes. "A cop came and talked to me. With a florist? He said I'd get better. Except it was all in my head. The florist kissed me." A tiny blush swam up through her pallor. "He was really hot."

"Well, it was Eros," Sylvie said. "I think hot goes with the position." The tears kept threatening, and she couldn't understand it. She pinched the bridge of her nose punishingly hard. Her nails dug into the skin.

"A god brought me flowers?"

"Two gods. I guess he didn't trust me with them," Sylvie said. Each of the orchids was potted, and didn't that boggle her brain—the idea of Dunne gardening. Even Bran— "I was going to mulch them."

"What? Why? They're beautiful," Alex said. "Beautiful." She rolled her head to look at them again. Pale spattered pink, violet, gold-tinged, elegant, radiating color in the sterile room, warming in sunlight.

"They're the satanists," Sylvie said. She hadn't meant to tell Alex, but she was tired of hiding things. If she was going to change, she would need help.

"What?"

Sylvie closed her eyes, leaned her head against the mattress. "It was my fee. For helping Dunne, he'd kill the satanists for me. . . . But he couldn't do it. *He's* not a killer." The last was a bare whisper.

Alex reached out an unsteady hand, and Sylvie handed her one of the plants, setting it carefully beside her. Alex stroked a petal. "This—was a person? One of the ones who killed Suarez?"

"That one's the red-haired bitch," Sylvie said. "The first one he transformed. *He* couldn't kill them."

Alex said nothing, still stroking the petals, giving them all her attention, and Sylvie stumbled on, well aware that Alex, for all her supposed abstraction, was listening very closely indeed.

"You were right," Sylvie said. "I've killed people, though I called them monsters. I've killed lots of things. And a lot of people die around me and because of me, and for—" Her voice gave out for a moment. "God, Alex. Demalion's dead. I let him in, and he died. I can't let that happen to you. That's why I never told. To keep you safe—"

"No," Alex said. "You were doing well there, Syl. Finish up right. You never told me, never let me know, hid what you had to do, because . . ."

Sylvie swallowed, pressed her face to the white sheets, breathed in faint hints of bleach and orchid fragrance. Alex leaned back and waited.

"I didn't want you to see I was a monster, too," Sylvie said.

Alex sighed. "We're going to talk, Sylvie. Before we open the shop again. Preferably with alcohol in hand." The sleepy daze had left her eyes, and she was getting that all-too-familiar martial look, the one that organized Sylvie's life for her.

"The shop?" Sylvie said. "I can't—"

"People *need* you," Alex said. "Did you think about that when you decided to close up shop?"

"People should take care of their own damn problems," Sylvie muttered.

"But so many of them can't, Syl. Not everyone can see what has to be done or have the strength to do it. You do both."

"I—" Sylvie shivered.

Alex turned her hand over, stroked her wrist, frowning. "You're all beat-up. More 'n usual. What have you been doing?"

"Surviving," Sylvie said. "At the expense of others. As usual." Alex's stroking stopped, but she made no other sign that she'd noticed Sylvie's words. "I'm sorry, Alex. The snakes were my fault. They came after me, too. I sent them away . . . set them on you. I didn't mean to." Another pitiful apology, better suited to a child.

"I know," Alex said. There was sufficient weight to her words that Sylvie looked up from their linked hands. Alex's eyes were tired, burdened. "The cop—that was your Justice, right?—he talked in my head while he brought the orchids. Told me what you've done. What you've kept from me. Told me about Lilith. About Demalion."

"And you still think I can help people? That Shadows Inquiries should stay open? I've killed *people*, Alex."

"It's another reason you *can't* close the shop."

"It's the best reason to close it," Sylvie countered.

Alex shifted in the narrow bed, pushing herself upward, trying to sit upright again. "And do what, instead?" Alex said. "You help people, Sylvie. That darkness in you gets focused on achieving results on the good side of the ledger. Without the job, how long do you think it would last before you snapped? Before you got into something else. Something blacker."

Sylvie shuddered, put her face down in her hands. "God, Alex. Don't let me fall."

"I won't," Alex said. She petted Sylvie's tangled hair. "You might be good at taking on the world. But I am good at taking care of you. If you let me. No more shutting me out."

"I'll try," Sylvie said.

"Good girl," Alex said.

Sylvie snapped, "I'm still the boss. And you're still the employee. Don't get cocky."

Alex bit her lip and laughed at her before her eyes grew thoughtful again. She touched the orchids nearby. "What are you going to do with them now?"

Kill them. Grind them to pulp. Why should they have any kind of life when they'd killed her friend?

New leaf, she argued with herself. They were no longer dangerous. They'd paid. They were plants, for God's sake. It wasn't like they could come back.

Best to be sure. They killed your friend. Tried to kill Alex.

I killed my lover, she countered, and silenced the growl in the back of her mind.

"I—"

"At a loss for words, Syl? That's not like you."

"Too many words," Sylvie said. "You decide." Her heart thumped. "You tell me what to do with those killers."

Alex dabbled her fingers into the soil a little, touched the pale petals again, traced the slender stem; fragile, it shivered beneath her touch. She let her hand drop, reached it out to Sylvie.

"We'll keep them alive. They're beautiful, Syl. Whatever they were before, whatever sins they committed—they're beautiful now."